The

HIGHWAYMAN

Also by
Kerrigan Byrne

The
*H*IGHWAYMAN

KERRIGAN BYRNE

St. Martin's Paperbacks

This is a work of fiction. All of the characters, organizations, and events portrayed in this novel are either products of the author's imagination or are used fictitiously.

THE HIGHWAYMAN

Copyright © 2015 by Kerrigan Byrne.
Excerpt from *The Hunter* copyright © 2015 by Kerrigan Byrne.

For information address St. Martin's Press, 120 Broadway, New York, NY 10271.

ISBN: 978-1-250-07605-2

Printed in the United States of America

St. Martin's Paperbacks edition / September 2015

St. Martin's Paperbacks are published by St. Martin's Press, 120 Broadway, New York, NY 10271.

10 9 8 7 6 5 4 3 2

To Darlene Ainge
You're the reason he survived.

$\mathcal{A}$CKNOWLEDGMENTS

Writing can be a very solitary vocation, and the right people to offer support, critiques, and encouragement are more than priceless. Cynthia St. Aubin, Tiffinie Helmer, and Janet Snell, thank you for being there morning and night. I've been able to count on you personally and professionally and it's meant the world to me.

One of the best days of my life was when my agent, Christine Witthohn, called to offer me representation. She's not only a stellar agent, but an incredible friend.

I'd be remiss if I didn't thank Monique Patterson, Alexandra Sehulster, and the team at St. Martin's Press for their patience and their incredible hard work on behalf of this series.

And thank you to my love. My very own hero. You are my everything.

CHAPTER ONE

Scottish Highlands, County Argyle, 1855

Blood ran down Dougan Mackenzie's forearms as he crouched against the ancient stone wall separating the grounds of Applecross Orphanage from the wild mountains beyond. None of the other children ventured here. The wall protected the stooped and faded headstones that rose from thick carpets of moss and heather fed by the bones of the dead.

Chest heaving, Dougan took a moment to catch his breath before sliding down to sit with his knobby legs drawn against his chest. Carefully, he opened his palms as far as the broken skin would allow. They hurt worse now than when the sharp switch had bitten into them.

Black emotion had kept him from crying out as Sister Margaret tried her level best to break him. It kept the tears from falling until now. He'd met her cold, bright eyes with his own, unable to stop his blink as the strap had come down again and again until the welts on his palms had split and bled.

"Tell me why you're crying."

The slight voice seemed to calm the intemperate wind into an invisible ribbon that carried the gentle words to him.

The craggy black and green highland peaks jutting from behind the gray stone of Applecross formed the perfect backdrop for the girl who stood not three spans away. Instead of lashing at her, the stormy wind tossed and teased at ringlets so astonishingly blond, they appeared a silvery-white. Round, pale cheeks, slashed with red by the cold, dimpled over a shy smile.

"Go away," he snarled, tucking his smarting hands beneath his arms and kicking a clod of dirt at her clean black dress.

"Did you lose your family, too?" she queried, her face a study in curiosity and innocence.

Dougan still couldn't manage to form words. He flinched as she lifted the hem of her white apron to his cheek, but he let her ever so carefully wipe at the tears and grime she found there. Her touch was light as butterfly wings, and entranced him so thoroughly, he stopped trembling. What should he say? Dougan had never spoken to a *girl* before. He could answer her question, he supposed. He had lost his mother, but he wasn't an orphan. In fact, most of Applecross's orphans weren't children but terrible secrets, hidden away and forgotten like the shameful mistakes they all were.

Whose secret was she?

"I saw what Sister Margaret did to you," the girl said gently, her eyes gleaming with pity.

Her pity lit a fire born of humiliation and helplessness in Dougan's chest and he jerked his head to the side, avoiding her touch. "I thought I told ye to leave."

She blinked. "But your hands—"

With a savage snarl, Dougan surged to his feet and

lifted his hand, ready to strike the pity from her angelic features.

She cried out as she fell backward on her rump, cowering on the ground beneath him.

Dougan paused, his face tight and burning, his teeth bared and his body coiled to strike.

The girl just looked up at him, horrified, her eyes locked on the bleeding wound on his open palm.

"Get out of here," he growled. She scrambled away from him, gaining unsteady feet, and scampered a wide berth around the fenced graveyard, disappearing into the orphanage.

Dougan slumped back against the rocks, his trembling knuckles brushed the back of his cheek. The lass had been the first person to ever touch him in a way that wasn't meant to hurt. He didn't know why he'd been so nasty to her.

Dougan ducked his head against his knees and closed his eyes, settling in for a right proper wallow. The chilly moisture on the back of his burning neck felt good, and he tried to focus on that instead of the stinging pain of his hands.

Not five wretched minutes passed before a bowl of clean water appeared in the space between his feet. A cup, this one full of a liquid the color of caramel, joined it.

Astonished, Dougan looked up to find that the girl had returned, except now she brandished a long and dangerous-looking pair of scissors and a determined wrinkle between her brows.

"Let me see your hands."

Hadn't he sufficiently frightened her away? Dougan eyed the scissors with suspicion. They looked both gigantic and sharp in her tiny hand. "What are those for? Protection? Revenge?"

His question produced that gap-toothed smile of hers, and his heart did a little leap and landed in his stomach.

"Don't be silly," she chided gently as she set them aside and reached for his hands.

Dougan jerked them both away from her reach, and scowled as he hid them behind his back.

"Here now," she coaxed. "Give them over."

"Nay."

Her brow puckered further. "How am I supposed to doctor your wounds if you insist on hiding them from me?"

"Ye're not a doctor," Dougan spat. "Leave me be."

"My father was a captain in the Crimea," she patiently explained. "He learned a little about doctoring cuts so they didn't fester on the battlefield."

That arrested his attention. "Did he kill people?" Dougan asked, unable to help himself.

She thought about this a moment. "He had good many medals pinned to the coat of his uniform, so I think he must have, though he never said so."

"I'll bet he used a rifle," Dougan said, diverted by thoughts he deemed manly and grown-up. Thoughts of war and glory.

"And a bayonet," the girl supplied helpfully. "I got to touch it once when he was cleaning his weapon by the fire."

"Tell me what it was like," he demanded.

"Let me tend your hands, and I will." Her sea-storm eyes sparkled at him.

"Very well." Cautiously, he pulled his wounded hands from behind him. "But ye have to start from the beginning."

"I will," she promised with a solemn nod.

"And doona leave anything out."

"I won't." She picked up the cup of water.

Dougan leaned forward and extended his palm toward her.

She winced at the broken flesh, but cradled his wounded hand in both of hers like one would a baby bird, before reaching for the bowl of water to trickle it over the cut. When he snarled in pain, she began to describe her father's rifle to him. The way the little coils fit together. The clicking noises of the levers. The silt and stench and sparkle of the black powder.

She poured the alcohol over his wounds, and Dougan hissed breath through his teeth, trembling with the effort it took not to snatch his hands away from her. To distract himself from the pain, he focused his blurring vision on the droplets of moisture collecting like diamonds in her abundant curls. Instead of making her hair heavy and straight, the rain seemed to coil the ringlets tighter and anoint the silvery strands with a darker gloss of spun gold. His finger itched to test the curls, to twirl and pull them, and see if they bounced back into place. But he kept absolutely still while she wrapped the strips of her petticoat around his palm with painstaking care.

"Tell me yer name," he demanded in a hoarse whisper.

"My name is Farah." He could tell the question pleased her because a tiny dimple appeared in her cheek. "Farah Leigh—" She cut off abruptly, frowning at the tidy knot she'd just produced.

"Aye?" he said alertly. "Farah Leigh—what?"

Her eyes were more gray than green when they met his. "I've been forbidden to utter my family name," she said. "Or I'll get me and the person I told into trouble, and I don't think you need any more trouble."

Dougan nodded. That wasn't so uncommon here at Applecross. "I'm Dougan of the Clan Mackenzie," he announced proudly. "And I have eleven years."

She looked properly impressed, which ingratiated her to him even more.

"I have eight years," she told him. "What did you do that was so wicked?"

"I—swiped a loaf from the kitchens."

She looked appalled.

"I'm so bloody hungry all the time," he muttered, not missing her flinch at his profanity. "Hungry enough to eat the moss off those rocks."

Farah tied off the last bandage and leaned back on her knees to inspect her work. "This is a lot of punishment for one loaf of bread," she observed sadly. "Those welts will probably scar."

"It's not the first time," Dougan admitted with a shrug more cavalier than he actually felt. "It's usually my arse that gets blistered, and I'd rather that. Sister Margaret said I'm a demon."

"Dougan the Demon." She smiled, thoroughly amused.

"Better than Fairy-lee." He chuckled, playing with her name.

"Fairy?" Her eyes twinkled at him. "You can call me that if you want to."

"I will." Dougan's lips cracked, and he realized that for the first time in as long as he could remember, he was smiling. "And what will ye call me?" he asked.

"Friend," she said instantly, pushing up from the damp ground and brushing loose earth from her skirts before she picked up her bowl and cup.

Peculiar warmth stole into Dougan's chest. He didn't quite know what to say to her.

"I'd better go inside." She lifted her wee face to the rain. "They'll be looking for me." Meeting his eyes again, she said. "Don't stay out in the rain, you'll catch your death."

Dougan watched her go, suffused with interest and

amusement, he savored the feeling of having something he'd never had before.

A friend.

"*Pssst!* Dougan!" The loud whisper nearly startled Dougan out of his skin. He whirled around, ready to deflect a blow from one of the other boys, when he spied a pair of owlish eyes sparkling at him from ringlets spun of moonbeams. The rest of her was cleverly shadowed behind a hallway tapestry.

"What are ye doing out here?" he demanded. "If they catch us, they'll whip us both."

"You're out here," she challenged.

"Aye . . . well." Dougan had tried to fill the emptiness of his stomach with water. Two hours later, while tossing in bed, the plan had somewhat backfired and he'd been chagrined to find that someone had hidden the chamber pot, forcing him to go in search of the water closet.

"I have something for you." Merrily, she hopped from behind the tapestry and linked her elbow with his, careful not to touch the bandages on his hands. "Follow me." A door at the end of the hall sat slightly ajar, and Farah shoved him through, closing it softly behind them.

A lone candle flickered on one of several small tables, the light dancing off walls comprised entirely of bookcases. Dougan wrinkled his nose. The library? What would induce her to bring him here? He'd always avoided this room. It was dusty and smelled of mold and old people.

Pulling him toward the table with the candle, she pointed to a chair tucked in front of an open book. "Sit here!" By now she was nigh on quivering with excitement.

"Nay." Dougan scowled down at the book, his curiosity dying. "I'm going to bed."

"But—"

"And ye should, too, before they catch ye and flay yer skin from yer hide."

Reaching into her apron pocket, Farah produced something the size of a tin of potted meat wrapped with linen. Setting it on the table, she uncovered a half-eaten slab of cheese, some dried roast, and most of a bread crust.

Dougan's mouth watered violently, and it was all he could do not to snatch it from her.

"I couldn't finish my supper," she said.

Dougan fell upon the offering like a savage, seizing the bread first, as he knew it would produce the most filling effect. He could hear the rooting, growling noises his throat produced around gaping mouthfuls, and he didn't care.

When she spoke again, her voice was full of tears. "Dear friend . . ." Her little hand pressed against his hunched back and patted it consolingly. "I shan't let you starve again, I promise."

Dougan watched her reach for the book as he shoved as much of the roast in his mouth as would fit. *"Waff's tha?"* he asked around the food.

She spread her tiny, pale hands to carefully smooth across the open pages, and nudged the tome toward him. "I felt bad for not knowing enough about the rifles this afternoon, so I spent all evening searching, and look what I found!" She mashed her wee finger next to a picture of a long Enfield rifle. Beneath it were smaller pictures of different parts of the disassembled weapon.

"This is a Pattern 1851 rifle," she offered. "And look! Here are the bayonets. The next chapter is about how they're made and how one affixes them to the top of— What?" She'd finally glanced over at him and something in his expression caused her to blush.

Dougan had almost completely forgotten about the

food, for his entire body was suffused with the most intense and exquisite sensation he'd ever known. It was something like hunger, and something like fulfillment. It was wonder and awe and yearning and fear encapsulated in a tender bliss. His chest expanded with it until it pressed against his lungs, emptying them of breath.

He found himself wishing there was a word for it. And maybe there was, lost in all these countless books for which he'd never before had use.

She turned back to the pages, clearing her throat. "They noted all the names of all the different components right below the pictures, see?"

"How do ye know?" He peered down at where she pointed and noted the markings below the pictures, but, to him, they were meaningless.

"It says right here. Can't you read it?"

Dougan filled the silence by tearing off a chunk of cheese and popping it into his mouth, chewing furiously.

"Did no one teach you?" she asked astutely.

He ignored her, finishing off the crust of bread whilst staring down at the pictures, wanting very much to know what they were about. "Will ye—read them to me, Fairy?"

"Of course I will." She leaned forward on her knees, the table too tall for her to sit on the rickety chair and see over the top. "But tomorrow when we meet here, I'll teach you how to read them for yourself."

Feeling full and satisfied for the first time in as long as he could remember, Dougan began to point to pictures, and she would tell him the caption beneath while he savored the cheese in little crumbles.

By the time they got to the chapter on bayonets, Farah's head had sunk to his shoulder as they huddled around their book and candle. He used one finger to point tirelessly at picture after picture, and the other found its way into one of her ringlets, idly pulling it straight and letting it bounce back into place.

"I was thinking," he said some time later as she paused for a drowsy yawn. "Since ye doona have any family to love anymore, ye could love me . . ." Instead of meeting her gaze, he studied the way the pristine white of her petticoat bandage made his hand look that much grubbier. "That is, if ye wanted."

Farah buried her face in his neck and sighed, her lashes brushing against his tender skin with every blink. "Of course I'll love you, Dougan Mackenzie," she said easily. "Who else is going to?"

"Nobody," he said earnestly.

"Will you try to love me, too?" she asked in a small voice.

He considered it. "I'll try, Fairy, but I havena done it before."

"I'll teach you that, as well," she promised. "Right after I teach you to read. Love is quite like reading, I expect. Once you know how, you can't ever imagine not doing it."

Dougan only nodded because his throat was burning. He put his arm around *his* very own fairy, reveling in the fact that he finally had something good that no one could take away from him.

Dougan learned much about himself in those two blissful years with his fairy. Namely that when he loved, he did it nothing short of absolutely. Obsessively, even.

She told him how her father had been exposed to cholera while visiting a friend at a soldier's hospital and had brought it home. Farah Leigh's older sister, Faye Marie, had been the first to die, and her parents had followed in short succession.

He told her that his mother had been a maid in a Mackenzie laird's household. She'd borne one of the laird's many bastards and he'd lived with her for about four years until she'd died violently by the hand of another lover.

One of the things Dougan had realized from an early age, which set him apart from other people, was that he remembered almost everything. He even recalled conversations he and his Fairy had a year later, and would shock and delight her by reminding her of them.

"I'd forgotten that!" she'd say.

"I *never* forget," he'd boast.

The ability made him a quick study, and he'd surpassed her reading skills quickly. Though he always sat attentively while she taught him, even when he didn't want to. Besides, she picked books that he would be interested in, ones about ships, cannons, and a barrage of historical wars from the Romans all the way through Napoleon. His particular favorite was one on the maritime history of pirates.

"Do ye think I'd make a good pirate someday?" he asked her once around a mouthful of hard cake she'd brought him as a special treat.

"Of course not," she'd answered patiently. "Pirates are wicked thieves and murderers. Besides, they don't allow girls on their pirate ships." She'd turned to him with moist, frightened eyes. "Would you leave me to go pirating?"

He'd pulled her in close. "I'd never leave you, Fairy," he vowed fiercely.

"Truly?" She'd pulled back, staring up at him with storm-cloud eyes that threatened rain. "Not even to be a pirate?"

"I promise." He'd taken a bite of cake and smiled at her with full cheeks before turning back to the book. "I might be a highwayman, though. They're a lot like pirates, but just on land."

After a short consideration, Farah had nodded. "Yes, I

think you would be *much* better suited to the life of a highwayman," she agreed.

"Aye, Fairy, ye'll have to resign yerself to being a highwayman's wife."

She'd clapped and sparkled delighted eyes at him. "Sounds like an adventure!" But then her face had sobered as though she'd remembered something particularly distasteful.

"What?" he'd asked anxiously.

"Only that . . . I think I'm supposed to marry someone else."

Dougan snarled, shaking her wee shoulders. "Who?"

"Mr. Warrington." She continued upon seeing the anger and puzzlement in his eyes. "He—he worked with my father and is the one who left me here. He said that when I'm a woman, he'll come to collect me, and we are to be married."

A cold desperation stole into his blood. "Ye canna marry anyone else, Fairy. You belong to *me*. Only me."

"What do we do?" She fretted.

Dougan thought furiously as they trembled against each other in the arid library, the threat of a future separation driving them together. Suddenly, he was struck by genius.

"Go to bed, Fairy. Tomorrow night, instead of meeting me here in the library, let's meet in the vestry."

Dougan had waited for her in the vestry with the only memento of his family he'd ever owned. A scrap of Mackenzie plaid. He'd bathed and scrubbed and yanked the tangles out of his straight black hair before tying it back with a string.

Farah's unruly curls poked around the heavy doors to the chapel, and when she'd spied him standing next to the altar, only illuminated by a lone candle, the brilliance of her smile had preceded her down the aisle. She wore her simple white nightdress that pleased him to no end, and her bare feet poked out from the long hem with her every step.

He offered his hand to her, and she took it without hesitation. "You look very fine," she whispered. "What are we doing in here, Dougan?"

"I'm here to marry ye," he murmured.

"Oh?" She looked around curiously. "With no priest?"

"We doona need priests in the Highlands," he scoffed gently. "Our weddings are bound by many gods rather than just one. And they come when *we* ask, not when a priest says."

"That sounds even better," she agreed with a fervent nod.

They knelt facing each other in front of the altar, and Dougan wrapped his faded plaid around their joined right hands.

"Just say what I say, Fairy," he murmured.

"All right." She looked up at him with those eyes, and Dougan experienced a pang of love so intense and ferocious it felt as though it didn't belong in this holy room.

He began the incantation he remembered from watching once from behind his mother's skirts when he was young.

Ye are blood of my blood, and bone of my bone.
I give ye my body, that we two might be one.
I give ye my spirit, 'til our life shall be done.

Farah needed a bit of prompting to remember all the words, but she said them with such fervency that Dougan was touched.

Slipping a ring of a willow herb vine onto her finger,

he recited the sacred *olde* vows with perfect clarity, but translated them into English for her sake.

> *I make ye my heart*
> *At the rising of the moon.*
> *To love and honor,*
> *Through all our lives.*
> *May we be reborn,*
> *May our souls meet and know.*
> *And love again.*
> *And remember.*

She looked lost and mystified for a moment, then announced, "Me, too."

It was enough. She was his. Sighing with the alleviation of a great weight, Dougan unwrapped their hands, and offered his plaid to her. "Ye keep this with ye, next to yer heart."

"Oh, Dougan, I have nothing to give to you," she lamented.

"Ye give me a kiss, Fairy, and then 'tis done."

She launched herself at him, puckering her wee mouth artlessly against his, and then letting go with a loud *smack*. "You're the best husband, Dougan Mackenzie," she announced. "I don't know of any other husbands who can make a frog jump so high, or come up with such clever names for the foxes that live under the wall, or skip *three* stones at a time."

"We musna tell anyone," Dougan said, still reeling a bit from the kiss. "Not—not until we're grown."

She nodded her assent. "I'd better get back," she said reluctantly.

He agreed, lowering his head to kiss her on the mouth once more, softer this time. It was his husbandly right, after all. "I love ye, Fairy mine," he whispered as she silently padded back down the aisle, clutching her plaid and crowned with the vibrant flowers.

"I love you, too."

The following night, a small body roused Dougan by lifting the covers and wriggling into his narrow dormitory cot. He opened his eyes to see a wealth of silver ringlets tucked against his chest in the dim light of the lone candle.

"What are ye doing, Fairy?" he whispered drowsily.

She didn't answer him, just clung to his shirt with uncharacteristic desperation, her body racked with shivers and wordless little whimpers escaping from her throat.

Instinctively, Dougan's arms went around her and pulled her in tight as panic pierced him to the bone. "What's happened? Are ye hurt?"

"N-no," she stammered against him.

He relaxed a little, but was distressed to find her tears soaking the front of his threadbare nightshirt. He lifted his head to see if any of the other twenty or so boys lined in the bunks next to and across from him noted her presence, but all was silent as far as he could tell. She'd never done this before, so whatever her cause, it must have been grave.

Curling back a little to look down at her, Dougan saw something in the silver moonlight that made the blood turn to ice in his veins.

She wore her brilliant white nightgown, the very same one he'd married her in the night before, except now the row of tiny buttons from her navel to the lace at her neck were missing. She held the gap together with one hand while the other one clutched at him. A desolate calm settled over him as he cradled his ten-year-old wife in his arms.

"Tell me," was all he could manage through a throat closing off with dread.

"He pulled me into his study and said such h-horrible things," she whispered to his chest, red with shame, still yet to bring herself to look up into his face. "Father MacLean, he told me all the things I tempted him to do to me. It was awful and vulgar and terrifying. Then he pulled me onto his lap and tried to kiss me."

"Tried?" Dougan's fists were buried in the back of her nightgown, shaking with the force of his rage.

"I—sort of—stabbed him in the shoulder with a letter opener and ran," she confessed. "I ran here. To you. The only safe place I could think of. Oh, Dougan he's after me!" She dissolved into sobs, her whole body shaking with the effort to keep them silent.

In spite of everything, Dougan's lips twitched with wry satisfaction in his wee wife. "That was well done, Fairy," he murmured, stroking her hair, silently wishing it had been Father MacLean's eye, rather than his shoulder, that she'd stabbed.

Applecross was a large, old stone fortress with many places to hide, but it wouldn't take the old priest long to come searching through the boys' dormitory.

"I don't know what to do," came the small voice from beneath his blanket.

A light appeared beneath the dormitory door and Dougan froze, placing a hand over her mouth and not breathing until it passed.

Dougan got out of bed and silently opened his trunk, extricating his two pair of trousers. He tossed one to her, along with one of his shirts. "Put these on," he commanded in a whisper. She nodded silently and began to struggle into them beneath her night shift. Swiftly, Dougan helped her to roll up the hem and the sleeves of the shirt and tied a bit of twine that he'd been using as a belt to lash the trousers to her nonexistent hips.

He donned his boots with rifts in the soles and decided

they would swipe a pair of the cook's boots for her from the kitchen when they gathered food for their journey. They couldn't risk going back to her dormitory to collect her things.

Her tiny hand felt fragile yet weighty in his as they made their way to the kitchens in the dark, pausing to peek around corners and creeping through the shadows. It was nigh on ten miles to Russel on Loch Kishorn. There they could rest and sleep and feast on the oyster beds before moving on to Fort William. Dougan only hoped his wee Fairy had the strength to make it.

Didn't matter, he'd carry her the full way if he had to.

Once in the kitchens, they gathered bread and dried pork, along with a bit of cheese, and wasted precious seconds stuffing cheesecloth into the toes of the cook's boots. The small woman had little feet for a grown woman, but Farah's were smaller still.

Dougan was glad to see that his Fairy had stopped crying, her face set with purpose and determination, if not a little anxiety.

Dougan tucked her in his thin jacket, hating that he didn't have anything warmer for her.

"Won't *you* be cold?" she protested.

"I've more meat on me bones," he boasted, opening the kitchen door and wincing when the hinges creaked loud enough to wake half of the souls in the graveyard. The loamy scent of dew reminded him that dawn would soon be upon them, but it also showed that the nights had stopped freezing, which was a good sign.

Searching the darkness, he noted which way was due east. They'd just have to walk as straight a line as possible and they'd be dumped onto the shores of Loch Kishorn. He was certain of it.

Her strangled whimper gave little warning before her hand was ripped out of his grip.

Dougan whirled to see the towering Sister Margaret restraining a struggling Farah as Father MacLean huffed into the kitchens, two stout friars close behind him.

"Nay," Dougan rasped, momentarily frozen in abject horror.

"Dougan, run!" his Fairy cried. Father MacLean approached Sister Margaret and sneered, reaching a thin, gnarled bloodstained hand to help subdue Farah's thrashing.

"Doona bloody touch her!" Dougan commanded. "She is *mine*." He pulled the knife he'd pilfered from the cook board, and thrust it in warning toward both of his adversaries. "Unless ye'd like to be stuck twice in a night." He took a threatening step forward and Father MacLean pulled his thin lips back from sharp, uneven teeth. His bald pate shone in the light from a torch one of the friars carried.

"This one's worth too much to let go." Quick as a hawk, MacLean wrapped long, bony fingers around Farah's delicate neck. "Ye should have picked another princess to prey upon."

Princess? "I'm not the predator here, ye are!" Dougan accused, unable to tear his eyes away from his Fairy's terrified gaze as she squirmed, and struggled to breathe. "Give her over. Or I'll cut ye both."

Farah gave a strangled sob as MacLean cut off her breath completely.

Dougan snapped. He barreled forward, kicked out, and drove his boot directly into Father MacLean's weak knee. The man went down with a tortured cry, and before Dougan knew what he was doing, he drove the knife into the priest's chest.

There were feminine screams, too deep to be his Fairy's, though he was sure he heard her crying, too. Suddenly, all the beatings, the starvation, and a surge of retribution on his Fairy's behalf thundered through him. Dougan pulled the knife out just in time to slash at the advancing friar, who leaped just out of his reach. He was so focused on the one in front of him, he didn't see the other swing the fire poker at his head until it was too late.

The last thing he heard was the sound of his Fairy, his wife, screaming his name. His last thought was he had failed her. He had *lost* her forever.

CHAPTER TWO

London, 1872
Seventeen Years Later

For nigh on ten years, it had been the custom of Mrs. Farah L. Mackenzie to walk the mile to work. She'd leave her small but fashionable flat above one of the many coffee-houses on Fetter Lane, and stroll down Fleet Street until it turned into the Strand, London's infamous avant-garde theater and arts thoroughfare. With Temple Bar, and The Adelphi Theatre on her left, and Covent Garden and Tra-falgar Square to her right, every morning was bound to be a particular feast for her senses.

She'd often take morning coffee with her landlord and owner of the Bookend Coffeehouse, Mr. Pierre de Gaule, who would regale her with stories of famous po-ets, novelists, artists, performers, and philosophers who would frequent his establishment during the evening hours.

That particular morning, the conversation had been about the strange Parisian author Jules Verne, and the ar-gument they'd had over their recently deceased mutual ac-quaintance, Alexandre Dumas.

Farah had been especially interested, as she was a great admirer of Mr. Dumas's work and was ashamed to admit she hadn't gotten around to reading Mr. Verne, but felt she should add him to her ever-growing book list.

"Don't bother," de Gaule spat in his thick French accent that, despite his expatriate status, had never diminished in the near decade Farah had known him. "He is another pretentious Deist novelist who considers himself a philosopher."

Leaving Mr. de Gaule with a smile, her month's rent, and a kiss on his considerable jowls, Farah had taken a croissant for her breakfast and nibbled on it as she made her way down the crowded Strand.

The only buildings on her route that didn't exhibit a colorful array of patrons were the handful of pleasure houses that, like many of their employees, only appeared deceptively tempting at night when the lighting was more favorable.

Farah found her morning stroll disappointingly dull, despite the dazzling bustle of London's most famous market street. That is, until she avoided Charing Cross by cutting down Northumberland Street to arrive at Number Four Whitehall Place through the rear entrance, notorious to all of English society as the "back hall" of the London Metropolitan Police Headquarters, otherwise known as Scotland Yard.

The mob surrounding the building was a great deal larger and angrier than usual, spilling out onto the main thoroughfare.

Farah approached the fringes of the crowd with caution, wondering if Parliament had passed another amendment to the Marriage Act. For that was the last time she could remember such an uproar at Scotland Yard, as it shared a building with the licensing commissioner.

Spotting Sergeant Charles Crompton atop the dappled

gelding at the west corner of the growing mob, Farah made her way toward him.

"Sergeant Crompton!" she called, placing a hand on Hugo's bridle. "Sergeant Crompton. May I ask you to assist me inside?"

Crompton, a burly man of maybe forty, scowled down at her from behind a bristled mustache that hung below the extra chins created by the strap of his uniform helmet. "You i'nt supposed to come frew the back hall on days wot like this, Missus Mackenzie," he called from atop his restless steed. "The chief inspector'll 'ave me badge. Not to mention me 'ead."

"What is all this?" Farah asked.

His answer was lost in a sudden roar rippling through the press of bodies, and Farah whipped around in time to see the shadow of a man cross the headquarters entrance toward the basement stairs. She couldn't make out any particular features, but caught the impression of dark hair, shocking height, and a long, cocksure stride.

The brief glimpse inflamed the crowd so intensely that someone threw a projectile through a window of the clerk's office.

Her office.

In a flash, Crompton was off his horse and propelling her by the elbow away from the crowd and toward the front of the building that faced Whitehall Place. "They've the very devil in there!" he hollered at her. "I've sent for bobbies from Bow Street and St. James precinct to 'elp."

"Who was that?" she cried.

But as soon as she was on the corner of Newbury and Whitehall Place, Crompton abandoned her to return to the crowd, his club raised in case of violence.

Smoothing her black wool uniform jacket over her dress, she was grateful for the lack of a bustle beneath the crinoline of her skirts. With the ever-shrinking offices at Scotland Yard, she'd never fit were she dressed fashionably.

Farah nodded to the licensing comissioner's reception clerk, and wound her way through the maze of hallways to the headquarters' connecting entrance, only to find the pandemonium inside Scotland Yard was barely tamer than the mob without.

She'd been in these kinds of situations before. There was the Irish riot of '68, and the time an explosive detonated outside of Parliament, not a stone's throw away, not to mention a constant barrage of criminals, thieves, and whores parading through Number Four Whitehall Place on a daily basis. And yet, as Farah elbowed her way through the Scotland Yard reception office, she couldn't remember a time she'd sensed such imminent disaster. A thrill of unease trembled through her, disrupting her usually infallible composure.

"Mrs. Mackenzie!" She heard her name rise above the din of constables, journalists, criminals, and inspectors all crowded within the back hall. Farah turned to see David Beauchamp, the first clerk, struggling toward her from the hall of offices. His slight, wiry build didn't meet the minimum physical requirements for an officer of the Metropolitan Police, so he'd been hired as a clerk, to his everlasting regret.

Farah pushed toward him, excusing herself along the way. "Mr. Beauchamp." She took his offered elbow and together they pressed toward the relative safety of the hall. "Would you please tell me what is going on here?"

"He's asking for you," Beauchamp informed her with an imperious frown.

Farah knew exactly to whom Mr. Beauchamp referred. Her employer, Chief Inspector Sir Carlton Morley.

"Right away," she replied, removing her bonnet and tossing it onto her desk. She grimaced at the shards of the window on the office floor, but felt guilty at the relief she felt when she realized most of the damage had been done to Mr. Beauchamp's desk, as hers was positioned closer to the door. Errol Cartwright, the third clerk, had yet to arrive.

"You'll need your instruments," Beauchamp needlessly reminded her. "There's to be an interrogation. I'm to stay here and deal with the press and coordinate the extra bobbies." He used the street name Londoners had dubbed the Metropolitan Police, which Farah found ridiculous.

"Of course," Farah said wryly, as she gathered her pen, inkwell, and pad of thick parchment upon which she took down minute notes, confessions, and drafted affidavits for criminals and coppers alike. Ignoring the sound of the mob outside the broken window took nerve, but she managed. Her office was high enough that they couldn't see her head as a target, though she could look down on theirs. "Will you kindly tell me just *who* is the reason for all of this hullabaloo?" she asked for what felt like the hundredth time.

Mr. Beauchamp gave a self-important sniff, pleased to be the one to give her news she hadn't already gleaned. "Only the man whose capture could make Sir Morley's entire career. The most *infamous* criminal mastermind in recent history."

"*No,* you can't mean—"

"Indeed I do, Mrs. Mackenzie. I can *only* mean Dorian Blackwell, the Blackheart of Ben More."

"Upon my word," Farah breathed, suddenly more than a little apprehensive to be in the same building with him, let alone the same room.

"Please do tell me you're not in danger of the vapors or some other such female hysteria. I don't know if you've noticed, but we're in the middle of a crisis, and I simply cannot cover for any missish behavior." Beauchamp regarded her with distaste.

"When have you *ever* known me to be plagued with the vapors?" she asked impatiently as she tucked her pad into the crook of the arm that held her pen and inkwell. "*Really,* Mr. Beauchamp, after all these years!" She huffed past him in a swirl of skirts, frowning with disapproval. Though he was the senior first clerk to her second clerk, perhaps it was time she usurped his authority.

First things first. Farah squared her shoulders and gathered her skirts to descend the stairs to the basement. Though not prone to the vapors, she did feel her lungs strain against her corset more rapidly than usual, and her heart felt like a trapped sparrow, fluttering around the walls of her chest, looking for an escape.

Dorian Blackwell, the Blackheart of Ben More.

Despite her apprehension, Farah realized she was taking part in something unprecedented. Certainly Blackwell had a number of arrests in his history, but he somehow always managed to escape imprisonment, and the gallows. Inwardly, she cited the information she had on Dorian Blackwell.

His countrywide notoriety had begun little more than a decade ago with disturbing and mysterious disappearances of half the criminals being investigated by Scotland Yard. During the initial inquiry, a name had amalgamated from shadows and whispers that rose from the most violent, treacherous bowels of the city such as Fleet Ditch, Whitechapel, and the East End.

The Blackheart. A new, almost Continental sort of criminal who ruthlessly seized control of the London underworld before anyone quite knew about it. All by means of infiltration and the curious organization of what amounted to a well-trained militia.

An incredible number of wanted thieves, pimps, book-makers, traffickers, slumlords, and the reigning heads of existing criminal enterprises had also disappeared, often reappearing as bloated corpses in the Thames.

A silent, hidden war had raged in East London, and it was only when the rivers of blood ceased flowing that the police even heard about it. According to increasingly unreliable sources, the Blackheart replaced these missing criminals with agents abjectly loyal to himself. Those who remained in their previous positions suddenly became wealthier and more elusive to justice.

Had the mystifying, so-called Blackheart stayed on his side of London, it was likely he'd never been pursued by the woefully underfunded, overworked police force. But once he'd secured the position of absolute control over squalid thieves' dens and gambling hells, the figure of a *man* emerged from the shadow and filth and blood of what was now known as the Underworld War.

And suddenly the Blackheart had a name. Dorian Blackwell. And that name became synonymous with an altogether *different* sort of carnage. The monetary kind. The police were still trying to tie together the seemingly random people Blackwell had elevated and/or broken with callous, precise efficiency. His battlefields were banks and boardrooms, with the swipe of a pen and a whisper of scandal that brought about the ruination of several of the London elite. To curb the rising terror gripping the city at all the upheaval, he smoothed some of the edges of apprehension by liberally giving to charities, especially those directed at children, sponsoring the careers of artists and performers, and stimulating the emerging middle-class economy with some very sound investments. He'd garnered somewhat of a Robin Hood-like reputation among the middle and lower classes.

He was rumored to be one of the wealthiest men in the

empire. He had a Hyde Park house, numerous properties and other holdings, either invested or seized in hostile business deals, and a rather famous castle on the Isle of Mull, from which he garnered the rest of his name.

Ben More Castle it was called, a secluded place in the Highlands where he reportedly spent a great deal of his time.

Upon reaching the dank brick-and-dirt basement, Farah checked out the porthole window through the iron bars covering it, distressed to see that the mob seemed to have doubled. It wouldn't take much longer for it to reach the Charing Cross circle. And what then?

She quickened her step, ignoring the calls and excited conversations of the dozen or so inspectors who loitered below stairs near the iron doors of the evidentiary, record, and supply rooms. All of their attention was centered on one point. The barred door of the first strong room, from which a series of curses and the unmistakable sounds of flesh connecting with flesh rang through the bars.

They were all talking about Blackwell. And *not* in favorable terms.

As an enigmatic public figure, all of the Blackheart of Ben More's business dealings were generally legal, if often unethical, and *still* the police might have left him to his personal devices.

That was, until *other* mysterious disappearances had begun to terrorize the city. A few prison guards. A police sergeant. The Newgate commissioner. And, most recently, a justice of the Supreme Court, Lord Roland Phillip Cranmer III, one of the most powerful judiciaries in the entire realm.

If Farah knew anything, it was that *nothing* incited the police to action like violence against their own. She'd known, of course, that Sir Carlton Morley had been following Blackwell since Morley had been a new inspector, almost ten years now, and the men had become embroiled in a sort of cat-and-mouse game that was swiftly escalating.

The chief inspector had even brought Blackwell to charges a few times, but that was ages ago when he worked the Whitechapel precinct. Still, the Blackheart of Ben More seemed to be a particular obsession with her employer, and Farah wondered if this time he'd finally cornered his quarry. She sincerely hoped so. Her feelings for Carlton Morley had recently become much more opaque. Complicated, even.

The smell below stairs was a complex combination of pleasant and repellent. The inviting scents of paper, musk, and cool, hard-packed earth underscored the more pervasive odors of the stone and iron strong room and holding cells which, the farther one ventured, strengthened to overwhelming. Urine, body odor, and other filth that didn't bear consideration assaulted her senses as it always did before she habitually compartmentalized it in order to do her job.

"I'm surprised Beauchamp let ye come down here, Mrs. Mackenzie." Ewan McTavish, a short but burly Scotsman, and longtime inspector, tipped his cap at her as she paused at the door. They had a good rapport with each other, as it was known among the men of Scotland Yard that her late husband had, indeed, been Scottish. "It's not every day we get someone as dangerous as the Blackheart of Ben More. He might forget to be respectful to ye." A dangerous gleam entered McTavish's blue eyes.

"I appreciate your concern, Mr. McTavish, but I've been doing this a long time, and I'm fair certain I've heard it all." Farah gave the handsome, copper-haired Scotsman a confident smile, and took her keys from the pocket of her skirts, unlocking the door to the interrogation room.

"We'll be stationed right out here should ye be in danger or have need of anything," McTavish said just a bit too loudly, perhaps for the benefit of those inside the room just as much as her own.

"Thank you, Inspector, thank you all." Farah gave one last smile of gratitude, and swept inside.

The smell intensified in the strong room, and Farah lifted a lace handkerchief dabbed with lavender oil that she kept in her pocket until the usual wave of nausea passed, before acknowledging the occupants of the room.

When she lifted her gaze, she froze, stunned in place at the sight before her.

Chief Inspector Sir Carlton Morley was in his shirt-sleeves, which he'd rolled to the elbows. The manicured hands clenched at his sides had blood on the knuckles, and his usually well-groomed hair was mussed into disarray.

A large, dark-haired man sat on a lone chair in the center of the room, his hands chained behind him, and his posture deceptively relaxed.

They were both panting and sweating and bleeding, but that wasn't what startled Farah the most. It was the almost identical expressions on their faces as they looked at her, an intense compilation of surprise and ruefulness, with a barely leashed undercurrent of . . . hunger?

Violence hung in the air between the two men with a tangible vibration, but as the prisoner in the chair studied her, all became extraordinarily silent and still.

Farah had once developed a fascination with exotic predators after seeing them on display in large cages at the World's Fair in Covent Garden. She'd read about them, learning that great hunting cats, such as lions and jaguars, could make themselves preternaturally still. Going so far as to conceal their frighteningly powerful bodies in shadows, trees, and tall grasses in such a way that their prey could pass by without even realizing a beast was about to pounce and rip out their throats until it was too late.

She'd pitied and feared them at the same time. For surely a creature so dynamic and powerful could do nothing chained in such a small cage but hate and whither and eventually die. She'd watched a particularly dark jaguar tread the scant four paces behind his bars as his wild yellow eyes promised retribution and pain to the brightly dressed masses who'd come to gawk at him. Their eyes had met, Farah's and the beast, and he'd demonstrated that unnatural stillness, holding her stare for an unblinking eternity. She'd been mesmerized by that predator while hot tears had scalded her cheeks. By the terrifying fate she'd seen mirrored at her in those eyes. He'd marked her as prey, as one of the weaker and more desirable morsels in the herd of people milling about them. And in that moment, she'd been grateful for the cursed chains that held the beast in check.

That exact, disquieting affectation suffused her now as she met the mismatched gaze of Dorian Blackwell. His features were those of cruel brutality. His one good eye had that amber quality that had belonged to the jaguar. The flickering lamplight made it glow gold against his burnished skin. It was his other eye, though, that arrested her attention. For starting above the brow, and ending at the bridge of a bladed nose, was a jagged, angry scar, interrupted by an eye leached of every pigment but blue by whatever had caused the wound. And, indeed, he stared at her like a predator recognizing his preferred meal, and lying in wait to pounce until she haplessly wandered into his vicinity. His cheek was split and bleeding along the sharp line of his masculine cheekbone, and another small trickle of blood dripped from his right nostril.

Catching her breath, Farah ripped her stare from the prisoner's compelling regard and sought the familiar, aristocratically handsome features of her employer.

Sir Morley, generally a self-possessed man, seemed to

be at the end of a frayed rope, clutching for control of his temper with both hands. This wasn't like Morley, to beat a man whose wrists were chained behind him.

"I see you've come prepared," he clipped, his tone belying the glimmer of warmth and yearning in his eyes as he gave her a curt nod.

"Yes, sir." Farah nodded, giving herself a stern shake as she fixed her gaze on the desk at the back of the room, and willed her shaking legs to carry her all the way to it without dropping something, or worse. She hid her discomfiture behind a carefully arranged mask of serenity as the heels of her boots clipped a sharp echo against the stones of the strong room.

"As much as I approve of your change in tactics, Morley, dangling this tasty piece in front of me still won't have the desired effect." Blackwell's voice reached out to her like the first unwelcome tendrils of frost in winter. Deep, smooth, caustic, and bitter cold. Despite that, his accent was astonishingly cultured, though a deeply hidden brogue rounded out the *r*'s, enough to hint that the Blackheart of Ben More might not have been London born. His neck swiveled on powerful shoulders as he followed her progress toward the writer's desk placed behind him at a diagonal. He didn't take those disturbing eyes from her once, even as he addressed Morley. "I warn you now that more brutal men than you have tried to beat a confession out of me, and more beautiful women than *she* have endeavored to bewitch my secrets from me. Both have failed."

The desk chair came up to meet her much faster than she'd anticipated as she dropped into it, nearly upsetting the items clutched in her arms. Unutterably glad she was stationed behind Blackwell so he could not see her unease, she smoothed the pad of paper in front of her with an unsteady hand, and positioned her inkwell and pen just so.

"You'll learn, Blackwell, that there *are* no more brutal men than I." Morley sneered.

"Said the fly to the spider."

"If *I* am the fly, why are you the one caught in my web?" Morley circled Blackwell, jerking on the manacles imprisoning his hands behind him.

"Are you certain that is what's happening here, Inspector? Are you quite sure it is *I* who am playing right into *your* hands?" Blackwell's demeanor remained unperturbed, but Farah noted that his wide shoulders were tense beneath his fine tailored jacket, and little rivulets of sweat beaded at his temple and behind his jaw.

"I *know* it is," Morley said.

The hollow sound of amusement Blackwell produced yet again reminded Farah of the dark jaguar. "Real knowledge is to know the extent of one's ignorance."

The man quoted Confucius? How unfair that a man such as he could be so clever, dangerous, rich, powerful, *and* well read. Farah stifled a sigh, then, alarmed by her reaction to him, straightened her spine and took up her quill, ready to swipe the efficient shorthand across her paper.

"Enough of this." Morley crossed to her. "Are you ready for the interrogation to begin, Mrs. Mackenzie?"

Her name seemed to zing about the room like an errant insect, hurling itself against the steel and stone and echoing back to the man chained in the middle.

"Mackenzie." Farah couldn't be certain, but she thought the word may have been absorbed by Blackwell and then uttered by him. But as she glanced through her lashes at a scowling Morley, she noted that he hadn't seemed to detect it.

"Of course," she murmured, and made a show of dipping her pen.

Morley turned back to Blackwell, his square face set

with grim determination. "Tell me what you did with Justice Cranmer. And don't bother denying it was you, Blackwell; I know he was the magistrate that sentenced you to Newgate fifteen years hence."

"So he was." Blackwell didn't so much as twitch a muscle.

Fifteen years ago at Newgate? Farah's head snapped up, her pen creating a loud scratch against the table. It couldn't be that he was there at the same time as—

"And those missing guards," Morley continued, his voice louder now, more desperate. "They were assigned to your ward during your stay there."

"Were they?"

"You bloody well know they were!"

Blackwell lifted a shoulder in a helpless gesture that seemed to say, I would help you if I could, which enraged Morley to no end. "All you bobbies look the same to me. Those ridiculous mustaches and unflattering hats. It's almost impossible to tell you apart, even if I wanted to."

"It's too much coincidence for the courts to ignore this time!" Morley said victoriously. "It's only a matter of time before you're dancing at the end of a rope from the gallows in front of Newgate, the very hole from which you slithered."

"Confirm one shred of evidence in your possession." Blackwell's soft challenge was threaded with steel. "Better yet, produce one witness who would dare speak against me."

Morley maneuvered around that pitfall. "The whole of London knows your penchant for swift and fierce vengeance. I could pick any half-wit off the street and they'd raise their hand to God and swear you'd done in the judge who'd sentenced you to seven years in prison."

"You and I both know that it will take more than heresy and reputation to convict one such as I, Morley," Blackwell scoffed. Craning his neck to look at Farah with his good eye, he addressed her directly, which caused her stomach to clench and her hands to tremble with even more violence. "Add my solemn, official confession to the records, *Mrs. Mackenzie,* and note that I swear by its absolute truth."

Farah said nothing, as always demonstrating her professionalism to the prisoner by ignoring him. Of course, though, he had her absolute undivided attention. That face. That savage, masculine face. All angles and intrigue and darkness. Handsome, but for the scar and the startlingly blue eye, which she found both repellent and compelling.

"I, Dorian Everett Blackwell, never have had any emotional antipathy toward High Court Justice Lord Roland Phillip Cranmer the Third. I was guilty of the crime of petty theft, for which he sentenced me to seven years in Newgate Prison, and I solemnly swear that I have learned my lesson." This was said, of course, in that ironic way that made one doubt the veracity of every word.

Farah could only stare at him, completely absorbed, trying to unravel the message burning at her from his one good eye with a foreign and alarming desperation. She felt as though the very devil was both toying with her *and* warning her. "You understand, don't you, Mrs. Mackenzie?" Blackwell murmured, his hard mouth barely moving as the intensity of his regard pinned her to her seat. "The deeds of a willful youth."

A thrill of danger kissed her spine.

"Horseshit!" Morley roared.

Dorian turned back to face him, and Farah was able to let out a breath she hadn't been aware she'd been holding as the black spell he'd woven over her suddenly dissipated.

"For shame, Morley," he mockingly chided. "Such language in front of a lady?"

"*She* is my employee," Sir Morley gritted through

clenched teeth. "And I'll thank you not to bother about her if you want to keep the vision in the eye you have left."

"I can hardly help myself. She's such a ripe piece of skirt."

"Bite. Your. Tongue."

Farah had never seen Sir Morley so angry. His lips pulled back from his teeth. A vein pulsed in his forehead. This was a man she'd never met before.

"Tell me, Morley," Blackwell calmly but ruthlessly persisted. "How much time does she spend at her own desk, as opposed to beneath yours, with her lips affixed to your—"

Sir Morley erupted, driving his fist into Dorian Blackwell's face with a force she'd not thought him capable of.

Blackwell's head snapped to the side, and an angry split tore into the corner of his lower lip. But to Farah's astonishment, the large, dark man made no sound of pain, not even a grunt. He simply brought his head back around to face the wrathful inspector before him.

Sir Morley glanced over Blackwell's ebony hair at Farah, a glint of shame touching his gaze.

"Gather your things, Mrs. Mackenzie. You are dismissed." His blue eyes lit with an anticipatory rage when he looked back down at his prisoner. "You don't need to see this."

Farah stood suddenly, her chair scraping with a jarring screech as she protested. "But sir, I—I don't think—"

"Leave, Farah! *Now*," he commanded.

Breathlessly, Farah gathered her paper, pen, and ink, surprised that her cold, shaking hands obeyed her. As she passed Dorian Blackwell, he turned his head toward her and spat a mouthful of blood onto the stones beside him, though it didn't reach the hem of her skirts.

"Yes, Farah Mackenzie, you *should* run." The voice was

so savage and cold Farah thought her mind might be playing tricks. That she may have imagined that when he said her name, a note of something like warm recognition thrummed through the words. "We're going to be here yet a while."

Turning back to him with a gasp, she was surprised to see that Blackwell wasn't watching her leave. Instead, his face lifted toward Morley, who stood over him, hands fisted at his sides.

Of all the evil Farah had had a chance to glimpse in this room, Dorian Blackwell's smile, full of his own blood and teeth and challenge, had to be the most frightening Farah had witnessed in her entire life. His eyes were dead, devoid of any hope or humanity, the milky blue one utterly motionless but for the reflection of the torchlight lending it an unnatural pagan gleam.

Farah turned from the sight and swept out of the room, past the silent inspectors who followed her progress with rapt attention.

It took everything she had, but she kept her trembling hidden until she was alone.

Chapter Three

Three nights later, Inspector Ewan McTavish struck a match on the gray stones of St. Martin-in-the-Fields and leaned against the rear of the building while feeding the embers of his well-worn cigar. He scanned the shadows of Duncannon Street thinking that, once he'd concluded his appointment, he might pay a visit to Madame Regina's down on Fleet Street. As always, after these clandestine meetings, he developed an itch born of the life-affirming feeling of having escaped the reaper. It would take two or three goes with a doxy to feel like himself again.

"Thinking of that new little Parisian skirt at Madame Regina's?" The voice that had become the stuff of his nightmares caused McTavish to all but jump out of his skin.

"Jesus kilt-lifting Christ, Blackwell!" he wheezed, retrieving his fallen cigar from the soggy ground with a petulant scowl. "How is it a man of yer size can slither through the shadows with nary a sound?"

If McTavish had his way, he'd never again have to see

the Blackheart of Ben More crack a smile, for the fine hairs on his body would stand on end for hours after.

"That was all well done of you," Blackwell remarked. "You executed your orders admirably."

"Wasna easy," McTavish groused, finding it difficult to meet the expression of bemused calculation on Blackwell's cruel features. "Disbanding yer mob and sneaking records into yer cell while trying to hide my actions from my precinct. Ye're lucky I'm not the only one loyal to ye at Scotland Yard."

If it was difficult to look Blackwell in the face, it was nigh impossible to meet his eerie, scrutinizing gaze. No one knew just how well the Blackheart of Ben More could see through his blue eye, but when it fixed on you, a man felt like his skin had been flayed open and his darkest sin exposed.

"I am a great many things, Inspector, but lucky has never been one of them."

McTavish found himself wishing he'd be as *unlucky* as the impeccably dressed blackguard in front of him. Rich as Midas, they said, powerful as a Caesar, and ruthless as the devil. So he didn't have a pretty face for the ladies to coo over, but a man such as Dorian Blackwell drew feminine notice wherever he prowled. Fear and fascination proved to be powerful tools of seduction, and women reacted one way or the other toward the dark giant.

"Why'd ye do it, anyway?" McTavish asked. "Why summon yer men for a riot only to send them away?"

Ignoring his question, Blackwell reached into his dark overcoat and produced a gold cylinder. From it, he pulled a brand-new cigar, which he handed to McTavish, who could only stare at it for a moment, hoping he lived long enough to finish it.

"I thank ye, sir," he said hesitantly, taking it and holding the fragrant treasure to his mustache before biting off the end. Blackwell struck a match with his gloved hand, and McTavish had to fortify himself to lean close enough to light it. His need won out, though, as he was pretty sure he'd never have the occasion for such an expensive smoke again. "Well, I only knew ye'd have to get yer hide in front of Justice Singleton and ye'd be walking the streets free as an alley cat. Morley didn't have a thing on ye."

"Indeed."

The flame of the match illuminated Blackwell's features and McTavish gave a little sympathetic wince. "He really went to work on yer face." He noted the healing lip and multiple bruises on Blackwell's cheekbones. "Whatever grudge he's holding against ye, it's powerful."

"As police beatings go, this was rather minor," Blackwell said almost genially.

McTavish blanched. "Let me be the first to apologize for—"

Blackwell held up a hand to silence him. "Before I pay you, I require some information."

Puffing on his own little piece of heaven, McTavish nodded. "Anything."

The Blackheart leaned down. "Tell me *everything* you know about Mrs. Farah Mackenzie."

Pausing mid-puff, McTavish asked, "Mrs. Mackenzie— the clerk?"

Blackwell was still and silent, but his droll stare was easy to interpret, even in the darkness.

Perplexed, McTavish scratched the back of his neck, trying to think of anything interesting to say about the woman. "She's been around as long as any of us can remember. Before me, even, and I started at Scotland Yard seven or eight years ago. Come to think of it, though, I havena learned much about her in all that time. She's efficient and well liked, but keeps to herself. Quiet. Which is a rare and commendable female trait, in my experience.

She works harder than the other two clerks, but gets paid less."

"What sort of *work* does Morley have her do?"

"Oh, the usual sort of clerical business. Bookkeeping, records, paperwork, supply orders, courier bookings, note-taking, filing documents at court, that sort of thing."

Blackwell remained motionless. Expressionless. But McTavish could feel the hairs rising on his neck again. He was trained to read people, and though the Blackheart of Ben More was an enigma, the inspector in him noted that his gloved hand was clenched just a little too tight.

"Her husband?"

"A Scotsman, if ye'd believe it."

"What do you know of him?"

"Next to nothing. Story goes she married young and he's a long time dead . . ."

"And?" Blackwell prompted, belying more impatience than McTavish had thought him capable.

McTavish shrugged. Intrigued, but knowing better than to show it. "That's pretty much all we know, come to think of it. Sure, we've speculated over the years, but she's never inclined to talk about it, and it's not polite to ask a lady about such matters."

"Is she . . . romantically involved with any of the men employed at Scotland Yard?"

McTavish found the idea so ludicrous, he laughed aloud. "Were she not such a pretty bird, most of us would forget she's even a woman."

"So . . . no one?"

"Well, the rumor is she's been spending an increasing number of evenings out with Sir Morley."

They simultaneously spat on the stones at the mention of the chief inspector, and Dorian's split lip curled with disgust.

McTavish froze. Something about the increasing intensity of Blackwell's demeanor caused his heart to kick. "I think he's sniffing around the wrong skirts for what he wants," he hurried to say, waving his hand as though it was of no consequence.

Blackwell's one good eye sharpened. "How do you mean?"

"Well, for one thing, she's a right proper widow, and I don't much know a man who's into that sort of thing."

"What sort of thing?"

"Oh, you know. The bluestocking sort. Cold. Straitlaced. Er—frigid, some might say. Besides, she's closer to thirty than twenty, and though she's the face of an angel, she's about as bedable as a hedgehog, if ye want my opinion."

"If I *wanted* your opinion, McTavish, I'd promptly inform you as to what it was."

"Fair enough." Heart really hammering now, McTavish puffed on his cigar, hoping with each breath that it wouldn't be his last. What did Blackwell want with Mrs. Mackenzie? Records access? Documents? Bribery? Couldn't be he was sweet on her. Men like Dorian Blackwell didn't go for upright ladies like Farah Mackenzie. Word about town was, he employed scores of foreign, exotic courtesans and set them up in his mansion like a private harem. What would a spinsterish widow like Mackenzie have to offer a man like him?

"Where does she live?" Blackwell demanded.

McTavish shrugged. "Couldn't say exactly. Somewhere off Fleet Street in the Bohemian sector, I think I heard."

Blackwell's nostrils flared with increased breath, remaining silent for a moment too long before McTavish thought he heard him whisper. "All this time . . ."

"Pardon?"

"Nothing." The Blackheart of Ben More seemed—shaken, for lack of a better word. McTavish couldn't believe his eyes.

"Here is for your services, and continued discretion." A note was pressed against his palm.

McTavish looked down and almost lost another cigar to shock. "But—this is half a year's salary!"

"I know."

"I—I couldn't take this." McTavish shoved it back toward him. "I havena done anything to earn it."

Dorian Blackwell stepped back, avoiding the money and any physical contact. "Let me give you some free advice along with that note, McTavish." It was amazing how the inflection of that cruel, cold voice never once changed, and yet the menace palpably intensified. "Scruples are a dangerous thing for men like you to have. If I can't trust your greed, then I can't trust anything about you. And if I can't trust you, your life is worthless to me."

McTavish snatched the note to his chest. "Right ye are, Blackwell, I'll be thanking ye for yer generosity, then, and be on my way." If his legs weren't shaking too much to carry him.

Blackwell nodded, donning an ebony felt hat that shadowed his eyes from any light, before turning toward the Strand. "Good evening, Inspector. Give Madame Regina my regards."

It was like the man had read his bloody thoughts. Foolishly, McTavish had assumed his habits too low on Blackwell's list of importance for the man to take any notice. When you're blackmailing dukes and bribing justices, how did one remember the proclivities of one in a hundred coppers in Blackwell's pocket?

Before he could stop himself, McTavish was seized by a fit of conscience. "Ye're not going to hurt her, are ye?" he called. "Mrs. Mackenzie, I mean."

Slowly, Blackwell turned, presenting him with his unnatural blue eye. "You know better than to ask me questions, Inspector."

Swallowing, McTavish took his bowler cap off, crushing the rim in his hands. "Forgive me . . . It's only that—well—she's a real gentle, kindhearted sort of bird. I couldn't live with meself knowing I had a hand in any . . . unpleasantness toward her."

The air around Blackwell seemed to darken, as though the shadows gathered to protect him. "If your conscience bothers you too much, McTavish, there are alternatives to living . . ." The Blackheart took a threatening step toward him, and McTavish jumped back.

"Nay! Nay, sir. I'll not get in yer way. I meant no disrespect."

"Very good."

"I—I didn't mean to question ye. It's just . . . not all of us are capable of such a black heart as yers."

Blackwell advanced further, and McTavish squeezed his eyes shut, certain this was the end for him. Instead of killing him, only that calm, cold whisper washed over him like the breath of damnation. "That's where you're wrong, Inspector. Every man is capable of a heart such as mine. They just need to be given the right . . . incentive."

Trembling, McTavish crushed the hat back on his head. "Y-yes sir. Though I'd not wish for such an incentive, if that be yer aim."

A callous, predatory enjoyment lit within Blackwell's eyes, and in that moment, McTavish hated the bastard for unmanning him like this.

"Come close, McTavish, and I'll tell you a secret. Something about me that few men know."

There wasn't a man alive who wanted to be privy to Dorian Blackwell's secrets. They were the kind that got one killed.

He stepped toward the dark, hulking man. "Y-yes?"

"*No one* wants *that* kind of incentive, Inspector. Not even me."

Blinking rapidly, McTavish nodded as he watched Dorian Blackwell melt into the mist and shadows of the London evening, certain that he'd not only escaped death, but the devil, himself.

CHAPTER FOUR

Farah enjoyed London at night. Mingling with the *beau monde* at Covent Garden, or attending lectures, concerts, and after-parties with the rather transitory crowd of novelists who came to England just long enough to get depressed and move back to Paris to write about it.

Today she'd worn her new finest sea-green silk polonaise over particularly ruffled and beribboned petticoats in deference to her plans to see the latest Tom Taylor production with Carlton Morley as her escort. Seized by a whim of recklessness, she'd pulled the puffed and filmy sleeves of her bodice wide to expose an extra expanse of clavicle and shoulder.

The moment the clock struck six, she rose from her desk and shrugged out of her professionally cut jacket which she replaced with a soft fringed shawl and white silk gloves.

Cartwright, the newest clerk, at least five years her junior, watched her with unabashed fascination. "I don't believe I've seen you wear that color before, Mrs. Mackenzie. It complements your eyes, if you don't mind my saying so."

"Thank you, Mr. Cartwright." She smiled, unable to help a small tingle of pleasure at the attractive young man's approval.

"Looking like that, you'll have Sir Morley down on one knee before the night is over," he continued, smoothing the thin golden mustache that teased his lip as though still delighted he could finally grow one. "If Morley doesn't, seek me out and I might be persuaded to give up my coveted bachelor status."

Farah's pleasure dimmed, so she brightened her smile. "I'd never dream of perpetrating such a tragedy, Mr. Cartwright, on either accord. I, for one, have no wish to be any man's trouble and strife." She used the cockney term for *wife* while she fiddled with the edge of her glove. It bothered her increasingly that almost everyone she knew seemed to think that her status as a longtime widow was so pitiable. Over the past decade, a multitude of men had offered to make her their wife if only because their conscience couldn't bear to think of her living, and sleeping, alone.

She'd deflected that behavior by wearing mourning dresses for nearly four years, until she'd reached an age where she was considered to be quite firmly on the shelf. It had abated after a while, and she was lucky enough to be employed in an environment where most of the men were either married or permanently disinclined to the institution. Which was just fine with her, as she felt similarly disillusioned toward the idea of a husband.

Her fortunes, modest as they were, remained her own. As did her time, her pleasures, her opinions, and, most importantly, her will. Being a middle-class widow of an ever-increasingly respectable age, she was afforded societal freedoms of which most women could only dream. She never required a chaperone, was allowed the most indelicate company, and could even take a lover if she liked, and no one but a vicar would so much as bat an eye.

No, Farah's brief and tragic brush with marriage was likely to be the only one in her lifetime. All to the good, in her opinion, for she had more pressing things to take up her time, not the least of which was the pursuit of justice.

Brushing a tightening of melancholy firmly into the past where it belonged, Farah bid Cartwright a good evening, and swept into Scotland Yard's rapidly vacating reception hall.

Sergeant Crompton and the desk sergeant, Westridge, emitted low whistles as she emerged from her office. "Well! Look 'ews trussed for a presentation to 'Er Majesty?" Crompton bellowed, his face ruddy from a chilly afternoon of making his rounds by the river.

"Gentlemen." She laughed and executed a deep and flawless curtsy.

"Don't you curtsy to the likes o' them, Missus Mackenzie!" Gemma Warlow, a streetwalker known to work the docks, called to her with a bawdy geniality. "They don't deserve to spit-shine your shoes!"

"Stuff your gob, Warlow!" Crompton called, though his voice lacked any true antagonism.

"Stuff it yourself, Sergeant!" Gemma shot back with a toss of her dirty-brown locks. "If you've enough in your trousers to reach me throat."

Farah turned to the holding square in the middle of the reception room and addressed Gemma. "Miss Warlow, what are you doing back here?" she asked gently. "Didn't I set you up at the reforming home?"

"Druthers found me and dragged me back to the pier. I got picked up for boffing during trading hours." Gemma shrugged as though it was of little consequence. "Was a bit o' kindness you did for me, Mrs. Mackenzie, but I should have known better than to think 'e'd let me go so easy."

Edmond Druthers was a pimp and a game maker who ruthlessly lorded over vice trade on the docks. His reputation for cruelty was only superseded by his greed.

"Oh, Gemma." Farah went to her and reached for her hand. "What are we to do about this?"

The woman's manacles rattled as she pulled her hands from Farah's reach. "Don't be soiling those lily-white gloves now," she warned with a cheery smile splitting her apple cheeks. Gemma had to be about Farah's age, but the years had been less kind, and she looked maybe a decade older. Deep grooves branched from her eyes and her weatherworn skin stretched tight over small bones. "Tell me where you're off to dressed so fine."

Farah tempered the sadness and worry for the woman out of her smile. "I'm turned out for a night at the theater."

"Ain't that grand?" Genuine pleasure sparkled in the woman's eyes. "Who's the lucky doffer wot's escorting you?"

"That doffer would be me." Carleton Morley appeared at Farah's side, his blue eyes twinkling at her from beneath an evening hat.

"Well, now!" Gemma exclaimed loudly. "Ain't that the 'andsomest couple in London?" she asked the handful of drunkards, thieves, and other doxies stashed in the box awaiting their turn for a cell.

They all readily agreed.

"Shall we?" Morley, resplendent in his evening coat, offered his arm to Farah, who took it with a delighted smile.

Turning back to Gemma before leaving, Farah said, "Please watch yourself. We'll talk in the morning about your situation."

"Don't you spend a minute worrying about me, Mrs.

Mackenzie!" the woman insisted, pulling a tattered red shawl around her scrawny shoulders. "I'll be spending a night on me back *sleeping* for once!"

Officers and criminals, alike, erupted into laughter that spilled into the early evening as Farah followed Morley toward the Strand. They were both silent for a time, their legs disrupting a soupy mist swirling off the river and hiding their feet from view. Gaslights and lanterns kept the dreariness of the gloaming at bay and gave the gray mist a golden glow.

The night was alive with music and merriment, but to Farah it seemed that she and Morley were apart from all that. Instead of being dazzled by the vibrant colors and merry music, they watched the street urchins dart between the legs of the wealthy, and the beggars reach out to callous and disinterested revelers. The city was ever split by an excess of wealth and poverty, of civilized progression and criminal erosion, and that weighed heavily on Farah's mind tonight in the form of Gemma Warlow.

"Sometimes on nights like this, I'd give anything for the sweet-smelling countryside," she said, feeling guilty for being distracted.

Sir Morley made a soft affirmative sound, and she glanced up at him to note that his light brows were also drawn into a preoccupied frown as he stared into the throng of people along the Strand, but focused on no one. He was very handsome in his evening clothes and white cravat. The consummate English gentleman. Tall, but not too tall. Trim, but strong. Handsome in a classic, aristocratic way that was both pleasing and approachable. His teeth were well cared for and not very crooked, and though he was nigh to forty, his gold hair was still thick and resisted gray. He walked in such a way that people parted for him, and Farah couldn't stop herself from thinking that added to his attraction.

Sir Carlton Morley was a man of distinction, if not blue blood, and was respected by most people on sight, not to mention by reputation, as one of the most celebrated chief inspectors in the history of the Metropolitan Police.

"I think I should like to drink two whole bottles of wine by myself tonight," she said, testing him, as neither of them ever had more than a glass with dinner.

He nodded and mumbled something, his aquiline jaw working in frustrated circles as though chewing on a thought.

"After that," Farah continued conversationally. "I shall very much enjoy a swim in the Thames. I'll most likely be nude. I wouldn't want to soil my new dress, you see?"

"Whatever you like," Morley agreed companionably, still yet to look at her.

Laying her other hand on their joined arms, she steered them into a doorway and out of the foot traffic. "Carlton," she said, turning to face him. "You're perplexed. Is everything all right?"

The casual way in which she used his first name seized his attention. This was a new intimacy between them, and they were both still adjusting to it.

"Forgive me." He lifted her hand to his mouth and pressed a gentle kiss to it. "I was being inexcusably discourteous. Do repeat what you just said?"

Not a chance, she thought, but her mouth relaxed into a smile. The kiss to her gloved hand settled a warm glow in her middle and she forgave him instantly. "I noticed Dorian Blackwell was acquitted at court today. Is that what weighs heavily in your thoughts?"

At the mention of the name, Morley's features tightened with aggravation and his grip on her hand tensed. "Every time I get him on something, he slips through my fingers! I know he has half the force in one pocket, and half of Parliament in the other." Releasing her hand, he took off his

hat and ran frustrated fingers though his hair before settling it back on. *"Damn him!"* he exploded.

"And do you know what that rotten Justice Singleton
had the audacity to do?" Morley asked, then continued
without pausing for her reply. "He publicly reprimands *me*
for malicious conduct toward the scum!"

Farah remained silent. She had her own opinion on that
score, but realized now wasn't the time to mention it. She'd
thought Morley a man of very strict principle, above beating someone with their hands chained, no matter how deserving the knave might be.

"Perhaps we should entertain a more relaxing diversion
than the theater tonight," Farah suggested gently. "A stroll
through the gardens maybe, or—"

"No," Morley interrupted, placing a gentle finger beneath her chin. "No. I think I require the distraction of a
comedy tonight. It will help to erase all thoughts of Dorian
Blackwell."

"Yes," she agreed, enjoying the familiarity of his touch.
"You'd do well to put him out of your mind for the evening." Though, even as she said the words, she accepted
that to rid the mind of one such as Dorian Blackwell was
a great deal easier said than done. As things stood, *she'd*
been attempting to do just that very thing for the better part
of three days. For the entire time Blackwell had been held
below stairs, he'd taken unbidden residence in her thoughts,
invading them like an unwelcome song until his presence
in the rooms beneath her had thrummed through her
nerves with a constant awareness.

"I shall. I shall focus only upon your dazzling company
tonight." Morley gazed down at her upturned face with an
intent sort of determination until his mood darkened again.
"It's only that, when he said those things about you and
me—I felt like I could *murder* him."

Farah tried her most disarming smile. "Don't let it

bother you overmuch, I've heard worse over the years, to be sure." And wasn't that the truth?

"Is that supposed to comfort me?" he murmured, his head drifting lower, lips hovering in the decreasing space above her own mouth.

"Yes," she said decisively, and nudged him out of the doorway and back toward the walkway to resume their evening. "Dorian Blackwell isn't even on the list of the most crude and vile persons who've addressed me in the strong room." But he was somehow the most frightening, she silently added. Which was strange, if she thought about it. Over the course of her career she'd been threatened, propositioned, degraded, and begged, and Dorian Blackwell had done none of those things. He'd merely said her name. Perhaps a few insinuations. Farah was certain she'd misread the subtle promise threaded through his voice, but it still sent shivers through her each time she remembered it.

"Do you enjoy working for me, Farah?" Morley asked in a tone that was almost boyish in its reluctance. "I often find myself wondering if you wouldn't rather be running a quiet and lovely home somewhere."

Farah waved a hand in front of her face as though swatting away a distasteful smell. "I like to be busy. I think I would go absolutely bonkers if I didn't have something productive to do with my day. I do enjoy working at Scotland Yard. I feel like I'm the keeper of London's records and all her dirty secrets. I take great pride in my work."

"I know you do." Morley nodded, seeming distracted by a whole new set of troubles. "But, do you want to work at Scotland Yard indefinitely? Don't you ever wish for family? For—children?"

Farah was quiet as the questions dug beneath her rib cage to get at her heart. She hadn't wanted to be at Scotland Yard at first, but had taken the position there because she hoped to someday get at what she needed. To unlock the secrets of her past. As time went by, she had begun to despair of that ever happening. As to the other question . . . she'd never allowed herself to think on it. Words like *family* and *children* had disintegrated when she was very young, and she'd never quite been able to resurrect them without her heart breaking. Though something deep inside her clenched and ached at the idea of a child of her own. A family.

"I'm famished," she said brightly, hoping to derail this topic of conversation. "Let's consider an early supper before the theater . . . something Italian?"

Reluctantly, Morley let the subject lie and agreed. "I know a place right next to the Adelphi."

"Excellent!" She beamed.

They avoided both the heavy topics of the Blackheart of Ben More and her future during their light Italian supper, instead allowing themselves to be serenaded by a roving violinist and gorging on a scrumptious Pasta Pomodoro with an excellent red table wine. They discussed inconsequential things like the construction of new underground railways and the increasing popularity of detective fiction. The play at the Adelphi was diverting and well written, and both of their spirits had vastly improved as they strolled down Fleet Street toward her apartments above Mr. de Gaule's coffee shop. As the night wore on, and the farther east they traveled, the streets of London became more dangerous, and Farah was glad that Morley always wore a weapon.

"I wager they'll write ha'penny novels about you next, Sir Morley," she teased. "Perhaps even include your chase of *he whom we shall not be naming for the rest of the evening.* How grand would that be?"

"Ridiculous," Morley muttered, but his blush could be

seen even in the lamplight, and his eyes were pleased as they glanced down at her.

Another one of de Gaule's poetry readings had dissolved into absinthe-soaked debauchery. The sound of Gypsy music and overloud laughter spilled onto the street and mingled with the calls of prostitutes and gin peddlers.

"I never understood why you chose to stay here, after all these years." Morley gripped her elbow more protectively as he escorted her up the dark back stairs to her rooms. "These—these so-called Bohemians are not the sort for a woman of your gentility to be trifling with."

Farah laughed merrily and turned to him, one stair above so she could meet his gaze straight on. "Can you imagine me trifling with anyone, Carlton? Though I'll admit to a certain fond fascination with Bohemians. They're all so creative and free-spirited."

Instead of charmed, Morley appeared concerned. "You don't ever . . . attend these soirees, do you?"

"And what if I did?" she playfully challenged. "What if I mingled with the brightest and most progressive minds of our time?"

"It's not your mingling that worries me, but something else altogether," he muttered.

"Dear Carlton." Her gaze softening, she reached out and rested her hand on his shoulder, letting her thumb graze the neat hair at his nape. "I'm too old to mingle or trifle or whatever other euphemism for scandalous behavior worries you." She glanced down the stairs toward the cobblestones painted in crossed golden squares by the windows of the café. "But I love this part of the city. It's so alive, so full of youth and art and poetry."

"And cutpurses and rakes and prostitutes."

That drew another warm laugh from her throat. "Most of whom know me from the Yard. I am careful and I feel quite safe here. Besides," she added lightly. "We can't all afford a terrace near Mayfair, now can we?"

She'd meant the jibe about his new home acquisition as a light tease, but her words seemed to sober him, and he regarded her there in the shadows with a new intensity. "Did you . . . enjoy yourself tonight, Mrs.—er—Farah? With me?"

"I find I hardly enjoy anyone's company more than yours," she answered honestly.

"Good." His breath seemed to be coming faster now, his eyes darting with indecision. "Excellent. That is—I had a very particular subject I wanted to discuss with you to-night."

A small tingle thrilled through her as Farah deduced just where this conversation might be headed. How on earth would she respond? "Of course." She sounded equally breathless. "Would you . . . like to come in for some tea?"

He stared at her door for a long moment. "I fear it would not be prudent to invite me into your home right now. Not with how much I—Christ. I think I'm going to bungle this."

Her fingers drifted from his shoulder to his cheek, as she tried to look as encouraging as possible, even though her heart raced away with her thoughts. "Just tell me what you're thinking."

His hand covered hers on his cheek. "I want to court you properly, Farah," he said in a rush. "We run such a successful enterprise together, just imagine how well we would run a society home. We enjoy each other's compan-ionship. And, I think, we have developed feelings stron-ger than friendship over the years." His hand curled around hers and brought it to his chest, right above his heart. "Nei-ther of us has to be lonely anymore, and I could think of no one else's company I'd rather have every night for the rest of my days."

That pleasant warmth returned to her stomach, though Farah found herself somewhat underwhelmed by his declaration. So he was no Rossetti or Keats. Should she hold that against him?

"Consider what you are offering," she said evenly. "I'm a widow well past the marrying age. A man of your position and deserving needs a young wife who will be content to make him a comfortable place to come home to. Someone to provide him with fat babies and respectable society. Everyone I know is either a criminal or a Bohemian." She smirked before adding wryly, "Sometimes both."

"You're seven and twenty," he argued with his own smile of bemusement. "That's hardly in your dotage."

"Eight and twenty last month," she corrected. "And I suppose I'm trying to warn you that I'm entirely too set in my ways to make you a dutiful wife." Though her stomach fluttered at the thought of children.

He was silent a moment, though he looked rather thoughtful instead of insulted. Reaching up, he brushed a ringlet from her bare shoulder to spill down her back, exposing the white skin uncovered by her shawl. "Your first marriage . . ." He hesitated. "Was it so awful?"

"Quite the opposite, actually." She smiled sadly. "Just . . . tragically short."

"I'd love for you to tell me about it someday."

"Perhaps," Farah lied as she focused on the warmth of his fingers as they hovered above her skin. Desire drifted about them like the London mist, a gentle, masculine form of it that was soothing and agitating all at once.

"I'd also like the chance to compete with your late husband for your affections. I would even strive to live up to his memory." Those elegant, gentle fingers finally closed around her shoulder, pulling her toward him. "The prospect doesn't frighten me like it would some men."

Touched, Farah allowed herself to drift against his lean body. "You are a very singular man," she complimented, her lashes sweeping down at this unexpected intimacy. "And quite handsome, too. These things are best never decided quickly. Give me a night or two to examine my feelings?"

"I should have known a woman as efficient and fastidious as you wouldn't get swept away. Give me some hope, Farah," he pleaded, his grip pulling her torso against his and his hand stealing around to the curve of her back. "Something my lonely heart can hold on to."

"I can't say it's not a dazzling proposition," she said sincerely. "Tempting, even."

His eyes flared with hope. With heat. "Tempting? Not half as tempting as you. *God*, Farah, you don't know how that word on your lips inflames me. Though, having been a married woman, I suppose you might. Damn, but your husband must have been the happiest man in all the empire, if only for a short time." His finger stole beneath her chin, his other hand pressing their bodies even closer.

Farah endeavored to keep the sadness out of her smile. "We were both happy, for a time." Though, she expected, not in the way that he intimated.

"May I kiss you, Farah?" The fervency in his question was at once frightening and exciting.

She considered it, then lifted her head.

Their first kiss was soft, tentative, and altogether pleasant. Farah was grateful for the relative darkness of her stairwell so she didn't have to worry about how to school her features, or whether her eyes should be opened or closed. She was able to simply enjoy the warmth of his closeness. The feel of the pressed linen jacket beneath her fingertips. The skill of his mouth as it danced and swept across hers in light, intriguing strokes. There was a momentary insistence before he gentled his pressure again. A hint of moisture as his tongue hovered close to her mouth, but never more than a whisper.

Dorian Blackwell probably kissed much differently than this, Farah found herself thinking. He was probably savage and hungry. Perhaps a bit too forceful and consuming in his passions. His mouth was so hard-looking. A cynical slash against an obstinate jaw. No, the Blackheart of Ben More would be selfish and demanding. Certainly not restrained or respectful like—Oh, Lord! What was she doing thinking about that criminal's mouth while entertaining the lips of a gentleman? Angry, more at Blackwell than at herself, she cursed the man for again invading her thoughts uninvited. Again. The unmitigated nerve!

Just as the warmth in her stomach bloomed into a more pervasive heat that spread a blush over her skin, curiosity and guilt nudged her toward exploration. Farah clutched at his shoulders and considered using her own tongue. Was that permissible? Would he recoil at the French manner of kissing? She'd really only heard of it from the mouths of prostitutes, but the idea had intrigued her for some time. Should she invite him inside again? Perhaps, in spite of whichever answer she decided to give him, she would still not reach the age of thirty untouched.

Just as that resplendent thought flitted across her mind, Morley pulled back, his rapid breath producing faint puffs of steam in the gathering chill.

"Come to church with me tomorrow," he gasped. "I don't want to wait until Monday morning to see you."

Farah let out a disappointed breath at the most tame request she could possibly imagine. How could he think of church at a time like this? She supposed, if he insisted on being a gentleman, she should be a lady.

"I'm not religious," she admitted. "Moreover, I do not

like churches. But if you'd like to meet for tea when church is over, you could call upon me in the afternoon." She smiled at the idea, liking the prospect of exploring more of these pleasant kisses with him. Of thinking about the future.

Stepping back, he released her, but not before lifting her gloved hand to his lips once more. "I would like that more than I can say."

Just as quickly as the warmth in her soul had ignited, the chill of the evening extinguished it, and Farah found herself wondering if the sensation had been in response to the kiss . . . or the intrusive thoughts she'd harbored about another man. Disturbed, she gathered her skirts, pulled her shawl more tightly around her shoulders, and slowly began to climb the stairs. "Good night then, Carlton."

"Sweet dreams, Farah Leigh."

Pausing, she turned very slowly back to where he looked up at her. "*What* did you call me?"

"Farah Leigh. What did you think I said?"

"I thought I'd heard you say *Fairy.*" She whispered the word.

Sir Morley's hair gleamed copper as he threw his head back and laughed. "That kiss must have affected you as much as it did me."

"Indeed." Farah turned and climbed the rest of the way to her door, unwilling to show him the sudden sadness washing over her. Because he'd been utterly wrong, her mistaken hearing had nothing at all to do with the kiss.

As she unlocked her apartment, her heart was heavier than it had been in months. An old and familiar grief twisted through her, its blade as sharp as it had been a decade ago. Closing the door behind her, she leaned against it and stood in the frigid darkness for a moment, her trembling fingers hovering above her lips.

How was it, after all these years, she could feel so . . .

conflicted? Like in some way she was being unfaithful? No, that was too strong a word. But, somehow, it still applied.

Stop this, Farah, she scolded herself. It had been ten years since the boy she loved had died. Seventeen since they'd been separated. She was nearly thirty. Surely she deserved to build a life with someone if she so chose. Certainly Dougan would understand.

Guilt compounded the sorrow until Farah felt so wretched she knew there would be no sleeping tonight. Crossing her cozy parlor, she took longer than usual to light the candle on the mantel so she could see enough to lay a fire in the stone hearth.

Lifting the candle, she reached for her basket of kindling. A swift movement in her periphery caused her to jump and turn around. The candle flame flickered, danced, and sputtered madly, as though trying to escape the devil whose face loomed above hers. His dark eye full of sin, the blue one with malice, he glared down at her with lips pulled back from white, predatory teeth to form a disgusted sneer.

Farah's screams crowded in her throat, preventing their escape as she groped behind her for the fire poker. To her shock and despair, two other large forms melted from the shadows and advanced from either side.

"I hope you enjoyed that kiss, *Mrs. Mackenzie*." Dorian Blackwell licked his finger and pinched the flame of her candle, plunging them back into darkness. "For it shall be your last."

CHAPTER FIVE

Ye could love me . . . that is, if ye wanted.

Of course I'll love you, Dougan Mackenzie . . . Who else is going to?

Nobody.

Farah drifted through a mist of memories punctuated by a swift but faraway click-clack rhythm that cut through the pleasant haze with loud and perplexing consistency.

I'd never leave you, Fairy.

Truly? Not even to be a pirate?

I promise. I might be a highwayman, though.

Click-clack. Click-clack.

Her head felt quite unattached to the rest of her as the softly floating mist began to swirl away and awareness permeated her pleasant dream.

"We're close enough to Glasgow, sir, that ye might want to dose her again so she'll be out for the ship ferry." A gruff Scottish voice that reminded her of sawteeth and strong drink cut through the sweet voices of her youth.

"In a moment, Murdoch."

That voice. Dark and cultured and smooth with just a touch of . . . something foreign and altogether familiar. Where had she heard that voice?

Will you try to love me, too?

I'll try, Fairy, but I havena done it before.

I'll teach you.

"Do ye really think she'll help ye?" The grizzled voice sounded closer now, along with those maddening rhythmic noises that seemed to heave her entire body this way and that.

"I'll leave her no choice." The dark voice was also closer. Terrifyingly close.

Farah was angry at them both. These men didn't belong here in the treasured memories of her past. They were corrupting it, somehow. Especially the smooth dark one. She wanted to tell it to leave her. Dougan Mackenzie was a precious tragedy who belonged to her alone, and she wanted to order this dangerous voice far away from him. She couldn't, though, as it reached into the miasma of her odd waking dream and wrapped cool fingers of dread around her throat.

Love is for fairy stories . . . No such thing.

They'd loved each other, hadn't they? Farah felt the need to reach out as Dougan's solemn dark eyes began to fade. His sweet boy's voice was ripped from her and replaced by something cruel and frightening.

Yes, Farah Mackenzie, you should run.

"What will ye tell her when she wakes?" the one called Murdoch queried.

"The question you should be asking, Murdoch, is what information does she have that will be useful to me?"

Troubled, Farah tried to make sense of what she was hearing, but her thoughts seemed to be swept from her reach like fallen leaves in the first winter storm. Her limbs felt just as stiff and treelike, heavy and unbending. But still she swayed like a branch would in an errant wind.

Click-clack-click-clack.

"Ye mean, yer not going to let her know—"

"Never." The dark voice carried a hint of passion in the vow, but pulled away from her.

"But I thought that—"

"You. Thought. What?" Cold. That man was so *cold*. Like the Thames in January. Or the deepest levels of hell where the souls too dark to burn went to keep the devil company.

A deep, long-suffering sigh could just be heard above the sound of the train. "Never ye mind what I thought." Murdoch sounded cranky and disappointed rather than frightened, and Farah thought that he must likely be the bravest man in the world.

The train! Recognition slammed into Farah with a jarring crash. The rhythmic clicking, the swaying movement, the faint smells of coal smoke and moisture. Seizing the knowledge of where she was with a desperate fear that she'd lose it again, Farah also mourned the loss as the last vestiges of her dream dissipated into nothingness. The mist upon which she floated formed into a soft velvet cushion with deep pockets every so often for fashionable buttons.

When had she decided to take a journey? Anxiety flared as Farah grasped for more recent memories. Had she packed a trunk? Was she traveling for work? Why couldn't she seem to surface from this fog long enough to open her heavy eyes or move her even heavier limbs?

The train whistle split the air and Farah noted that they began to slow. Oh, dear, she needed to move. She couldn't very well be caught sleeping once she reached her destination, could she? Just who were her companions?

Another word slashed through her gathering consciousness.

Glasgow.

What in the world was she doing in Scotland?

Her eyelids began to flutter and she felt her muscles tense, which she took as a sign that she might be coming out of whatever fugue state she'd been trapped in. This was so unlike her. She never took any substances to help her sleep. Nor did she ever drink to excess for fear she'd be in this very position. Just what was going on? Had she been poisoned?

Fear lanced through the holes in her memory and she felt as though she barreled toward the truth with the speed of the train's steam engine.

Let me kiss you, Farah.

She'd been with Carlton. He'd proposed—after a fashion—and she'd said . . . what?

"All right, then." Murdoch's grizzled voice interrupted her concentration. "I'll go get everything prepared, Blackwell, whilst ye see to the lass."

Blackwell. Farah's heart raced and her mind struggled to catch up. It was almost there. Blackwell . . . Scotland . . . Kiss . . . Oh, *why* couldn't she put it together?

I hope you enjoyed that kiss, Mrs. Mackenzie . . . For it shall be your last.

Dorian Blackwell, the Blackheart of Ben More. He had her. He'd *taken* her!

Farah's eyes flew open in time to see a silver flask pass between two black-clad gentlemen who, once she looked at their faces, didn't appear to be gentlemen in the least.

They were alone in a private railcar, the luxury of which she'd never before seen. Blurry images of wine-red silk damask and velvet dripped from windows and upholstery and startled her overwhelmed senses. The color of blood. Aside from the hulking shadows of the men in the middle of the car, the color pervaded the décor to excess.

That didn't make any sense, Farah thought. If anyone

were drenched in blood, it was Dorian Blackwell. From everything she'd heard, he swam in rivers run thick with the blood of his enemies. So why did it seem so incredibly wrong that his silk cravat and collar rose so pristine beneath his hard jaw?

Farah's lids fought her, but the urgency that thrummed through her told her to run. To fight. To scream.

"Doona forget to dose her before the train pulls in," Murdoch reminded before his shadow opened the door to the railcar, letting in a blast of frigid air and daylight.

"Worry not." Dorian turned to her, the particulars of his face lost to the shadows of her unruly vision. "I *never* forget."

The next time Farah woke, she found the transition from dream to reality much easier, for no alarming voices or movement jarred her body. The sensation of floating on a cloud lingered for quite some time, and she stayed as long as she was able in that soft and safe in-between place. Not yet awake. Not quite asleep.

The first thing she registered was the sound of the ocean being tossed about by a storm. Thunder growled in the distance. A howling wind threw rain against a window in strong gusts, and the air hung heavy and cold with clean but briny moisture. Farah breathed it in, letting it evoke the memory of a place she'd left behind seventeen long years ago.

Scotland.

Her eyes flew open. Night greeted her with a heavy, velvet darkness. Windows told her that her chamber was large, but only with minimal outlines as the moon and stars were hidden by storm clouds.

Still a little too muddleheaded to panic, Farah flexed her numb limbs, testing their movements, and found, to her great relief, that she was not bound or restrained. Sending a silent prayer of thanks, she tried to gather her thoughts. She was on a bed with the softest linen she'd ever felt beneath her cheek. More movement told her she was still fully dressed, though her corset felt as though it had been loosened.

Who'd done that? Blackwell?

The thought sent a shiver through her, despite the warm, heavy covers. She needed to get moving. She needed to figure out just where he'd taken her and how to escape. The middle of the night felt like a good time to try, though the storm could definitely be a problem. If she guessed correctly, she'd be at the Blackheart's fortress, Ben More Castle. Which meant the ocean surrounded the Isle of Mull and that made escape more than just a little tricky.

Maybe impossible.

First things first. She recited one of her mantras, unwilling to let fear incapacitate her. One had to be able to stand in order to escape anything, so she shouldn't get too far ahead of herself. Wondering just *what* he'd given her, she carefully slid her feet from beneath the covers. How would she find her slippers in the dark?

Perhaps she could feel around for a lamp or candle.

Her arms trembled weakly as she attempted to push herself into a sitting position. The room spun, or was it her head? She blinked a few times and clutched at the bedclothes to keep herself from pitching back over.

A silver streak of lightning arced through the diamond-paned windows and flashed several times. The impression of a tall, sprawling bed and a fireplace that would fit a rather large man in it barely registered as she locked eyes with the shadowed figure sitting motionless in the high-backed chair close to her bed.

Dorian Blackwell. He'd been watching her sleep. He'd been close enough to reach out and touch her.

The lightning passed, plunging them both back into

darkness, and Farah froze for the few seconds it took for the thunder to shake the stones of the keep. Though she could see nothing, she blinked several times, trying to rein in the beats of her runaway heart.

Any moment, she expected him to leap on her like the predator he'd evoked in her memory, and she knew she didn't have the strength to fight him, or to run.

"Please," she whispered, hating the weakness in her voice. "Don't—"

"I'm not going to hurt you," the darkness said. He was so close, she thought she could feel his breath on her skin.

Farah wasn't certain she believed him. "Then why? What am I doing here?" She wished for an impression of movement, but the shadows remained still and absolute.

A few silent moments passed before the voice reached for her through the inky black. "There is something very important I need to do. You have the capacity to either help me or be in my way. Regardless, it's better to have you where I can keep an eye on you."

"What makes you think I would ever help *you*?" she asked imperiously, as outrage began to smother her panic. "Especially after you've taken me from my home, my *life*. That was a reckless move. I work for Scotland Yard, and they'll be looking for me." Farah hoped her threat struck home. She remembered Blackwell in the strong room. He'd been collected, seemingly fearless, but she'd seen the sweat in his hairline, the tension in his coiled muscles, the pulse throbbing at a vein in his strong neck. "You don't like enclosed spaces, I think," she ventured. "If they find me here, you won't be able to avoid kidnapping charges. They'll send you back to Newgate for certain."

"You don't think I can make it so that you're never found?" His inflection remained the same—cold, uncaring—but Farah gasped as though he'd slapped her. Silently, she fought a tremor of terror. Had he meant they wouldn't find *her*? Or her body? She had to remember that the Blackheart of Ben More left a mountain of devastation in his wake in the form of the dead or missing. Regretting her threats, she groped inside her murky thoughts for something to say.

"Do you love him?"

The question caught her completely by surprise. "Pardon?"

"Morley." The name could have been blocked in ice. "Were you going to accept his proposal?"

Farah had the oddest sense that the question had astonished them both. "I fail to see how that's any of your—"

"Answer. The. Question."

Farah resented being ordered about. However, something about the shroud of night made her uncharacteristically frank. "No," she confessed. "While I have a great deal of respect and fondness for Carlton, I do not love him."

"You let him kiss you." The dispassionate words still managed to convey accusation. "He put his hands on you. Are you in the habit of allowing men you do not love to take such liberties?"

"No! I . . . Morley's the first man I've kissed since—" Farah blinked rapidly. How could a man such as Dorian Blackwell put her on the defensive over a measly kiss? Didn't he have a harem of beautiful courtesans? Wasn't he the most notorious blackguard in the realm? "I don't have to explain my actions to you! I'm not a thief, a kidnapper, or a murderer. I'm a respectable, employed, self-possessed widow, and may allow whatever liberties I deign appropriate." Her head still swam, and the more excited she became, the worse she felt. Whatever he'd dosed her with was making her reckless, impulsive, and emotional.

The darkness was silent and still for so long, she wondered if his specter had been a hallucination brought on by the drug in her veins.

"A widow?" Dorian Blackwell murmured as though bemused. "You may play the respectable matron with others, *Mrs. Mackenzie,* but you are a woman with terrible secrets. And I happen to know what they are."

The arrogance in his tone provoked her, but Farah's heart kicked behind her ribs at his words. That was entirely impossible. Wasn't it? Her secrets had died ten years ago and were buried in a shallow, unmarked grave.

Along with her heart.

"What is it you think you know?" she whispered. "What is it that you want from me?"

Another streak of lightning forked through the storm, illuminating his bulky shadow, turning the ebony of his hair a blue-black and his scarred eye an unnatural silver. Farah only caught his expression for a moment, but it was an unguarded moment, and what she saw stunned her into silence.

He was leaning closer, his head dipped down, but his deep-set eyes burned at her through dark lashes. His hand hovered in the space between them, his expression a mixture of exquisite pain and longing.

The vision was gone as swiftly as it had appeared, and Farah sat in the dark, awaiting the pressure of his fingers.

He left her untouched, his shadow appearing as a wide outline against the window as he stood and moved away from her. "Yours are questions best left for the morning."

Confused, Farah couldn't dispel the image of his eyes as he'd reached toward her. His scar marred the chiseled symmetry of his swarthy features. It added to his menace, to be sure, but the naked, yearning agony she'd glimpsed colored her fear with mystification.

Had it been an effect of the storm and her unruly vision?

A door opened on the far side of the room and Farah

was once again astonished. He'd moved so stealthily in the pitch-blackness, without running into furniture or making a sound.

"How long do you intend to keep me prisoner here, Mr. Blackwell?" she asked, her hands fisting in the sheets, her eyelids heavy.

"I do not intend for you to be my prisoner," Blackwell said after a slight pause.

"Captive, then?" She had the impression that she'd amused him, or was it exasperated? The sound he made was impossible to correctly interpret without seeing his face.

"Get some sleep, Mrs. Mackenzie," he prompted. "You're out of danger tonight, and everything will be clearer on the morrow."

He left her then, to contemplate just what he'd meant by, *You're out of danger tonight.*

CHAPTER SIX

Dorian Blackwell's words proved prophetic, Farah realized, as she woke from a dreamless sleep with sunlight spilling across her bed and pleasantly warming her skin. Her thoughts and vision had, indeed, cleared away with last night's storm clouds, leaving her rested and restless all at once.

Blinking against the brightness of the morning, she became aware of busy, rustling noises coming from *inside* her room. Gasping, she sat up like a shot as a fire flared to life in the gigantic fireplace, set by a short but husky man dressed far too well to be in the service profession.

He turned to face her, his graying beard split into a cheerful smile. "Why, good morning, Mrs. Mackenzie! What a pleasure it is to finally meet ye." He crossed the room with startling speed for such a short, stout man.

Alarmed, Farah snatched the covers to her loosened bodice, though only her silk chemise was revealed beneath the opened buttons. "Don't—don't come any closer." She held up her hand in what she realized was a ridiculous motion to stop him.

Surprisingly, it proved effective, and he paused near the foot of the bed.

Soft blue eyes gentled as did the grooves in his cheeks, lending him a very fatherly appearance. "Ye've nothing to fear from me, dear lass, I'm only here to lay yer fire and bring ye breakfast." He motioned to the tray set by his left hand at the foot of the bed. "No doubt yer belly's a wee dicey, so I brought ye some rice pudding, a quail's egg, toast, and some tea."

As Farah eyed the artfully arranged plate, her stomach let out a hungry sound of protest, then pitched unsteadily.

The smile returned to the man's cheeks, glowing with pleasure. "'Tis as I thought." He grabbed the tray and carefully carried it toward her, setting it over her lap. "Ye can breakfast like a proper lady." He beamed, handing her a linen.

Automatically, Farah reached up to accept the linen, settling it where it belonged while he poured tea into a delicate china cup the most lovely shade of mint green.

"You're—Mr. Murdoch," she said, recognizing his grizzled voice. "From the train."

The look he cast her from beneath his lashes was impossible to interpret. "Aye," he said finally. "Though I was hoping ye didna remember anything from the journey. We kept ye out so as to cause ye the least amount of distress."

Farah gaped at him. *Distress?* Who could not feel distress when they were kidnapped and taken to this isolated part of the world? And what was this man about, treating her as though she was a welcome guest instead of a hostage?

"Sugar? Cream?" He solicitously gestured to the matching tea service full of foamy fresh cream and lumps of cubed sugar.

"No, thank you." Manners dictated she be polite, even to her captors. She studied Murdoch as she lifted the cup to her lips, freezing mid-tilt as she realized there might be something other than just tea in the brew.

"Have ye no fear, lass, 'tis just a breakfast tea, no more." He correctly deciphered her thoughts.

Farah drank. If he were going to dose her again with whatever had knocked her unconscious, he'd likely hold the cloth over her mouth and nose as they'd initially done. The tea was strong and good and, though she was used to coffee in the morning, it helped to dispel the lingering cobwebs in the corners of her mind.

"Isn't there a chambermaid who could attend me?" she asked, hoping for sympathetic female company, along with a chance to escape. "You are obviously too important and well appointed to be in service."

A sliver of knowing mischief slipped into his ever-present smile. "He said ye'd be as bright as ye are beautiful," Murdoch praised, picking up the spoon and handing it to her while nudging the crystal dish of rice pudding toward her.

Farah hoped he didn't see her blanch at the compliment, knowing the source to which he referred.

"There are no women here at Ben More, ye see, and I'm the only man the master of the castle would allow in yer boudoir to attend ye. Now eat up. Gather yer strength."

This was a command Farah didn't disagree with. If she were to escape her present circumstances, she needed to keep a cool head, gather information, and indeed, regain her strength. "Why you?" she asked, before taking her first bite of the honey-sweet pudding that melted in a mélange of spices on her tongue. She couldn't help but savor the confectionary taste of what had looked like a boring dish, in spite of everything.

Murdoch shifted his weight a little uncomfortably.

"Well, lass, that would be due to my lack of . . . er . . . romantic proclivities . . . toward women . . . that is . . ."

"You prefer men," Farah deduced around a second spoonful.

He blinked, obviously not expecting her to be so blunt. "That's the way of it," he admitted. "Hope that doesna offend ye."

"That doesn't offend me in the least," Farah said. "Though I do take exception to the part about you being a kidnapper, and who knows what else, for the most notorious criminal on the isle."

At that, Murdoch threw his head back and laughed until he was gripping the sides of his suit coat as though to hold the seams together. "Ye're a brave lass for someone so wee," he said. "Ye'll need it in the days to come, I think."

That gave her heart a kick, and Farah found it hard to swallow the next mouthful. "What do you mean by that?" she asked, remembering Dorian Blackwell's words about being out of danger. Or had it been *in danger*? Last night seemed like a dream at this point, and faded just as readily. Except for the lightning in his eyes, and the way he'd reached toward her. Like a man in the desert reaches for a mirage.

"That's a simple question with a complicated answer, lass, best leave it to Blackwell to explain it all to ye."

Farah's stomach erupted into a flurry of moths at the thought of facing Dorian Blackwell again. "Mr. Murdoch," she began.

"Just Murdoch, ma'am."

"All right. Murdoch. Could you not just . . . give me an idea about why I've been brought here?" she implored. "All I can do is dream up the worst possible scenarios, and I'd like to be prepared to see your—employer."

"I'm sorry, lass, but orders are orders." To his credit, the man did seem genuinely regretful. "But I want ye to know that not one of the inhabitants of Ben More Castle will raise a finger to do aught to ye but yer bidding."

"As long as I don't escape," Farah pointed out, cutting into her quail's egg.

Murdoch's smile disappeared. "Right. Yes."

"And only if I behave like a proper hostage." She popped a bite in her mouth, delighted to find the egg had been cooked in butter.

"Well—that's not—I mean—we'd all be obliged if ye'd—"

"And insomuch as my request doesn't contradict with Blackwell's orders."

"Also . . . that." Increasingly uncomfortable, Murdoch backed toward the door. "But ye're safe, is what I was saying, no matter how frightening any of the blokes around here appear."

"Well, then, I shall strive to be the best possible prisoner this castle has ever incarcerated." Farah took a dainty sip of her tea, enjoying Murdoch's discomfiture. He deserved it, the knave, despite his solicitous manner. He'd had a hand in her kidnapping and she'd do well to remember that. It would help her to fight the growing urge to like him.

"Och, lass, I'd ask ye not to see things in that way," he said seriously, a wrinkle of worry appearing between his brows. "Give Blackwell a chance to explain the situation and maybe . . . ye'll see things a bit differently." Putting his hand on the doorknob, he regarded her as she ate her breakfast as though waiting for a response.

"Very well, Murdoch," Farah said, hoping she was convincing enough.

He seemed to relax. "There are some ladies' clothes in the attic," he supplied. "How's about I go searching for some while ye eat and finish yer tea, then I'll come back and gather yer dress to launder it. Would ye like me to see about a bath?"

She nodded around a bite of toast, and the husky Scotsman scuffled out of the room.

Farah listened for the sound of his boots to carry him away from her door before she shoved the remaining bites of toast into her mouth and washed it down with scalding gulps of tea. He hadn't locked the door behind him. This could be her only chance. If Farah knew anything, it was that women who went missing were rarely ever found, and though the best and brightest investigative minds would be looking for her, no one would ever imagine she'd been taken to Ben More Castle. Liberation was her responsibility, alone, and she intended to take the risk rather than await her fate in the silk-draped luxury of her castle chamber.

Finishing the perfectly cooked quail's egg in two bites, she set her tray on the ground and leaped out of the bed, her fingers flying to fasten the buttons on her bodice. It really was a shame that she'd have to attempt escape in her lovely evening wear, but at least the extra layers of her full skirts would help keep her warm.

She found her purse, shawl, and slippers draped over a soft blue velvet chair next to the beckoning fireplace, and she checked inside the satin bag to find enough coin to hopefully secure her passage back onto the mainland. After that, she would try to find a local constable, and see if she couldn't return to London on a little credit and professional courtesy.

After a fruitless check of the white wood wardrobe, she despaired of finding a cape or pelisse and prayed the sunshine would hold for a few more hours. Crossing to the large windows, she investigated the castle grounds.

The dazzling sight that greeted her stole a sigh from her lips. Ben More Castle lorded over a wide peninsula from atop a foundation of craggy gray and black rock. Farah followed the gentle slope of the hill as the emerald grass crawled toward the coast where the sun glinted off the calm gray-blue waters of the sound. Grazing sheep dotted the pastoral view, and the beauty of it distracted her from the urgency of the moment. The mountains of the Scottish mainland were visible across the narrow channel, close and yet unattainable.

The windows faced east, which meant land was to the west and north of here. Where there was a castle, a village always hunkered nearby, and if she had any chance of finding someone to help her across the channel, she'd find it among the fishermen and porters who doubtless lived there.

Farah wrapped her shawl around her disheveled curls and stepped into her slippers on her way to the bedroom door. She only looked over her shoulder once, pausing to consider her options. Despite her rush to escape, a niggling curiosity seized her. Why had the Blackheart of Ben More brought her here? What possible use could she have been to him?

A dark fear whispered to her that she likely didn't want to linger long enough to find out. With a pounding heart and a surprisingly steady hand, Farah eased open her door and pressed an eye to the crack, checking for a guard. Finding none, she slipped through the opening and softly shut it behind her.

Instead of cold gray stone, the halls of Ben More Castle were updated with plush burgundy carpets and Italian marble floors. Farah silently followed the dark wood panels along the hall toward a grand open gallery stairway. The carpets muffled her light footfalls, but it would do the same for anyone deciding to trail her, so she was careful to look out for Murdoch or any of the other frightening characters who might be in Blackwell's employ. The front gallery must have been an older wing of the structure, because it could have been the great hall of any medieval castle. The chilly stone was warmed by lush woven tapestries and a wrought-iron chandelier dangled over a wide stone staircase.

Farah barely paid her expensive surroundings any heed as she crouched to the level of the chiseled stone railing, as a side door opened on the floor below the curved stone staircase and two booming male voices echoed through the hall. Footmen, she realized, as they crossed the foyer in their heavy boots and left by way of the impressive and ornate front doors.

Well, she hadn't expected to escape by just walking out the front doors, had she? She remembered back to another escape attempt . . .

The kitchens. They'd be on the ground floor or below, and have places to hide if need be. And if she was caught on the way there, she could claim to be in search of food.

Farah didn't breathe as she tiptoed down the grand staircase and dashed across the wide stone entry. The kitchens would be in back of the keep if this castle were built like any of those in England, which would be, thankfully, on the north and west sides. Feeling as though providence was with her, she wound her way through the ground floor among a maze of hallways, past an intriguing library, a neglected rectory, and numerous sitting rooms. When she found the dining hall, she knew she'd come in the right direction. Other than the footmen, she didn't meet another soul.

A large, fragrant stewpot simmered over a cookstove in the kitchen, and on the flour-covered island, steaming fruit tartlets rested in neat, scrumptious rows. Farah's mouth watered at the scent, and her fingers itched for the tarts, but she resisted, knowing that her window for escape narrowed with each passing second. Murdoch would return to her rooms eventually, to find her gone, and she needed to be at least a mile away by then.

The door across the large and well-stocked kitchen actually stood ajar next to an open pantry door adjacent to it. Perhaps the cook was down in the cellars or the larder.

Her timing couldn't be better.

Toes barely touching the floor, she flew past the island, the ovens, and the simmering food, clutching her shawl to her chin and lifting her voluminous skirts. Sunshine spilled over the stones and touched her face for a glorious moment as she pulled the heavy door wide enough for her to slip through.

Farah's shoulder was nearly wrenched from its socket as her only hope of escape was slammed shut by a meaty hand.

"No," said the sloe-eyed giant, wagging his other finger as though scolding an ill-mannered hound. "No leaving."

Farah leaped back, banging into the sharp edge of a counter. Biting back a curse and a cry, she clutched her hip and tried not to cringe away from the hulking, ill-formed bald man who resembled something like Frankenstein's monster, complete with scars, marks, and very gentle brown eyes.

"Please," she implored him desperately. "*Please* let me go. I'm being held here against my will. No one will know that you let me leave. Have pity on me."

In response to her pleas, the man shut the pantry, and positioned himself in front of the kitchen door, a silent sentry against her escape.

"I have money," Farah tried, dumping the coins in her purse onto the counter. "It's yours if you'll just let me pass."

Frankenstein remained quiet, crossing his arms over his belly and still regarding her with a mixture of patience and pity.

Spying the cutlery, Farah lunged for the largest knife she could find, and brandished it at him. "You *will* let me go, this instant."

The infuriating quirk of his lips told her she'd just amused him.

"I—I mean it. I don't want to hurt you." The thought of doing anyone violence made her ill, but she tried to put on the most determined expression she was capable of producing.

His amusement turned into a disconcerting smile uncovering sharp teeth spaced at alarming intervals. "You won't," he said in the relaxed voice of a simpleton. An English simpleton. Strange, that.

"I most certainly *will* if you don't step aside and—"

With a movement much too quick for such a slow-talking beast, he relieved her of the knife without so much as touching her, and set it on the counter out of her reach.

What would he do now? Farah could feel the blood draining from her face, but the man's eyes sparkled at her as though she'd pleased him somehow. "He needs you," Frankenstein informed her genially. "Go to him."

"I'd rather go to the devil!" she spat, again not needing clarification regarding just who *he* was. Turning from him, she faced the cook island behind her, seething with indignation and not a little bit of fear.

A sigh evoking a bovine character emitted from the bull-statured man behind her. "You were Dougan's Fairy," he said, his voice touched with a bit of awe.

Farah whirled back around. "What?" She gasped.

"He told me you looked like one. With silver curls and silver eyes and tiny freckles." He pointed at her hair as though to show her the color.

Farah blinked rapidly at the hulk of a man in front of

her, tears pricking at the corners of her eyes. "You knew Dougan Mackenzie?" she breathed.

"I's in prison with him. We all were. Long time ago."

"Tell me," she begged, all thoughts of fear and escape evaporating at Dougan's name. "Please, sir, can you tell me what he said? Tell me about—"

"Go to *him,* first." Frankenstein's meaty hand scratched a large scar on his head. "In the study. That will give me time to remember words."

"I can stay here while you remember." Farah stalled, wondering if this man had been born so handicapped or made so by his many obvious head injuries. Searching for anything to distract him, she eyed the tartlets. "You made my breakfast, didn't you?"

He nodded.

"It was very good," she said truthfully. "Do you think that maybe—"

"Go. Now. Talk later." The cook's expression became stubborn as he thrust a finger toward the door.

"I don't *want* to go to Blackwell. I want to go *home*!"

"He needs you, Fairy." He blinked at her and nodded in encouragement.

"Don't *ever* call me by that name!" Without realizing what she was doing, Farah took a threatening step toward him and he backed up into the door, his eyes wide and mystified. "Do you understand me? You haven't the right to call me that!"

Farah had the notion she'd surprised them both with the intensity of her reaction, but this situation infuriated and, she'd admit it, intrigued her. So many questions about her past were left unanswered, and perhaps those answers waited for her in this isolated castle. And yet, what if there was nothing here for her but danger? What if, behind the solicitous staff and handsome décor, awaited a Machiavellian predator who was simply playing with her before she became his next meal?

She couldn't take much more of this. "I'll go to him," Farah snapped. "You leave me no choice."

He nodded again, as though oblivious and satisfied. "You can take some tarts if you'd like," he offered.

"Not a chance." Farah swiped her coins back into her purse and huffed to the door, thoroughly exasperated. Why was it that every time she came close to answers, to truth, she was thwarted by thickheaded men? It was inconceivably irritating.

Pausing, she turned back around. "What kind of tarts?"

"Strawberry." Frankenstein wiped his hands on his apron and held the tray out to her.

Cursing her inability to refuse pastries, she took one of the bite-sized confections. "This doesn't mean I forgive you for being a kidnapping criminal."

" 'Course not," he agreed.

"Just so we're clear." She popped it into her mouth, and instantly butter, sugar, and the tartness of spring strawberries delighted her palate. "Oh, Lord," she moaned, unable to help herself.

His teeth, or lack thereof, appeared again as his lips peeled back in a genuine smile. Farah considered the man in front of her as she chewed. He looked so out of place in the Parisian-style kitchen stocked with the latest and most expensive of instruments, like he'd be better suited to a blacksmith's stable or—well—a prison hulk. Regardless of that, he was a very talented chef.

"What is your name?" Farah couldn't stop herself from asking.

"Walters."

"Walters." She took another tart, and then another. "Is that your first name, or your last?"

He took longer to answer than the question warranted.

"Can't say as I remember. Just Walters, though I'd like to have a first name, I expect."

Farah thought about it for the space of another tart before deciding. "What about 'Frank'?" she suggested, switching her third tartlet to her other hand before reaching for a fourth.

"Frank Walters." He savored the name like she savored his tarts.

"A right proper name," she told him. *For a right proper Frankenstein.* "Now, if you'll excuse me, I apparently have an appointment with a blackhearted criminal mastermind."

Farah got lost taking one too many turns through the winding halls before finding the study. She'd dawdled in the library for a few minutes, distracted by the floor-to-ceiling bookcases and the iron spiral staircase leading to the second floor. The study was, as she predicted, located in a resplendent room off the grand entry. Though when she peeked her head in—apparently no one closed doors in this blasted keep—she found the handsome massive room empty.

No, not empty, per se. Though devoid of anyone else, a strange and dynamic presence lingered in every corner of the masculine study. Farah could smell it in the pungent notes of cigar smoke clinging to the supple dark leather furniture. The aroma mixed with cedar and whatever citrus oil was used to clean the enormous desk flanked by even more dark wood bookcases. No sunlight pierced through heavy drawn wine-red velvet drapes. The only light in the room was provided by two lamps on the neat desk and another fireplace that could house a small family from Cheapside.

Drawn by unseen hands, Farah took a tentative step into the study, and then another. The rustling of her skirts and rasp of her breath disturbed the halcyon purity of the stillness. The beats of her heart echoed as loud as cannon blasts in her ears as she entered the private lair of Dorian Blackwell.

Farah tried to imagine a man such as the Blackheart of Ben More in this room, doing something as pedestrian as writing a letter or surveying ledgers. Running the fingers of her free hand along a bronze paperweight of a fleet ship atop his enormous desk, she found the image impossible to produce.

"I see you've already attempted escape."

Snatching her hand back, Farah held it to her heaving chest as she turned to face her captor now standing in the doorway.

He was even taller than she remembered. Darker. Larger.

Colder.

Even standing in the sunlight let in by the windows of the foyer, Farah knew he belonged to the shadows in this room. As if to illustrate her point, he stepped into the room and shut the door behind him, effectively cutting off all sources of natural light.

An eye patch covered his damaged eye, only allowing glimpses of the edge of his scar, but the message illuminated by the fire didn't need both eyes to be conveyed.

I have you now.

How true that was. Her life depended on the mercy of this man who was infamous for his *lack* of mercy.

The black suit coat that barely contained his wide shoulders stretched with his movements, but what arrested Farah's attention was the achingly familiar blue, gold, and black pattern of his kilt. The Mackenzie plaid. She hadn't known that a man's knees could be so muscular, or that beneath the dusting of fine black hair, powerful legs tucked into large black boots could be so arresting.

She backed against his desk as he stepped toward her,

evoking once more the image of a prowling jaguar. The firelight danced off the broad angles of his enigmatic face and shadowed a nose broken one too many times to any longer be called aristocratic. Of course, despite his expensive cravat, tailored clothing, and ebony hair cut into short and fashionable layers, nothing at all about Dorian Blackwell bespoke a gentleman. A fading bruise colored his jaw and a cut healed on his lip. She'd missed that last night in the storm, but knew it was Morley's fists that had wounded him. Had that only been days ago?

What had he just said to her? Something about her escape? "I—I don't know what you're talking about."

His good eye fixed on the tarts she'd all but forgotten she clutched in her hand. "My guess is you attempted to leave through the kitchens, and were thwarted by Walters."

Oh, damn. The air in the study was suddenly too close. Too thick and full and rife with—with *him.* Determined not to be cowed, Farah raised her chin and did her best to look him square in the eyes—er—eye.

"On the contrary, Mr. Blackwell, I was hungry. I didn't want to face you without being—fortified."

That earned her a lifted eyebrow. "Fortified?" His callous tonelessness set the hairs on the back of her neck on end. "With . . . pastries?"

"Yes, as a matter of fact," she insisted. "With *pastries.*" To make her point, she popped one in her mouth and chewed furiously, though she instantly regretted it as moisture seemed to have deserted her. Swallowing the dry lump, Farah hoped she hid her grimace as it made its slow and unpleasant way into her stomach.

He moved a little closer. If she wasn't mistaken, his cold mask slipped for an unguarded moment and he regarded her with something like tenderness, if a face such as his could shape such an emotion.

Farah had thought it wasn't possible to be more

confounded. How wrong she'd been. Though the lapse proved fleeting, and by the time she blinked, the placid calculation had returned, causing her to wonder if what she'd seen had been a trick of firelight.

"Most people need much stronger fortification than a strawberry tart before facing me," he said wryly.

"Yes, well, I've found that a well-made dessert can do anyone a bit of good in a bad situation."

"Indeed?" He circled her to the left, his back to the fire, casting his face into deeper shadows. "I find I want to test your theory."

Of all the conversations she'd expected to have with the Blackheart of Ben More, this had to be the absolute last. "Um, here." She extended the tart toward him, offering him the delicacy with trembling fingers.

Blackwell lifted a big hand. Took a deep breath. Then lowered it again, clenching both fists at his sides. "Put it on the desk," he instructed.

Puzzled by the odd request, she carefully set the tartlet onto the gleaming wood, noting that he waited until her hand had been returned to her side before reaching for it. It disappeared behind his lips, and Farah didn't breathe as she watched his jaw muscles grind at the pastry in a slow, methodical rhythm. "You're right, Mrs. Mackenzie, that *did* sweeten the moment."

A burning in her lungs prompted her to exhale, and she tried to push some of her previous exasperation into the sound. "Let's dispense with pleasantries, Mr. Blackwell, and approach the business at hand." She put every bit of crisp, British professionalism she'd gained over the last ten years into her voice, quieting the tremors of fear with a skill born of painstaking practice.

"Which is?"

"Just what is it you want with me?" she demanded. "I thought I'd dreamed of you last night, but I didn't, did I?

And there, in the darkness, you promised to tell me . . . to tell me why you've brought me here."

He leaned down, his eye touching every detail of her face as though memorizing it. "So I did."

CHAPTER SEVEN

"Would you like some scotch?" Dorian asked, moving to a table topped with a tray of crystal decanters and glasses situated between the two high-backed leather chairs.

Grateful for the space between them, Farah's first inclination was to decline, but upon second thought she said, "Yes, thank you."

"It is compliments of your relation, the Marquess of Ravencroft."

Farah blinked. "Relation?"

Watching her carefully, he retrieved two identical glasses, splashing them liberally with thick, caramel liquid. "Liam Mackenzie, the current laird of the Mackenzie clan. A kinsman of your late husband, I'm certain."

Searching her memory, Farah struggled to quell her racing heart. "I—never had the chance to meet him," she said. Which was the truth.

Blackwell gave her an enigmatic look. "Please, sit." He motioned to the chair closest to the fire.

Cautiously, Farah sat, unable to take her eyes off him

for a moment, just in case. In case he—what? Flew into a murderous frenzy? Lured her into a false sense of security and then—

"You mustn't attempt escape again," he said conversationally. Instead of handing her the drink, he set it on the small table at her elbow before lowering his tall frame into the chair across from her. It was a little like sitting across from the devil, preparing to make an arrangement and trying not to consider the eternal cost of such a bargain. Your heart. Your life.

Your soul.

"I told you," Farah began. "I was hungry."

Blackwell leveled her a droll look. "Let's not insult either of our intelligences by lying to each other."

To cover her guilt, Farah reached for the scotch and took a larger gulp than she should have. Gasping, she held her hand over her mouth as the liquid burned into her chest and brought tears to her rapidly blinking eyes. So much for keeping her composure.

Amusement toyed with the corner of his lips, but a smile never claimed them. "You nearly frightened poor Murdoch to tears."

Farah opened her mouth to retort, but only a hiccup emerged. Clamping her lips shut, she cleared her throat, and tried again. "In circumstances other than these, I would be sorry to hear my actions caused another any distress, but to kidnap a lady in the middle of the night and not expect her to attempt escape *already* calls your intelligence into question." She took another sip of the strong liquor, a much smaller one this time, having learned her lesson.

Blackwell had yet to drink, he only swirled the liquid about in his glass, never once taking his eye from her. "I thoroughly anticipated your flight, and had one of my men watching each possible exit to the castle," he informed her.

"I only warn you against further attempts for your own safety. If you happen to slip past one of my guards, I shall very much dislike to send the hounds after you. It would make all of this much more unpleasant for both of us."

"You wouldn't!"

"Wouldn't I?"

Farah gaped, unable to fathom his brutality. She shouldn't be shocked, she'd been around the worst sort of criminals for more years than she'd care to admit. But, somehow, it astounded her that one so cultured, so relaxed and wealthy and tailored, could issue such a threat with a civil tongue. The criminals of her acquaintance were dirty and foul with explosive tempers and crude language. Blackwell threatened violence as though discussing the price of Irish potatoes.

"I'm beginning to understand, Mr. Blackwell, that there are no depths to which you wouldn't sink to get whatever it is you want."

At last, Blackwell lifted his glass, to his lips and drank, effectively hiding his expression. When he lowered it, he regarded her with an unapologetic smirk. "Then you are finally beginning to know me, Mrs. Mackenzie."

"I shouldn't like to," she said stiffly.

"You don't have a choice."

Farah finished her drink in one reckless swallow, this time braced for the burn. "Go on, then," she challenged, the scotch adding smoke to her voice. "Let's have it."

Resting his drink on his knee with one hand, he leaned forward, watching her features intently. "Do you know the one thing a man must do to achieve all that I have in such a short time?"

"I'm sure I don't."

He ignored the note of sarcasm in her voice. "He must *always* repay his debts, and he must *always* fulfill his promises."

"That's two things," Farah challenged.

"Not necessarily."

Biting her thumbnail, she puzzled over his words. "But you don't owe me anything, nor I you. We've never made promises to each other."

At that, he was silent for an uncomfortably long time. Farah squirmed in the large, overstuffed chair, feeling like a child whose feet barely touched the ground.

"Do you remember what Morley said in the strong room those few days ago?" he asked.

"Should I?" Of course, she remembered every word.

He made that sound again, one that could have been amusement or annoyance. "Seventeen years ago, I was sentenced to Newgate Prison as a lad for theft. Because of some prior indiscretions, I was given a hefty term of seven years' hard labor."

His build began to make more sense. If he'd spent a great deal of his youth digging tunnels, breaking rocks, and hauling ties for the new London underground railway, as many English prisoners did, such work would form his wide shoulders and heavy bones.

"Among my new fellow prisoners was a transferred orphan boy from the Scottish Highlands. A murderer too young for the gallows, as he was all of thirteen, and the public revolted to see anyone younger than sixteen with his neck snapped by a noose."

Farah flinched, then stared. "Dougan," she whispered.

"Precisely." He finished his drink in one swallow, but made no move to pour another. "How we hated each other, at first. I thought he was a sniveling weakling ripe to be picked upon, and he thought I was a witless bully."

"Were you?"

That provoked the whisper of a nostalgic smile. "Of course I was. I used to throw rocks at his hands while he carried buckets of dirt. Tried to make him drop things and cause his knuckles to bleed."

Farah could feel her face hardening and a very foreign, frightening sort of anger bubbling through her blood. If Blackwell noticed, he ignored it and continued.

"One day, my rock missed his hands and caught Dougan between the legs. He fell to the ground, vomited, trembled for at least five long minutes while we all stood and laughed at him, even the guards. And then he did something quite extraordinary. He reached for the rock, stood up, and hurled it so hard at my head that it felled me. Then he leaped on me and beat my face so bloody, my own mother wouldn't have recognized me."

Farah set her glass back on the table as the trembling in her own hand become violent. "Good," she forced through lips stiff with outrage. She began to detest the sight of him. What was once intriguing and dangerous was now not just her enemy, but Dougan's as well, and that she could *not* abide.

Instead of taking offense at her anger, a barely perceptible softening of his features relaxed the hard line of his mouth. "I respected him after that, enough to leave him alone. Not just me, but all of us boys. He was one of the youngest among us, but the hate and violence he harbored burned the brightest. We all saw it that day, and we all feared it."

Farah's throat tightened. She didn't want to hear any more of this, didn't want their beautiful memories tainted with a confirmation of the details of his suffering. Yet, this was her penance, wasn't it? To be faced with the consequences of the reckless actions of her youth. If Dougan's memory deserved anything, it was to have his story told, and she would force herself to sit and listen. She still owed him that much.

Owed him *everything*.

"The day came when we were to be assigned to the labor lines. Initially, most of us younger lads were put in the lines to be sent to the prison ships stationed off the coast. Hellish, rotting hulks that neither the navy nor shipping companies could use anymore, with a prisoner mortality rate of more than seventy percent. We were separated into four lines, ours bound for the ships." Here, Dorian paused and considered her intently. "None of us knew it at the time, but Dougan Mackenzie was the only one among us who knew how to read the signs or the guards' registers. We all would have marched to our deaths had he not plucked my two best mates, Argent and Tallow, into the railway worker line. To this day, I don't know what made him do it, but at the last moment he grabbed me, too, without a guard noticing, and very likely saved my life."

Farah couldn't fathom it, either, but still hadn't recovered her voice well enough to say so.

"We were inseparable after that, Dougan and I. We formed a band of boys who worked the railways, just the four of us at first, protecting each other when we could from the older men and sometimes the guards. Teaching each other how to survive in such a place. For seven years, we gathered favors, debts, allies, and a few enemies among the boys and men who came and left Newgate Prison. We were leaders among them, young and strong, feared and respected. They came to know Dougan and me as 'the Blackheart Brothers,' as we both had black hair, dark eyes, and sharp fists."

Now that Farah looked at him, *really* looked at him, she attempted to superimpose her memory of Dougan's boyish features on the sculpted, cruel face of the man in front of her. Couldn't be done. Though the hair was black, and the one eye was dark, the resemblance ended there. Swallowing, she forced her frozen tongue to form words. "How do I know you're not deceiving me?"

"You don't," he answered simply. "Nor does it matter, because here's where all this information becomes relevant to you."

"I fail to see how."

"Let me ask you something," Blackwell said intently. "How do you believe Dougan Mackenzie died?"

A knot of dread formed in her stomach. "I was told it was consumption that took him, that he fell ill and never recovered."

"And who told you that?"

"The reception guard at Newgate," she answered honestly. "The day it happened."

Blackwell became very still, the hand on his glass turning white. "What were *you* doing at Newgate Prison ten years ago on the day Dougan Mackenzie died?" he demanded, emotion coloring his voice for the first time since they'd met.

"That's none of your business."

"You *will* tell me, Farah, if I have to force it out of you," he said through clenched teeth.

She blanched at his forceful use of her first name, but stubbornly pressed her lips together.

"Damn it, *why* would you go there?" he roared, surging to his feet and hurling his crystal glass into the fireplace. Farah flinched as it exploded against the stones.

He stalked to her chair, and to her everlasting shame, Farah cringed away from him in fear. He didn't touch her, though, just towered over her, panting and raging. "Why would you set foot in that wretched place on that day of all days?"

"I—I . . ." She could barely form a thought, let alone words.

"Answer me!" he bellowed in a voice that she swore rattled the windows.

Farah couldn't look at him anymore. Couldn't see the

wrath piercing at her with an archer's precision. Couldn't face his lies, or more petrifying, his truths. "It wasn't just that day. I went to Newgate *every* night for seven years and left Dougan cheese and bread."

"No." He retreated a step, staggered was more like it, giving her the moment she needed to gather her courage.

Farah stood, her head barely reaching his cravat so she had to crane her neck to look up at him. "You see, Mr. Blackwell, your kind are not the only ones who keep their promises. I, too, made a promise years ago, that I'd never let Dougan Mackenzie go hungry, and I kept that promise up until the day he . . . the day . . . he . . ." Her composure finally broke and she retreated to stand in front of the desk, swallowing frantic gulps of emotion.

He allowed it, gathering his own armor to him in front of her eyes in the form of cavalier tranquility. "He never knew that extra food was from you. We thought the other prisoners' families left it as offerings, or some kind of payment for our continued favors or good graces."

"But I wrote him letters every week and delivered them with the food," she protested.

"He never received them."

That, alone, was enough to break her heart. Farah's shoulders lost all their ability to keep her head up, and she slumped over. "I thought I'd at least give him a little bit of hope. That he would know that, even locked away, he wasn't alone in the world." She didn't look at him but for a glance from beneath her lashes. He still stood where he had before, with more information she didn't want, but had to discover, locked behind his cruel lips.

"Tell me how he died," she ordered softly. "If not by illness, then by what means?"

"He was murdered." With those three cold words, Blackwell pierced her heart.

"How?" she whispered.

"Beaten to death in the middle of the night by three prison guards."

Farah clamped a hand over her mouth as the tartlets churned in her stomach and crawled up her throat with an acid burn. She swallowed, then again, grateful the food couldn't pass the lump of tears in her throat to end up retched all over the study's expensive carpets.

"Why?" she gasped.

"That is the eternal question, isn't it?"

Farah was too shocked, too disconsolate to be angry at the lack of emotion in his voice. She couldn't be sure how long she stood staring at the hem of her lovely dress, one she'd had on for much too long that now felt tight and confining and bit into her skin. She wanted to be rid of it. To be rid of this room, of the past, of everything. She wanted to be back in her office, where she ought to be, shuffling paperwork and making ordered sense out of chaos. Pretending that she had no time for emotion, for grief, for guilt, only responsibility and an endless list of things to do to keep the dissonance of her thoughts occupied.

She didn't hear Blackwell approach until he was standing beside her.

"Why are you telling me this now?" Her question came out more of an accusation.

He submitted her to another one of his protracted silences before finally answering. "Because I've owed Dougan Mackenzie a debt, one it has taken me ten years of careful execution to repay. When I saw you in the strong room, when I realized who you were, I thought, who better to share his revenge with than you? You can help me wreak vengeance on everyone who tore your lives apart all those years ago."

Farah stared at him, searching for a lie on his pitiless face. Finding none, and still doubting her instincts. Dorian Blackwell was a thief, a liar, and a criminal. Could she believe him? Was he, even now, playing some kind of terrible, merciless game?

"Take my hand, look me in the eye, and *promise* me you're not lying to me." It came out more of a plea than a command. Morley had told her once that one could detect a lie by the tension in a man's hand, the dilation of his pupils, and the direction of his gaze. Farah was not skilled in the practice, but she wanted to try.

Blackwell regarded her offered hand as though she presented him a slug or a spider. "No," he said shortly.

"Then you *are* lying," she insisted.

"No."

"Prove it," Farah challenged. "Why would you deny this innocuous request if you have nothing to hide?" She thrust her hand farther toward him, and he barely concealed a flinch.

"I have plenty to hide, but in this, you can be assured I am in earnest."

"I could never trust someone who couldn't even offer a handshake upon his honor."

Blackwell considered her outstretched hand for a disturbingly long time. "I'm afraid I won't be able to oblige you."

She let her hand drop. "I can't say I'm surprised." So had he been lying about Dougan's death? About all of it? What should she believe?

After a time, he seemed to come to a decision. "I will, however, give you a gesture of good faith. I will give you information about myself that few beyond the two of us have ever or will ever know."

Farah found the gesture odd, but she stood silently, waiting for him to continue.

"The years I spent in prison, shall we say . . . disinclined me toward any contact with human flesh. That is why I do not shake your hand." He presented this information as though informing her of the weather but, for the first time, his eye did not meet hers. "I also admit that I'm not above lying to you to get what I want; however, in this I'm certain our purposes are aligned, and therefore I have no need to manipulate you. I think you want those who have harmed Dougan, and you, to pay for their crimes."

"Revenge." She tested the word, an ideal she'd always abhorred and yearned for at the same time. "And you consider yourself as what, some sort of Count of Monte Cristo?"

He gave a nonchalant shrug. "Not particularly, though the book is a favorite of mine."

Farah frowned. "I thought you said you couldn't read."

That Dorian Blackwell could laugh at a time like this astounded her. But he did. The sound so devoid of true mirth, it caused goose pimples to rise on her skin and her nipples to tighten painfully. It was a dark sound, like the rest of him, and it washed over her with chilling totality. "I don't see what's so funny, it was only a question."

"You must think me a fool," he said.

"I think you're a lot of things."

He stepped closer. A moth's wing wouldn't have survived in the space between them, and still he never touched her, though she could feel the sensation of him on every inch of her skin.

"I'll tell you this," he began darkly, his eye swirling with all the intensity of last night's storm. "There are immense differences between the Count of Monte Cristo and the Blackheart of Ben More. Edmond Dantes was given his treasure. He never had to stoop to the things I did in order to take it. In prison, he was only whipped on his anniversary. He was isolated in his own cell, which Alexandre Dumas never imagined would be preferable to what *we* had to endure. He was never stabbed, raped, publicly flogged, humiliated, beaten within an inch of his life, or taken ill and left for dead."

With every word, Farah's eyes widened and she again found herself cringing back, but he didn't allow her to retreat, bending until his compelling face was mere inches from hers. "And that is just what the gaolers did to me."

She'd been able to control her tears until that moment, but no longer. They spilled over her lashes and washed down her cheeks, causing her breath to tremble in her chest and rattle through her lips. To no longer be able to abide the comfort of human contact. How did he stand it? No wonder he was so very remote. How could warmth touch your heart when it wasn't even allowed near your skin?

It could have been regret that softened his features, but it was still impossible for her to tell. "You're thinking of Mackenzie," he murmured.

Ashamed that she'd been thinking of Blackwell and not her Dougan, Farah nodded, not trusting herself to make a sound.

For the second time since they'd met, he raised his hand to her face, only to pull it back again. "Is there no pity in your heart for me?"

Farah turned from him then, dashing madly at her cheeks. There was, of course, but she didn't dare show it to him. "Do you deserve my pity?" she asked, her voice thick with her tears.

"Probably not," he answered honestly. "But the boy I once was might have."

The next tear that fell was for him, though she'd die before letting him know it. "Dougan. He was—he was small for his age. So skinny and starving. It would have been easy for anyone to . . . to prey upon him."

"It was," Dorian confirmed. "But he learned quickly."

The sobs she'd been fighting so valiantly began to burst into tiny explosions in her chest. They cut off her breath unless she let them free in a flood of hot tears and desperate gasps.

"His death was years ago." Dorian's voice softened, and she dare not turn to him. "A decade at least. The pain cannot be so fresh as all that."

She agreed. She'd thought that with time, the stinging grief and the crushing guilt would fade, but it didn't. It was as though Dougan Mackenzie refused to die, and because of it, she was doomed to relive the blessings and horrors of their time together again and again. "You don't understand," she wailed. "It was *my* fault. My fault all of this befell him. Didn't he tell you why he was incarcerated in the first place?"

"He killed a priest."

"For me!" She whirled around, shocked at how close he still stood. "He killed that priest for *me*. He was subjected to all the suffering and indignities you just described and more because he was only trying to protect me. You don't understand how much I regret that every day of my life! I think about it all the time. I hate myself for it!"

"He never blamed you." For the first time since she'd met him, Dorian seemed to be at a loss. Unsure, maybe, of how to handle a distraught woman. But Farah didn't care, she was purging something so terrible in front of someone who may be an enemy, or might prove an ally.

"You can't know that!" she insisted. "It was just a few kisses from the priest, a horrid touch or two. If I'd never gone to Dougan that night. If I'd only submitted to a small ignominy . . . perhaps it would have saved his life. Perhaps we'd still be . . . together."

"Never." Blackwell's features hardened again, and he looked as though he wanted to shake her. "Dougan would rather have submitted to his thousand tortures than to have you submit to one. He wouldn't have survived your suffering. He loves you that much."

"Loved," she sobbed. "*Loved* me, and because of it, he *didn't* survive! His love for me got him killed." A smothering nausea overtook her, images of the boy she loved suffering in the graphic ways Blackwell described assaulted her imagination until she wanted to crawl out of her own skin to escape them. She needed to escape this room, to flee the darkness and the man who was shrouded by it. "Forgive me," she gasped. "I—I must . . . go." Her vision blurred by tears, she lurched in the direction of the doors, relieved that he made no move to stop her. Light flared through the windows of the grand entry and blinded her as she was so accustomed to the shadows. She caught the scent of muffins or toast wafting from the hulking figure silently shocked by the sudden opening of the study door.

Farah seized upon the sunlight with a mad desperation, and pulled the heavy doors of the keep open. The two footmen stood as sentries on either side, and they moved to stop her, but paused as though someone had given them a staying command.

Farah launched herself past them, running blindly for a gazebo perched on the edge of the tallest rocks, and shaded by a copse of trees. From the vista, she could stare across the channel and see the black rock and green mosses of Scotland's Highland shores. She watched the churning waves break upon the cliffs with power enough to crush the mightiest of ships. The shards of her churning emotions were tossed about thusly inside of her. And, for the first time since those months after Dougan Mackenzie had died, she cried with all the strength her broken heart could muster.

Dorian stood in the archway of his castle and watched the woman flee as if for her life. "Let her go, Walters," he ordered, stopping his cook from going after her and hauling her back.

"Name's Frank," Walters insisted, though he obediently returned to Dorian's side.

It took a moment for the words to penetrate Dorian's concentration, so focused as it was on the retreating form running with desperate abandon toward the pavilion, her skirts the color of sea foam billowing out behind her.

Finally, he glanced over at his biggest and most pliable employee. "Frank?"

Walters inclined his head toward the pavilion. "She named me this morning."

"Of course she did," Dorian muttered.

Walters looked after her, as well, his doe-brown eyes becoming very troubled. "What's wrong with your Fairy, Dougan?"

Dorian sighed, running into this problem more often than he cared to. "It's me, Walters. It's Dorian. Dougan is dead, remember?"

"Oh." Confused, the giant man took a long moment to study his features, his brows drawn together. "I forgot. I'm no good at remembering things."

"It's all right," Dorian soothed.

"She misses Dougan," the big man said, sniffing down at his muffins.

"Yes. Yes, she does."

"I do, too, Dorian."

Dorian could feel a familiar darkness surge in his veins. These days, it was tinged red, for blood, with a greater frequency. It no longer disturbed him, he told himself as he retreated to his study. "We all do, Frank," he said before he closed himself in. "We all do."

CHAPTER EIGHT

It was Murdoch who nudged her limp, despondent form from the planks of the pavilion and tutted over her until she allowed him to guide her back inside. The arm that kept her upright was solid beneath his suit coat, and he all but carried her up the steps.

"I've drawn ye a warm bath, lass, and found ye something suitable to wear whilst I launder yer dress." Absurdly, he reminded her of a clucking mother hen, hovering nervously over her chick.

Farah nodded her thanks, her throat still too raw to say much of anything.

He went on, deciding to ignore or forgive her escape attempt, solicitous as ever. More so, now that tears streaked her cheeks and reddened her eyes. Once ensconced back in the bedroom, Murdoch relieved her of her shawl and purse, setting them on the jewel-blue chair.

"Did Blackwell frighten ye?" he queried with a false brightness. "Because although he's a dangerous-looking bastar—er—villain, he's really not so—"

"You were in Newgate with Dougan Mackenzie." She didn't pose it as a question, more of a soft declaration, one he couldn't deny without perjuring himself.

Murdoch froze. His stout form working through a shiver as he found something arresting about her shawl draped across the chair. "Aye," he gruffly confirmed. "For five long years."

"What was your crime?"

He turned to her slowly, his face a mask of shame and pain. "My only crime, dear girl, was love." He must have read the lack of comprehension on her face, because he continued. "I had a prolonged affair with the son of an earl from Surrey. When his father found out, charges were brought against me, and the man I loved turned on me in court, branding me a . . . predator."

Farah's already bruised heart jolted as another pang pierced it through, this one for the torment mirrored at her in the features of the wide Scotsman. "I'm sorry," she whispered, surprised by how much she meant it.

"It's ancient history, now." He shrugged, summoning a wan smile for her.

"The past can long stay with us, Murdoch," she murmured.

"Right ye are, lass."

"Were you and Dougan . . . friends?" Farah ventured, knowing his rendering of the past would be kinder than Dorian Blackwell's.

Murdoch shifted, retreating to the washroom door. "I owe him my life, many times over. And, as such, I owe my life for yers, as well."

"How is that?" she whispered, uncomfortable with the veneration on his gentle face.

"Well, ye're his Fairy, of course, his lady wife for all intents and purposes. We promised Dougan Mackenzie that we'd find ye. That we'd protect ye. That, if we could, we'd give ye back the life that ye're owed, the life he would have wanted for ye."

Tears threatened again and Farah fiercely blinked them away. "He told you about our handfasting when we were young?"

"Aye, it was one of our favorite stories."

"Truly?" A soft wonder began to expand through her chest and she seized upon it. "Are you saying Dougan told you stories about me? That must have been incredibly tedious and uninteresting."

Murdoch came forward and gently took her hand, drawing her toward the adjoining washroom. "Ye canna understand what prison is like, lass. When a single night passes in fear and despair, a week might as well be a lifetime, and a year becomes an eternity."

Farah's bare toes curled against the cold white marble floors of the washroom, streaked with silver and blue. Gilded silver mirrors and dainty white furniture upholstered in the boldest cobalt littered the room almost to excess. More windows spilled sunlight through gauzy sapphire curtains that fluttered in a spring breeze. A porcelain bath stood on a dais surrounded by the softest blue paisley rugs.

Murdoch busied himself by dragging a silk-and-iron changing screen from the corner and placing it next to the bath, talking all the while. "In Newgate, a story to make the time pass with greater alacrity has more value than gold." He draped a large robe of heavy blue fabric over the silk of the screen. The draw of the steaming bath overcame her misgivings about disrobing in the same room with a relatively strange man. Of course, this would never be done back in London, but when one was a prisoner of the Blackheart of Ben More, one didn't worry about paltry scandals.

"Thank you." Stepping behind the screen, Farah undid

laces of her bodice and pushed her dress from her shoulders. She could hear Murdoch bustling about the room, keeping himself busy for her benefit, she guessed. "Would you tell me about it, Murdoch, your time in Newgate with Dougan?"

The restless movement ceased and the older man gave a gusty sigh, or maybe it was whatever dainty chair he lowered himself into that produced the sad noise. "As I said, the nights are the worst," he began in a faraway voice. "The hours of darkness break even the bravest of men, let alone frightened wee boys. We'd be finished with a day's worth of work on the railway and return to our world of iron bars too exhausted to move, let alone defend ourselves from the dangers the night might bring. The sounds. The cries. The whispers from the shadows . . . they're dreadful. If ye didna have friends to help protect ye . . ." He trailed off, leaving the rest to her imagination.

"I'm sorry," Farah whispered, stepping out of her skirts, and draping the stiff dress over the sturdy screen.

"Thank ye," Murdoch acknowledged. "By the time I arrived at Newgate, Blackwell and Mackenzie had been there nearly three years. Thick as thieves and twice as shrewd, they were, each of them dark as the devil and just as ruthless. It always amazed me that ones so young could learn such cruelty."

Luckily, Farah's corset was laced in the front, and she went to work on that as she absorbed Murdoch's words. "It's hard for me to imagine a cruel Dougan," she admitted. "But . . . he was kind to you?"

"Eventually," Murdoch said evasively. "But once I proved myself useful, I was taken into their gang's protection and that made life much easier for me, most especially at night. As ye likely know, Dougan had a gift for words and an eerily accurate memory. On the darkest and coldest of nights, he'd tell us about books he'd read with ye, and often he'd be sidetracked from the memory of the book and just go on about some adventure or another the two of ye had together."

"He did?" Farah breathed, pausing before peeling off her chemise and exposing her breasts to the chilly air. Once she'd finished that, she bent and tucked her only treasure beneath the washroom rug, not wanting anyone to find it.

Warmth stole into Murdoch's voice at the memory, and Farah's heart clenched at the picture of her Dougan not yet a man, and yet not a boy, regaling a room full of hardened prisoners about the graveyard capers and bog adventures of a ten-year-old girl in the Scottish Highlands. "He described ye so many times, I feel as though any of us would have recognized ye had we seen ye on the streets. He told us of yer kindness, yer innocence, yer gentle ways and boundless curiosity. Ye became something of a patron saint to us all. Our daughter. Our sister. Our . . . Fairy. Without even knowing it, ye gave us—him—a little bit of sunshine and hope in a world of shadow and pain."

"Oh." Farah again lost the battle to her tears, and she stood behind the screen, naked and shivering, her arms wrapped around herself as she drank in Murdoch's memories as though she could make them her own. She barely noticed her nakedness, as it was her insides that felt so entirely exposed and vulnerable. "Are you quite certain he was never angry with me? That he never—blamed me for his incarceration?"

The older man was silent for a time, and tendrils of panic snaked through her. "Please. You must tell me the truth," she begged.

"Get in the bath, first," Murdoch nudged gently.

Farah complied, stepping up and into the fragrant tub and lowering herself into lavender-scented water that lapped at her shoulders.

"The truth is, lass, that it would have killed Mackenzie to ever hear ye ask that question," Murdoch continued when he seemed certain that she was situated. "It was only we who were closest to him who knew the particular depths of his fears for ye. He never told anyone but Blackwell and me yer name. To everyone else, ye were his Fairy, and that was all the information they ever got. He guarded ye like the jealous husband he was."

"Our marriage was never legitimate, Murdoch," Farah confessed, letting the hot water and lavender soothe the chill and the aches from her stiff muscles. "You must know that, as well."

Murdoch's rude noise echoed off the stone and marble of the washroom, amplifying his contempt for her words. "Dougan Mackenzie was as faithful and devoted a husband to ye as there ever was," he insisted. "And after all these years, *Mrs. Mackenzie,* seems to me ye've stayed as true a bride to his memory as ye would have if he was alive."

Farah's hand skimmed across the still, clean water as his words pricked her with needles of guilt. "That's not entirely true," she acknowledged. "You know that I—kissed another man the night you and Blackwell took me from my home."

"Aye, well . . ." If a voice could convey a shrug, Murdoch's did so. "For a woman who, for all intents and purposes, had been widowed nigh on a decade, no one can blame ye for trying to fill the loneliness with company."

"Your Mr. Blackwell certainly didn't see it that way." It disturbed her to think of the master of Ben More whilst naked. Suddenly needing a vocation, Farah picked up a bar of soap that smelled like heather and honey and began to vigorously scrub the past few days away.

"Blackwell's as tied to Dougan Mackenzie as we all

are," Murdoch said cryptically. "He may be meaner than a coiled snake, and twice as deadly, but out of anyone alive, he's the best chance ye've got."

"That's something else I don't understand," Farah began, lifting a leg above the water to rub the bar of soap all the way down to her toes. "You all seem to be convinced I'm in some sort of danger, but I can't readily imagine what that would be, and no one is inclined to explain it to me."

"Blackwell didna get around to that, eh?"

Farah pinched her lips together with a frown. "That was my fault, I suppose. I fled him before he was quite finished."

"Ye wouldna be the first," Murdoch grumbled, sounding more like an exasperated father than a loyal minion. A creak of furniture told her that Murdoch had risen and was coming closer. She tensed, but as soon as she heard him gathering her things from the screen, she relaxed again. "Mrs. Mackenzie . . ." he began.

"You might as well call me Farah," she instructed, lifting her arms to pull the pins from her hopelessly disheveled bun and let her curls fall into the bath. "I feel we're far beyond societal constraints at this point, Murdoch."

His pregnant pause conveyed a shifting reluctance that piqued her curiosity. "When it comes to the danger, I doona want ye to feel like it can touch ye all the way out here. In this castle, ye have nothing to fear."

"Yes, you've said that already." Farah dropped her head back, wetting her scalp, and began to work the suds through her thick waves.

"I mean to say, I know it doesna seem like it now, but ye can trust *him*. The rest of us, we'd lay down our lives for yers, but Blackwell . . . he'd do that and more. He'd rip the beating heart from his chest. He'd give up his soul if ye'd only—"

"It is making a rather large and fallacious assumption that I have a heart to give . . . *or* a soul." Dorian Blackwell's smooth voice didn't echo through the washroom as theirs did. He slithered into their midst with a serpentine stealth, striking before Murdoch's words uncovered any of his secrets.

Gasping, Farah sank deep into the bath, thankful the water was now cloudy with soap, though she did draw her knees under her chin and anchor them with her arms, just in case. "Get out!" she insisted in an unsteady voice. "I'm indecent."

"That makes two of us."

He'd moved closer. So close, in fact, that Farah knew if she looked behind her, she'd find his mismatched eyes staring down at her from his towering height. Perhaps, despite the opaque water, he could see the flesh that quivered just below the surface. The thought sent bolts of heat and mortification through her.

"Leave," Farah ordered, unable to face him for fear she'd lose her nerve.

"Stand up and make me."

She sank deeper into the water, her rapid breaths creating ripples on the surface.

"Blackwell," Murdoch cajoled. "If ye'd like to wait in the chambers, I'll have her dress and—"

"That'll be all, Murdoch," Dorian said.

"But, *sir.*" Murdoch's emphasis on the word was puzzling. "I doona think this is any way to—"

"You're *dismissed.*" Only a man with a death wish would have argued, and Farah couldn't bring herself to blame Murdoch one bit for abandoning her. The click of the washroom door felt like the slide of iron bars, locking Farah in her gilded prison with the most blackhearted criminal. Helpless, trapped, and naked.

If Farah had learned anything from her job, it was that

those who took the offensive usually kept the high ground. "What could you possibly want that couldn't wait until I was finished bathing?" she asked impatiently, proud that she kept any apprehension or weakness out of her voice.

Blackwell stepped from behind her, running long fingers along the rim of the tub. Dressed in only shirtsleeves, the dark kilt, and a vest, his lack of coat did nothing to detract from the startling width of his shoulders. He'd taken off his eye patch, she noted, and his blue eye glinted at her in the spring sunlight. "It occurred to me, whilst contemplating the unfortunate turn of our previous conversation, that our next communication might be better served if you are not in a position to run from me."

Even in the steaming heat of the water, Farah's blood turned to ice in her veins, but she stiffened her spine and lifted her chin. "You're sadly mistaken if you assume that I will not run, or fight, if provoked."

He positioned himself at the foot of the tub, the sunlight casting a blue aura over the thick ebony of his hair as he leaned down to grip each side of the basin. "Then by all means, consider yourself provoked, but do be careful, marble tends to be slick when wet." His gaze touched the ripples of the water with suggestive interest, and Farah's temperature swung wildly from chilled to overheated. A sheen of moisture bloomed in her hairline and above her lip.

He was calling her bluff, *damn him,* and he seemed infuriatingly unconcerned by the strength of her disdainful glare. She'd never been very good at nasty looks or confrontation, but she had an idea that before she and Dorian Blackwell were through with each other, she'd have a great deal of practice with both. "Well . . . say your piece, then," she prompted, hating that her eyes couldn't rest on him for any length of time without being quite overwhelmed.

"I intend to do *exactly* that." His voice, usually the texture of cold marble, roughened with a husky note that was intriguing and alarming all at once. "I will talk whilst you finish bathing yourself."

"Impossible!" she huffed, drawing her knees in tighter to her chest.

One dark eyebrow lifted. "Is it?" His fingers skimmed the milky water, sending ripples toward her that lapped against her knees. "I'd be happy to assist if you find yourself unequal to the task."

Farah remembered what he'd said in the study. That he didn't particularly like physical contact. Though the pads of his fingers idling in her bathwater suggested he may have been lying. Or was he bluffing now? Was she brave enough to test the veracity of his own admission?

"Touch me, and I'll—"

"You'll what?" His voice cooled as did his regard, but he pulled his fingers from the water.

Farah desperately grasped for something to say, but her mind was suddenly blank as a sheaf of paper.

"You'll learn that I do not respond favorably to threats," he said rather drolly as he wiped his fingers on a hand towel hanging from a rack at the foot of the tub.

"Neither do I," she countered, and watched his other eyebrow rise to join the first. "I gather that you want something from me, Mr. Blackwell; well, let me inform you that this is *not* the way to go about obtaining someone's cooperation."

"And yet, I always manage to get what I want from people."

"I highly doubt very many of those people are self-respecting *women*."

Blackwell smirked and rubbed his hard jaw, smooth from a morning shave, as some of the ice receded from his eyes. "I'll grant you that," he said, turning and stepping from the dais toward a plush velvet chair. "But, as you know, my world is ruled by many laws, not the least of which is quid pro quo." He settled his long frame into the chair, his legs falling open and his hands resting on the arms with the indolence of a royal. "I can give you *everything* you want, Farah Leigh Mackenzie, and all you have to do is wash." He gave the bar of soap a meaningful glance.

Farah couldn't think of anything she wanted badly enough to warrant such humiliation, but then she remembered what Blackwell had said before. Dougan may have been brutally murdered. Blackwell was seeking vengeance for his death and wanted her help. If there was any truth to those words, Farah needed to hear them to ascertain it.

Bracing herself, she stretched her legs along the bottom of the bath and lifted her hand to reach for the soap. Her neck and jaw seemed an innocent enough place to start washing, as long as she was careful to keep the swell of her breasts below the murky water. "Tell me what it is I want," she demanded, chagrined to hear that her voice had become husky and low, the words sounding like an altogether different command. A lover's command. But they both knew better.

Blackwell's anomalous eyes glinted as they followed the path of the soap down the column of her neck but, surprisingly, he complied. "Seven years is a long time to spend almost every moment with someone. Over the course of our time together, Mackenzie and I became like brothers. We not only fought, worked, and suffered alongside each other, we shared everything to keep our bond as leaders— as brothers—strong. And to help pass the endless time, I suppose. He shared with me the food you left, though now I doubt he'd done it if he'd known it was you who'd left it. We shared every sordid detail of our pasts, every name, every story, every . . . secret."

Farah's head snapped up, the soap pausing halfway down her shoulder. "Secret?"

Blackwell's head dipped in a single, meaningful nod, though his eyes remained locked on the bar of soap. He didn't continue until the soap resumed its glistening path along her flesh.

"In prison, needs, emotions, and fears are only weaknesses to be exploited," he explained. "Mackenzie's primary fear was for you. It tortured him that he didn't know what had happened to you after his capture. His only consolation was that he'd killed Father MacLean, and thereby knew you were out of danger from him, at least."

Blackwell turned his head to a slight degree, so his good eye focused on the soap she slid along her other arm. Farah became acutely aware that she was running out of skin, and the anticipatory intensity of Blackwell's stare proved he relished that fact. Her arms could only get so clean, before she had to wash elsewhere.

How absurd this situation had become. The humiliating memories and dank, raw pain of Newgate Prison didn't belong in this sunlit room with the fragrant, moist heat settling around them, turning the atmosphere hazy with steam. To Farah, the effect was something of a dream, blurring the lines between reality and imagination. Blackwell spoke of hard and valid truths, but the way he watched the soap turn her flesh into slick paths of glinting silk evoked the most sinful and debauched renderings her thoughts could devise.

"How fortunate for you that the water obscures so much." Blackwell shifted in his chair, his knees falling wider and his nostrils flaring.

"Would Dougan Mackenzie forgive this coercion?" she challenged, doing her best to ignore the stirrings of her own body. "If you owe him as much as you claim, would he not wish you to spare my modesty?"

The spark of heat in his eyes died for a moment, before flaring brighter than before. "When we meet in hell, I'll ask his forgiveness." His mouth pulled into a harder line, his skin tightened over the sharp angles of his cheeks and jaw. His dark eye gleamed triumphant and also dissatisfied, his blue one conflicted and aroused, and both were locked on the soap hovering at her shoulder.

Farah understood what she must do to urge him to keep talking. Lips parting on an anxious breath, she slowly washed the slim expanse of her chest before dipping the soap below the water's surface, running it over her breast.

The immediate reaction of her body was both unexpected and acute. Sensation ripped through her, starting at her nipple as the soap grazed it, and coursing through her limbs before settling between her clenched thighs. Farah forced her eyes not to flutter closed as she savored this new and profound awareness. Instead, she studied Blackwell for any signs that he recognized the effect he'd had on her. That she'd had on *herself* in his presence.

So intent was he on the spot where her hand had disappeared, she doubted he noticed her reaction at all.

"Go on," she demanded breathlessly, hoping to keep him distracted as she sorted out the insistent pressure now burning through her blood and combating the chill in her bones brought on by the content of their conversation.

True to his word, he complied. The dispassionate tone of his voice again conflicting with the intensity of his bold regard. "Since Dougan would likely spend twenty years in Newgate before the crown revisited his case, he asked me to swear a vow on the debt I owed him of my life." He trailed off when her breath caught as she washed her other breast.

"Which was?" she prompted.

"That when they released me, I would hunt you down and make certain you were safe and cared for."

"As you can see, Mr. Blackwell, I'm quite unharmed and well cared for. You may return me to my life with a clear conscience." Farah laughed a little. "That is, if you even have one."

"I suppose it does remain to be seen," he said mildly, though he still hadn't lifted his notice above the slight ripples in the water. "My seven-year sentence was completed almost a month to the day after Dougan's death. And the first thing I did was go looking for you." He leaned forward then, like a great cat readying for his lethal blow. "Do you know what I found?"

"No." A slice of dread began to tangle with the heat in Farah's belly, just beneath where the soap hovered in her trembling fingers. "Tell me."

"I will. As soon as you resume washing."

"I—I'm finished," she lied. "I'm clean."

Flames licked at the ice in his blue eye. "You missed a spot."

An answering heat bloomed deep inside her. Low in her belly, no, lower—in her womb. Farah wanted to hate him. He held her captive. Manipulated her emotions. Used this wicked compulsion to gratify his own perversions.

And yet . . .

As the soap slid through sparse curls and into the cleft between her thighs, ribbons of unexpected sensation stirred from her most intimate flesh and unfurled across the expanse of her skin. Her mouth dropped open, but she caught the moan before it escaped.

Their gazes collided, the flames in his eyes darkened as his pupils dilated.

He knew. Though he could see nothing, he knew exactly where her fingers drifted, and precisely where the soap slicked over already moistened skin.

Despite her mortification, Farah also marveled. She'd been bathing for almost three decades and, while she'd found a tremor of pleasure whilst lingering here, it had never been so achingly insistent, so full of demand and promise.

That demand, those promises, were mirrored in the stare of Dorian Blackwell.

Whatever he read in her eyes caused him to slam his lids shut, giving Farah an unimpeded view of the angry scar across his brow and eyelid. The wound looked deep and angry. It was a wonder he hadn't lost his eye. When he reopened them, she found herself staring at his wounded blue iris with rapt attention. To her disappointment, he'd conjured his signature chill again, though he cleared his throat before speaking.

"I will tell you that I found you had your own share of secrets, and not ones best left to the darkness, like mine, but secrets that would rock the entire British Empire."

The soap slipped from her fingers, trailing down her womanhood and disappearing into the water. All the warmth and pleasure dissipated, and Farah shook her head in shocked denial. "I don't know what you're talking about." The frightening speed with which the atmosphere between them heated and cooled was enough to make one consumptive. Hadn't she just been having one of the most intimate moments of her life? And now he wanted to resume talking about the past. Revealing secrets. Tearing open old wounds.

She'd changed her mind. She *did* hate him. She hated how he was shaking his dark head, but in a mock semblance of righteous censure.

"Applecross was, of course, where I started my search. The orphanage's records showed that one Farah Leigh *Townsend* succumbed to a bout of cholera, her tolerance having been weakened by her family's fatal disease."

Farah knew all this, but found herself riveted, wondering if the Blackheart of Ben More was really going to sit in the only shadows of the bright room and uncover the only concealment she'd thought she'd had left. He'd used her real last name. Something she'd never disclosed to anyone, not even Dougan Mackenzie.

"A terrible disease, cholera," he continued, watching her reaction carefully. "It spreads through tight quarters like Applecross, leaving mass devastation in its wake. A single case is unheard of. So, with a little coercion, as you call it, I learned that a fortnight after MacLean's death and Dougan's arrest, a ten-year-old girl vanished from Applecross and Sister Margaret covered up the disappearance, using the excuse of burning a diseased corpse to cover the lack of a body."

None of this was news to Farah. Having worked next to the records commissioner for nearly a decade, she'd been able to sneak a look at her very own death certificate. "Where did you go after?" she queried breathlessly.

Dorian gave her a wry look. "A complicated search such as that takes money, of which I had none. So, I immediately set out acquiring some, and found a little success."

Farah rolled her eyes to encompass her lavish surroundings. "Only everyone in the world knows how you set about it."

"Not initially. For a few years I made my living as a highwayman. In those days, the trains didn't go so far, and the wealthy often traveled the rest of their distances in carriages."

Farah straightened in the water before realizing that a dusky nipple bobbed above the surface before she ducked down again. "A highwayman? Did you hurt anyone?" she asked, hoping he hadn't noticed her mistake.

He had, of course. "I've hurt a lot of people," he told the swell of her bosom. "But we can discuss that later. We're talking about *your* past right now. I feel we've quite exhausted the subject of mine."

Farah's heart leaped like a startled rabbit. "I have no past. I was an orphan and then I ran from Applecross, made my way to London and—"

"*Don't* lie to me, Farah." His soft voice was so terrifying, she'd rather he shouted. "You're terrible at it."

She busied herself by groping at the bottom of the tub for her missing soap, using it as an excuse not to look at him. "I don't know what you mean."

"I know who you were . . . who you *are*."

"Impossible," Farah insisted. "I'm nobody." There. She'd found the soap, but pretended to still be looking, as she chased it with slippery fingers.

"You are *far* from nobody. Farah Leigh Townsend, daughter of the late Robert Lee Townsend, captain of the Prince Consort's Rifle Brigade in the Crimea, *and* more importantly, Earl Northwalk. You are the only living heiress to what has to be the most controversial, contested fortune in Britain until quite recently."

His every word pinned her to the floor of the tub. She sank to her chin, wishing she could just slip below the surface and hide in the murky safety of the water without lethal consequences. He saw too much. *Knew* too much, and that could ruin everything.

"You're mistaken," She made another attempt at denial, hoping that she could convince him of her identity. "Farah is a common enough name, and Leigh a very ordinary middle name, so your mistake is understandable. But, in case you were unaware, Farah Leigh Townsend was recently discovered in a hospital in London, having miraculously recovered from amnesia." She finally mustered the strength to meet the skepticism bleeding from Blackwell's every pore head-on. "She married a Mr. Harold Warrington, Esq., not a month ago, to whom she'd been long betrothed. So you see, Mr. Blackwell, it is infeasible for me to be who you claim."

His eyes narrowed on her and he spoke his next words very carefully, though caustic reprimand leaked like venom from his lips. "Imagine my surprise when I saw the banns in the papers. The long-lost heiress of Northwalk secretly married, the title of earl bestowed upon her husband, who happened to be her deceased father's steward and of little to no blue blood. Naturally, driven by the oath I'd made all those years ago, I arranged a meeting with Mrs. Farah Leigh Warrington, and knew the moment I laid eyes on her that she was an imposter."

"That's ridiculous," Farah scoffed. "How would you know a thing like that?"

A secret smile threatened the bleak lines of his mouth. "I know a thing or two about imposters, con artists, thieves, and greed."

"Yes, I've heard you're something of an expert." Farah usually didn't possess much in the way of a temper, but it seemed that ire made her feel less helpless than fear.

"Indeed," Blackwell confirmed. "So believe me when I say that I recognized a soul as black as my own and just as devious."

"I find it highly improbable such a thing exists." Farah began to seriously consider an attempt at escape, modesty be damned. It only took one glance at Dorian Blackwell's long and powerful limbs to squelch the panicked impulse immediately.

She wouldn't get far, and she could only imagine how he would punish her this time. Farah couldn't tell if her barbs had affected him or not, but she couldn't think of another reason he would silently study her for such a long time. "Believe it or not, there are villains out there more evil than I," he said finally.

"Doubtful."

The upholstery of the chair protested as Blackwell's

strong fingers tightened on the arms. "I haven't hurt you, have I? Touched you, even?" His smoky voice echoed with challenge. "I know men who would tear you apart just for the pleasure of hearing you scream. They would make you beg for death before they finished with you. They would use every part of your body and soul until they both shriveled and died and they'd leave you in the gutter like so much filth." Blackwell stood then, his boots impossibly quiet on the marble as he stalked closer. "I may be a villain and a reprobate, but I am *not* like *them*."

"No, you only associate with and employ them." Farah's bravado began to fail, and she grasped it with the desperation with which someone about to be swept downriver would reach for a rope. "Your hands may appear clean, but everyone knows you're tainted with rivers of blood." And she'd do well to remember that.

"That is where you're wrong, Farah. If blood needs to be spilled, it is *my* hands that do the spilling." Frost glazed over any of the warmth and interest he'd shown before, and suddenly her bathwater felt chilly and stale.

"I'm not going to help you hurt anyone," she vowed.

"I wouldn't ask you to." He again stood at the foot of the tub, staring down at her with his unholy eyes. "I only require that you claim what is rightfully yours."

"Someone else has already claimed it! The rightful—"

"Deny it again, and you won't like the consequences." Farah was fast coming to realize that the more toneless his voice became, the more dangerous he was.

"All right, yes!" she hissed. "I am—was—Farah Leigh Townsend. But don't you think there's a reason I never claimed to be her? That I took on the name of someone else and a life of relative obscurity?"

"I assumed it was Warrington."

"It's not *just* Warrington. Much of my father's wealth

was obtained the same way yours was. The spoils of war, the deaths of enemies, the cloak-and-dagger of lies and espionage."

"How do you know this?"

"I remember him and my mother fighting about it when he returned from the Crimea." A band squeezed Farah's chest as it always did when she thought of the past. "My parents loved me, at least, I remember them loving me. So why they would betroth me to a toad like Warrington is a complete puzzle."

Blackwell shrugged. "Sometimes greed is stronger than love."

"No, it isn't," she argued. "Not *real* love. Only fear is stronger than love . . . and even then only if you allow it to be. My parents must have been afraid of something, in trouble, somehow."

"And then they died."

"Precisely." She returned the soap to the tray, and didn't miss the glimmer of something like regret that touched his features as he watched the action.

Deciding to ignore it, Farah ran her wet fingers over eyes made tired and puffy by her prior tears. "I could never stand the idea of marrying Warrington. He was my father's age, and always unsettled me as a child. I was told my family died of cholera . . . Though as I grew older I always wondered if maybe . . ." She let the thought trail off into the steam, unwilling to give it life with her words. Could her life be that cruel? Was everyone she loved taken from her by the evil deeds of another?

Distracted from his ire, Blackwell gripped his chin in a thoughtful gesture. "This is all beginning to make sense."

"I don't see how it possibly can. My head is spinning."

"A week ago, a member of the peerage approached one of my men, Christopher Argent, about a business contract of a rather sensitive nature." Blackwell cast her a meaningful look.

"Argent." The name pricked Farah's memory. "One of your friends from Newgate."

"One of my closest business associates," he corrected slyly. "Argent contacted me right away. A king's fortune was offered for the disappearance of a certain employee of Scotland Yard."

Astounded, Farah gasped. "You can't mean . . ."

"You. Mrs. Farah Leigh Mackenzie. Warrington found you, after all, and he wanted you dead."

"No." Farah began to shiver in the tub, and Blackwell folded his arms tightly across his broad chest, as though to force them to be still.

"You see, there is no returning you to your old life," he said victoriously. "If I hadn't made you disappear, he would have hired someone else to do it."

"Why would he want me dead? He already has everything he could desire, I'm no threat to him."

"On the contrary," Blackwell said. "You threaten everything. You could *ruin* everything and expose him by claiming your title."

"But . . . I wasn't going to!"

"He couldn't be certain of that. A risk is better taken care of before an actual threat presents itself."

Farah couldn't believe her ears. "Is that how *you* conduct your affairs?"

"Absolutely." He said this without shame or remorse, and Farah found she didn't want to look at him anymore. She hid behind her eyelids as her thoughts raced. What did she do now? She'd been happy—well, contented in her life. She'd had a purpose and knew her place in the world. Now everything had changed. There was no going back, and yet she couldn't see any options on how to move forward.

"I haven't anything to prove that I am Farah Leigh Townsend," she began. "Especially now that someone else has adopted the name. Also, a woman can't claim the title and lands of the peerage without being married. On top of everything, I'll have to explain why I was posing as a widow all this time, and I have no evidence of any foul play in my family's death. I don't even know where to begin!"

"Leave all that to me," Blackwell offered.

Farah's head snapped up. The way he stood, like a general surveying his massacre over a battlefield, made her uneasy. "And you'll take care of it all for a debt to a friend a decade gone?" she asked dubiously.

"Of course not," he scoffed. "I am, after all, a businessman. I can return your fortune to you, in exchange for access to the only part of London society still denied me."

"I—I don't understand," Farah stuttered. "How will I do that?"

Blackwell leaned over the tub, bracing his hands on both sides, his powerful shoulders bunching as they supported his considerable weight. "Simple," he purred. "You'll marry me."

Chapter Nine

Aye, Fairy, ye'll have to resign yerself to being a highwayman's wife.

Sounds like an adventure!

Farah stared mutely at the man looming above her with disbelief while memories stole through her bones like a soul lingering in a graveyard.

Dougan's earnest dark eyes, alight with love, possession, and tender vulnerability, glowed at her through the obscure veil time cast on all reminiscences. How romantic the prospect had seemed when they were children, without the understanding of reality to temper their exuberant dreams of the future. But an entirely different set of eyes glowed down at her now, these displaying arrogant calculation and the possession of a much more adult variety.

A highwayman's wife, indeed.

"What makes you think I'd marry the likes of you?" she declared with vehemence when she again found her voice. "That's easily the most ridiculous proposal I've ever heard."

"Please," he scoffed, lip curling in distaste. "You forget I was there when Morley proposed to you. Besides, a proposal denotes a question, and I have yet to ask you one." He pushed away from the tub and turned from her, his shoulders bunched tighter than before. "I informed you that you'll marry me, and marry me you will."

Farah squelched the childish impulse to splash him with water. "I most certainly will not!"

"It is foolish to deny the inevitable," he threw over his shoulder.

That did it. Farah stared daggers at his broad back, knowing they were sharp enough for him to feel them, even though he faced the windows. "Explain to me how becoming the wife of the Blackheart of Ben More improves my circumstances. Other than your ill-gotten money, what else have you to offer me that I could possibly want? You said yourself you have no heart, no soul. A tarnished reputation. You don't love me. You can't even stand to touch me. Why would a woman like me *ever* want a life with a man such as you?"

"Why, indeed?" He turned to face her and Farah's lips snapped together. She realized now just *how* he incited fear in the very souls of his enemies. He didn't scald with a fiery temper. He didn't intimidate with his superior size and brutal strength, though that couldn't be ignored. It was the absolute rigid placidity of his arresting features. Bereft of animation, emotion, or acknowledgment, as though he considered the life in front of him as beneath his notice as that of a harmless insect. He'd be as likely to pass you by as he would to crush you beneath the sole of his boot and not even bother to scrape you off into the gutter. He was beyond arrogance. Above condescension. He would watch a cruel child pluck your limbs off, or survey the carnage of a civilization without a crack in his smooth façade.

Was he truly so cold? Had her words not affected him

in the slightest? She wished he'd meet her ire with the evidence of a wound, with anger, with passion, with *anything* to show her he wasn't as soulless as he claimed.

"I can offer you protection from the man who wants you dead, the safety and stature of my name, and the restoration of your parents' legacy to you. In return, you can offer me the title of earl and a seat in Parliament." Though his voice and deportment bespoke ambivalence, Farah had a notion of how much this meant to him. "Along with avenging Dougan Mackenzie's death, there is quite a lot we can accomplish by joining forces."

Joining forces? "You speak of marriage like a military commander discusses battle strategy," Farah accused.

"In this case, that's not a bad comparison. We'd be two allies with our own set of advantages, strategically aligning against an opponent for a mutual benefit."

"Your benefit seems to outweigh mine. As I'm certain you're aware, if I marry you, my parents' title, wealth, property, and *legacy* wouldn't be returned to me, it would legally belong to you."

He waved a large hand to show how inconsequential her argument was to him. "I have wealth and property enough of my own. What need have I of an estate and a few tenements in Hampshire and a Mayfair mansion? I own more profitable land than the queen. I'll sign a document giving you full rights to your father's holdings before we marry. They would be yours to do with as you wish."

A strange, paralyzing numbness born of shock and disbelief weighed down Farah's limbs even in the buoyant water. Her sweet Dougan's memory avenged. Her father's beloved home restored. Her mother's jewels and priceless art hers again, to cherish and admire. To pass along to further generations. With such resources, she could uncover the truth behind her parents' deaths. Could demand justice for the usurper Warrington and his pretender bride.

Oh, Lord. Was she really considering this—this lunacy? She measured the man in front of her, a study in strength and darkness and ruthless control. Just what would agreeing to be the wife of the most infamous man in the empire entail? The very thought chilled the blood.

And yet . . .

"What do you want with a title and a seat in Parliament?" she queried.

He gave her a droll look. "What does every man want? Prestige. More power. Access to the elite. There are still some investments and schemes almost impossible to achieve without a title behind your name and the blessing of the queen. Even Americans, as dogmatic as they are about their lack of nobility, are more likely to conduct affairs with a titled English gentleman, thus making my ventures overseas a great deal easier."

"No one would ever mistake you for a gentleman," Farah quipped.

That produced a dark sound from deep in his throat and a twinkle of amusement from his good eye. The Dorian Blackwell version of a smile and a laugh. "A full minute passed between insults. Does that mean I've succeeded in convincing you to reconsider your refusal?"

"Do I have a choice?"

"Do you really need one?"

Perplexed, aroused, insulted, astonished, Farah couldn't decide which emotion to land on. How could she make such an important decision in the bath of all places? A woman should at least be clothed appropriately upon considering a marriage proposal—command—or whatever this was. Blackwell was as persuasive as the devil, and just as tempting, truth be told. But she prided herself on being practical, didn't she? Was there no other solution to the danger in which she found herself? She refused to accept that marriage to a criminal was her only option. What about her career? Her life? What about Morley? He'd be looking for her now. He might not have been too worried by her absence for tea on Sunday, as plans often changed, but when she didn't show for work this morning, he'd already have started the search for her.

Could Morley not also offer her protection against someone who wanted her dead?

Perhaps, but despite her qualms regarding the Blackheart of Ben More, she couldn't deny his merciless ferocity nor his intelligence or ingenuity. He ruthlessly vanquished his enemies; he could rid her of hers, as well.

But who would protect her from him?

Moreover, could she trust him to keep his word? What did he hold back from her? What angle of his hadn't she considered? Farah knew Dorian Blackwell had his secrets, ones buried deep enough to be licked by the flames of hell. Could she be tied to them as his wife? Did she dare?

Ye canna marry anyone else, Fairy. Ye belong to me. Only me.

Her heart clenched and dipped, pulling the lids of her eyes down with the weight of an old and heavy burden. "This isn't what *he* would have wanted," she told herself in a wavering voice.

"You're wrong." Something about the hard words in a softer tone forced her to look at him, but when she opened her eyes, he'd turned away from her again. "Besides you, I was the only other person Dougan loved and trusted in the entire world. And, in turn, he was the only person who ever meant anything to me . . . because I had no Fairy to occupy my heart."

Was that because he had no heart to occupy his chest?

Farah wished he would look at her. That she could see the coldness of his cruel features. That his frightening visage would chill the subtle warmth stealing into her chest, threatening to melt her resolve.

He remained facing the window, a swarthy shadow bathed in pastoral sunlight. For someone who sounded so English, he certainly seemed a part of this wild, sharp, treacherous landscape.

"What are you saying?" she prompted.

"Do you not think that had he lived, he would have wanted us to know each other? To get along, even. His closest friend and his beloved wife?"

His question rendered her speechless. The implications were something she hadn't considered, something that could alter her entire perspective.

"I told you, he asked me to find you . . . Isn't it a possibility that, in the event of his death, he might have granted a marriage between us his blessing? That, perhaps, he might have even wanted us to—care for each other?"

He made a disturbingly compelling point. "Care for each other? Is that possible?" she breathed, immediately wishing she had the presence of mind to keep her thoughts inside her head.

Dorian Blackwell's silences had begun to be more meaningful than any words, and Farah's mind whirled as he surveyed the emerald shores kissed by spring, and the clouds gathering in the distance.

Farah felt that with her age and experience came no small bit of self-awareness that the young rarely possessed. Most of her life, she'd considered her capacity for caring and compassion one of her strengths. Could she care for Dorian Blackwell? Of course she could. He was a person, wasn't he? With needs and ambitions and—feelings. Though that last one might be up for some debate. The danger became, what if Blackwell transformed her ability to care so much from one of her greatest strengths into a profound weakness? If anyone would do something like that, it would be him, most likely without remorse or pity.

"Regardless of how we felt about each other, I would

vow to *take care of* you. Could that not be a place to start?"
He finally turned back toward her. In the sunlight, his scar
looked whiter, deeper, somehow. Even in the light, a
shadow lurked in his wounded eye, a shadow that hinted
at a cavernous, abysmal rift that one could stare into and
never find the bottom of. A reckless part of her wanted to
try, and that had to be the most frightening impulse she'd
had in her adult life.

Farah found herself wondering if anyone had ever taken
care of him.

"I could allay a few of your fears," he continued, obviously interpreting her silence as contemplative. "It would
be a marriage in name and title, only. I would spare you
the more—intimate duties of a wife." He didn't meet her
eyes when he said this, and rushed on rather quickly. "Also,
after we'd taken care of the threat to your life, I'd only
require you to live with me here at Ben More Castle a
month out of the year, and in London a month of the sea-
son. For appearances and what-not. Other than that, your
time and fortune would be yours to do with as you wish.
You could occupy one of your father's residences, or any
number of my own."

"How . . . many are there?" she asked curiously.

It took him a moment to tally, which meant his holdings were vast. "I assume you're wanting me to include
my international residences. So counting the Mediter-
ranean villas and the vineyard in the Champagne region
of France—"

"*Villas?*" She gasped. "As in plural?"

The ghost of a smirk haunted his lips.

Farah pressed her hands to her overheated cheeks. The
wife of a highwayman. A disgustingly wealthy highwayman, granted, but a criminal all the same. Had she and
Dougan truly been so prophetic as children? Was she actually considering this? Considering . . . him?

Seized by the sudden need to reconcile, she wanted to smooth out the bunching of constant tension at his shoulders. To warm the patina of frost from his stare. To produce a crack in the smooth, armored mask of his features. If she were to give this any further thought, she needed to find something human about the Blackheart of Ben More.

She skimmed wrinkled fingertips across the surface of the water. "Before I say anything else, I feel it's right to say that I didn't mean to be so insulting to you earlier. I'll admit to being rather out of my depth here. Being so ordered about doesn't bring out the best in me, I'm afraid."

Blackwell made a dry noise. "Don't be ridiculous. I'm the last man alive who would condemn bad behavior. In spite of that, I concede you have every reason to doubt, despise, and fear me."

"I don't despise you . . ." Though she couldn't honestly deny the doubt or fear part.

"Give it some time," he muttered wryly.

That coaxed a smile from her, and she studied him from beneath her lashes, noting with some pleasure that she'd been effective. Blackwell had unclenched his fists and his unsettling eyes conveyed, if not warmth, an acceptable amount of equability.

Her heart began to pound with such strength that her whole body vibrated with it. The beat could be heard in her noisy exhales as they stared at each other. The entire island, the ocean beyond, the Highland air, itself, seemed to catch on her inhale and hold, waiting for the word hovering at the tip of her tongue to escape the prison of her lips.

Once this particular convict was set free, it could never again be reclaimed.

Yes. Not usually such a terrifying word, but at this moment it seemed to equally represent either salvation or damnation.

Of course, she could always say *no*.

Though the way Blackwell was staring at her now, she had a feeling that word meant very little to him. Not many people denied Dorian Blackwell and lived to tell about it.

Oh, Dougan, why send me this dark horse? Farah inwardly railed. *Why ask the devil in the flesh to find and protect me?*

Young Dougan couldn't have known how the man in front of her would affect her. How dangerous he truly was, because of the reckless impulses pouring through her veins and settling in the most secret of places.

He couldn't have known how much Dorian Blackwell secretly thrilled her. How his eyes on her made her feel helpless and powerful at the same time.

She would never tell Blackwell that it was his words about Dougan's wishes that had persuaded her in the end. Had he lived, would this all have turned out differently? Would Dorian Blackwell still be the lesser half of the so-called Blackheart Brothers? Dougan would, even now, be a mere three years from his release from that hellish place. Would the three of them have made some kind of life together?

She'd never know.

Either way, it seemed her destiny to end up the wife of a highwayman.

The devil in question stood silent and motionless as she argued with herself, but the need to breathe overtook both sides of the debate and Farah realized it was now or never.

"I have one condition." The words rushed out on a gusty exhale.

"This ought to be interesting." Blackwell impatiently crossed his heavy arms against a heavier chest, but his eyes lit with a victorious spark. "Let's hear it."

"I will not reclaim the Northwalk fortunes just to lose them again to some distant relative when I die. So, if I am to marry you and give you the title of earl, then you will provide me with something else I want."

"The Townsend wealth, the title of countess, and relative autonomy." He ticked these off on his fingers. "What else could you possibly want of me?"

"Other than Dougan, I've been without a family for over twenty years." Farah pushed herself up until she stood before the Blackheart of Ben More completely nude. "What I want from you is a child."

CHAPTER TEN

Dorian couldn't recall the last time someone had shocked him. Years. Decades, perhaps. He'd seen so many variants of naked women, so many other things that would break most people, and over time the ability to feel surprise had abandoned him.

Or so he thought.

His thoughts became as scattered and aimless as the rivulets sluicing down her lush curves. She was a goddess rising from the water. Like Botticelli's *Birth of Venus,* except with heavy silver hair darkened by her bath that, unlike Venus, she didn't use to hide her feminine secrets. She stood with her chin held at an obstinate angle, her shoulders straight in an observance of good posture, those soft gray eyes staring at him with a mixture of resolution and expectation.

Farah was offering her body to him. She wanted him to say something. To respond to her demands. But how could he, when all that glorious skin was bared to him, flushed pink with heat and not a little shyness? The condensation in the atmosphere blurred any sharp lines or bold colors with a dreamlike ambiguity that drew him closer to the bath.

Struggling to maintain his mask of nonchalance, Dorian pulled himself up short, gluing his boots to the marble and refusing to take another step. Wasn't there a saying about losing control of situations like this? Moth to a flame? Flying too close to the sun?

Those breasts, that was what. Silken globes of pale perfection tipped with tight nipples the most flawless shade of pink. The delicate dip of her waist, the small divot in the center of her stomach that seemed to draw his eye ever downward to the thin nest of golden curls between her—

"No," he declared through teeth that would not unclench no matter how much he ordered them to.

"No?" she echoed, her light, delicate brows drawing together. "Don't you want me?"

"No." It wasn't a lie. It wasn't exactly the truth, either. From the moment he'd entered the room and seen the way her hair brushed her bare shoulders, his body had betrayed him. As she washed for him, his cock had become heavy, full, and hard. And now? Now even the lightest brush of his kilt caused him inconceivable pleasure and agonizing pain.

Her lashes fluttered down, her expression the only thing hidden from him. "What about me do you find distasteful?"

"It isn't that." The instinct to protect her from hurt was a hard one to smother.

"Then . . ." Her gaze bounced to the side, her arms inching up to cover her breasts, now quivering with a chill. "Are you and Mr. Murdoch somehow involved—"

"Christ, no!" Running frustrated fingers through his hair he paced away from her, needing to fill his eyes with something other than the bounty of her glorious skin, and then back toward her, already craving the sight of it. How often since they met had he secretly fantasized? How much torment had this woman already caused him? How much more could he take?

"Then . . . why?" she asked, the boldness seeping out of her voice.

Another man, a better man, would have covered her to spare her modesty. Would have warmed her from the chill now visible on her delicate flesh. Would have swept her slick body into his arms and carried her to the bed, sinking into her softness before the moisture on her skin had time to dry.

But the only man here was him, and he was incapable of giving her what she asked for because . . .

"It's simply out of the question," he insisted, through teeth still ground together.

Her eyes softened and she cast a surreptitious glance at his kilt, and Dorian had never been more grateful for his sporran to shield what his manhood was doing. "Is it that your body is not—able?"

The noise his throat produced sounded more cruel than he'd meant it to, but he couldn't explain that he'd meant to direct it at himself. "My body . . ." His body wasn't the problem. Even now, as he forced himself to look at her, a wave of aching pleasure made an agonizing journey down his spine until his every muscle clenched and the tip of his cock wept a tear of yearning. "My body could take yours until you begged me for mercy."

Her full lower lip dropped open, and the silver of her irises overtook the green as he knew it was wont to do. "Then do it," she whispered in a quivering voice. "I'll marry you, and you have my permission to—take me however you'd like, until I am with child." She blinked often as she said this, and held her tiny fists tightly at her sides, but her posture, her expression, remained resolute.

To any other man, her offer would have been like receiving the keys to the Kingdom of Heaven. To Dorian, it was like being thrust into the deepest pit of hell.

He fought to retain his composure, to tear his eyes away from her, but the feat proved biblical. His eyes had never feasted like this. His body never responded to any sight like it did to her.

And why wouldn't it? She belonged to him.

Only him.

All this time, a part of him had expected that little silver-haired fairy whose stories still haunted his every night. Dorian hadn't prepared himself for the bold, elegant woman who stirred his blood and inflamed his body.

No, his body wasn't the problem.

It was his mind.

The flames that had licked at the ice encasing his heart were quickly doused in a rush of frustrated fury and self-disgust. "We will not lie together," he enunciated darkly, red beginning to seep into the periphery of his vision. "I decline your conditions."

Eyes narrowing, Farah turned, giving him a view of her heart-shaped rear before she lifted her leg and stepped out of the bath.

If a man like Dorian Blackwell whimpered, he would have then. Could fate be any more cruel?

She reached for her robe and belted it over her lovely nudity. "If you decline my condition, then I decline your proposal." Grabbing a towel, she began to work the excess water from her luxurious curls.

"You forget, it wasn't a proposal," he reminded her. Dorian also hadn't expected her to be so strong. So willful. As a child, wasn't she the sweetest of cherubs?

She cast him an irritated glance, still ministering to her hair. "Regardless of what you call it, I'll refuse. I'll marry Inspector Mor—"

"You will not!" he roared, stalking toward her. "You don't love him." Crazed, he reached for her shoulders, to shake some bloody sense into her, but before he could bring himself to do it, his fingers curled in upon themselves, the joints cracking with the force of his rage.

Fear flared in her lovely eyes, but she didn't back away from him. "I don't love *you,* either," she reciprocated. "That isn't part of this discussion, is it?"

His lungs emptied of breath as an exquisite ache speared them, and he had to struggle to fill them again.

"I want to give someone the childhood that was taken from me," she said more softly. "And the man I marry *must* agree to that."

"You. Don't. Understand."

"I understand that you are the boldest and most feared man in the realm. You can kill someone without a second thought, or ruin entire families with the stroke of a pen. If you are brave enough to do that, then you can summon the courage to lie with your wife the few paltry times it will take to get me with child."

They glared at each other, their wills clashing with palpable force.

"Is your body promised to someone else?" she asked.

"God, no."

"Is your heart?"

"I thought we'd quite established that I don't have one."

She was getting better at those irritated glances that conveyed her impatience. "Then explain this to me, if I don't understand it."

Dorian couldn't put it into words. Not to her. "I already did."

She studied him for a moment, then extended her hand toward him.

He retreated out of her reach.

Her brow furrowed in thought. "Dorian, how long has it been since you've allowed someone to touch you?"

His stomach clenched at the sound of his name on her lips. He couldn't tell her, not without giving away too much. "A lifetime," he answered.

"And honestly, is that why you cannot have—er—relations with me?"

He glanced away from her, regretting that he ever revealed such a weakness. When he'd avoided contact with others, he'd turned it into a power play, insinuating that he found them too beneath his dignity for a handshake or an offered arm.

That wasn't so in this case. Not with *her*.

"How do you kill people if you do not touch them?" she asked curiously, then shook her head, a peculiar expression twisting her mouth. "I never thought I'd ask such a question."

"I often wear gloves," he answered honestly. "Also, not every weapon requires physical contact."

"Of course," she said automatically, though her brows furrowed as if puzzling out a problem. "But, with your gloves on, you *have* come into contact with others?"

"Rarely. If it can't be avoided."

She nodded, deep in thought. "Though I live as a widow, I remain a virgin. Despite the issue of a child, our marriage would *need* to be consummated in case its validity was ever called into question."

Dorian's mouth went dry. He'd thought he'd considered everything, but a sexual relationship had been so far out of the realm of possibility, this one detail had escaped him. Beneath the panic, a whisper of pleasure beamed at the knowledge that another man hadn't touched her.

Tapping the tiny divot in her chin, she set her towel down and picked up a brush from a dressing table and began to work it through her curls. "I—suppose if I was being completely practical, I could take a lover. That would solve both of our problems, wouldn't it?"

"I would kill any man who dared touch you," he informed her coldly.

"Well, that isn't being very solution-oriented, is it?" She sighed, exasperated. "Would it please you to watch? That seems to be a proclivity of yours."

He took a threatening step toward her, smarting at her observant insinuation. He'd been nothing his entire life but an observer and manipulator of human will and desire. Should it be such a surprise that the inclination extended to his troubled sexuality? "I will force you to watch as I dismember whatever part of his body he dared to touch you with, and feed it to him," he declared tightly.

"Then it has to be you," she insisted.

They glared through another impasse for the space of a few moments.

The thought of another man touching her brought out his most evil, sinister impulses. He'd felt them when she'd kissed Morley, and had barely stopped himself from snapping the man's neck in front of her.

Despite his anger, he loved looking at her like this. Flushed from her bath, her hair a heavy curtain of coils around eyes the color of moonbeams. How could any man deny her? He *wanted* to touch her. Craved it.

But he couldn't bring himself to taint her like that. Why did she refuse to see it? How could she invite the Blackheart of Ben More into her bed? Marriage was one thing. Sex was something else altogether. Did she really want a child so badly that she'd lower herself to allow someone like him inside her glorious body? Did she not know who he was? Had he not painted a clear enough picture of what he'd done?

Of what had been done to him?

"Your gloves," she murmured, as though struck with a bit of genius.

"What?"

The pink of her cheeks deepened and she visibly gathered her courage to explain. "I've spent a great deal of time over the last ten years in the company of street and dock prostitutes," she began. "And I've learned from them that to conduct their business out in the open like they do they rarely have to disrobe. In fact, I gather that very little in the way of contact is required."

The idea angered Dorian, because it tempted him. "You want me to treat you like a bloody dock walker?"

She leveled him a droll look, though her cheeks still burned with timidity. "Not particularly. My point was that I think we could achieve—intercourse—without a great deal of touching."

His lip curled, but his thighs clenched in response. "You aren't serious?"

"You could wear your gloves, your shirt, your kilt or trousers, indeed, your vest and evening jacket if you were so inclined."

"And that is what you want? To be fucked like an East End doxy and then tossed aside? Because that is what I will do," he warned, the darkness gathering in his heart as answering clouds gathered in her features.

Her eyes were liquid silver as they narrowed at him, swirling with as many mysteries as the stars in the night sky. "I want a *family*," she murmured. "And I'll do what I must to get it."

The naked, aching honesty in her voice pierced him with a poisoned arrow, and he could feel the toxins spreading through his blood. Soon he would be completely paralyzed, a victim of the opposing forces now quarreling inside him like two wolves fighting for dominance. The two strongest emotions known to man.

He took in a deep breath, the scent of her honey soap and the lavender water invading his senses with the subtlety of a Roman legion.

"Then on your head be it." He stalked past her toward the door. "We'll marry in the morning," he announced, then slammed out.

CHAPTER ELEVEN

It astounded Farah that Frankenstein—er, Frank Walters couldn't remember his given Christian name, but could recall the recipe for Indian curry with the endless measurements of exotic spices.

Once Murdoch had returned to dress her in a clean if somewhat dated white lace shift and a skirt of long and heavy wool Mackenzie plaid, she'd done what she could to soothe his worry that she was quite well after her confrontation in the washroom with Blackwell, and then promptly wandered to the kitchens.

Perhaps what this situation needed was more tarts.

She'd found Frank patiently slaving over a sumptuous feast, and she'd spent the rest of the afternoon taste-testing his fare, sampling the wine, and doing her best to forget that tomorrow she sealed her vow with the devil in a church.

And then she would belong to him. Her *body* would belong to him.

At half past eight, she stood in the lavish dining room studying a landscape canvas of Ben More that looked suspiciously like a Thomas Cole painting. A footman—whom she learned through a rather severe stutter was Gregory Tallow—lit an obscene amount of candelabra for a person dining alone. The clouds and sunset over the Highland peaks of the painting almost jutted out of the canvas, and Farah reached out to it, hoping to catch the evening before it disappeared.

"I have a fondness for Americans who paint in the Romanic fashion," Blackwell said from the shadows of the entry.

Farah snatched her hand back, and turned to face him. "Oh?" It unnerved her that every time he announced his presence, she had the notion that he'd been watching her for some time, and she only became aware of him when he decided he wanted her to.

She took a bracing sip of wine, ignoring the fact that her face already felt flushed and her blood flowed warm with a few prior glasses from the expanse of the afternoon.

"M-M-aster Blackw-well!" The footman hopped to attention as though in the presence of a British colonel, adjusting his bow tie and smoothing his thinning blond hair. "We'd th-thought you'd dine in-n your study. Like u-u-u . . ."

"I understand," Blackwell said softly when the other man's speech failed him.

Tallow, who was slight of build and stature, blushed furiously and refused to look in Farah's direction. "W-Walters already sent a t-tray."

This keep certainly had a curious amount of Englishmen for a Scottish castle. Had they all been criminals? Farah felt pity for the little man, who vibrated with the nervous energy of a woodland deer and seemed just as apt to bound into a thicket at the slightest provocation.

"I can see that. But I've decided to join my fiancée for dinner."

Farah was uncertain whose eyes widened more at the use of the word *fiancée,* hers or the footman's. Tallow promptly disappeared without another arduous word.

Even in his impeccable black dinner jacket and collared shirt and tie, Blackwell evoked the image of the piratical highwayman. It could have been the kilt, Farah mused, or more likely the eye patch, as he'd donned it again. Or maybe the way his thick hair fell just a little too long to be completely fashionable. Though, she expected, it was most likely the manner in which he surveyed the opulence of his surroundings, as though he didn't recognize them as his own, but would kill to keep them safe.

He looked at her that way, too. Like a possession he coveted.

She couldn't imagine why; she'd promised to be his, hadn't she? A wife was a legal possession, and the fact enticed her more than it should.

She set her wine glass down, deciding she'd had quite enough.

"What's all this?" He gestured to the table laden with trays.

"Dinner."

His snort conveyed absolute disbelief. "This is *not* dinner. It's . . . gluttony."

Frowning, Farah surveyed the table. The Indian lamb curry centered the meal as the main entrée, surrounded with fragrant flat breads. Partridge compote steamed next to a fried savory forcemeat pastry made of garlic, parsley, tarragon, chives, and beef suet enclosed in a buttery crust. The appetizer included oysters cut from their shell, sautéed, and then returned to be arranged in a bath of butter and dill.

The footman reappeared, and while he set a second place, Farah counted the admittedly obscene amount of desserts. Perhaps they should have left out the cocoa

sponge cake, or the little cream-and-fruit-stuffed cornuco-
pias with chocolate sauce. She absolutely couldn't have
chosen between the almond cakes with the sherry reduc-
tion or the coriander Shrewsbury puffs or . . . the treacle
and vanilla crème brûlée. Oh, dear, perhaps she and Walters had gotten a *little* carried away this afternoon.

Glancing at Blackwell, she suppressed a grimace. His
one eye fixed on her slender waist enhanced by a thick black
belt as though marveling at her intentions for the evening.

"I like food," she said defensively, omitting that she
tended to overeat during times of stress or anxiety.

"Everyone *likes* food. It's what keeps us alive. But I was
expecting a lamb and vegetable stew, like I always have
on Mondays." He stared at the fare as though he didn't
quite know what to do with it.

Farah wrinkled her nose. "I'm certain the lamb stew is
very—nutritious," she conceded diplomatically. "But you
must admit the distinction between food that nourishes the
body, and food that nourishes the soul."

"But I have no soul, remember?" He took one glance at
her narrowed eyes and the corners of his mouth twitched.
In a grand gesture, he stepped around her and pulled out
the tall chair at the table's head. "My lady."

"Is that not *your* place?"

"Where I dine at my own table doesn't mark or eliminate me as master of this castle." He lifted the linen and
swept his gloved hand at the chair. "This place was set for
you tonight. I don't wish to oust you from it."

Farah had to fight very hard not to be astonished and
charmed at the same time. "How very gauche of you," she
said as she took her seat, catching her breath when he
draped the linen across her lap.

"Yes, well. I can afford to be."

The understatement amused her more than she wanted
it to.

He took the seat to her left, positioning himself to see both entrances, and arranged a linen across his kilt. Though the table was long enough that the far end all but disappeared into the horizon, Dorian Blackwell made whatever place he occupied the unquestioned head. "Why is the food not on the sideboard with the footman serving you?" he asked, surveying the courses piled in front of them.

"I told them it was ridiculous to stand by and serve a dinner to just one. It's late, and I'm certain they have better things to do." She transferred some oysters to her plate.

"They don't," he clipped, tossing a disapproving look at the empty door frame toward the kitchens. "It is their first priority to serve and please you."

"And I told them it pleased me to dine alone."

"I'm sorry to disappoint," he said blandly, reaching for the forcemeat pastries and the curry.

Farah regretted her words. She hadn't meant that she preferred he not be there, only that she didn't want to be watched by hovering staff whilst dining. Though she might be the daughter of an earl, she certainly hadn't been raised as such. Her mouth felt too slow to form the correct reparation, so she watched in troubled silence as he served himself generous helpings of both main dishes with crisp movements.

It was often impossible to tell if her words affected him. She'd only glimpsed momentary slips in his façade, and at times such as this, she had only a slight feeling that she'd displeased him because of a chilly shift in the atmosphere. Yet, his features remained smooth and cold as glass, causing her to wonder if she imagined everything and he was truly as heartless as he claimed.

He glanced up at her and caught her staring. His eye a fathomless pool of secrets.

The enormity of what she'd agreed to blindsided her, so she averted her eyes and popped an oyster in her mouth, chewing to release the sweet flavor of the meat. "If I may ask—your eye—does it cause you pain? Is that why you cover it sometimes?"

He paused in cutting his pastry and considered her before answering. "I do not see well out of it in low light, which often gives me headaches. The eye patch prevents them, and also makes it easier for me to read."

"Of course," she murmured, lifting another bite to her lips, stilling the impulse to ask how he'd obtained the wound.

His hand paused in the middle of bringing his first bite to his lips. "You still say that," he breathed, a bit of the chill lifting from the air.

"Pardon?"

He paused. "Dougan told me that was your answer for everything. 'Of course,' as though all you learned was as it should be, and so you accepted it."

"He told you that?" At Dougan's name, she opted to drink the rest of her wine.

"Yes."

She wanted to ask what else Dougan had said about her, but didn't want to seem narcissistic.

Instead she finished her appetizer as Blackwell folded into the pastry, his sinuous jaw transfixing her as he chewed with an onerous pace, as though testing the food.

Farah busied herself by dishing her own curry and bread.

"Obviously, I've been underutilizing Walter's talents," he finally observed. "I tend to eat for function rather than pleasure. I think you have shown me the error of my ways."

"I find it hard to believe you do anything that isn't just as you please," Farah said around a bite of tender, spiced meat and soft, hearty bread.

His expression relaxed into a resemblance of amusement. "Why is that?"

"You have the reputation of a hedonist."

"Maybe so, but you have the palate of one." He indicated the overladen table.

A reluctant smile interrupted her next bite. "Touché."

Heavens, was she actually enjoying herself? Only yesterday she despised this man. Only hours ago she feared him, their every interaction overwrought with emotion, revelation, confession, and finally submission. It had all left her quite exhausted and, apparently, hungry.

Three chandeliers glittered with Irish crystal over the long table, only the one at their end adding its light to the flickering candelabra. The sounds of expensive cutlery against the elaborate china provided the accompanying music to the dance of the flames casting the atmosphere with a golden glow.

Farah found herself mesmerized by the way the shifting light shadowed the stark angles of Blackwell's masculine face, and gleamed off the rare ebony of his hair.

Was this what life as wife of the Blackheart of Ben More would be like? Luxurious. Decadent, even. Fraught with intrigue and secrets, banter and the clash of wills. Memories of a painful past, loved ones lost, and the shadow of an uncertain future.

She tore her curious gaze from him and fixed it on the table. Oh, well, at least there would be confections and chocolate sauce, and thereby hope for a sweeter outcome.

Pushing her nearly finished entrées aside, Farah filled her dessert plate with one of everything and pulled the chocolate sauce close, which greatly improved the potential of the moment.

A shame she was out of wine.

Farah savored a bite of the dark, bitter cocoa cake, swinging her gaze away from her enigmatic companion and observing all the opulent accents of the masterful woodwork and luxurious burgundy and gold textiles adorning the dining room.

"Everyone speculates about what goes on here at Ben More Castle," she ventured. "I'm quite surprised at the lack of virgin sacrifices and torture chambers. Though you do have your share of interesting characters in your employ."

"Torture chambers are generally below stairs, I don't believe you've seen that part of the castle yet." The devilish twist to his lips made her wonder if he were truly joking.

"You never entertain people here?" she queried.

"You mean for reasons other than ritual sacrifice or torture?" His lips twitched again, curling higher this time than she'd ever seen them.

She leveled him a mock-exasperated stare around a bite of the crème brûlée. A muffled moan was lost in the heavy layers of sweet custard exploding with vanilla and kissed by a hint of molasses.

Much as he'd done in the washroom, his gaze locked on her mouth, more fascinated with her actions than her words. "No." The word was huskier, tighter. "I invite no one here."

"But it's so spacious and lovely," she protested, gesturing to the table that could easily seat an entire regiment.

His gaze also touched the china, the candelabra, the heavy drapes, and expensive art. "I have other properties used for guests. Ben More has become something of a refuge, for me and the others who live here."

Farah nodded with sudden understanding. It seemed that most of the men who ended up here were in need of a sanctuary. Murdoch, with his sad eyes and misunderstood heart. Frank, who was lost anywhere but the kitchens. And poor Tallow, who trembled more than he talked.

"Then why bring *me* to your sanctuary?" she ventured.

"Seemed appropriate," he said cryptically, watching her cut into her almond cake for a moment before diverting the conversation away from his thought-provoking words. "I'm aware of what people speculate about me, but I hope you realize that not every story of my hedonistic villainy has merit."

"Of course. For example, I've seen no evidence of a harem of exotic courtesans warehoused in your secret Highland castle." *And thank God for that,* she added silently, and then wondered where the errant prayer had come from.

"Is this where they think I keep them?" he asked.

Her head snapped toward him and prepared to deliver a derisive reply before she caught the twinkle of gratification in his eye and the first real semblance of a smile widen the brackets around his mouth.

"You are every *bit* the villainous knave!" He was teasing her or telling the truth. Either way, he deserved to be publicly flogged. Farah tossed her napkin at him in outrage.

He caught it. "You don't love me," he said lightly. "What does it matter?"

"I—well—it doesn't," Farah stammered, cutting a profane bite of cake.

"No, indeed?" He stabbed at his plate only to find it empty, then looked down as though surprised he'd finished his entire meal. Pushing the empty china aside, he said, "What would a man such as *I* do with a harem of courtesans?"

"I'm sure I don't know," she evaded. "But perhaps one of them could have enticed you to do something other than watch."

His expression turned serious. "You're the only woman I'd even consider bedding."

Farah blinked at him, frozen in place, unsure of what to say. Every conceivable interpretation of the intention behind his words caused her heart to jump like a fox-hunt rabbit.

"At any rate, a great deal of the things said about me are utter rubbish."

"Such as?" she challenged, hating the breathless note in her voice.

"That I've killed more than a thousand men with my bare hands. That I broke out of Newgate by bending the iron bars. That I defeated the Duchess of Cork's husband in a fit of jealous rage. Oh, and my most favorite, that I personally assassinated the infamous crime lord Bloody Rodney Granger with a quill pen."

Farah searched her memory. "Rodney Granger was assassinated thirty-five years ago."

"Before I was born," Blackwell confirmed, lifting a glass of red wine to his lips.

"Why don't you refute these untruths, then?"

He made a nonchalant gesture, the muscles in his throat working over a swallow. "They're more of a help than a hindrance. The more people fear me, the more power I hold."

"That's terrible."

He gave her a rakish half-smile. "I know."

Farah added a bit of the cream-filled cornucopia to her bite of cake. The wine fed a ribbon of recklessness and she stretched her lips wide over her dessert, overflowing her mouth with a mélange of sweet decadence.

Blackwell's unblinking eye honed in on her mouth as it struggled to contain the overload of fluffy whipped cream.

The skin around his lips whitened.

Farah searched for her napkin. *Right,* she'd thrown it at him, because he'd deserved it, and the ill-mannered villain never gave it back to her.

Shrugging, she swiped at the corner of her lips with a finger and lapped at the cream with her tongue.

The wine glass shattered in his grip.

A breath passed before either of them reacted. The wine spread across the gold tablecloth like plum-colored gore. Shards of glass reflected light from the candles in various dishes.

Dorian's eye blazed with a black flame. Not with fury, but with a more complex, darker emotion. His nose flared on deep, uneven breaths, like a stallion that'd raced through the night.

"You're bleeding!" Farah gasped as rivulets of red oozed from his clenched palm and thickened the wine stain with blood. She stood and reached for his hand, searching for a napkin to stanch the flow.

"No." Blackwell pushed to his feet so forcefully, his chair tipped and crashed to the ground. He towered over her, yanking the wounded hand behind him, and warning her off with a dangerous glint in his eye.

She gestured toward him. "If you don't get that seen to—"

"Do *not* reach for me," he growled, both fists still clenched tight, one undoubtedly around a sharp piece of glass. "Is. That. Clear?"

"I just—"

"Never."

The ice in his command shriveled what little warmth had bloomed between them. Inwardly, Farah shrank from him, though she thrust her chin forward. "You won't have to worry about me making that mistake again," she retorted.

His upper lip curled in a chilling sneer. "See that you don't."

"B-Blackwell!" Tallow lunged around the corner of the kitchen, looking very much like a scarecrow in footman's garb, followed by a red-faced Murdoch. "W-we heard a-a-a-a . . ." At the sight of the shattered wine glass and blood, Tallow's speech seemed to stall out indefinitely.

"We heard a crash, are ye all right?" Murdoch touched Tallow on the arm and Farah wasn't too distressed to note the protective gesture.

"We've concluded our meal." Dorian made the cold announcement as though a steady stream of blood wasn't dripping from his fist onto the expensive carpet beneath him, and the shattered corpse of his wine glass didn't cause the leftovers to sparkle. "See to Mrs. Mackenzie and make sure all is prepared for tomorrow." The last of his order was given over his wide shoulder as he turned away.

"Blackwell," Murdoch began, "let me—" One look from his employer silenced him, and then Blackwell was gone, leaving behind only shadows and blood.

Dorian's jaw ached from clenching it. The tremble in his hands had nothing to do with the hooked needle he used to sew the fleshy pad of muscle that controlled his thumb closed, as he'd stitched more of his own wounds than he could count over the years, but he couldn't seem to calm the shaking.

After he'd removed the piece of wine glass embedded in his muscle, blood had soaked through two makeshift bandages and dyed the water in the basin next to his bed a dark pink before he'd stanched the flow.

The fire in his blood had felt like a betrayal. The force of his need shocked him. Indeed, shock didn't seem like a strong enough term for the pure, hot energy singeing along his skin, but he couldn't conjure another word. Which was odd, because he'd read the dictionary and memorized all of them. And their meanings. And their synonyms, antonyms, variations, and conjugations.

"Fuck," he swore as he jabbed the needle too deep into the muscle. Luckily, he'd been drinking with his left hand when the arousal had struck him with all the strength of a Viking's cudgel, causing his fist to clench and the flimsy glass to explode. Stitching a wound with your dominant hand always afforded a neater scar.

If only he hadn't so many wounds. Some that no stitch could reach deep enough to repair and so they remained open and bleeding, festering until they poisoned the body with their putrid filth.

Dorian focused on the sharp jab of the needle, the sting of the thread pulling through skin and meat. The pain provided an inadequate distraction from the lust pounding through him. It dulled the persistent ache in his loins, but didn't eliminate it.

Nothing did.

Since the day he'd seen Farah glowing like a silver angel in the dank, gray strong room of Scotland Yard, he'd wanted her. His body, long thought immune to bindings of lust, came alive with stirrings and sensations he'd never before felt.

Dorian had learned too young that love and lust had very little to do with each other. Love was pure, selfless, kind, and consuming. It came naturally to someone like Farah. Lust, on the other hand, was tainted and selfish. It overwhelmed one's humanity and transformed them into a dark creature full of impulse and instinct.

Women used it to manipulate.

Men used it to dominate. To humiliate.

Even now, he could feel the desire to press her beneath him and demonstrate to her his superior strength. To claim that mouth that had so tortured him at dinner as his own. The milk-white cream she licked off her lips and finger had evoked unwanted images of branding her mouth with the creamy evidence of his release while she licked at it with as much relish as she had the dessert.

Farah had been right. He was a villain, a monster, a killer, and a thief. A man without conscience or mercy. His past had twisted his desire into something dark and deviant.

He liked to watch her. To scrutinize her when she had no idea she was being observed. He loved how her expression lit with the unguarded curiosity he knew she'd been born with. The way she reached for things that intrigued her, needing to touch with her hands and not just her gaze. The way she ran her fingers over her discoveries with an almost carnal relish as though, in her own innocent way, she found a sensuous delight from the entire world.

The sight inflamed him beyond his comprehension. Her slim, pale, elegant hands and clever, nimble fingers. Exploring. Discovering.

Stroking.

His cock twitched and flexed, demanding something from him that he could not give. He'd tried in the past to relieve his body's need. But even the feel of his own hand repulsed him.

Desire and disgust roiled in his gut, leaving very little room for the sumptuous dinner he'd shared with Farah, and intensifying the trembling in his limbs.

Tonight would be another eternity.

He could already feel the itching and prickling beneath his skin. The heat would follow. A feverish, pulsating torture. His body and mind locked in a stalemate of desire and hostility. His natural instincts to fuck overcome by memories of thrashing shadows and violent lust. Brutality. Helplessness. Weakness. Screaming. Memories of whispering a beloved name against the cold, fetid ground by his desperate, bleeding lips. He would disassociate from the pain. Imagine the feel of a small hand within his own. Moonbeam curls made of silk. Eyes like pools of liquid silver. A dimpled smile that held the light of the far-reaching cosmos.

One duty had kept him from succumbing to the darkness in that dank, rotting prison.

One vow.

It had given him the strength to lead, the bravery he transformed into ruthlessness, and the desperation he wielded like a blade until it was his *enemies* with their faces in the dirt.

On nights like this, before *she* slumbered beneath his roof, Dorian gave up attempting sleep. If it claimed him, so would the shadows, thrusting into his psyche until he woke sweating and screaming, a blade in his hand. Other nights, flames would lick at him instead of the shadows. Rip at his skin and hold him in their muscle-wrenching grip until he would wake to the wet shame of his release soiling his sheets.

On those mornings, he'd bathe in scalding water, scrubbing until the flames died, until his skin was red and raw and bleeding.

Instead of sleeping, he'd taken to roaming the halls, usually ending up in the library to escape into a book.

Dorian looked at his bed, neatly made and turned down for his comfort. The red linens a constant reminder of the blood he spilled. Of the blood he lost.

He suddenly didn't want to look at it, let alone climb between the covers. He would not be fodder for the terrors of the past tonight.

Finishing his last stitch, Dorian inspected his handiwork. It would heal and scar nicely.

A different scar caught his eye, and he ran a finger across the long-healed wound. He had to make sure she never saw this, for it would expose a secret he could never reveal.

For it could be the destruction of them both.

Dorian wrapped the wound as he walked toward the door. There would be no sleep tonight.

Tonight, he would watch.

CHAPTER TWELVE

Heavy clouds threatened to drench Farah's wedding day.
She'd fought the pull of sleep until very late, and so she
hadn't woken until noon, which generally would have distressed her. Instead, she lay beneath the cozy counterpane
and watched the storm clouds crawl over each other in
their haste to reach the shore, congregated by the wind and
clashing like unruly children in a school yard.

Reaching for a glass of water on the bedside table, she
paused, noting how the high-backed chair crowded the
bed. Had it been pulled that close when she'd turned in?
She didn't think so, but then, she'd been rather distracted
the night before, puzzling over the events at dinner.

She'd uncovered another crack in Dorian Blackwell's
façade, a rather large one. A chink in the armor of ice he
encased around his humanity. Regardless of his aversion
to touch, and despite the vow that bound them both to this
course of action, Blackwell's eyes were drawn to her. His
body responded to the sight of her mouth. Her tongue.

Watching her eat, enjoy, lick her fingers and her lips, those things inflamed him.

Farah hadn't meant to entice him with her actions over dessert. But she knew she had, she'd seen the heat in his eyes. The alarm. The banked passion.

And his body wasn't the only one affected by whatever this was between them. Something had awakened within her, as well. Something previously missing, or perhaps merely dormant all this time. Lying in wait for the perfect mix of shadow and intrigue to draw it out. Some wicked, playful thing comprised of equal parts curiosity and womanly knowledge. Of timidity and desire.

All she knew was that she came alive beneath Dorian Blackwell's inscrutable gaze. He watched her with an intensity she'd never before seen, and she wanted to fill his insatiable mind with images he'd not likely forget.

The urges frightened her. Elated her. Stole her breath and sped her heart until it kicked against her ribs.

Tonight. Their *wedding* night. Would he be able to go through with it?

Would she?

Murdoch arrived with a gown of pristine cream silk, trimmed at the neck and sleeves with expensive handmade lace and adorned with nothing more than an endless row of pearl buttons that ran from the high neckline to the waist where the skirt flared and fell in simple, elegant layers.

Farah recognized the dress, as it had hung in her own closet back in London where she'd figured, if her marriage had ever come into question, she could produce the simple gown as corroboration to her story.

It wasn't meant to be a wedding dress, she knew, but it had called to her from a shop window on the Strand, and she'd been lost to it the moment her hand had drifted over the pearly silk.

Blackwell had been in her wardrobe. He'd touched her things. A picture of him running his rough hands over her clothes, across her silky delicates, flared in her mind, and she had to focus very carefully on dressing and her conversation with Murdoch, lest he guess the direction her thoughts had taken.

Pinning her hair into a braided bun at the crown of her head, she left a few ringlets to fall against her cheek and neck. There, if she wasn't ready to be married, at least she looked it.

Ben More Castle's chapel was arid with disuse, and Farah announced her presence with a sneeze that disturbed the veil of white lace Murdoch had produced for her.

No prelude music preceded her and Murdoch down the aisle, just the sound of her heels on the aged stones, the staccato of heavy rain beginning to fall against the roof, and the pulsing rush of blood in her ears.

Murdoch whispered something that she didn't quite catch, but Farah gave a stilted nod, and he seemed to take that as an acceptable answer.

The castle's hodgepodge of outcasts lined the first pew closest to the bare and largely unused altar in front of which stood a rather harried-looking young priest. His round spectacles rested at a crooked angle on his nose, and his unruly red hair stuck out in such a way, Farah was reminded of baby chickens when they began to lose their fuzz in disorganized tufts.

The men stood when they entered, and Frank courteously and inappropriately blessed her sneeze in his booming voice. Dressed in a suit that must have fit him in the days he consumed fewer pastries, he fidgeted with his crooked tie while, next to him, Tallow watched their steady progression down the aisle, not facing the bride, but Murdoch.

Farah counted five other household staff, along with

the stable master, Mr. Weston, and his stable hand. The groundskeeper, a shifty-eyed man with a Greek-sounding name, and a couple of other faces with which Farah was unacquainted.

She was grateful their expressions were blurred from behind the veil, and that it obscured hers from them, as well. It helped conceal the fact that she had yet to look at *him*.

Her bridegroom stood motionless to the right of the priest, a tall, broad figure swathed in black. The shadows and angles of his strong jaw and shock of ebony hair were visible, but little else. Farah found the veil made the whole ordeal easier. She could pretend that today was a happy day, long awaited and full of words like *hope* and *promise* and *future* instead of shadowed by vengeance, duty, and the past.

Reaching the priest, Farah turned to face Dorian once Murdoch had given her away. They both stood silent during the ceremony, still but for her quaking legs, while the priest solemnly recited scripture in an airy lilting Scottish accent and adjusted his glasses enough times to dub the behavior obsessive.

When the priest asked for the ring, Frank stepped forward gripping both sides of a small wooden box as though he presented them with the Holy Grail.

Blackwell opened the box and extracted from the black velvet a white-gold ring adorned with a single diamond fashioned in the shape of a tear. Well, a tear only if Goliath ever cried. Or Cyclops, maybe.

The massive diamond wasn't white, but a silvery-gray that caught each facet of the wan light filtering in from the chapel windows, its sparkle underscored by darker shadows that made the gleam more brilliant somehow.

"It's lovely," she breathed, holding out her trembling left hand.

Dorian held it up in his black-leather-clad fingers so it would catch the light. "Gray diamonds are the rarest and most valuable in the world," he said. "It seemed appropriate that you should have one."

Were she not in the middle of her own wedding ceremony, Farah would have snorted. Of course he would think that the wife of the Blackheart of Ben More should have some obscenely expensive ring to demonstrate his wealth and power to all the world. Regardless of the reason, Farah had to admit she would be glad to wear it, having never owned something so lovely or valuable in her life.

"Well, put the blasted thing on her bloody finger, lad, we're all going to die with purple faces if we're forced to hold our breaths verra much longer." Murdoch's impatient prompt broke the mesmerizing spell of the ring, and Blackwell studied her extended fingers.

He cast Murdoch a dark look and the priest flinched at the old man's profanity, but they all watched in fascinated silence as Dorian visibly prepared himself. Pinching the bottom and diamond between his thumb and forefinger, he slid the ring onto her hand with hardly a brush of his leather glove, before snatching his fist back.

Farah learned that Dorian decided to forgo a ring, as was the husband's prerogative, and they got on with the ceremony. Her mind drifted to another wedding, in a different small, dusty church. This one attended only by the two souls who wanted to bind their destinies together. Farah was glad that this ceremony was Christian instead of the more archaic fashion like she and Dougan had. She couldn't have said those words to another.

"Do you take this woman to be your lawfully wedded wife . . ."

Ye are blood of my blood, and bone of my bone.

Blackwell's "I do" was more decisive than hers. In fact, when she spoke the words, she may have been answering a question like, "Do you mind sitting next to the Marquis de Sade and discussing literature?"

It counted, though, and before she knew it, the priest pronounced them man and wife. The final words read in his hushed voice from his Bible sent little shocks of dread and desire through her.

"And they two shall be one flesh: so then they are no more two, but one flesh . . ."

I give ye my body, that we two might be one.

One flesh, the Bible said. Joined. Cleaving. The righteous words caused a wet rush of warmth to spread like a sin between her legs. Tonight they would be joined by more than words. Their two bodies moving as one. Surely such wicked thoughts were blasphemous in the church. Farah stared across at the dark form of Dorian Blackwell. Of course, when one was marrying the devil, what was one or two other blasphemies?

"What therefore God hath joined together, let no man put asunder . . ."

I give ye my spirit, 'til our life shall be done.

"Amen," Dorian agreed.

"Amen," echoed the congregation.

"Um, Mr. Blackwell, sir, that part in the canon doesna require an *amen.*"

"To me, it did."

"Well, then, I suppose . . . ye may kiss yer bride."

It took Dorian an eternity to lift her veil. And another to lean down to her, his eyes two mismatched pools of determination.

Farah held perfectly still, as though one tic of a muscle might change his mind. Both of them breathed rather hard, though his inhales labored through his chest more deeply than hers. He smelled of soap and spice with a hint of wood smoke, as though the flames of hell had singed his tailored suit.

His lips parted a whisper above hers. His breath brushing her mouth in soft bursts. She could read the yearning in his eyes. The doubt. The need. The panic. And she did what he needed her to do. She closed the infinitesimal gap between them with a slight reach of her neck, and pressed her mouth to his in a chaste but undeniable kiss.

His lips were warm, hard, and still, but he didn't pull back. In fact, he didn't move until she pulled away and turned to a grinning Frank, not missing the surreptitious swipe Murdoch made at his watering eyes with the handkerchief Tallow had pressed into his hand.

Farah had done it. She was Mrs. Dorian Blackwell. For better or worse.

Until death parted them.

Dorian's cock was hard. It pressed against the fabric of his tailored trousers with an aching persistence that made walking damned inconvenient. He'd been worried it wouldn't be, that the blood rushing in his ears and pounding in his chest and throat might not leave enough for his manhood.

It had happened before.

But, though he'd legally taken Farah as his wife, he could not truly call her his own until he claimed her body and planted his seed in her womb. She knew it, demanded it. And so did his cock.

He stood outside of Farah's room for what could have been a few minutes, or may have been an hour, the door handle gripped in his leather glove.

She was his, her name no longer tied to the past, but to *him*. The sweet, innocent girl who'd become a Newgate legend, now an unspeakably desirable woman about to be sullied by his corrupted, repellent, vile body.

He couldn't let her touch it. Or look upon it, even. She would be revolted, disgusted, or worse.

Of all the things Dorian had coveted, a wedding night had never been among them, and yet, here he was. But what of his bride? Had she dreamed of this day, this night? Did she have mysterious and romantic expectations of the virginal explorations of a tender lover? Or had she accepted that he was incapable of both love and tenderness? His wife was no fool. She had agreed to marry the Blackheart of Ben More. A man who gave nothing. No compassion and no mercy. A notorious thief who only *took* and only when it pleased him to do so.

He'd made the promise to take her tonight, and Dorian Blackwell *always* kept his promises.

Farah had passed restless and settled on anxious a half hour ago. At first, she'd arranged herself in a pretty picture on her blue and cream counterpane with a book, the first button or two on her high collar undone, and her skirts spread about her legs in a pool of silk. She pictured herself posing for a Marie Spartali Stillman painting, serene and mysteriously aloof, but approachable.

That had lasted all of five minutes.

Slipping off the bed, she'd lit candles and placed them on various surfaces about the room, hoping to cast just the right amount of flattering golden light. That done, she'd positioned herself on the edge of the bed, her hands folded in her lap, and decided not to move a muscle until he entered.

Oh, dear, what if she was supposed to go to him? What if, even now, he awaited her in his own lair? They hadn't really discussed the particulars after the meal that neither of them had touched, as they'd listened to the sound of masculine merrymaking around them.

A slightly drunk Murdoch had escorted her back here, announcing loudly that he'd been waiting on this day for decades and it was about bloody time she and Dorian seized their happiness, and each other.

Farah knew enough not to argue with a Scotsman in his cups, so she declined to remind him that she and Blackwell had only known each other a few days, and that neither of them were particularly happy about the marriage.

She wasn't *unhappy*, though, which amazed her. One would expect to feel morose trepidation about such a match. But she didn't. In fact she felt surprisingly calm, hopeful, even. Almost as though—as if—

If Dorian Blackwell didn't show his face soon, she would go raving mad.

What if he didn't come to her tonight? What if he'd been lying to her when he promised to get her with child?

I'm not above lying to you to get what I want.

Oh, she would skin him alive. If Dorian Blackwell meant to stand her up on her own wedding night, she had more than a thing or two to say about that! Farah paced the floor for a few minutes, organizing her rant into specific and chronologically important points, the last one beginning with *and furthermore,* because when one predicated a statement with that, it was impossible to ignore it. Even if you were the bloody Blackheart of Ben More.

Having worked up a sufficient amount of righteous indignation, she marched for the door.

It burst open, missing her face by inches.

Farah shrieked.

Blackwell stared.

"What do you think you are doing?" she demanded.

"Where do you think you are going?" he said at the same time.

She answered first. "I was coming to find my husband."

"Well, here I am," he said with a droll glance around her room, twitching his nose at the rosewater scent she'd sprayed on the pillows and curling his lip at the carefully placed candles.

"You could have knocked," Farah indicted, unwilling to show the hurt that squeezed within her breast.

Blackwell entered her room, forcing her to take a step back. "I'll be a dead man before I knock on a door in my own castle."

"What if I wasn't ready?"

He speared her with those eyes. Ones that could be so full of mystery and flame. Ones that could be so dead and cold.

Like now.

"There's no amount of preparation for what we're about to do." He strode past her, barely giving her an assessing glance, and claimed the seat by her bed as though he owned it. Which he did, of course. Shadows gathered near him as they were wont to do, despite the candles she'd so carefully placed. Cold menace and a dangerous, unstable element rolled off him and reached for her like the mist that blanketed the Highland shores of a morning, shrouding the dangers of the ancient volcanic rock and the shapes of predators.

For a predator he was, that had never been clearer than in this moment.

"Now," he said in that deep, chilly voice, examining the fine leather of his fitted gloves. "Take off your dress."

CHAPTER THIRTEEN

Farah clutched the bodice of her dress, even though the buttons were still doing their job, and stared at the large, dark man in the chair.

He met her look with a level one of his own. "Second thoughts already, my dear?" The endearment was not meant as such, and they both knew it. His words were a challenge, an answer to one that she'd issued initially. She'd offered him her body, almost demanded that he take it, and now he'd come to collect.

It would be foolhardy to think that he might make this easy for her.

Farah lifted her chin. "No. I merely thought that you might want to take it off, yourself."

She was playing a dangerous game, and she saw that danger flash in his eyes. "If that were the case, I'd have ripped it off you immediately. Stop stalling and take. Off. Your. Dress."

Of course. He'd want to watch. It excited him. Aroused him.

Very well, Mr. Blackwell, Farah thought. *Watch this.*

Dorian could tell she pretended it wasn't the trembling of her fingers that stole the dexterity from her movements. She tried to keep his gaze locked on her challenging eyes, flashing with little gray storm clouds, but Dorian couldn't manage to stop from visually devouring every hint of skin each release of a button revealed. The slim column of her throat. The soft expanse of thin flesh stretched over her chest and collarbones, so rife with nerve endings.

She took her time, *damn her.*

The light from the candles kissed her silvery hair and her creamy ivory skin with gold as though King Midas had given in to temptation and touched her with his cursed fingers.

Regret tried to lick at him, to stir the humanity buried down deep beneath the layers of greed, self-loathing, violence, hatred, and anger he walled within that impenetrable casing of ice.

This was Farah. His wife. Should he objectify her like this?

Another button worked free, exposing the first hint of the swell of her bosom.

The question was: Could he stop himself if he wanted to?

Dorian already knew the answer.

Not for all the money and power in the empire.

As she exposed the valley of shadow in between her breasts, Dorian felt the intoxicating, almost chemical mixture of thrill and shame he imagined tortured the waifish opiate addicts that haunted the back alleys of the Chinese immigrant shops on the East End.

His body was going to get something it pined after. Burned for. Screamed with the intensity of its need.

And he'd hate himself in the morning.

Hell, she'd probably hate him, too. But she'd progressed

in getting the buttons undone to her navel, and Dorian spied one nipple outlined in pink-tipped perfection against the thin white silk of her chemise, presented to him by her tightly laced corset. All coherent thought dissipated like the mist before the sun's rays, and everything around him receded but for her. His next breath hinged on the next button being set free. The next expanse revealed for him to consume like a starving man.

He wanted to stop her. To demand that she continue. But for all his composure, words had become lost to him, communication beyond his ability. All he could do was sit helplessly and await her next move. Watching.

Farah found it strange that the more she revealed, the bolder she became. Perhaps it had something to do with the way Blackwell's gloved hands gripped the chair arms when she allowed her dress to slide down her curves and puddle at her feet. Or the flare of his nostrils as she reached up, aware of how the action lifted her breasts even higher beneath her sheer chemise, and took the pins from her hair, one by one.

She unraveled the heavy braid that fell over her shoulder, shaking the curls loose to fall to her elbows.

Farah could tell Blackwell fought it, but desire began to melt the ice in his stare, causing his lids to fall heavy over his eyes, and his lips to part in order to allow for the quickening of his breaths.

She hesitated only a moment before moving to untie her laces.

"Don't," he ordered. "Not yet."

Blackwell was a statue, but for the lift of his jacket in deep, heaving movements. His eyes traveled the expanse of her exposed flesh with all the tangible deftness of a caress, branding their way to the waist of her drawers.

"Get rid of them." His voice barely recognizable now, he filled his chest as though it would stop the little twitches of muscle she could see by his eye, below his collar, in his fingers.

Heart thudding wildly, Farah tucked her thumbs into the band of her drawers, preparing to draw them down.

"Wait," he clipped through gritted teeth.

Farah paused.

"Turn around."

Puzzled by the request, she silently complied, determined to follow his instruction. She somehow understood that if Blackwell felt in control, he'd be more likely to go through with this. Farah was prepared and unprepared. Afraid and yet not afraid. Embarrassed and emboldened. The need lurking beneath the chill in his eyes drove her to abandon her characteristic modesty. She was too old for virginal shyness, had seen too much of the horrors this world thrust upon others.

Men were visually stimulated creatures, and females were lovely. It seemed only natural that Blackwell would feel the desire to look upon what he found difficult to bring himself to touch. She understood that in order to conceive the family she wanted, she needed to entice him to do more than look, and that was her prerogative. To push him to a place where desire overcame fear, where the animal instinct to mate controlled the machinations of the body.

And so she faced the fire banked low in the hearth, closed her eyes, took a deep breath, and bent to push her drawers over her hips.

"Slowly." He hissed the command.

A hazard lurked in her plan, though, Farah realized as she languidly swept the lacy drawers over the swell of her rump and down the quivering muscles of her thighs. For a man such as Dorian Blackwell to be driven mad enough with lust to break the bonds of the past.

He might be driven to break her, as well.

Dorian had often studied the female form in every

modality from paintings to prostitutes. He'd seen them all. Appreciated a few, despite himself. But *nothing* could have prepared him for the vision of Farah's body, a dark and flawless silhouette against the backdrop of the flames.

His weak eye blurred detail in the direct contrast with the firelight, and so instinct drew him to lean closer. She flared out in all the places a woman should, dipping to create curves that were the soft answer to a man's hard angles.

Bent as she was, her ass was so exposed to him, the slight outline of her womanhood a dark secret in the low light.

Dorian's mouth went dry. His racing heart sped like a stallion on the last sprint toward the finish line. Impossibly faster. Pushed to the limit of its capacity. His breath sawed in and out of his chest in tight, painful bursts, burning like it did when he ran in the winter. Frost and heat. Ice in his blood and fire in his loins.

It had been almost twenty years since anyone had touched him in a way not meant to cause pain. To humiliate, incapacitate, and control. It had been just as long since he'd used his hands for a purpose other than defense, violence, or domination.

Farah's skin. Her flawless, unmarked skin. Free of scars, branded by no one, and belonging to *him*.

At last.

How could any man bring himself to desecrate such unblemished skin with his touch?

How did he stop himself from doing just that?

Dorian's gloves creaked as he physically held himself to the chair. He wasn't certain which impulse compelled him more, the one to seize her or the one to run.

So he sat. And watched. Savoring the torturously slow movements of her body like she'd enjoyed her dessert the night before. The pleasure not confined to her tongue, but a full-bodied, visceral experience.

Dorian had never in his life felt as much anticipation or found as much pleasure as she had for her cake and cream. Not his wealth, not his luxury, not in the victory over his many enemies. Not until this moment, when the round, tight curve of her hips and ass were presented to him like the spoils of war.

And yet he could not claim it, for the battle was not over. It raged within him. There were blood, casualties, losses of ground and gaining of the upper hand. It was violent. The outcome unsure.

So he sat.

And watched.

Farah did her best to ignore the whisper of chilly air against the moist, warm folds of her body as she stepped out of and discarded her drawers. Lifting her torso, her unsteady fingers plucked at the ties on her garters in order to rid herself of the cream stockings.

"Leave them," he rasped.

She straightened, clad only in her corset, chemise, and stockings, unsure of what to do next.

"Lie down on the edge of the bed," he commanded tightly.

Her gaze flew to the bed, a comfortable, finely appointed, fairly innocuous piece of furniture. Unless one knew that the next time she left it, she would be forever changed.

Though, truth be told, Farah was relieved that Dorian informed her what he wanted of her, as she had no skill or practice in the art of seduction, and felt quite lost until he gave his commands.

A strange, ever-shifting balance of power, this. Her feminine instinct told her that *she* commanded every synapse in his brain, every beat of his heart whilst she carried out his requests, but once she'd finished, the control ebbed back to him, and she held her breath in anticipation of his next demand.

She tiptoed to the bed on unsteady legs and gingerly lowered herself to sit on the counterpane. She sought his gaze for reassurance, but he was fixed on the thin wisps of golden hair at the apex of her thighs as though the answers to the mysteries of the universe could be found between her legs.

Farah froze, real fear blocking her throat for the first time. Even when he sat, Blackwell managed to loom. Even when silent, he threatened. Though candles illuminated his tall, wide frame, he seemed a specter of muscle and darkness and shadow.

She'd been wrong just now. So very wrong. Any control she'd imagined had been an illusion. Dorian Blackwell never allowed anyone else to wield it in his presence.

She faced him, wondering what came next. She understood the culmination, knew where this ended. But he needed to come to her, to come *inside* her.

"Lie back." His voice was brimstone raking over the souls of the damned. "Open your legs."

This was it. Shaking, Farah rolled slowly to her back. Her fingers grasped the fluffy covers at her sides as though she could find bravery in their seams, and squeezed her eyes shut, unable to look at him.

She felt his eyes on her as she stretched her body across the bed. Knew he was looking at her in places no other man had seen.

Bracing her heels on the bed frame, she took a deep breath and parted her knees.

As the silent seconds ticked by, Farah opened her eyes and stared up at the canopy. Her husband truly was pitiless. Barbaric. Unforgivably cruel. He left her like this, an artless innocent bared for the first time without comfort or care. Gathering her annoyance like a cloak, she summoned the courage to look down at him.

What she saw froze her and melted her all at once.

Between the valley of her breasts and the V of her thighs, Farah saw Dorian Blackwell, the Blackheart of Ben More, *quake*. Not just a shiver, or even a tremble. But great, shoulder-heaving shudders that affected his breath.

Expressions she hadn't thought his brutal features capable of producing played in rapid succession across his face, gone before she could even identify them all. Longing. Apprehension. Privation. Frenzy. Control. Despair. Lust.

Worship.

She breathed his name and his head snapped toward her. "Come to me," she ventured. "Tell me what to do."

He shook his head, but his eyes remained fixed upon her. "You're not ready," he said without moving his clenched jaw.

"I am," she encouraged. "I want—"

"You need . . . to be . . . wet." Every word of his sounded like a labor, like it caused him pain.

Farah frowned. She couldn't help that. It was anxious work seducing a husband who didn't want to be seduced, baring herself to a man for the first time, all without the arousing of his lips or any soothing consolations. "How do I—"

"Pleasure," he growled. "Touch."

Farah knew exactly what he meant. She'd felt it in the bath when she'd washed for him, those first wet stirrings of pleasure, the moisture that bloomed from her body. She needed to produce that again.

Prying her fingertips from where she'd dug them into the bedclothes, Farah let the curve of one nail drift across the sensitive skin of her chest.

His eyes flared.

Her body responded.

More fingers joined the first, playing their way down the curve of her breast, flatter now that she was on her back, the nipple still jutting upward, insistent as ever. Then she reached the edge of her corset, also done in cream silk, and toyed with the barrier before dipping beneath it.

Farah couldn't believe what she was feeling. The thrills of sensation, the moist whisper of pleasure to come. She no longer cared that he could see, that he was watching. Farah wanted him to. She was not only a bashful virgin, but a bold exhibitionist, and in some way that made all of this much more tantalizing.

At the sound that escaped her parted lips, Blackwell completely lost the cold, observant look of a bird of prey and gained the ferocity of a beast. Hot-blooded. Prowling. Stalking. Waiting to leap. Teeth bared in a grimace of pleasure and pain, he strained as though he fought back a monster with the strength of his own will.

He was her black jaguar, and he just might tear her apart.

Dorian knew he trembled more than she did as her hand drifted from the perfection of her breasts and down the unyielding expanse of her corset. Her touch light and fingers gentle as they followed the candlelit path to her hips, and below.

Could *he* touch her like that? With this need for domination pounding through his veins? Could he learn that softness, that gentility, by watching her perform it on herself?

For surely he could not allow her to touch *his* flesh in that way.

Surely—she wouldn't want to. Not if she ever looked upon it.

She would be revolted, and he would be rejected. Of that he had no doubt.

Beautiful. She was so fucking beautiful. Her thighs long creamy cylinders of pale, taut muscle. The blue bows on her garters drove him to the brink of sanity.

Her sex. Pink, pretty flesh nestled between a light dusting of fair curls. His mouth watered. His blood roared. His cock pulsed behind his trousers in a rhythmic and uncontrolled clench and release of muscle.

Her curious fingers paused before dipping below the soft hair. When she encountered the feminine folds, she gasped.

Dorian stopped breathing.

She tested that place lightly, finding a place that quivered and pulsed at the apex of that pliable skin. Awe speared Dorian as her feminine muscles clenched in the exact rhythm his own loins did. He could see them working through the skin unique to her sex. Her hips rolled with instant little movements, her breath catching on sighs of appreciation.

If Dorian was a lesser man, unused to patience, torment, and agony, he would have released his seed then and there. But he grappled his orgasm back down, thinking of her hands on his repulsive flesh, letting the fear throw ice into the flames.

Then she parted the inner cleft, dipped inside, and let out a moan that could have aroused Eros, himself. Her finger came away glistening as she pulled it back toward the nub that seemed to demand more attention than anywhere else. When she swiped the moisture across it, her muscles all tensed, and she threw her head back onto the counterpane, letting loose a sound so visceral Dorian's will snapped.

And he lunged.

CHAPTER FOURTEEN

An animal sound warned Farah a moment before Blackwell seized her hands and pinned them both to the bed at her sides.

His face hovered above hers as he bent at the waist from where he stood in between her parted legs. He wore the savage look of a man about to lose his greatest battle, but unwilling to put down his weapon.

"I'm going to give you one chance," he threatened. "Do you understand? *One* chance to deny me, to stop me. So consider this carefully, wife. Is *this* what you want?" He turned his blue eye to her, affording her a closer look at the angry scar.

If he had treated her thus at any moment before, she might have retreated. But now her body had been awakened to its most primitive desires. Need and heat seethed within her, and overcame the trepidation she should be feeling. Not many a man came this close to the Blackheart of Ben More and survived.

Would she?

Farah met his wounded gaze with absolute conviction. "I want you to . . . take me."

"Then God help us both."

His dark eye flashed the moment before his hard mouth bore down on hers. His kiss felt like a punishment, but for what she couldn't be sure. Because he wanted her? Because she wanted him?

When the pressure became too much, Farah made a sound of distress, and he broke the kiss.

"Damn you," he accused, then descended again.

This time, though, he was more careful. Not gentle, per se, but the press of his mouth became another pleasure she'd not previously experienced. He kissed every part of her lips, the corners, the rims, the pillowing fullness, devouring her with the efficiency of an experienced man. Instead of becoming more severe, his movements began to slow. He sampled her like a man sipping and measuring a fine scotch. What his mouth lacked in fullness, it made up for in innate skill. Eventually, those hard lips softened, opened over hers, and his tongue thrust past her closed lips, demanding entrance. His trembling began to subside, though the tension coiled in the muscles beneath the jacket of his fine suit intensified.

Farah opened for him on a sigh of acquiescence, her muscles pooling beneath his body in a puddle of anticipatory submission. If their consummation was anything like this wet, probing kiss, she looked forward to it.

His fingers relaxed their punishing grip on her wrists, the fine leather peeling off her skin, and he pulled away just far enough to look down at her.

In the midst of the frenzy of need building inside them, bloomed a quiet moment. One of stillness and acceptance. His disbelieving eyes searched her face and his lips parted as though a confession hovered on his tongue, but could not breach the hardness of his mouth.

"What is it, Dorian?"

"Don't call me that," he admonished gently. "Not here."

"What shall I call you, then?" she asked, puzzled that the intimacy of his first name could be forbidden from the intimacy of their marriage bed.

"Husband." The word caressed her cheek. "Call me *husband*."

Farah felt a tender smile touch the corner of her lips. "What is it, then—husband?"

"Your mouth," he confessed with all the reverence of a saint and the torment of a martyr. "I've dreamed of this mouth." He lifted a hand to her face, his breath hitching as he traced her lower lip with his glove. "I've imagined that word on your lips more times than you realize."

Touched, Farah pressed her lips together. Could it be that Dorian Blackwell didn't just need her for his devious ends, but he desired a life with her, as well? She wanted him to take his gloves off, more than she wanted anything in the world, but knew better than to ask it of him. She desired his skin against her skin, the warmth she could feel radiating from him absorbed by her flesh. *Maybe someday,* she thought with a twinge of hope, *but not tonight.*

"Put your body against mine, husband," she invited. "And kiss me again."

His eyes pasted to her lips, he released her other hand. "Do not—reach for me," he warned.

Farah nodded, once again knitting her fingers into the covers.

Placing both of his hands on the side of her head, he leaned on his uninjured hand to lower his body in measured increments. His eyes locked with hers, onyx and ice, reaching for her like a pious man would reach out for a relic, or a godless man would reach for salvation. Farah didn't dare blink, for fear she'd lose him. That this moment would slip through her fingers, the first of its kind, where

Dorian Blackwell lifted the shroud of mystery and didn't use words to wield shadow and misdirection. Instead, he whispered truths against her skin.

Neither of them breathed as his long, heavy torso pressed against her. Even through the layers of his clothes and the bindings of her corset, she could feel his tempered strength. His solid, lean frame built by years of forced labor and honed by a decade of violent dominion.

She'd do well to remember that. To keep in mind what he was capable of.

They both gasped when his hips settled into the cradle of hers, forcing them wider. A thick ridge of steel pressed against her cleft, and even through his trousers she could feel the heat of it. It pulsed in rhythm with his heart, and the slight movements sent little shocks of pleasure through her already sensitized core.

Eyes peeling wide, she clenched the covers so tightly, her fingers ached.

"Are you frightened, Fair—Farah?"

"Are you?" she asked breathlessly. "Should I be?"

"Yes."

She didn't have time to contemplate which of her questions he answered as his head dipped to claim her mouth once more.

"I want to see all of you," he demanded before plunging his tongue back inside her mouth, caressing her answering tongue with deep, delicious strokes. Without breaking the fusion of their mouths, he lifted his chest off her enough to jerk at the laces and stays imprisoning her rib cage. The movements created more friction where their sexes pressed against one another, and Farah could tell by the tightening of his features that he felt at least an echo of the pleasure the movement caused her.

When the pressure of her stays gave, Farah filled her lungs with a delicious inhale, as she always did, this one flavored with his masculine scent and warm with his breath.

Her throat clenched, trapping the breath inside as she remembered her treasure. "Wait," she gasped against his mouth, wrenching her head to the side. "Wait!"

But she was too late. He'd already pulled back to inspect what he'd found corseted to her. He clutched it in his fist and stared at it with all the shock of a man struck by a deadly viper.

"I—I'm sorry," Farah whispered.

"Why?" Dorian asked as he ran a black-clad thumb across the folded, faded strip of plaid with a very odd intensity. It didn't seem to anger him, though neither did it seem to please him. Did he mean why did she still have it? Why was she sorry? Why didn't she keep it hidden from him, this keepsake of another marriage? Of a much different wedding night, this one only sealed by a few chaste kisses and a vow of forever.

The opposite of this night.

They both stared at it, this memento of a boy long dead and love that could not be.

"I promised to never be without it," Farah ventured. "Are you angry?"

Dorian glanced at her, then back at the plaid, schooling his features. "No," he said, perhaps more fervently than even he meant to while carefully placing the folded plaid next to the lamp. "Perhaps—it can now symbolize both him and me. A reminder of what binds us."

She stared at the plaid, feeling naked for the first time that night. "The law binds us."

He settled back over her, a dark gleam in his one light eye. "We both know how much regard I hold for the law."

Their next kiss they shared with the tilt of a smile, their teeth softly rasping against one another's as he spread the corset beneath her and pinched the hem of her chemise.

The arch of her back seemed to tantalize him as she undulated in order for him to peel the garment from her prone body, baring the last of her secrets for his hungry gaze.

The barrel of his erection ground at her from behind the seams of his suit, as his mouth returned to hers like it was her lips from which an oasis sprang, and not below.

"Your trousers!" she gasped when he followed some curiosity he found down the curve of her jaw. "They're wet." She could feel how drenched they'd become, absorbing the moisture of her desire, the friction creating a stronger, slicker surge followed by a shocking burst of pleasure as he ground them harder against her.

"I don't care," he growled, passing his thumbs over her pebbled nipples in tandem, claiming her mouth and swallowing her startled cry as he rocked his hips against her again, and yet another time.

Her thighs trembled, her stomach clenched, and a delight for which she had no name spread like a flood of fire through her limbs.

"This pleases you?" He did it again, his own groan rumbling against her lips.

Pleased her? More than strawberry tarts and decadent desserts. More than she'd pleased herself with him watching. More pleasure than she'd ever imagined her body capable of producing. But she could say none of those things, so she just hissed a "Yes!" as her muscles began some sort of ascension she didn't yet understand.

With each of his movements, and every one of his kisses, the glorious sensation intensified, electrified, until, unable to help herself, her head dug into the bed and her hips peeled off it. Her body bowed with a jerking, pulsing ecstasy so acute, she felt as though she was lost in an apoplexy. Her heart raced, forcing her blood into each extremity, and then stalled, only to charge again.

She thought she heard her name. She knew she gasped

illogical things. Maybe screamed words, but couldn't hear them, or for the life of her, remember what they were. Perhaps the same incoherent tongues spoken by the evangelicals whilst taken in rapture, for surely that's what this was. The pulses became so powerful that if she didn't stop it, she'd see the face of God, because it would kill her.

Frantic, she clutched at him, clawed at him, struggled to find a voice lost in the agonizing bliss of her release.

"No!" He recoiled with a violent curse, ripping himself from her to stand over her quivering body. He'd just reduced her to little more than a corpse, dying beautiful little deaths as each aftershock singed along her nerves.

Farah realized what she'd done too late, as she watched him yank off his tie.

"I'm sorry—"

She was suddenly in his clutches, dragged to the headboard by merciless fingers, her arms wrenched above her head.

"I told you not to reach for me." Those eyes so alive and expressive only moments ago, returned to what she'd become accustomed to. Cold. Calculating. Lifeless. He secured one wrist to the intricate headboard with alarming swiftness before casting his gaze about the room.

When his eyes fell upon the plaid, Dougan's plaid, he sneered, then reached for it, using it as a binding for her other wrist.

She'd been wrong. She wouldn't have seen the face of God, because she'd been lying beneath the devil.

Panic surged beneath the satiation. He didn't understand. She hadn't meant to betray his fledgling trust. Her body had no longer been her own, but possessed by the pleasure he inflicted on her. "Dorian, I—"

He covered her mouth with his gloved fingers. "This is how it has to be."

Dorian tried to suppress the blackness threatening to

smother his desire. He'd passed some line of demarcation. A point of no return. No matter how much his skin crawled and his mind shrank from the grasping hands of another, the hard flesh between his legs still insisted he see this to fruition.

He tightened the final knot on her wrist, and then inspected it for weaknesses, not lifting his other hand from her tempting mouth. She could not touch him. She could not scream. She could not escape.

Dorian breathed deeply, able to gather a bit of his humanity back from the abyss.

A fragrant essence stole his attention from the guilt threatening to reach beneath his armor. It lingered on the tips of her elegant fingers, the ones that had tantalized him with the innocent discovery of her pleasure.

Dorian refused to look at her. If he saw fear, he might take mercy. If he saw submission, he might take advantage. If he saw pity . . . there was no telling what he would do.

He swallowed the excess of liquid in his mouth, the sides of his jaw aching with the force of it, and stared at the well-kept nails of his efficient clerk of a wife. Acting on pure instinct, his lips closed over her index and middle fingers, framed as they were by the Mackenzie plaid.

They were cold inside the heat of his mouth. After a twitch of surprise, they stilled.

And he savored.

She tasted of salt and musk and . . . woman. He slid her fingers deeper into his mouth, splitting them with his tongue.

To his utter shock, she whimpered and bit down on the leather of his glove, her hips clenching and lifting off the bed. He freed her fingers with a nibble at the tips. Once released, they curled into a tight fist.

He still didn't meet her eyes. Instead, his entire being focused on the golden-covered folds of her body. He kept his hand secured over her mouth as he lowered his lips to her ear, watching the trembling of the flat plane of her belly.

"I tasted your cunt," he warned her. "And I'm hungry for more."

Her breaths became manic, heaving her breasts apart with each desperate expansion of her ribs. The nipples trembled like little pink confections atop the pale mounds. He was as shocked as she at his words, and yet, not surprised.

An hour ago, the very thought of any human contact repulsed him.

But this was Farah. And he'd made her a promise.

His body responded to her as it had to none other. The sight of her release nearly drove him over the edge.

If *only* she'd not touched him. If only his skin didn't feel like it was on fire, and every wound he ever had ripped open again, the sensation of blood trickling down his gashed flesh warring with the intensity of his body's need.

Someday he'd tell her that he wasn't angry. That she was tied up for her own protection. In case, in her pleasure, she clutched at him again, and he couldn't control his reaction.

The thought was enough to turn his veins to ice, but scent was a powerful sense, and hers now entrapped him as no other had.

In order to reach her sex, he had to release her mouth. "Don't say a word, or I'll gag you, as well."

Christ, he was a monster. But Dorian knew that he couldn't deny her if she pleaded for mercy. That he couldn't face her if she rebuked or rejected him. And so he could allow her none of those options.

He'd warned her, hadn't he? Before she demanded this night.

Her nod beneath his palm was enough. He let her go and she didn't make a sound.

Thank God.

Heart pounding, mouth still watering, and cock pulsing with need, Dorian was glad she offered little resistance as he parted her knees.

She glistened. *So. Fucking. Beautiful.* He smoothed his wide hands down the insides of her thighs, pushing them open all the way, fingering the garters of her stockings and wondering if her skin was as soft as it looked.

His hunger was a ferocious thing as he lowered to his elbows and let the yearning clench deep in his belly. The slickness of her desire beckoned him. He split her cleft with his gloved finger, coating the tip with her nectar.

She trembled, but remained silent, as she'd agreed to do.

Curious, he rubbed his thumb and finger together, testing the glossy consistency. Soon his cock would be coated with this, slick and wet and—

Christ, if he didn't get his mouth on her soon, he'd go mad.

Dorian had no fucking idea what he was doing, but her scent lured him down until he pressed his lips to her sex.

Her hips flinched beneath him, arched a little, and he could tell she fought to remain passive, but her body betrayed her. *Good.* Because his betrayed him, as well.

She tasted like heaven. Like desire and release. Like want and fulfillment. Like woman. *His* woman. The predator in him was going to dine until he'd had his fill.

And he had a lifetime of hunger to satiate.

The frantic need to struggle against her bindings had leached away from Farah the moment her husband's mouth had closed over her fingers.

When he'd issued his vulgar threat in her ear, arousal had raced through her with crippling strength. Now his wide shoulders overflowed the space between her parted thighs, and his mouth was doing things that made her bite her lip so hard she tasted blood.

His tongue split her in one long lick. He growled against her, and Farah whimpered in reply, unable to stop herself.

But she didn't say a word. Not. One. Word.

Blackwell had become that jaguar she'd evoked the first time she'd laid eyes on him. His shoulders rolled and bunched just so as he settled in for a feast. He left no part of her unexplored. His bold tongue found places she'd never known she possessed. He parted her with his fingers, exposing her in a way so absolute, she could barely stand it. And yet, she read the veneration on his face as he looked at her, as he tasted her, as if he committed every single crevice and protuberance to memory. He learned very quickly what made her gasp, what caused her to arch or retreat. He played like a man who'd only just learned how. Testing her reactions, re-creating sensations, enjoying a bit of cruelty as only the Blackheart of Ben More could. Driving her to the edge of her wits and then pulling back, leaving her groaning, straining, and sweating.

She jerked as his finger found its way inside her slick channel, and the vibration of his groan against the soft hood of flesh he'd sucked into his mouth with a flattened tongue shattered her composure.

Farah screamed with the force of it. The need to grip, to knead, to flail seized her, and she tested the strength of her bonds. The harder she struggled against them, the more potently the bliss ripped through her blood and out her throat in desperate screams. He stayed with her, riding the frantic thrusts of her hips as she ground her heels into the mattress and arched. For a moment, she thought the release would break her in half, but he was there, pressing her hips back down and forcing her to experience the devastating finish. She closed her eyes, but light still burst behind her lids. She could feel the muscles of her sex gripping and releasing his gloved finger. Pulling him deeper.

And then he was gone.

Farah collapsed, panting and shivering with exhaustion. Feeling trapped and yet released.

Her head lolled to the side, and she looked down at him from beneath heavy lashes. What she saw made her eyes peel wide.

Dorian had undone his trousers, and knelt between her quivering knees palming his turgid erection. The act they were about to commit hadn't intimidated Farah until now.

His dark features both ruthless and almost apologetic, he bent and prowled up her body, stopping to slick a bit of moisture from his glove on one nipple and then proceeding to lick it off.

"God, the taste of you. I'm drunk with it." He moaned, his eyes alight with accusation as he held himself above her, still fully clothed but for the arousal now pressing against the slit of her body. "What have you done to me?"

What had *she* done to *him*? "I—I—"

His glove covered her mouth again, stopping words she never would have found.

"I never wanted to hurt you," he whispered against her ear. "I'm sorry."

Farah didn't have time to contemplate just which of his many offenses he was apologizing for before he surged inside her, breaching her virginity.

His glove muffled her cry of pain as Dorian branded her with hot, hard flesh, searing all the way to her womb, or so it seemed.

He cursed, spewing blasphemies Farah hadn't even encountered in all her years at the Yard. Though her flesh stretched and bled, his scarred face contorted into what appeared to be a mask of pain.

Farah strained against her bonds, against his hand,

wanting to escape the pain, wanting to soothe him, wanting control of her limbs back.

But control was something the Blackheart of Ben More would never allow.

Dorian forced himself to look at her. To witness the pain in her eyes. The pain he inflicted. How cruel was a God that made entering her body the sweetest pleasure for him and the sharpest torment for her?

She wanted this, he reminded himself.

Not as much as you, whispered a dark voice.

I never wanted to hurt her, he argued. *And never like this.*

You wouldn't have stopped until you claimed her. Until you'd tasted her like this, until you'd invaded her like this.

She'd never deny me, he thought frantically.

Then take your hand off her mouth.

He didn't. *He couldn't.*

So locked in a battle with himself, Dorian almost missed the gradual give of her intimate flesh locked so tightly around his own. In warm, slick little pulses, she accepted him into her body. The fight and fear drained out of her muscles until they were soft and pliant beneath him and the pain and panic leached from her gray eyes until they were pools of silver again.

He remained motionless, his every sinuous muscle wound tight as a coil. He was on the edge of a precipice, one he couldn't bring himself to leap from.

If he'd learned anything, it had been that reality never lived up to a memory, or even worse, a fantasy. But that long-held belief shattered as he held himself inside of his wife. Her body only sheathed a part of him, but her warmth suffused him, surrounded him, until he knew beyond a shadow of a doubt, that once he lost himself inside her, he'd lose himself *to* her, as well.

She let a soft sigh of relief through her nose and her lashes fluttered as her hips flexed, testing the feel of him inside her.

A hot ripple of lust tore through him, followed by a tidal wave of pleasure. Instinct won over intellect, and Dorian lifted his hips, only to sink again, and again.

Ecstasy crawled over the pleasure, clawing at his flesh, ripping him apart, draining the very essence from him, and bathing her womb with it. Rendering him an empty vessel, a dark void of bliss and hunger, sated but not satisfied. He was a powerful man swimming against a riptide, realizing too late that he battled a force of nature stronger than himself.

And he was lost.

Farah felt him swell inside of her, stretching her already taut flesh. It only took a handful of movements for him to find release. He ducked his head against her neck, silent, not breathing for longer than she thought possible as each shudder racked his powerful body in unrelenting waves. He held his weight on one hand, as he had all night, his wounded palm still fixed over her mouth, the pulses echoed in the clench of his fingers.

When the storm subsided, he released his captive breath on a gasp against her hair. She hadn't known what to expect after he'd found his pleasure, but what he did was absolutely not it.

Blackwell didn't pause, or even abate. He maintained a slow, rippling rhythm, his manhood just as hard and unyielding as that first thrust. His gasps became pants that melted into groans.

He lifted his torso to look down at her, disbelief a foreign expression for his sharp, unsettling features. The fine wool of his jacket abraded her sensitized nipples. The leather of his glove, a buttery-smooth reminder of his fortunes, trailed from her mouth to her jaw, her throat, and her breasts. His seed further eased his way as he slid into her untried body with long, deep strokes.

Farah had thought her part over, that he'd coaxed from her body all the pleasure it had to give. But, to her ultimate surprise, a tight, aching heat bloomed low in her belly, starting in her womb and reaching for the shaft of branding heat plunging and retracting from inside her.

Her lips parted of their own accord, and a small sound of delighted surprise escaped.

Blackwell's eyes sharpened. Questioned.

Farah's body answered without thought. A lift of her hips, a press of her thighs, and a soft moan of encouragement.

It was all he needed.

Blackwell didn't kiss or taste her. Instead he watched her face with an intensity that abashed her. Every flutter of her eyelid, or intake of breath, the way her lips parted or pressed together. His body again became a conduit of her gratification.

It shocked her how he could support his heavy frame all this time on one powerful arm, but the thought dissipated as he used his other hand to explore her, rendering her mind useless and directing her awareness like a symphony conductor. He traced the line of her jaw, the curve of her cheekbones, as though committing her to memory, or visiting one, she couldn't be sure.

As the slow pressure mounted, her moans became mewls, her mewls became cries. His finger drifted along the outline of her lips, slipping past her teeth and leaving the taste of sex on her tongue. Sex and leather. She closed her lips and rolled the glove between her tongue and the roof of her mouth, feeling the hard ridge of his finger beneath.

He hissed, growled, and pulled his hand away, drawing it down to her hip and gripping the curve of her ass, spreading her wider for his accelerating thrusts.

Farah's head tossed against her pillow, her eyes rolling back into their sockets, retreating from sight, as her other overwhelmed senses demanded her attention.

Leather and sex. Darkness. Spice. Chilly air. Hot Blood. Textiles. Smooth, slick flesh. Wide, hard male.

A mouth on hers. A tongue thrusting inside, tasting the essence of her he'd left there, lapping at it.

Farah could feel the waves of sensation pressing against her spine. She feared it, like the first stirrings of an earthquake, or the silent breath after a lightning strike.

She waited for the answering thunder which was certain to resonate through her bones. Straining against her bindings with weak and trembling muscles, she wasn't sure she could survive another earth-shattering release.

But there was no escape. It rushed over her helpless body like a rogue wave, drowning her in crash after crash of sensation. Blackwell swallowed her frantic cries until abruptly, he ripped his mouth from hers and reared back, letting loose a deep, hoarse roar, and then another. Calling his second release to the sky like a prisoner set free.

A languorous satiation turned her bones to liquid. Farah would have wondered if she were still connected to her body if not for the ties still binding her wrists to the headboard, or the small, errant twitches of exhaustion pulsing in her limbs.

Dorian Blackwell, her *husband,* lingered over her as they both fought to regain their breath. Peering up into his mismatched eyes, she shared an unspoken moment of awe with him.

Something in their world had shifted. Some sort of cosmological knowledge, or a secret thought lost at sea floating to the surface. In this quiet, unfettered moment, she *knew* him, truly saw him for what he was. Hard, ruthless tyrant. Abused, wounded boy. An empty heart full of promise, and a soul of shadows in need of sunlight.

Not only did her eyes feel more opened, somehow, but her heart, as well.

Curse her expressive face, he must have read her probing thoughts. Because before he even withdrew from her body, he drifted back behind his screen of shadows and ice, leaving her cold and vulnerable and alone.

Don't go, she thought desperately. She'd unlocked something. Exposed it. But couldn't decipher what it was yet, or what it meant. She needed more time, just another moment with him. Beneath him.

"I must," he clipped, drawing out of her body and off the bed.

Farah frowned at his back as he adjusted his clothing and buttoned his jacket over the front of his trousers. She hadn't realized she'd spoken aloud until he answered her.

"Why?"

Dorian retreated from the question, walking over to the basin and pitcher and pouring water over a towel.

Why? The reasons were innumerable. He was both protector and coward.

Protector, because his nightmares, while physically harmless to him, might prove lethal to her. If he woke in a panic, fighting off his memories, he'd likely break her before he'd fully become aware.

Coward, because he couldn't face her hatred in the morning. Couldn't see the marks the bindings had left on her wrists. Couldn't bring himself to witness the regret and disgust when she realized what she'd done. What he'd done to her. That he'd taken her precious innocence and left his tainted seed inside of her.

Twice.

He wrung the excess water from the towel and returned to her. She looked like a captured goddess. Like the spoils of an ancient war, tied and displayed for her new lord's pleasure.

He'd treated her as such.

And he deserved to die for it.

Releasing his necktie that bound one of her hands, he pressed the cloth into it. He should stay and wash her. But the sight of her broken virginity might send him over the edge. Better that he escape, while he still could. While he was still together, because surprisingly, he was. He was strong. He'd kept his word. His duty was absolved. She could untie the knot of her plaid with relative ease.

Of Dougan's plaid.

His composure cracked.

"Stay?" she prompted softly, her eyes almost obscured by heavy lids and thick lashes. "I'll not—reach for you."

"Sleep now," he commanded, turning away from the beckoning halo of her curls. Dousing candles on his way to the door, he didn't look back as he left her in darkness.

Once the latch clicked behind him, his control gave. Imported carpets muffled the sound of his knees hitting the floor. He'd been a fool to think he was strong. A bloody fool.

He had an evident fucking weakness. One with liquid gray eyes and silver curls.

And God help him if she ever found out.

CHAPTER FIFTEEN

"Good morning, Mrs. Blackwell!" Daylight burst into the room, jarring Farah awake as drapes slid along their rails, grappled by a cheerful Murdoch. "I trust ye slept well?"

The sun battled its way through high white clouds and low gray mist, but still managed an illuminating brilliance.

Only in the Highlands.

"Good morning, Murdoch." Farah yawned, blinking the film of sleep from her vision. "What time is it?"

"I let ye sleep as late as I dare, lass, but Blackwe—Jesus Christ Almighty, the bloody oaf tied ye up?"

Startled, Farah tested the movements of her arm, only just becoming aware that her left hand was still above her head, secured by Dougan's plaid to the headboard. She must have been so exhausted last night that she'd drifted off without untying herself.

Farah looked up at the hand that had since lost all feeling resting limply against the mattress and headboard, wrapped in a faded cloth woven with black, gold, and blue.

A reminder of what binds us, she thought. The interpretation of her husband's words now alarmingly literal rather than just figurative.

Murdoch rushed to her side, reminding her that she'd also fallen asleep quite nude. Grasping the bedclothes to her chest, she allowed him to work the knot free.

"No wonder he lit out of here this morning like the devil chased him. He knew we'd all turn on him and flay his skin from his bones with a dull knife for treating ye like this. And on yer wedding night! I doona care if he is Dorian *bloody* Blackwell, when I see him I'm going to—"

"It's all right, Murdoch," Farah soothed, testing her tingling fingers once they were released and wincing as the blood rushed back with little needles of fire. "It needed to be done in order to—You see, I reached for him in a moment of . . ." Farah closed her eyes against the blush heating her skin. When she opened them again, Murdoch regarded her with a mixture of regret and understanding, carefully handing her plaid back to her.

"He didna hurt ye, did he?"

Farah shook her head, sitting up and inspecting the faint bruises around her wrists, and testing the twinges and aches in muscles she'd never before been aware of. "I rather think last night was more difficult for him than for me."

"Aye." Murdoch nodded his agreement. "I imagine so. This isna like him . . ."

Farah's lips lifted in a sardonic smile. "I would have guessed this is *exactly* like him."

"Not when it comes to ye," Murdoch insisted.

"What do you mean?"

The burly Scot cast his eyes away and turned from her, gathering familiar lacy underthings from where they draped, and laid them out for her at the foot of the bed along with her silk polonaise that she'd worn the night of her abduction. "I only meant that ye're Dougan's Fairy. He should have been gentle and taken great care with ye."

Memories of the previous night singed through her with a vibrant thrill. Dorian hadn't been gentle, per se, though . . . "He was—careful," Farah acknowledged. "There's no reason to be cross with him. As you see, I am well." She offered him a smile, a little surprised, herself, that it was genuine. Until Murdoch's earlier words struck her. "Did you say that Mr. Blackwell—er, my husband left this morning?"

Murdoch turned to set a fire and offer her privacy. "Aye. He's procuring our passage back to London on the late afternoon train."

"London? So soon?" Farah had wondered if they might not take a few days to adjust to married life. To, at the very least, get acquainted with one another. Perhaps take a few nights like the one before, and discover what other pleasures might be found in the marriage bed.

"There's a hot bath waiting in the washroom for ye." Murdoch poked at the fledgling fire, urging it to ignite. "And I'd advise ye to hurry. I'll not want to be the one to tell Blackwell that we derailed his plans, as it were." He chuckled at his own pun.

Of course, Farah thought as she gingerly stood on shaky legs and reached for the silk wrapper next to her bed. Now that he'd claimed her, Blackwell would be in a great hurry to also claim the Northwalk title. Which meant dragging her back to London and parading her in front of a villain who'd once desired her as his wife, but now just wanted her out of his way.

By murdering her, if necessary.

Farah bit her lip, wondering, not for the first time, if Dorian Blackwell kept his promises as obsessively as he claimed. After she procured what he wanted, would her life mean anything to *him*? Was he truly any less of a villain than Warrington? Whose word did she have, other than a castle full of convicts and criminals, that her new husband and Dougan Mackenzie were as close as he claimed?

Farah held a hand to her lips, watching Murdoch's un-hurried movements. She'd been so quick to believe them. So desperate for a connection with her past, with the boy who had been taken from her, that she'd readily accepted anything they'd said. Had already begun to care . . . What if she'd just made the gravest mistake becoming the wife of the Blackheart of Ben More?

What had she been thinking?

Doubt unfurling in her sore muscles, she glanced at the bed, remembering the reverence on her husband's face, the savage possession in his touch, the longing pleasure tinged with awe and wonder.

Such things could not be fabricated. Could they? Certainly not on her part. No, what happened between them last night had been real. So real that he'd retreated from it. From *her*.

Farah had spent the better part of a decade around criminals and liars. And she believed, as much as she could trust her own judgment, that Blackwell had been telling her the truth when he promised to keep her safe.

God, she hoped so, because as much as she loved and missed Dougan Mackenzie, she wasn't ready to join him in the grave just yet.

The train from Glasgow to London whistled its final warning. The warm rush of steam colluded with the fog to obstruct the vision of the late-afternoon passengers. A footman turned the fine latch and handed Farah up into Dorian Blackwell's private railcar.

"We stowed Mr. Blackwell's luggage, but I doona see any here for ye. Should I hold the train while we fetch something?" The young man's wide brown eyes matched his constellation of freckles as he steadied her on the step.

Only for a man like the Blackheart of Ben More would they throw off the entire train schedule. And now, she supposed, for his wife, as well. "No, thank you, Mr. McFarley, I am not traveling with a trunk." Reaching into her bag, she pulled out a coin and tipped him.

"I thank ye, Mrs. Blackwell." His eyes sparkled at her. "Going to enjoy some shopping in London, eh?"

Mrs. Blackwell. Why was it that the counterfeit name of Mackenzie had felt more accurate than the valid name of Blackwell?

She glanced down at her evening dress, the loveliest she'd ever owned, and realized that for people of the upper class, such garb would be acceptable traveling clothes. "I suppose I will have to, won't I?" Surely her everyday dark Scotland Yard clerk uniforms wouldn't do for a countess.

"Will ye be returning to Scotland soon, ma'am?"

"I am bound to visit regularly," she answered honestly.

"Very well, Mrs. Blackwell, enjoy yer journey." He tipped his cap and stepped back, hurrying toward the other rail workers milling on the platform next to the office door. Once she glanced over at them, they jumped and pretended they'd been looking elsewhere or were going about business other than staring at her. Something she'd have to get used to, she supposed. Anonymity had worked splendidly for her, and Farah mourned the irrevocable loss as she turned and latched the door on the conductor's last "All aboard" call.

In every room Blackwell occupied, a large chair seemed to take a central location, from which he sprawled and towered at the same time. He looked like a dark autocrat who soaked velvet and damask in the blood of his enemies and then adorned the textiles with gold tassels and illuminated them with a crystal chandelier. A despot with a taste for luxury.

His eye patch slanted across his forehead and shaped

his glossy hair into a rakish wave. The good eye was fixed on some invisible vexation on the floor in front of him. A forgotten crystal glass of caramel liquor rested on one knee, clutched in a black leather glove that caused Farah's feminine muscles to clench.

Were those the same pair of gloves he'd worn the night before?

He stood when she moved from the shadow of the narrow hallway and passed the two long, lavish chaise longues that served as the alternate seating, accompanied by a small dining table with delicate Louis XVI chairs. He tossed his drink back and set the glass on the sideboard. A long silent moment passed as he began a thorough inspection from her sedately knotted hair all the way down to her one good pair of slippers, a questioning anxiety lurking behind the ever-present frost.

Long legs ate up the distance between them in two strides and he stopped just far enough away to be out of her reach. "Are you—I—"

Certain that catching the Blackheart of Ben More stuttering and speechless was a rare and marked occasion, Farah quirked her lip and eyebrow at him. "Yes?" she encouraged.

He blinked the moment away and brackets appeared around his hard mouth as it turned downward into a troubled frown. "We're visiting a seamstress the moment we get to London."

"Oh? Why the moment we arrive? Don't we have rather more pressing concerns?"

His lip curled in the fashion that announced he was about to say something cruel. "I dislike that dress immensely, and I noticed you have none better in your wardrobe."

"What's wrong with my dress?" She looked down at herself, smoothing a hand over the foamy green fabric that had cost a month's savings. "I thought the color rather suited me."

"Yes, and so did Carlton Morley."

Farah's smile returned. For someone so notoriously indifferent, her husband certainly had a jealous nature. The revelation shouldn't please her as much as it did. "Well, if my wardrobe insults you so, I suppose I'll have to resign myself to a new and expensive trousseau." She gave a long-suffering sigh. "Such is my burden."

Farah could tell she'd flummoxed him by his alert stare. "That . . . displeases you?"

Did it matter to him? "While a woman never likes to have her taste in fashion questioned, one can never go wrong by offering her a chance to buy a new dress." She flashed him a cheeky smile. "Or several, in your case."

Dorian studied her smile as his frown deepened and two furrows appeared between his ebony brows. It seemed that her good humor darkened his mood, almost as though he'd expected her to be cross or angry. "You should sit," he ordered, gesturing to the plush chair he'd just vacated.

"Is that not *your* place?"

"Take it," he insisted, his intent scrutiny oddly restless. One moment he was staring at her wrists, protected by silk gloves. Then he squinted at her left breast as though he could see through her layers to the plaid protecting her heart. He inspected other parts, her lips, her waist, and her skirts.

"I think I'd prefer the chaise," she said, wondering at his strange behavior.

He glanced at the wine velvet chaise with something akin to alarm. "Are you . . . unable to sit?" A muscle twitched beneath his eye, and then in his jaw.

"Why would I be?" Clarity cut through Farah's confusion and she had to clench her fists in her skirts to squelch the almost overwhelming urge to reach for him. Her husband was concerned about her well-being after their wedding night. Touched, she took a step toward him, glad to see he didn't retreat. "My corset makes sitting for an extended period of time quite uncomfortable," she explained gently. "I find that reclining is much more pleasant."

His suspicious regard bespoke disbelief, but the first jarring launch of the train stopped him from replying.

The movement caused Farah's already unsteady legs to give, and she stumbled backward, her arms flailing as she realized she wasn't going to steady herself in time.

She was in his arms before she registered his movement, and her hands gripped at his shoulders to regain her balance.

They both froze.

"I'm sorry," she gasped, releasing his shoulders immediately, but not before she registered that his arms were even more solid than she'd originally thought.

To her surprise, he didn't let her go, but drew her closer, closing his arms and locking her elbows to her sides before lowering his head and claiming her lips.

His kiss had all the possession of the previous night, all the constrained passion, but something else lurked behind it. A frustrated restraint. A probing inquisition.

Moaning, Farah relaxed into the kiss, opening beneath his lips and leaning against the unyielding strength of his chest. Perhaps if he didn't like her dress, he could rid her of it, and they could pass the long train ride from Glasgow to London as newlyweds ought to.

An insistent length pressed against her through her skirts, the evidence that his body supported her plans for the afternoon. She purred into his mouth and rubbed against his swelling erection, signaling that she was not just receptive, but aroused.

She found herself thrust onto the chaise, and her panting husband standing across the railcar from her, pouring himself another drink. A rather large one.

"Dorian," she began.

He pointed a shaking finger at her as he tossed back enough whisky that it took two gulping swallows for him to finish it. "Don't. Move."

"Or what, you'll throw yourself from a speeding train?" Oh, dear, perhaps it wasn't the best idea to plant that suggestion. The train wasn't speeding as of yet.

His eye narrowed into a dangerous slit. "Take care with what you say to me, wife."

Chastened, Farah realized her words had been unnecessarily inflammatory, but she wasn't one to avoid a situation. "One can only be rejected and discarded so often before one starts to take offense."

"Discarded?" He enunciated the syllables with a dumbfounded artlessness.

"You left me last night. Why?" The moment Farah asked the question, she wanted to take it back. What right had she to act like a jilted bride? He'd said he would get her with child, but affection hadn't been part of the bargain, had it?

He poured himself another drink and gave her his back. "You wouldn't have wanted me to stay."

"I wouldn't have asked you to if I didn't want it."

"You don't understand."

"You keep saying that." She huffed. "But I comprehend more than you realize!"

Dorian stilled, his broad back tense and immobile as a mountain. "What do you presume to know about me?" he asked coldly.

Farah chose her next words with care. "Only that last night was a first for both of us, and I think it was a rather rare and unexpected experience. I suppose I anticipated—I don't know—an acknowledgment of the pleasure we shared."

"I thought our pleasure was acknowledged rather loudly," he commented wryly, tossing back another scotch.

"It was," she agreed, heat rippling across her skin at the memory. "And then you were gone almost without another word."

"And it will always be thus. I will *not* sleep with you. Ever. I'll thank you not to ask me again."

"You will not? Or you cannot?" she prompted gently.

His glass made an angry sound as he slammed it on the table. "*Christ,* woman, can you leave no wound unsalted? No shadow unilluminated?" He stalked to where she perched on the chaise, looming over her. "Do you have no darkness or secrets that you'd rather not expose to me? Do you not fear I'll use them against you? Because that's what people do. What *I* do." His features were more uncertain than angry, more desperate than dangerous.

"You are the only person to whom all my secrets have been bared," she answered honestly. "And I had no choice in the matter. I have not only been naked in front of you, but also exposed to you, in every way." She let that sink in, watched him realize the truth in her words. "And," she continued, her eyes drawn to the snug fit of his trousers and the ridge beneath. "I found some of those expositions rather liberating."

His gaze darkened, taking on that dangerous glint that she'd come to understand was unpredictable. She liked him this way, anything was better than the wall of ice.

"You see, husband, I have nothing left to fear but death."

"*That* is where you're wrong." His usually silky voice thickened to the texture of the jagged Highland stones. Whether from the strong liquor or the bleak memories swirling in his eyes, she couldn't be sure. "There are so many things more terrifying than death."

In that moment, Farah was certain he'd been exposed to them all. She tilted her head back, feeling the stretch in her exposed throat as she gazed up the expanse of his torso to meet the dark glitter in his devilish eye. "What is it that you fear, husband?" she asked, allowing herself to lean toward him in infinitesimal degrees. "Why do you deny me your company at night?"

He watched her move toward him, making no attempt to stop her. Nor did he retreat. "My dreams," he muttered. "Often they're nothing more than memories. They follow me back to this world and they're—violent. I could hurt you, Farah, badly, and not even realize what I was doing until it was too late."

That was why he'd left? To protect her? "Perhaps we could work on it. Next time we could try—"

"There may not need be a next time."

She frowned. "What do you mean?"

"You could already be with child."

Farah's hand flew to her abdomen. "Surely, but that doesn't mean that we won't—you know. It likely takes more than once."

"We'll revisit this discussion when we know if it's relevant or not."

"But, don't you *want* to?"

He leaned closer as well, that cruel sneer affixed to his features. "Do you? Do you want me to defile you like that again? To tie you up and use your body as a receptacle for my seed, an object for my pleasure?"

Of course she did. Without question. But the way in which he worded his queries perplexed her. "You weren't the only one who found pleasure."

"What if you hadn't?"

"But I did."

"Not in the way you were supposed to, not for your first time."

Farah shrugged. "Who gets to say how we find our pleasure together?"

"I *hurt* you," he gritted out, his lips drawing tight, even
as his body responded to the conversation.

"Yes, for a moment, but as I understand it, all virgins
experience a bit of discomfort at first. You also pleased me
beyond words. And I'd like to think that—I could do the
same if you'd let me." Farah curled her fingers within her
gloves. It was epically difficult not to reach for him. His
body, so at odds with his mind, strained and beckoned to
her, and she'd promised not to reach out, no matter how
badly they both craved it. So she kept leaning forward,
toward the flat expanse of his stomach, a flesh-colored
shadow beneath the crisp white of the shirt tucked into
snug dark trousers. Beneath the dark wool, that long ridge
of his manhood flexed and strained, and her body answered as she imagined it always would.

Last night, her husband had put his wicked mouth on
her, causing her unimaginable pleasure. Could she have the
same effect on him? What if she pressed her mouth against
that hard length? What would he do?

She turned her head, running her cheek along the
slightly abrading fabric, feeling the heat of the flesh beneath.

"Farah," He growled a warning.

"Yes?" she breathed, her chest suddenly tight, filled to
the brim with anticipation, her body releasing a slick rush
of desire.

"I brought ye tea and snacks!" Murdoch announced as
the door to the bridge joining the railcars burst open with
a blast of cold early-evening air. "They call this first-class
fare, but if it is, I'll eat my own hat." He kicked the door
closed. "Be glad ye left Frank at home; he'd be appalled."

"Mr. Murdoch!" In her surprise, Farah stood abruptly,
bringing her almost chest to torso with her husband, who

stepped back. If Dorian Blackwell could look guilty, he almost pulled it off just then.

Murdoch stared for a beat longer than necessary. "I've—interrupted something."

Searching her husband's enigmatic face, she looked for the hope of regaining the moment, but his mask was back in place, and she gave a disappointed sigh. "Not at all, Murdoch, tea sounds just lovely." She turned back to Dorian. "Join us?"

Dorian regarded the delicate table with even more delicate chairs and scowled. With the three of them, they'd have to sit rather close. "I have paperwork to attend and business to set in order before we reach London." He abandoned them to their tea for his plush throne, ignoring them as effectively as though he'd shut an invisible door.

Farah watched his retreat with smarting eyes. Was he able to shut off his body's response to her so completely? Would he always leave her so unsatisfied?

Regardless, tea and conversation with Murdoch was a lovely break from the ceaseless intensity of her husband's company. They talked of pleasant things, books, theater, the Strand. Farah couldn't help but steal glances at Blackwell as he wrote over a mobile desk, bent above ledger books and breaking the seals on important-looking documents. If he marked their conversation, he gave no indication.

After tea, she and Murdoch settled into a card game and laughed over some more amusing tales from the Yard along with more ridiculous happenings at Pierre de Gaule's café beneath her flat. After one of her lively stories involving a Parisian painter and an English poet's fight over a rather famous Russian ballerina, Murdoch held up his hand and begged her to stop, wiping tears of mirth from the corner of his eyes.

They took a moment to sober and he stood to pour them

a glass of wine. "May I ask ye something that we've all been wondering, my lady?"

Farah lifted the wine to her lips and paused. "I'm not a lady yet, Murdoch, but you may ask me anything you like. I'm an open book." *Unlike some,* she thought, her eyes sliding over to study the sinew of Dorian's curved neck. Despite all they'd done last night, he was still such a mystery. She'd barely glimpsed more flesh than his face and throat, and hardly that. There was a powerful, masculine form beneath the layers of finery. Would she ever have occasion to gaze upon it?

Murdoch settled with his own glass and retrieved his hand of cards. "Where have ye been, lass?"

Farah paused, rolling the sweet blended red wine in her mouth before swallowing, trying to drag her thoughts away from her husband. Lord, would she ever get used to that word? "What do you mean?"

"Ye left that orphanage seventeen years back. Where did ye go? What did ye do to get by?"

Dorian's fist made them both jump as it slammed down on his desk. *"Murdoch,"* he growled.

"Oh, doona pretend ye havena been dyin' to know!" Murdoch was likely the only man alive who could wave a dismissive hand at the Blackheart of Ben More and keep the offending appendage.

"Have you considered that it may not be something she can bear to tell, or that you can bear to hear?" Her husband's low voice rumbled from between gritted teeth.

"It's all right," Farah offered, setting her glass on the table. "The tale is neither terribly amusing, nor traumatic. I don't mind telling you."

"I'll have no part of it," Dorian stated without looking up from his desk.

"Then regale *me,* lass. How did the daughter of an earl come to work at Scotland Yard?" Murdoch asked.

Farah stared into the wine, a lovely plum color in her dainty crystal glass. It had been ages since she'd thought about those hellish, angst-ridden weeks after they'd taken Dougan away. "I found out from Sister Margaret that they'd taken Dougan to Fort William. On that same day I also learned that she'd informed Mr. Warrington of my— attachment to Dougan and that we'd attempted to run away, and he was on his way to collect me."

"So ye ran?"

Farah smirked. "After a fashion. I was small enough to stow away behind the trunk strapped to the luggage rack on the rear of Mr. Warrington's coach. Once they'd stopped looking for me, I rode behind Warrington's conveyance all the way to Fort William, certainly a less comfortable journey than this one."

Murdoch chuckled. "Bastard didna even know ye were there. Clever lass."

Clinking Murdoch's offered glass with her own, she gave him a wry smile. "Once I reached Fort William, they'd already sent Dougan off to a prison in southern Glasgow called 'the Burgh.' And so I stowed on a post carriage from Fort William to Glasgow."

"And ye didna get caught all that way?" Murdoch asked.

"Of course I did." Farah laughed. "I was a terrible stow-away. But I told the post carrier who caught me that my name was Farah Mackenzie and my brother and I were orphans and I needed to find him in Glasgow. The man took pity on me, bought me a meal, and let me sit up front for the rest of the way beneath a blanket."

Blackwell snorted from across the car. "You're lucky that's all he did."

"I know that now," Farah conceded. "I was rather naïve at the time."

"I can't believe you were foolish enough to strike out

on your own," he continued darkly, flinging a letter to his table. "It's a miracle that—"

"I thought ye were having none of this conversation," Murdoch quipped, winking at Farah.

"I'm *not*. But the idea of a tiny, sheltered ten-year-old girl on the streets of Glasgow—"

"If ye want to be involved, come over here and involve yerself, otherwise, kindly *shut it* and let the lady finish her story."

Farah was certain Murdoch had signed his death warrant, but Dorian only muttered a foul blasphemy under his breath, dipped his pen in ink, and resumed his work.

"Ye were saying?" Murdoch prompted.

"Oh, yes, um, where was I?"

"Glasgow."

"Right. I found the same story at Glasgow that I did at Fort William. The Burgh was only built to house forty people and currently incarcerated over a hundred. So they'd already shipped Dougan off to Newgate to work on the railways. The post carrier, Robert Mackenzie was his name, told me he had a cousin in London who worked as a grocery delivery man. He said that he couldn't leave a little one from his clan undefended, so he bought me a ticket on the train and sent me to London. Sweetest man," Farah recalled. "I sent him letters every month for a decade until he passed from a heart problem."

"And his cousin was kind to ye?" Murdoch asked.

"Oh, yes. Craig Mackenzie and his wife, Coleen, were only ever able to have one child, a rather sickly girl named Agatha. Seeing as how I boasted the same last name, no one particularly questioned my presence in their home. He needed help with his deliveries, and so I made certain my rounds took me by Newgate, where I left food and such for Dougan which was subtracted from my own wages.

I worked with Mr. Mackenzie for seven or so years, and didn't mind it so much. Until the year Dougan—died. Everything seemed to change after that. Craig left Coleen for a Spanish dancing girl. They ran off to the Continent and so his business went under. Coleen's sister said she'd heard that they were hiring maintenance staff at Scotland Yard, and so, at seventeen, Agatha and I went to work there as maids."

Dorian's quill scratched to a halt on his desk, but he still didn't look at her. "I was searching all over the damned Scottish Highlands for you, and *you* were scrubbing the cesspool floors of Scotland Yard?"

"Not for very long," Farah announced proudly. "Before Carlton—"

Dorian's head shot up and he skewered her with his glare.

"I mean before *Chief Inspector Morley* took office, a man by the name of Victor Thomas James held his post. You see, because of Agatha's poor health, I often stayed late to finish her chores, as well. One of which was laying all the fires for the Yard offices. Chief Inspector James was one of the most decorated detectives in the history of the Yard; however, his eyesight had begun to fail, but he wasn't ready to retire. One night, while tidying his office and stoking the fire, I helped read a particularly untidy document. The next night, he had a stack for me to read and an extra ha'penny for my troubles. Over the course of two years, I became indispensable to him, and he installed me as a widowed clerk at twenty." Farah lifted her shoulders. "The nature of the work at the Yard is rather transitory. Men come and go, are transferred, sacked, killed, or promoted. After maybe five years, Agatha had married and no one who knew me as a maid still worked at that office. I was merely Mrs. Farah Mackenzie, a widowed bluestocking. Chief Inspector James retired six years hence, Morley took his place, and there I have remained until, well, until a few days ago."

The two very differently featured men shared identical expressions of abject disbelief for long enough to make Farah want to squirm.

"To think of the trouble we went through to find ye this wee fairy, Blackwell, and all this time she was right under our noses. All ye would have had to do is the one thing ye swore ye wouldna." Murdoch turned to toss his employer a pained and ironic look.

"What's that?" she asked.

"Get arrested."

"That *is* how you found me."

Murdoch chuckled. "Aye, but we orchestrated that, so it doesna count."

Farah thought a moment, wondering whom they had on the inside who would have helped with said orchestration. "Inspector McTavish?"

Murdoch laughed and slapped his thigh. "Dougan always said ye were a witty lass!"

She remembered the beating Blackwell had taken whilst locked away in the strong room. The echoes of a bruise and the all-but-healed cut on his lip reminded her of the lengths he must have gone to. "I am sorry you were mistreated by Morley," she offered. "I don't know what got into him."

Dorian's gaze touched her in places that made memories dance along the nerves of her skin until she was overwarm and aching. "I do."

As her face heated, she ducked it down and retrieved her own cards. "Just a point of curiosity, were you responsible for the deaths of those three Newgate prison guards Morley accused you of?"

Her husband didn't lift his head from his work, his pen never pausing in its relentless scratch across the page. "No, I wasn't *responsible* for their deaths," he said darkly.

Farah blew a quiet but relieved sigh.

"I killed them each, myself."

CHAPTER SIXTEEN

London certainly looked different when one knew their life was in danger. Though street mobs obeyed and shadows parted for her influential new husband, Farah still found herself shrinking from dark alleys and checking around corners for a murderer, or for Warrington, himself, to seize upon her.

"Stop that," Dorian ordered from the shadowed corner where he watched Madame Sandrine turn her into a human pincushion.

"I haven't moved one iota in nearly three hours' time. I'd first have to be *doing* something in order to cease doing it." The endless standing had made Farah irritable, and after this fourth garment, the novelty of such fine apparel was beginning to wear off.

"You keep checking out the window for danger," he accused.

Drat, she *had* been doing just that. Eyeing the richly attired citizens of the West End in a ridiculous search for a would-be assassin. Gritting her teeth against an itch on her collarbone, she fought the overwhelming urge to scratch at it. How would she even know what an assassin might look like? "Can you blame me under the circumstances? Perhaps being a target for powerful enemies is all very typical for you, but I've still yet to adjust to it."

"And you won't have to," he said casually. "It won't be long before we have Warrington's head displayed on a spike from the London Bridge."

"Not—literally?" Though the image didn't disgust her as much as it should.

He cast her a look of droll exasperation.

"Well, one can never tell with you, can they?"

Her infuriating husband looked pleased with himself, and Madame Sandrine chuckled. "You picked a good wife, Monsieur Blackwell. She is, as we say, a *femme forte.*"

Farah inwardly felt guilty for all the discourteous thoughts she'd been having about the woman whilst submitting to her ministrations. "You are too kind, Madame Sandrine."

"Hah! Your husband knows better than that, *n'est-ce pas*?"

Farah's smile disappeared at the sly look the lovely brunette slid toward Blackwell. A few extra discourteous thoughts stunned her as Dorian awarded the dressmaker a civil nod, which was akin to an all-out declaration of affection for him.

Farah's eyes narrowed at the woman, who didn't notice because she was calculating the remarkable breadth of Blackwell's shoulders. Just how *well* did they know each other? Had the lady put her hands on him? Had he allowed her to take his measurements and dress his impressive physique? It seemed oddly galling that, though she'd coupled with her husband, whoever tailored his clothing would still be more intimately acquainted with his body.

He was regarding Farah with the queerest expression when she couldn't stop herself from lifting her disapproving gaze toward him. Could he read the odd mixture of curiosity and suspicion on her face? The knave's own look hovered between disbelief and satisfaction.

He almost seemed contented. Most men wouldn't dare think of accompanying their wives to a dress fitting, let alone refuse the distractions of a paper or book.

But not Dorian Blackwell. True to form, he *watched,* looking on with mild interest as Madame Sandrine tucked, pinned, measured, wrapped, and hemmed. Sometimes it seemed he couldn't stop himself from staring, as if he drank her in with his gaze. Savored her. The intensity of it left her more than a little discomfited.

Her husband. A thief, a highwayman, a criminal.

A coldhearted killer.

But she'd known that, hadn't she? Somehow, it seemed excusable for him to take down the dregs of society. To disappear men more villainous than himself; monsters, crime lords, and pimps. But officers of the law? Men she might have known and maybe even befriended.

She remembered their first conversation back in his study at Ben More. His devastating description of the hellish tortures he and Dougan had endured as boys.

And that was just what the guards did to me.

Swallowing strong emotion, Farah locked eyes with him. The wounded one glimmered with blue fire from the shadows. Swirling with things he would never say out loud. He couldn't bear to be touched. Couldn't relinquish a modicum of composure or control.

It was difficult to imagine the strong, lethal predator in front of her as a small boy, let alone a victimized one. Somehow, with a man such as Blackwell, it would be easy to assume that he'd always been the force of nature he currently was. That maybe, through some Olympian feat, he'd appeared on this earth in his mature, powerful body, birthed by a potent, mystical darkness.

But that wasn't the case, Farah thought, her chest clenching for him. He was as much a product of the past as she, more so even, and he'd spent many of his formative years helpless, wounded, and afraid.

In a clever strategy, he'd crafted his vengeance around hers, so that she couldn't separate herself from him if she wanted to achieve it. Dorian Blackwell wasn't the sort of man to kill needlessly. Those guards whom he'd confessed to killing, if they'd mistreated Blackwell, they'd also likely victimized Dougan and countless other incarcerated boys. How many of those children had been innocent, as Dougan was? If that was the case, then Farah not only understood his lethal actions, she fought back a dark sort of approval. It was surely wrong, but she couldn't bring herself to condemn him for it.

How strange that she felt more indignation for the genial tilt of his lips toward Madame Sandrine, than the deaths of three people. What sort of woman was she becoming?

"Madame Sandrine's father, Charles, is my tailor," he explained, a pleased smile toying with the corner of his mouth. "He spent a span with me in Newgate. I've known the family for some time, including Sandrine's *husband*, Auguste." He put undue emphasis on the word.

"Before we were tailors, my family were smugglers," Madame Sandrine announced proudly. "But my father was wounded by the police and incarcerated. He always tells me that he could not have survived in an English prison without the Blackheart Brothers. And even after that, Monsieur Blackwell bought and leased us this palace in the West End, and now we are among the most elite tailors and dressmakers to the *ton*. The only payment he accepts is the *exclusivité* of my father's expertise, and now, mine for you, Madame Blackwell."

"*Merci,*" Farah murmured, swinging back to regret for her ire at the French woman as she still stared into the eyes of her husband. How was it that she was beginning to consider him more of a philanthropist than a philistine? Was he corrupting her somehow? Or was she finally seeing the truth? That the Blackheart of Ben More just might have a very big heart, indeed.

"I think this dress will stun the nobility, and leave them stupefied with envy and lust," Madame Sandrine announced with relish.

"I'm just glad it's not crimson, like everything else you drape," Farah said to her husband as she glanced at her transformation in the floor-to-ceiling mirrors across from the raised podium on which she stood. The creation of blue silk evoked the midnight sky, as it wrapped her bosom and waist in bejeweled gathers before cascading from her hips in a dark waterfall. The shamelessly cut bodice was lent a hint of respectability by folds of a shimmering diaphanous silver material draping from a choker of gems about her neck and flowing down her shoulders like moonbeams. To call them sleeves would have been a mistake, for all they concealed.

Madame Sandrine threw a teasing look over her shoulder at Blackwell. "How fitting that the color of blood is the one you prefer the most."

"Not for *her,*" Dorian rumbled.

The seamstress lifted a winged eyebrow, but didn't comment. "*Voilà.* I believe that is all I'll need from you today, Madame Blackwell. I can have these finished in the morning, and in the meantime I have a lovely soft gray frock hemmed with tiny pink blossoms that will bring out the color in your cheeks."

"Thank you, Madame Sandrine. I apologize for the imposition upon your time."

"Nonsense!" The woman gathered herself from the floor in a pool of skirts. "In this shop, time stops for Dorian Blackwell, and now his *femme,* as well." Gingerly, she helped Farah out of the dress, leaving her only in her corset and underthings. "Next I shall bring an assortment of *lingerie.*"

"Oh, no, that's quite all right," Farah protested. "I have plenty of respectable—"

"Yes, bring them," Dorian interjected. "Only your best."

"That goes without saying. A newly wedded husband wants nothing to do with *respectable* undergarments." The dressmaker tossed a lascivious smile toward Farah. "I have *just* the things that will keep the mistresses' beds empty and cold." She bustled out, sweeping the blue gown with her.

Mistresses? Farah glanced at Blackwell. He wouldn't ever have mistresses, would he? No. He could barely bring himself to lie with *her.* But what about the future? What if he developed a taste for sex that she could not fulfill? What if he found someone whose touch did not repel him?

A brightness glimmered back at her from where her dark husband sat in the shadows. A look not of laughter or joy precisely, but a rearrangement from his usual cold calculation. A sense of reclining and recreation, and dare she say joviality?

"Don't tell me you're enjoying this," she warned.

His smug look became a full smirk.

"She thinks you have a harem of mistresses."

"I believe you've pointed out before, it's a common misconception."

"I'm fairly certain Madame Sandrine would like to apply for a position within the ranks," Farah muttered.

"I find that jealousy becomes you, wife." The suggestion in Dorian's voice caressed all the way down to her respectable knickers.

"Don't flatter yourself." She was *not* jealous. Though,

she had to admit, the suggestion that she couldn't please a husband such as the Blackheart of Ben More enough to keep him from straying hurt more than she'd expected.

"You can assign me a great many sins, but self-approbation is not among them." Dorian's voice danced with amusement, and Farah had to fight back a threatening smile.

"If self-approbation were your only sin, you'd be an honest and virtuous man," she quipped, lowering her lashes to hide her enjoyment.

"You weren't looking for virtuous when you found me," he said softly.

She made a sound of mock outrage, and chucked a balled-up stocking at him and he caught it. "You know full well I didn't find you! *You* took *me* captive!"

"Is that how you remember it?"

"That's what *happened*," she insisted.

"I recall being quite captivated when first we met," he said lightly. "Helpless, I daresay."

Farah's snort turned into a reluctant laugh. "Don't be charming. It doesn't suit you."

The glimmer in his blue eye became a twinkle, the curve of his mouth lifted a little too far to be called a smirk anymore. But a smile? Almost . . . "No one's ever accused me of being charming before."

"You don't say." Lord, were they—flirting?

Madame Sandrine's swishing skirts announced her arrival. "Here we are! The latest in Parisian fashion." She selected a particularly thin bit of lace chemise in the palest shade of lavender from her cart, stocked with everything from corsets to drawers, stockings, garters, and nightgowns that barely covered enough to deserve the name. "This would go with these stockings—"

"Wrap one of everything," Dorian ordered.

Farah imagined her dumbfounded look was just as

ridiculous as the seamstress's. "But, that's a small fortune in *underthings,* for which I really have no need."

"As it so happens, I have a small fortune to spend on underthings."

Madame Sandrine's throaty laugh set Farah's teeth on edge. She reached into the cart and picked up a long sheer gown comprised of fine black lace.

Farah didn't miss the tightening of her husband's features.

Perhaps these would push him over the edge, entice him to "defile" her again. A blush climbed up her cheeks as Farah imagined herself in nothing but this bit of lace, drawing the lustful mismatched gaze of her husband. The garment was almost more indecent than being naked. Something a *mistress* would wear. Or a prostitute.

A horrific realization seized her, and Farah gasped, letting the garment slip from her fingers before she covered her suddenly burning eyes with both hands.

Prostitute. "Gemma!" she groaned. Tears squeezed from her clenched eyelids as she considered all the terrors the woman faced in her absence. Farah had promised the poor prostitute that she'd be there before her release from Scotland Yard. That she would help her escape the clutches of Edmond Druthers. She'd been so busy what with getting drugged, kidnapped, and subsequently married, that she'd all but forgotten. "What have I done?"

"What are you talking about?" Dorian's voice was closer, alert, and concerned. "What's the matter?

Slowly, Farah lowered her hands, revealing the wide form now towering in front of her. A dark notion swirled in the periphery of her moral conscience. Her *husband* was none other than the formidable and notorious Blackheart of Ben More. His name struck fear into the hearts of the most hardened criminals, to say nothing of his menacing features and powerful frame.

She only hoped that her outlaw husband would be willing to place his ill-gotten skills at her disposal. Sucking a bracing breath into her lungs, she prepared to speak the words that might just strike her final alliance with the devil. "Dorian, I need your help."

A silent, expectant aura lifted the fine hairs on the back of Dorian's neck as he surveyed the foul-smelling mists of the London docks. He didn't have time for this. Furthermore, he didn't like bringing Farah here. The dangers of the London neighborhood of Wapping didn't exactly rival that of Whitechapel, but one didn't bring their treasures here and hope to keep them. At least not at this hour of the early morning with all the river pirates and smugglers making use of the dark wharfs along the Thames.

Three things kept his shoulders relaxed as he strolled down Wapping High Street with Farah beside him.

The first was the thick copper hair, wide shoulders, and long stride of Christopher Argent, who guarded Farah's other side. Dorian's London assassin had the eyes of a hawk and the reflexes of a mongoose. Nothing would leap from the shadows that Argent didn't see coming.

The second was that Murdoch flanked Farah and, despite his stout frame and advanced years, he was handy with a pistol or two. Though Dorian saved pistols as a last resort, as they tended to rouse the coppers if fired within the city. No need for that, tonight. Or ever.

The third, and most important, was that he remained Dorian Blackwell, and he owned the interest, goods, and loyalties of more than half the dock smugglers and river pirates along the Thames. This was his world. Not because he belonged here, but because he *ruled* here. Anyone they'd likely meet would either owe him fealty, money, or blood. And if someone stepped in his path, he'd collect his due.

If the Thames was a river of filth and sewage, Wapping

High Street was a river of brick and stone. The structures here were comprised mostly of moldy warehouses and crumbling manufacturing buildings made obsolete by the new industrial revolution. The cobbles shone blue from the full moon, as street lamps were spaced much less liberally here than back on the lively Strand or in wealthy Mayfair. The moonlight never reached the deep alleys or narrow roads that led from the thoroughfare out to the docks.

This was a place for men who lived in shadows. Men like him.

Dorian glanced down at his wife. Her upswept ringlets glowed in the moonlight like a silver beacon against the seedy grime barely concealed by the night. He should not have brought her. Should have insisted she stay back in the safety of his terrace.

They shouldn't be here at all, chasing after errant prostitutes. They'd interviewed over a dozen between Queen's Head Alley and where they now stood on the corner of Brewhouse Lane. Farah had offered them coin, resources, and a place to sleep for any information about her friend Gemma Warlow.

Dorian couldn't understand her grim determination. There were too many prostitutes to save. Too many orphans and urchins to house. Too many of the wretched and starving to feed. Chances were they'd go to all this trouble and the whore would run back to her master the moment her bruises healed and the man called her to him with a flippant apology.

Dorian had known and hated Edmond Druthers for years. The man was the human equivalent of the toxic sludge that gathered along the banks at low tide. No one wanted it there, but no one knew quite how to rid the city of it.

Gods, this was a bloody waste of time.

But Farah's acute distress and earnest tears had unstitched him, and Dorian had known for some time that he could deny her nothing. Not even this fool's errand. Christopher Argent kept stealing disbelieving looks at Farah, his blue eyes reflecting the ambient glow like an alley cat's. Dorian understood why the man would dare in his presence.

First, because Christopher Argent was an unfeeling, fearless killer-for-hire.

And second, because most of the incarcerated men at Newgate had considered Dougan's *Fairy* some mythical creature, a sight too rare and beautiful to be beheld by a common man. Maybe even a fancy born of an imagination keen enough to take possession of the prison. To meet her was to gaze upon a fantasy realized, to remember the desperate yearnings of a lonely prisoner bereft of kindness, mercy, or beauty. To be blinded by the embodiment of all three of those things. For a man like Argent, one born into incarceration, the sight might have him reassessing some long-held cynical philosophies.

But judging from the curious yet calculating look sparkling in Argent's pale eyes, Dorian realized he could be mistaken. Seventeen years and he still knew next to nothing about the man other than the fact that Argent would kill without question and was abjectly loyal to him.

Farah was oblivious to the man, so intent was she on the rescue of her friend. She likewise ignored the sounds of drunken dockworkers spending what they won in many belowground gin hells for a cheap fuck, and approached the women who stood in the streets, brave enough, or desperate enough, to service thieves, smugglers, and dock pirates. Her composure was impressive as she conversed with these women without fear or judgment, even recognizing some of them by name. They might have been respectable ladies meeting in a city park, rather than unwashed wraiths stinking of sweat, sex, and in some cases, disease.

Problem was, Farah was getting nowhere, and with each dead end, her shoulders would lose a bit of their starch, and her eyes lost a bit more hope. Dragging Blackwell and Argent in her wake guaranteed her loose tongues, as no one would dare deny them, but it seemed that Gemma Warlow was nowhere to be found.

"I'm beginning to wonder if Druthers hasn't—killed her," Farah worried. "And it would be all my fault."

"How in God's name would it be your fault?" Dorian asked, staring down two sailors who leaned against an abandoned building. Hired muscle, possibly, awaiting an incoming shipment of smuggled goods, pocketing what would have been paid to the crown in import taxes.

Not his freight. They didn't have anything scheduled until a company fleet arrived from the Orient in a week's time.

Dorian heard his name spoken in awestruck whispers and knew the men wouldn't be a bother. But they shouldn't be looking at his wife like they did, so he didn't break his glare until they found something interesting to study about their boots.

"I told Gemma when I left Scotland Yard with Morley that I would return in the morning to help her figure out how to escape Druthers for good. When I didn't show she must have felt so—Wait a moment." She stopped walking and her vanguard paused as well as she turned on Dorian. Her eyes, once wide and luminous with tears, now narrowed with accusation. "This isn't my fault, this is *your* fault."

Argent hid his amused smile behind the upturned collar of his long, black coat, but Murdoch didn't bother hiding his undignified snort of laughter.

Dorian blinked. "I fail to see how."

"If you hadn't kidnapped me, I'd have been there for her."

"You also might have been murdered on the way to work," Dorian reminded her stiffly. "There is a price on your head, you know."

"Yes, but Gemma Warlow might be the one who is murdered now. Is my life any more important than hers?" Farah challenged.

"It is to me."

Three pairs of eyes widened in the blue darkness, and Dorian narrowed his in challenging response. He'd step over a mountain of murdered Gemma Warlows if it meant saving Farah, and didn't feel one drop of shame for the truth of it. Though her features told him shock had turned back into reprobation, and therefore Dorian wisely remained silent.

"I 'ear you're lookin' for Gemma," a voice cooed from the stairs that led down to the Hangman's Pub and emptied onto Brew House Lane.

His wife instantly forgot her ire, and rushed toward the top of the stairs, her eyes beseeching as she gazed down at an aging dark-haired woman dressed in little more than tatters. "Yes! Gemma Warlow. Have you seen her?"

The strumpet pushed matted hair away from eyes alight with calculation. She looked through Farah to Dorian, and saw opportunity.

"Wot's it werf to you, Black'eart?" she asked in her thick cockney. "We all know just how deep your pockets be lined. And you know there in't no questions on the docks wot's answered for free."

Dorian stepped forward, taking a coin from his pocket and holding it up to the bit of wan streetlight from the adjacent corner.

"I'd take on all four of you for that," she said, greed and want flooding her suggestive words.

Dorian swallowed revulsion, wondering how long it had been since the woman bathed. Chances were she only got the most blind or desperate of customers anymore, her age and years of use sitting heavy on her skin and rotten teeth. "Warlow," he reminded her.

The prostitute shrugged a bony shoulder. "'Er face is too busted to work, so she's standin' lookout for a shipment for Druthers. She's s'posed to send a runner to fetch 'im from the Queen's 'Ead Pub when it gets 'ere."

Dorian tried to ignore Farah's horrified gasp. "Where?" he demanded.

The woman extended a bony finger toward the river where Brewhouse Lane ran straight into the Executioner's Dock.

"Excellent." He tossed the coin to the woman.

"You take care, Black'eart," the whore crowed at him as her hand snaked out and caught it. "The shadows be too full tonight of men wif dark coats and shiny weapons. They've driven ev'ryone inside."

"Good," Dorian clipped. "Let's hope they stay there and out of my way."

The woman's cackle ended on an airless cough. "Wif you and Argent on the street, they'll all fink a war's brewin' in Wapping."

"If there was, I'd have brought an army with me." Dorian turned away, hoping to get to Warlow before whatever shipment she awaited arrived. "Stay off the Executioner's Dock, just in case," he threw over his shoulder.

Farah hurried after him, and he slowed his stride so she could keep up. "Executioner's Dock?" she queried. "Sounds ominous."

"It isn't used for its original purpose anymore," Dorian said, attempting to soothe her obviously jangling nerves. "The crown used to hang river pirates and smugglers from the Executioner's Dock in centuries past, and leave them there as a deterrent to others. Nowadays that's rather out of practice."

"And that very dock is used for smuggling?"

Dorian smirked. "The warning failed. Most criminals saw it as a challenge. Wapping, specifically this dock, has been the epicenter of underground trade ever since."

At the mouth of the pier, where the stones became planks beneath their feet, Dorian nodded to Argent, who melted into the shadows and disappeared down a side alley, with an almost mystical silence.

The dock running parallel to the river was wide enough for a freight cart or about a handful of men standing shoulder to shoulder. Smaller piers branched from it with various boats and planks bobbing in the lazy black ribbon of the Thames. Upon long-standing order of the crown, the pier that completed the Executioner's Dock was to remain as empty as it was now. But night after night, dark boats and darker men made it their port to London's commerce.

"I think I see her!" Farah indicated a stack of crates loosely covered with a canvas blocking more than half the dock one pier to the north. Perched atop the haphazard pile was a smallish boy of maybe eight and a taller feminine form, hunched together against the chill.

"You are to stay by my side, unless I tell you otherwise. Is that understood?" he commanded his wife.

She craned her neck to look up at him and stunned him with what shone from her soft gray eyes. Gratitude. Trust. "Of course," she promised.

Dorian lost himself to it for a moment. Perhaps this wasn't such a colossal waste of time, after all.

Murdoch cleared his throat. "The whelp already spotted us and scampered off," he warned. "I expect we doona have much time before we've unwanted company."

Dorian tore his eyes from his wife. She was too much of a distraction out here. He needed to be sharp and ruthless. Not for the first time, he cursed her presence. She'd insisted Gemma wouldn't go with them unless she came along, and neither of them was familiar with the prostitute, so they'd not be able to identify the real Gemma. And yet, Dorian couldn't help feeling like he should have insisted they take the whore, willing or no, and deliver her to Farah's feet safe and sound.

How did his wife keep talking him into foolhardy things? After tonight, he'd have to look into that.

The crates were in a shadowed swath of walkway equidistant from the gas lamps doing their best to illuminate the pier. As they approached, the plump figure hopped down from her perch, preparing to bolt.

"Gemma!" Farah called. "Gemma, wait!"

The figure froze, and Farah held her hand out, though the woman was not yet within reach.

"Mrs. Mackenzie?" A shocked reedy voice struggled through split and swollen lips. "Wot are you doin' out here?"

Farah quickened her step and reached for her friend, despite Dorian's orders. The women collapsed against each other with different versions of relief. Though the grimy prostitute was taller and much larger than Farah, Dorian watched his wife pull her friend into her bosom and hold her there in a very maternal gesture. She didn't seem to spare a thought for her fine new gray dress or the fact that the woman had dried blood matted to her dirty hair.

It was Gemma who spoke first. "I been sick wif worry over you," she scolded Farah against her shoulder. "You didn't tell no one you was leaving, Mrs. Mackenzie."

"*You* were worried about *me*? You dear thing." Farah stroked the woman's hair, her cream silk glove coming away soiled, as she flicked her eyes toward Dorian. "And it's—Mrs. Blackwell now."

"As in, Dorian Blackwell? If you're married to the Black'eart of Ben More, I'm the bloody Duchess of York." Gemma popped out of the embrace, staring at Dorian with the one eye that wasn't swollen shut as if she'd only just noticed him. "I'll be boffed," she breathed.

"Your Grace." Dorian dipped his head at her, inwardly wincing at her injuries.

"Oh, Gemma! Look what that fiend did to you!" Farah gingerly smoothed dirty brown hair away from the angry wounds.

Druthers had left no part of the unlucky whore's face unpunished. A dark anger surged inside of him, and he instantly respected the tough woman.

" 'Ow'd a lady like you shackle Dorian fucking Blackwell? I'd already bet me garters you'd brought Morley to heel."

"We'd best leave if we don't want any trouble," Murdoch warned.

"You're coming with us." Farah linked her arm through Gemma's. "We're taking you away from here."

Gemma wriggled out of her gentle grasp, casting fearful looks up into Dorian's scarred eye. "Better not, kind girl," she denied gently. "You don't want Druthers after you, now. He's already sore you got to me the first time."

"I'm not a girl," Farah protested. "We're the same age."

Gemma stepped back from Farah's second advance and Dorian hated the hurt confusion on his wife's face as she paused. He knew what the prostitute was thinking even before she said it.

"No, we in'nt," the woman said wearily. "I'm as old as the sea and tired of this game. Barely werf the trouble to fuck anymore."

"Don't say that, Gemma!" Farah insisted. "I refuse to be shocked."

The whore took another step back. "It's true. Druthers don't 'urt your face if 'e finks it'll still make 'im money."

Farah would not be deterred. "Gemma, come with us this instant, we must hurry. We must go *now*."

Gemma shook her head. "Go where?"

"My home, of course. We'll give you shelter and food and safety."

"Then wot? 'Ow will I keep meself? I don't live off charity, and who'll 'ire the likes of me? You?"

Farah nodded emphatically. "Of course I will!" At Gemma's skeptical look, she rushed on. "As it so happens, I've acquired a household from my father. I'll need it staffed."

Gemma threw up her hands. All the talking had caused the cut in her lip to reopen, but she didn't seem to notice. "Don't know 'ow to do much else than lie on me back and spread me legs. Wot would you do wif a whore in a fine 'ouse? Get out of here, all of you, before there's blood spilt."

Only someone with a death wish spoke that way in his presence, and Dorian read that wish in Gemma's hard, dead eyes. She was beyond caring, her spirited demeanor more a habit now than anything.

"Gemma—*please!*" Farah's voice thickened with confusion and tears. "Please come with me? I couldn't bear it if you stayed here." The desperate, frustrated admonishment tore at Dorian's guts. He stepped forward, but paused when the prostitute took a frightened retreat.

"We'll send you to Ben More so you can recover," he offered lowly, trying not to frighten the woman further. "While you're there, Walters can show you your way around a kitchen. We'll join you once our business here in London is concluded."

The look of adulation Farah sent him gave him strange stirrings in his chest. Like someone had released an army of moths in there.

Gemma Warlow regarded him with something else, entirely. Skepticism, or more accurately, outright disbelief. "Why? Why would the richest thief in England stick his neck out for a frowaway like me? You're not known for your mercy, Blackwell."

Dorian met her glare, but couldn't say the words, so he looked down at Farah who'd clasped her hands hopefully in front of her. She was the only reason. His only reason.

For everything.

A distinct bird whistle warned Dorian they had company before he heard pairs of heavy boots on the planks. Argent had found his perch.

"If your woman fancies a bit of quim, Blackwell, she'll have to pay for it, like anyone else."

Dorian and Murdoch turned toward the grainy voice behind them.

Edmond Druthers was a sewer rat with delusions of grandeur. Despite the physical resemblance, he was repulsive, smelled of rubbish and refuse, and had the knack for survival and resourcefulness that kept him on the top of his own little dung heap.

Druthers wasn't alone. Three wide-shouldered sailors strode the length of the Executioner's Dock, all of them armed.

"Don't come near her." Farah took a protective step in front of Gemma.

Dorian, in turn, stepped in front of his wife. He didn't have to tell Murdoch to use his girth to help corral the women back behind the crates. The sound of Murdoch's pistol cocking told him that should he fail, six bullets were waiting for four men. In Murdoch's hands, those were good odds.

Dorian placed himself between the crates and the wall, creating a semieffective bottleneck. Only two of them could come at him at a time, and unless he did something foolishly out of character, it was impossible for him to be flanked as the only alley for a great span was an abyss in his right periphery.

Once the women were secured out of sight, Dorian

made a few quick calculations. He counted three weapons. A knife held by a lanky man he recognized by the street name Bones, as his gaunt skin stretched over a frame more heavy bone than heavy muscle. A cudgel brandished by a hard-bodied, long-haired sailor of African or Island descent. And, if Druthers was a sewer rat, then the monster running his thumb down the sharp edge of his kukri was nothing less than a bear. Immense, lumbering, and all ungraceful brawn beneath the thick pelt of dark hair. The size didn't fool Dorian, though. George Perth was one of the deadliest men alive.

Druthers had heard the Blackheart of Ben More was at his door, and brought the most lethal of his men out to brawl. The kind of brawl that someone wouldn't be walking away from.

Four someones, to be precise.

If anyone carried a pistol, it would be Druthers, but if he was expecting a shipment of goods, the last thing he'd want to do was fire it and alert the night patrol.

Dorian may just have to stake his life on that. "Gentlemen," he greeted them ironically.

"What you sniffing around my cut of snatch for, Blackwell?" Druthers barked, his accent clearly marking his peasant Yorkshire ancestry. He motioned to Gemma and Farah through the slats in the crates. "Don't you got enough of your own?"

"What I have is a business proposition for you." Dorian attempted to communicate in a language the bastard would understand.

Druthers motioned to Bones and the African to step ahead of him, which they did. "What makes you think I'd discuss business with a cornered pretender and a few whores? If I took down the king of the London underworld, I'd never have to buy me own drink again, not to mention the rest of the London docks would be up for grabs."

A shadow shifted in the alley, and Dorian stepped back a few paces, drawing the criminals closer. "Think about your next move carefully, Druthers," he warned with the arctic calm that had sent many a would-be attacker scrambling away. "I see this ending with your death."

Bones and his compatriot passed the alley and reached the pile of crates, though they threw each other covert looks of uneasiness.

"You don't see nothing out of those eerie eyes, Blackwell." Druthers addressed him but sneered at the women who remained wisely silent behind the crates. He wedged himself behind his advancing men, the bear with the kukri remaining at his side like a giant scarred sentinel. "What *I* see is a few cunts needing to be taught a lesson."

"I couldn't agree more," Dorian replied, tucking his hands behind his jacket to offer his chest as a target.

"My whore's too ugly for the four of us." Druthers wet his cracked and peeling lips with a swipe of the tongue, his eyes snagged on what he could see of Farah. "But as soon as I've rid the world of Dorian Blackwell, your pretty, tight slut will be looking for a new man to ride."

Some men felt fire lick through them when they were about to kill. It turned their skin red, made them sweat, filled their muscles with strength and heat and burned away all sense of logic and control.

With Dorian, it was ice.

It hardened his muscles and crackled through his veins, freezing everything that made him alive. *Human.* It expanded to fill the empty spaces and reinforced any brittle parts. It dulled pain until people could chip away at him again and again, only to be bit by shards. The cold kept him sharp. Alert. Fierce.

And didn't slow him down one bit.

With this many opponents, the fight would *need* to go quickly. Once a body hit the ground, another would replace it, and he couldn't take the chance that someone might stand up and come at him again. No time to waste with punishing or wounding.

Lethal blows. Open veins. No survivors.

As Bones's knife arced at his throat, Dorian crouched and wrenched the two long knives from their scabbards hidden against his back beneath his coat. He spun them so his thumb capped the pummel, and the blades rested along his forearms. On his way back up, he sliced through the meat beneath the pit of his attacker's arm.

The man dropped his knife immediately as he severed the muscle and rendered his opponent's knife arm permanently ineffectual. The piercing scream was cut short by Dorian's second knife embedding deep into his throat.

Dorian was too focused on the next threat, the cudgel held in the coffee-skinned man's leathery hand, to feel the warm arterial spray as he wrenched the blade out of Bones's neck. The bleeding man made a terrible gurgling sound as his momentum carried him forward, and the body landed somewhere out of view.

Dorian almost missed the flash of auburn hair as Christopher Argent materialized from the alley and struck like a viper. One moment, the bear, George Perth, was just behind Druthers readying his kukri to strike, and the next, his limp feet were disappearing into the black alley.

Another unsuspecting victim of Argent's famous garrote.

Dorian rushed the dark assailant, giving him a chance to raise his right arm for a blow that would have all the force of a speeding steam engine. That was, if Dorian had allowed it to land. Throwing his left knee into the unguarded torso, he heard the satisfying sound of the man's breath leaving his body as he collapsed at the waist over his knee. One strong thrust of the knife to the back of the neck was enough to sever the man's spinal cord.

He looked up from discarding the body, and found Druthers had pulled his pistol. "Not another move," the brigand warned, his eyes peeled wide with fear. "I don't want to shoot you, it'll bring the coppers."

"Then what do you propose?" Doran queried, fighting the need to look back and check on Farah. She'd never seen him kill before. What did she think of him now?

"Hand me the whore, she's mine, and I'll be on my way."

"It's too late for that, I'm afraid." Dorian shook his head, slinging drops of blood from his blade with a flick of his wrist. "A man like me can't leave an attack like this unanswered and hope to retain his place at the top."

"I still have George," Druthers threatened. "He's the deadliest man in Wapping. You can't kill us both before eating a bullet."

Dorian's fist tightened on his knife, positioning it for what he needed to do next. "I'm assuming you meant George *was* the rather large gentleman with the kukri."

Druthers didn't miss Dorian's use of the past tense, and his brow dropped with confusion as he did exactly what Dorian needed him to do. He turned his head and looked toward the empty spot from which the bear of a sailor had disappeared.

The moment Druthers looked away, Dorian let his knife fly. It embedded deep into the man's right shoulder, and the force of it drove Druthers to his knees. The slimy bastard tried to raise his gun, but the knife impeded all movement, and Dorian was on him before he could grab for the weapon with his other hand. Druthers's face made a satisfying crunch beneath Dorian's boot, and the man crumpled to the planks with a pathetic noise. After kicking the gun across the dock and into the river, Dorian crouched over Druthers with his remaining knife pressed against his throat, one knee grinding down on the pimp's uninjured shoulder.

Blood poured from Druthers's nose and mouth, leaking into his eyes and ears. A man once thought dangerous now squirmed and writhed like a trapped snake, emitting little mewling sounds of pain.

Feeding a mean-spirited impulse, Dorian reached out and twisted the knife still protruding from Druthers's shoulder. Pleasure speared through him at the hoarse noise that ripped from the pirate's throat. Sometimes the pain was too great to take in enough air to produce a proper scream.

Dorian knew that all too well.

"I'm going to slit your throat," he murmured to Druthers in a seductive whisper. "I'm going to watch the life drain out of your eyes as you struggle to draw breath and your lungs only fill with your own blood."

"Don't!" Farah's desperate plea stayed the draw of his knife across the throat. Light footsteps ran up behind him.

"Stay back, Farah. Let me finish this."

"You can't kill an unarmed man."

"Actually," he gritted out, his knife nicking into the thin, stubbled flesh of Druthers's neck, "the killing goes more smoothly once I've disarmed them."

"Dorian . . ." She let his whispered name trail into the quiet sounds of the river. "Please."

"He *threatened* you, Farah." The cold rage surged again. "He should not be allowed to live."

"It would be murder." Instead of censuring, her voice was gentle behind him, using warmth to slowly melt the ice instead of force to bash up against it. "If you kill him in cold blood, this horrid man will be another black stain upon your soul. Must you grant him that?"

Dorian stared down into the disgusting, broken face of Edmond Druthers, and knew he didn't want to add the man to the many that haunted his nightmares. Moreover, he didn't want to turn back around and have the blood that Farah saw on his hands be a stain of dishonor.

Retrieving his knife from Druthers's shoulder produced another tortured sound, but Dorian didn't stop there. He sliced through the tendon in the man's dominant arm. Edmond Druthers would never wield a weapon again.

"Dorian!" Farah gasped.

After wiping the blood from his blades on Druthers's coat, Dorian stood and faced his wife. "Not a stain, my dear," he said while replacing his weapons in their scabbards tucked beneath his coat. "But what's one more smudge?"

Farah's seemingly unearthly moonlight glow intensified as the corners of her mouth trembled before she fought off the mirth and pressed them together, adopting a stern look.

"Lord, you're a wicked man," she said wryly, as though she could think of nothing else and so she just shook her head in abject disbelief.

"So I've been told."

A gunshot shattered the darkness. Shouting downriver echoed across the piers. A splash. Repeating shots.

Dorian thrust Farah behind him and backed them both toward the crates where Murdoch had drawn his pistol.

Irritation stabbed through him as he identified the dark shapes with buttons that reflected the brilliant moonlight spilling onto the Executioner's Dock.

The tavern slut had been right when she said the night was full of shadows. In fact, those shadows had been full of the London Metropolitan Police.

A tall figure emerged from the army of coppers, wearing an impeccable gray suit and an air of superiority. "Lieutenant?" Carlton Morley's pistol was aimed right where Dorian's heart would go, his finger caressing the trigger with sensual promise.

A large blond bobby stepped from the line. "Yes, Chief Inspector?"

"Arrest them."

"Which ones?" the lieutenant asked, his eyes flicking from Farah with astonished recognition to Dorian with apprehension.

Morley wasn't glaring daggers at Dorian, but at Farah. "All of them."

CHAPTER SEVENTEEN

Farah clenched her hands in her lap and stared at the myriad of commendation certificates hanging behind Carlton Morley's intimidating executive desk. Next to her, Gemma sat in a similar posture, quiet and subdued.

Instead of taking his place of authority in the high-backed chair, Morley paced in front of it, his long legs eating up the space as he inspected the document held in hands shaking with rage. His collar was loosened, his unbound tie hanging limp around his neck. Without his jacket, Morley's gray vest accentuated the width of his shoulders against his lean waist. He was more disheveled than Farah had ever seen him, and guilt pricked at her skin and stuck in her throat.

Perhaps she should start with an apology. "Carlton—"

He held up his hand in a silencing gesture, not bothering to glance up from where his shrewd eyes flew across the official piece of paper.

Pressing her lips together, Farah winced. She hadn't wanted him to find out this way.

She thought of her husband and poor Murdoch stuck in the dank strong room directly below them. It cost so much for them to be locked away in a cell after all they had suffered, and she had to use her wits to get them released as soon as possible.

This was her fault, after all. She'd begged for their help.

After a moment Morley tossed the document onto his cluttered desk, thoroughly disgusted, and ran a hand through his already tousled hair. "Tell me this is some kind of joke." He whirled on her. "Or a nightmare."

"I can explain," Farah soothed.

"You're goddamned right, you'll explain yourself!" he thundered, his blue eyes swirling with storms. "Starting with just where the *bloody* hell you've been for four days!"

"I was hiding at Ben More Castle on the Isle of Mull," she answered honestly, her eyebrows lifting at Morley's uncharacteristic profanity. "There was a threat against my life."

"Where you—*married* the fucking Blackheart of Ben More?"

Farah bit her lip. "Yes."

Morley balled his fist and looked around his office decorated in a sort of organized chaos of paperwork, evidence, and a few intricate antique clocks that he had a passion for collecting and restoring. He obviously wanted to hit something, but couldn't find a place where the damage would be worth the cleanup.

That was Carlton Morley as Farah had known him for six years. Always considering the consequences of his actions. Calculating the risks and weighing the cause and effect of every decision.

Jamming both fists into his trouser pockets, he leaned against his desk and glowered at her. "Did he force you?"

"No." She didn't want to lie to him, so she promised herself she would tell the truth.

"Hurt you?"

"No." At least, not more than necessary, and not at all on purpose.

"Coerce you?"

Farah swallowed. "No," she lied. *Damn*. She needed to get them out of this so that she didn't end up as corrupted as her husband before the night was through. "I'm sorry that I've been absent, Carlton. If I haven't already been sacked, I need to resign my post as a clerk for Scotland Yard, collect my husband and his . . . valet, and take Gemma somewhere safe."

"The *hell* you will!" Carlton exploded. "Half of Scotland Yard witnessed your *husband* slaughter two smugglers. In addition, Edmond Druthers is being stitched up and having his broken jaw set by the surgeon." He grimaced at the word *husband* as though it tasted foul. "Then there's the unexplained, and no doubt connected, death of George Perth, whose body was found strangled on Executioner's Dock. Did you have anything to do with that?"

"You don't seriously believe I could strangle a man the size of George Perth?" Farah asked.

Gemma chortled beside her, but wisely refrained from remarking.

"Do you know who killed him?"

"I can honestly say that . . . the man who is responsible for George Perth's death is no legitimate acquaintance of mine," Farah hedged, certain she was digging her own pit in hell.

Morley's eyes narrowed to slits of pure skepticism. "That isn't what I asked."

"Furthermore," Farah continued, hoping to distract her former boss with more important things than the elusive and mysteriously frightening Christopher Argent, "if your men witnessed the encounter, they may add their statements to Miss Warlow's, Mr. Murdoch's, and mine that Mr. Blackwell was only defending himself, and Miss

Warlow and me, against attacking dock pirates who deserved every bit of what they got."

Morley's jaw jutted forward as he ground his teeth together. "I was too far away to see much of the particulars," he muttered. "But I didn't miss the part where you barely talked him out of committing cold-blooded murder." Morley pushed himself away from the desk with his hip. "You saved his life, because the moment he cut Druthers's throat, I'd have had the fodder to finally see him hanged."

"I owed him for saving my life," she replied carefully. "May I ask what you all were doing *en masse* at the docks at that hour?"

"We'd a tip that Druthers had a large shipment of smuggled goods arriving tonight. We'd staked out the position in the hopes of making a mass arrest."

"And so you did." Farah offered a solicitous smile. "Druthers and a large contingent of his smugglers are either dead or in your custody. The night was a success, and if you don't mind, I'd like to collect my party and go home." She stood, gathering her skirts.

"Sit. *Down*," Morley ordered.

Damn, she thought with a sigh. She sat.

Morley studied her for a long time, and Farah resolutely met his gaze. She'd done nothing of which she was ashamed. Only, Morley, a kind and honest man, had been hurt in all of this madness, and that was her one profound regret.

"I'm sorry for disappearing, Carlton. I realize the trouble and angst it must have caused not just you, but everyone here. It is unfair to you, especially after the evening we spent together." She remembered the kiss, the proposal. If she'd accepted it right then, would she still be alive? "I was—am in danger. Say what you will about Dorian Blackwell, he did save my life."

Morley flicked an uncomfortable glance at Gemma

Warlow before he said, "You could have come to me. *I* would have kept you safe."

Farah realized she must tread these waters carefully, for the sake of everyone involved. "I wasn't given that option. And I'm not sure that you could have, given the circumstances."

"But—Dorian Blackwell? You belong to *him* now? The marriage is legitimate?"

Farah knew he was asking if it was consummated and she blushed as she nodded, unable to say a word.

"*Why?* He's a monster. A murderer. I thought you were smarter than this. Better than the likes of *him.*"

A surprising protective defensiveness swelled in her breast for her criminal of a husband. "You don't know him, Carlton."

The disgust returned to the inspector's clear eyes. "God, Farah, listen to yourself! You sound like a bad cliché."

The words hurt because he meant them. Farah didn't mind losing Morley's romantic attentions, but losing his respect was one of the hardest things she'd had to face in a long time.

"Maybe I do," she murmured. "Maybe I am. But you don't understand what's at stake here, Carlton. Through Blackwell, I have the chance to regain something very precious that was taken from me a long time ago."

"And what's that?"

"My past."

He snorted, circling behind his desk and buttoning his collar. "Be a little less vague, if you please," he asked crisply.

"It will all make sense in time," Farah said gently. "But time is something you must grant us. You have no legal call to keep us here. If Dorian hadn't fought off those river pirates I'd probably be dead, or worse." The truth in her words sent a cold shudder down Farah's spine.

Anger seemed to drain from Morley's shoulders and he paused in the middle of retying his necktie, looking nothing more than tired and sad. "Do you love him?"

Farah had to look away. Her eyes found Gemma, who seemed just as interested in the answer. Her feelings for Dorian had become increasingly complex and opaque. But, as Morley had pointed out, she'd only known him four days. She'd begun to care for Dorian. To understand him. No. They were a long way from understanding each other. She was grateful to him. Wanted to help him and heal him. The *desire* to know and understand the enigma that was her husband drove her to hope for good things to come of whatever future they were to have together. Though he'd barely touched her body, he'd definitely left a mark on her heart. But . . . Love?

"I couldn't say." It was the most honest answer Farah could give him. "But I do know that although I like and respect you a great deal, I don't love you, and that you don't love me." She said this gently, the words devoid of cruelty or pity. "Accepting your proposal would have been a mistake. We both would have come to regret it, in time."

Morley finished tying his cravat and shrugged into his suit jacket, his attention on the discarded certificate of marriage on his desk. Picking it up, he studied it once more. "Perhaps you're right. You are a woman with more secrets and shadows than a man in my position could live down."

Distressed, Farah frowned. She'd never thought of herself in that way. It was Dorian Blackwell who owned the secrets and shadows, not she. Though, thinking back, she could count more than a few rather large secrets. They'd just been a part of her for so long, she'd begun to think of them as the truth.

Because the real truth had been not only painful, but dangerous.

Somewhere along the way, she'd lost Farah Townsend completely, and had become Mrs. Dougan Mackenzie.

Morley stepped around his desk and pushed the paper into her hands, slapping his finger against her name on the certificate. "Townsend?" He cocked a disbelieving eyebrow. "As in, the about-to-be-inaugurated Countess Farah Leigh Townsend? What is all this about? Some scheme you cooked up with your delinquent of a husband?"

"Don't be cruel, Carlton," Farah reprimanded sharply. "You'll lose the moral high ground."

"It would still be a long way to fall to reach *his* position."

"Maybe so," Farah conceded. "But regardless of all that, I was born Farah Leigh Townsend, and through the name of Blackwell, I'll be able to reclaim my title and my birthright."

"Do you realize how impossible that sounds? They found the missing Farah Townsend weeks ago. She's already met the Queen of England."

A familiar fear bubbled in Farah's middle. She wrapped one arm around herself as though to contain it, and met Morley square in the eye. What if this was a mistake? What if they failed? "The woman everyone knows as Farah Leigh Townsend is an imposter."

"Prove it."

"That'll be easy," Gemma cut in with a lift of her dirty shoulder. "Every whore in East London knows she's Lucy Boggs from 'er picture in the paper. More'n a few of us planned to blackmail 'er when she came into 'er money." Gemma cut off when she noticed both Farah and Morley were staring at her with twin expressions of incredulity.

Farah regained her voice first. "What—what did you say her name was?"

"Lucy Boggs. She's a whore, same as I, only younger and prettier. Was picked from the streets to work at some uppity place on the Strand called Regina's. Next thing we 'ear, she's a bloomin' countess in all the society papers." The wounded prostitute guffawed a few times, not appearing to feel the pain in her swollen lips and cheeks. "If Lucy Boggs is nobility, I'm the bloody Virgin Mary."

"Gemma!" For the second time that night, Farah threw her arms around the woman. "You may have just saved the day!"

"Awright, awright . . ." The woman shrugged out of her embrace, uncomfortable with the genuine show of affection. "Can't 'elp you out there in the real world. No one would take the word of a lot of cocksuckers like us over that of 'er magistrate 'usband, Mr. Warrington."

"What about Madame Regina, herself?" Farah asked, both her excitement and trepidation building in tandem. "As Lucy Boggs's employer, wouldn't her word have some clout?" She looked back at Morley who stood over them with his arms folded and a rather dazed expression frozen on his features.

Shaking his head as though to clear it, he didn't look at Farah, addressing Gemma, instead. "Miss Warlow, if you'd give us a moment alone. Mr. Beauchamp will give you tea and something to eat until the surgeon is available to see to your injuries."

"Fank you, Chief Inspector." Gemma flicked a concerned one-eyed look to Farah, who nodded, before sliding off her chair and stepping out of the office, closing the door behind her.

Morley shook his head, looking at her as though he'd never seen her before in his life.

"She's right, you know. Everyone knows it's too easy to pay a prostitute, or a madam, to do or *say* anything you like."

"I do realize that. We'll go about it in a different way."

"The official Queen's Bench decision on the case is tomorrow morning." Morley pointed at a discarded newspaper on his desk.

"Don't remind me." Farah held a hand to her fluttering stomach. This all seemed to be happening with the speed and inevitability of a runaway locomotive. The miraculous recovery of a very fake Farah Leigh Townsend. Escaping Warrington in the Yard. Her abduction and subsequent marriage to the Blackheart of Ben More. Returning to London. And tomorrow she would claim her birthright.

"All this time?" Morley asked. "A countess? Why didn't you . . . ? How long did you . . . ? What happened?"

"That is a very long story." Farah moved her hand to her head, a needling ache prickling behind her eyes.

"One that involved Dorian Blackwell?"

"Interestingly enough, yes, in a roundabout way." She sighed and stood, bringing herself closer to Morley's handsome, downturned face. Heart clenching, she reached up to his jaw. "I promise to explain when all of this business is handled."

Recovering from his shock, Morley closed his eyes, but then backed away from her touch and retreated to his territory on the opposite side of the desk. "In reality, I was never officially more than your employer. Regardless of what I said before, you don't owe me an explanation." He took in a deep breath, picking up a file and staring at it, though Farah was certain he couldn't even read the name in front of him at the moment. "How do you propose to reclaim your legacy?" he asked genially. "I assume Blackwell has some nefarious plan?"

Farah smiled a little. "All I have to do is prove that I'm the real Farah Townsend. I lived her life as a child, I'll know things about my parents, my home, my past, that the imposter couldn't possibly know. I only have to convince the court."

"It'll take more than that, I fear." Morley shrugged. "Paperwork. Documents like records of birth and records of where you spent your childhood as an orphan."

Farah blanched. "How did you know I was an orphan?"

He gave her a droll look and she realized the idiocy of the question before he answered.

"Farah, *your* childhood, *your* miraculous resurrection, has been all the society papers have reported on for weeks."

Farah had heard, of course, but she rarely wasted her time reading the society papers when there was a book to be had.

"I could help you," he offered without looking at her. "As you know, the records commissioner's office is attached to this building, and since it is the middle of the night I could—"

"Mr. Blackwell already has that well in hand." Farah grimaced.

Morley's eyes narrowed and she could almost hear him thinking. "When we brought him in, somehow he . . ." Morley squeezed the bridge of his nose and growled. "I should have known. It was too damned easy an arrest for the likes of him."

He looked up at her and they shared a knowing, frustrated chuckle over the infuriating man to whom she was now married. And just like that, the tension between them was dispelled, and the past became the past. A melancholy idea of what might have been and could never be.

"I'll release your husband and his valet," Morley said on an exhausted sigh. "But that doesn't mean I'm still not watching his every move."

"I know." Farah gave in to the impulse to hug him, but kept it brief and distant, for both their sakes.

"You're a good woman, Farah. I've always admired you." Morley paused, a muscle in his jaw working to hold something back. "If he ever hurts you—hell, if he makes you unhappy in any way, come to me. I'll sort him out."

Farah felt every ounce of tenderness she put into her smile. "Thank you, Carlton. And, you were wrong, you know, about only being my employer. You were—are also a very dear friend."

He gave his desk a wry smile. "Don't twist the knife any further."

"Good-bye," she murmured, reaching for the tarnished, well-used handle of his office door.

"Farah."

She turned back at the serious tone in his voice. "Yes?"

"Look into Madame Regina's. You happen to know the owner quite intimately."

"I don't. I've never met Madame Regina," Farah said.

"She's just the proprietor." An amused smile quirked his lips. "The owner is your husband, Dorian Blackwell."

CHAPTER EIGHTEEN

Farah had never felt so small and insignificant in her entire life. She'd been to the Royal Courts of Justice innumerable times in her career with the Yard, and walked past the impressive Gothic white-stone building on her way to work every day. But her presence had always been part of the silent workings of the legal process, on hand with documents and such. Never had her voice echoed in the hall of Her Majesty's High Court, and *never* in front of the Queen's Bench.

It amazed Farah that even here, in the imposing buttressed stone of the great hall, men, women, and nobility alike avoided the path of Dorian Blackwell. Though the hall bustled with more members of the *ton* and agents of the crown than Farah had ever seen, she and her husband were still able to make a rapid pace.

Up until the previous year, the King's Bench had held its court in Westminster Hall, as it had since the eleventh century. Now, by royal writ of Queen Victoria, herself, the

King's Bench became the Queen's Bench and moved from Westminster to the Royal Courts of Justice on the Strand. Though, as it had for hundreds of years, the High Court of Justice remained the epicenter of the sovereign's official word and royal administration in the realm. The office of lord chief justice had long since replaced the presence of the regent at court proceedings, and as such became one of the most powerful seats in the empire.

Farah found it difficult to look anyone in the eye as all who'd gathered followed their progression toward the Chambers of the High Court. The byzantine cathedral feel of the great hall intensified as voices hushed upon their approach. The hush wasn't full of reverence, but curiosity and speculation.

Farah was certain her heartbeat could be heard by all as she watched the intricate geometric designs of the marble floor disappear beneath the billowing skirts of the midnight silk dress Madame Sandrine had delivered late last evening.

The prior night hadn't done much, if anything, to dispel the anxiety tightening an iron band around Farah's lungs. Once she'd collected her husband and Murdoch from the reception sergeant at Scotland Yard, they'd taken a cab to Dorian's luxurious terrace in Mayfair. The blood had been wiped from his face, but it still stained the crisp collar of his shirt and darkened his already black jacket.

Her husband had yet to utter more than a crisp, monosyllabic reply to the myriad of questions, gratitude, and apologies she'd showered upon him.

"Are you all right?" she'd asked.

"Quite."

"Did they hurt you?"

"No."

"You saved our lives at the docks, you know."

"Yes."

"I'm sorry for involving you in such a dangerous misadventure. But Gemma and I are supremely grateful for what you and your men did."

"Hmm." Once his pathetic communication dissolved to nonexistent, Murdoch had picked up the conversation on his behalf.

"Think nothing of it, lass," he'd soothed, casting a dark look at Blackwell. "We'll get Miss Warlow on the way in the morning."

"I'm just glad I was able to persuade Chief Inspector Morley to release you so quickly. I couldn't bear the thought of your incarceration overnight, or longer."

"Ye canna know how much we appreciate it." Murdoch had patted her hand in a fatherly gesture.

At that, Blackwell had leaned forward, unlatched the door to the cab, and leaped out before the driver had fully come to a stop. He disappeared into the night and Farah had not seen him again until he came to collect her and Murdoch the following morning to convey them to court.

Murdoch had assured her again and again that their short time in the strong room had been not only uneventful, but rather amenable. "The bobbies were fair and civil, and Dorian even conversed with one of his contacts, though I didna catch what was said."

"Then why is he so upset?" Farah had asked.

Murdoch shrugged and regarded her with a little pity. "Canna say, lass, just that Blackwell has his moods sometimes. Doona fash yerself over it. Just get some sleep, we've a big day tomorrow."

Sleep had been next to impossible, even in the elegant, luxurious bed. Finally, Farah had drifted into a restless sort of limbo, tossing about in the darkness, her stomach rolling and her jaw clenching as images of the past haunted her dreams. Her father's pale, waxy face at his wake, the

cheeks sunken in from dehydration brought on by the devastating illness. Warrington, who'd seemed like a giant to
a seven-year-old, bending down to inform her of their en-
gagement. Sister Margaret's intimidating robes and wim-
ple. Father MacLean's thin, lascivious mouth. Dougan's
dark eyes and sharp features. Small and symmetrical,
twisted with boyish mischief and incessant curiosity.

She'd called out to him in her dreams, begged him to
run. To survive. To live on so she didn't have to face this
horrid world with only a dark and broken man beside her.

"I'm right here," Dougan had crooned through her
dream, his face sad and fierce. But his *voice*. His voice was
nothing like she remembered. It melted into something
dark and cavernous. A man's voice. Sinister, dangerous,
and smooth. Like brimstone gliding over ice.

You're not *here,* Farah had thought as she felt herself
sinking into the void of oblivion. *I'm so lost. So lonely.
So—afraid.*

"Sleep, Fairy mine. You're safe." A slight tickle at her
scalp told her that Dougan had wound his finger into a
ringlet, pulled it softly, and watched it bounce back into
place before winding it again. Like always.

He *was* here. She was safe.

She'd slept then, and awoke with the crisp, salted tracks
of dried tears running into her hair.

Farah knew she should be thinking on the enormity of
what was about to happen as they stood in front of the
gilded doors of the High Court. But she found herself
studying Dorian's profile, interrupted by the black strap of
his eye patch, and wondering if Dougan ever featured in
the terrors of *his* dreams.

Or if she did.

She wanted to cry out for him to wait when he reached
for the doors to the courtroom, but she forced herself to remain stoic. Like him. If Dorian Blackwell could maintain

his composure after everything he'd been through, she could, too. Throwing her shoulders back and steeling her spine ramrod straight, she tilted her chin a notch above stubborn to pretentious.

Eschewing polite behavior, Dorian preceded her into the courtroom instead of holding the door open for her.

Farah couldn't have been more grateful.

Proceedings had already begun, and Farah realized with a start they were technically committing an act against the crown.

An astonished hush blanketed the dark wood of the stately High Court room. Those who crammed the pewlike benches turned back at their entry, very much like an audience at a church wedding. Except, no one was pleased at their arrival. The kindest expression Farah could find was one of shock. It all disintegrated from there to disapproval, disbelief, and in some cases, outrage. She followed him up the wide aisle, the thick burgundy carpet muffling her steps.

"Mr. Blackwell!" bellowed a smallish man with an inappropriately large head made all the more bulbous by a long, curled, snowy wig. He sat behind the tall dais, the middle of three such attired men, his station dignified by the silver seal affixed to the middle of his black robes. "What is the meaning of this impudence?"

Of course Lord Chief Justice Sir Alexander Cockburn was acquainted with Dorian Blackwell, or at least knew him on sight. The justice had a reputation for sport, adventure, socializing, and womanizing. Though he was something of a legal genius, it was a subject of much contention how the Scotsman had risen to such an illustrious position with his besmirched reputation.

Farah stared at the broadness of her husband's back with stunned amazement. Did Dorian have anything to do with Lord Chief Justice Cockburn's stunning career trajectory? It wouldn't surprise her in the least.

"My lord." Dorian executed a formal bow in a manner that could arguably be called mocking. "May I present to you the Right Honorable Farah Leigh Townsend, Countess Northwalk."

An audible gasp echoed through the courtroom and beyond, as some of the crowd outside the doors pressed forward behind Farah to witness these highly unprecedented happenings in an already high-profile case.

"This is an outrage! I demand these insolent criminals be arrested at once!" Harold Warrington perpetually appeared to have just sucked on a lemon. In spite of that, he had the handsome and hearty form of someone born to farmer's stock rather than the historically incestuous aristocracy. An infamous hedonist, his skin and hair hadn't fared well against the years of overindulgence, but his stature evoked that of Goliath as he surveyed the court with the air of a royal rather than the civic servant he was.

The sharp rap of a gavel pierced the bench, but it was not the lord chief justice who'd employed its use. The man to his left sat behind the nameplate of Justice Roland Phillip Cranmer III, though everyone knew Justice Cranmer had recently and mysteriously gone missing.

Farah recognized the face behind the gavel as Sir Francis Whidbey, a newly appointed justice of the High Court. He exchanged covert glances with her husband as he addressed Sir Warrington. "Sit down, Warrington. I'll remind you that you're not a member of the peerage as yet, and are still an officer of this court who should know better than to speak out of turn!"

Farah was acutely aware that she and Dorian had only just committed that selfsame act, but she wisely kept her own counsel. Besides, she couldn't have spoken if commanded to at the moment. So much for her self-possession.

Dorian approached the bench without being invited,

which elicited more gasps and even brought the two red-coated queen's guards posted at the edges of the bench rushing to restrain him.

"My lords, I have here official documents supporting the validity of our claim." He brandished a file of paperwork he'd pulled from his coat. "Including Lady Townsend's birth certificate, church records of her years at Applecross Orphanage, the falsified record of her death, and also—"

"Where did you obtain these records, Blackwell?" the lord chief justice demanded, holding up his hand to stay the guards.

"I also have included a copy of our marriage license." Blackwell blithely ignored the justice's question. "The importance of which we can discuss later." He threw a look to the assembly that had a ripple of ironic laughter passing around the room.

"Impossible! I have a legal and binding betrothal contract signed by her father!" Warrington exploded to his feet, ignoring the grasping entreaties of his wigged lawyer.

The third justice leaned forward. "And so you've *claimed* that you have already married her, Warrington. So, why the objection?"

"You—you're right, my lord." He motioned to a dainty, well-dressed blond woman at his elbow with wide and vacant blue eyes. "This is my *wife*, Farah Leigh Warrington, Countess Northwalk. Formerly Farah Leigh Townsend. How dare you try to usurp her birthright, you conniving liar!" Warrington turned his wrath toward Farah, his already ruddy skin taking on the patina of a tomato.

Farah, however, was transfixed by the third justice, recognition storming through her that had nothing to do with her past seventeen years as Mrs. Mackenzie.

"Rower," she breathed, reading the nameplate in front of his wizened face.

"Speak up, lady," the lord chief justice commanded.

Farah glided toward the face from her past that was lined with two lost decades of age, but still had very much the same piercing eyes and severe features. "You are the Baronet Sir William Patrick Rowe, whose estate is in Hampshire," she said. The crowd strained to hear her low voice; such was the silence that a loud breath could be heard grating out of someone's lungs. "You—you were a lieutenant in the Queen's Rifle Brigade under my father, Captain Robert Townsend, Earl Northwalk. You sculled together at Oxford, and my father called you 'Rower.'"

The man in the wig looked stunned and narrowed his eyes at Farah. "Come closer," he ordered.

Farah approached the bench. "I remember your thirtieth birthday party," she murmured to him, "because you were kind enough to share a piece of spice cake with me, as it was my fifth birthday on the day after. Yours is September twenty-first, I believe. And mine is September twenty-second."

"Good Lord," Justice Rowe exclaimed, peering into her eyes with a similar recognition. "I do remember that!"

"Anyone could have attained that information!" Warrington protested. "Don't let this—this renowned brigand and his doxy make a mockery of this esteemed court!"

"I've heard enough out of you, Warrington!" the lord chief justice warned. "Next outburst and I'll have you banished from this courtroom!"

Warrington's red color intensified to a purple hue, but he sat, shaking with barely leashed rage.

And not a little bit of fear, Farah assumed.

Lord Chief Justice Cockburn turned back to Dorian, affording Farah less than a cursory glance. "Mr. Warrington has a point. He's provided documents identical to those you have and has the added superior claim. He was steward to the late Earl Robert Townsend and trustee of his estate. He's known Farah Townsend since birth, and has a long-standing betrothal contract. What cause have we to doubt his wife's claim to the Townsend legacy?"

Farah glared at Lucy Boggs, who was silently twirling a ringlet, obviously fabricated by a curling iron, around one anxious finger.

"I have witnesses, my lords." Dorian swept his hand to a pew at the back of the court.

Warrington's lawyer finally objected. "This is highly irregular and I would like to request that we meet in chambers to discuss how to further proceed."

"Bollocks!" Warrington's chair scraped against the floor as he leaped to his feet once more. "There is no reason to delay this any further. Blackwell has fabricated witnesses and I want a chance to refute them. After almost twenty years I have uncovered the missing Northwalk heiress and I *demand* to be granted what is mine!"

Justice Whidbey turned his hawklike face toward Warrington. "Don't you mean, for your wife to be granted what is hers?" he queried. "Surely you know that when one is not born a peer of the realm, as husband to a countess, one's title as earl will be a courtesy only. One would be called 'Lord' and granted stewardship of the properties, but the other rights and privileges of peerage will only be granted your heir and issue."

Farah gaped, turning a wide-eyed glance over her shoulder at Blackwell. He stood at the mouth of the aisle with his hands clasped behind him, seemingly unaffected by the justices' words.

His sable eye met hers and Farah gasped. He *knew*. He'd known all along that he wouldn't be granted the rights and privileges of nobility. He'd gone to all this trouble, played this dangerous and complicated game of chess, possibly even manipulating the seats of the High Court of England, to help her reclaim her birthright.

And for what?

Certainly his name would be prefixed with "Lord," but as far as she could tell, that didn't come with half the power and esteem his wealth and reputation already afforded him.

Why had he done all this? What was his intention?

"We'll hear your witnesses, Blackwell, but let me warn you that you stand on unsteady ground with this court. You and this lady are very much in danger of egregious consequences." The lord chief justice gave them each a practiced warning glance.

Warrington glared daggers at her, but allowed his lawyer to wrestle him into his chair.

"So it has ever been, my lords." Dorian bowed at the waist and then turned to the pews in the back with a sweep of his arm. "Let me present to you Signora Regina Vicente, sole proprietor of a rather popular gentleman's club here along the Strand."

A tall, stately woman in a grand dress of dark plum stood and excused herself to make a procession up the aisle toward them. Her caramel skin and exotic bones proudly stated her Italian heritage, and she looked like a bronzed Roman goddess in a sea of pasty Brits. Her train was as long as any countess's and her dark eyes sparked with intelligence and mirth.

At least someone was enjoying themselves.

"Madame Regina is prepared to testify that she has employed this woman who claims to be Farah Townsend as Lucy Boggs in her establishment some five months, before turning her employ to Warrington for a large sum." Dorian gestured to the sheaf of paper in the woman's silk-gloved hand.

Warrington pounded the table, but barely restrained himself.

"Is this true?" Justice Whidbey asked of the woman known as Madame Regina.

"It is, my lord," she purred in a sultry Italian accent. "I have brought you the documents of legitimacy I demand from my employees, and also the receipt for money exchanged between Mr. Warrington and me."

Whidbey held out his hand for them, and she glided toward him, handing over the crisp, official papers.

Warrington's lawyer stood. "This is a joke. This story, these documents, they could both be forgeries produced by the infamous Blackheart of Ben More and this purveyor of filth and sin!" He gestured to Regina, who only quirked one dark eyebrow.

"He makes an excellent argument, Blackwell," Lord Chief Justice Cockburn stated.

"I suppose he does." Blackwell gave a very serious, meaningful look to Whidbey and Cockburn, ignoring Rowe. "Madame Regina has many, *many* stories to tell. Who's to decide whether they're truth or slander?"

Was it her imagination, Farah wondered, or did the two men behind the bench pale a little? Had Dorian just issued a veiled threat to the highest judiciary branch of government in the British Empire? In front of *everyone*? Farah felt like she might be sick.

In the silence that followed, Dorian gestured to another woman in the pew. "If you're in need of another witness, how about this one?"

Another rumble of surprise mirrored Farah's inner feelings as a stooped old woman in a black-and-white habit shuffled toward them. "Sister Margaret?" she breathed.

"Its Mother Superior now," the woman corrected in her unmistakable crisp tone of cold piety.

Farah narrowed her eyes at the woman, remembering all of the harsh words and even harsher beatings she'd piled upon Dougan. Farah didn't want to look at her, couldn't fathom why the crotchety nun would speak in her defense.

"That is your witnessing signature on the death certificate of Farah Leigh Townsend dated seventeen years ago, is it not?" Dorian asked in a voice that had lost all of its prior mockery or even brash arrogance. His gloved hands fisted.

"Aye," she affirmed.

"Explain to the court, then, why you falsified this official document," Dorian ordered, returning the nun's sharp look with a jagged one of his own.

"She was a precocious, heathen child." Though the nun referred to her, she spoke of Farah as though she didn't stand right in front of her. "She always followed the troublemakers and ruffians, one in particular, who had the very devil in him."

"He did not," Farah defended.

"He killed a priest!" the woman hissed. "Even ye canna deny that. Ye were there in my arms whilst he did it. Screaming his name like a possessed banshee."

"You knew that priest was a—"

"That isn't relevant," Dorian interrupted them both, his voice hard and cold. "What is pertinent to the moment is that you knew Farah Leigh Townsend *wasn't* dead."

"She ran off after that devil Dougan Mackenzie when the police took him away." Margaret sneered. "I had fifty other children in my care. I couldna risk the reputation of Applecross over one missing girl. And so, yes, I falsified the document at the request of Sir Warrington." She pointed her gnarled, arthritic finger at the man.

Those congregated in the courtroom gasped, and turned their collective heads toward the accused.

"Lies! *I* married Farah Townsend! The Northwalk fortune belongs to me!" Warrington exclaimed, leaping up again. "Tell them, Farah, tell them who you are!" With crazed eyes, he shook Lucy's shoulders with bruising force, and she uttered a soft cry of fear.

The lord justice's gavel pounded a deafening repeat

against the dais. "I warned you, Warrington, you will be removed at once!" He motioned to the queen's guard who seized a shouting Warrington and removed him from the room.

"I will have what's mine! I will have justice!" Warrington threatened. "Farah, prove your worth! Prove to them who you are!"

Lucy stood, her blue eyes wide with fear and tears, looking like she wanted to bolt.

The chief lord justice pointed his gavel at her, his large head swiveling on his almost comically diminutive shoulders. "The next word spoken out of turn will earn the speaker a week behind bars, is that understood?"

Lucy nodded mutely, and the court's notice seemed to return to the nun in tandem.

"Tell me," the lord chief justice began. "You might be stripped of your habit and honorable name within your papist church for your lies. Not to mention the likelihood you'll be brought up on charges of fraud. Why come forward now?"

Sister Margaret glanced at Dorian before answering. "When one lives as long as I have, one realizes it is almost time to face God and answer for my sins. This is one less mark against my soul. I care not for earthly things. I only want peace with the Lord."

"And it is your sworn oath that the woman standing before us here is Farah Leigh Townsend?" Justice Rowe asked, gesturing to Farah.

"Yes, she hasna changed in almost twenty years." The nun flicked a glance full of hatred at Dorian. "Still canna resist the draw of the devil."

A tremor sliced through Farah at the old woman's words. Dougan had called himself a demon the first time they'd met. If that sweet boy had been a demon, then Dorian Blackwell certainly was the devil.

And Farah was, indeed, helpless to resist his dark allure.

"I'll admit, Blackwell." The lord chief justice eyed them both. "I rather don't know what to make of this. Two women claiming to be the Countess Northwalk. Each of them married to a self-serving scoundrel. I'm almost convinced to grant your wife's claim. But I'm not sure it would hold up if appealed to the lord high chancellor, or Her Majesty."

Dorian lifted a large shoulder in a debonair gesture. "Anyone who knows me knows I would marry no imposter. My lords, *this* was Farah Leigh Townsend, now Farah Leigh Blackwell. Of that I am certain. Tell me what you require for further proof, and I'll provide it to you."

Justice Rowe stood, reaching beneath his wig to itch at his scalp. "I can settle this," he declared. "With your permission, my lord chief justice."

"By all means." Cockburn gestured for him to continue.

The French army could have invaded London and the congregation still would have remained where they sat, silent and riveted on what was to happen next.

"Both of you approach," Rowe ordered, pointing to the carpet in front of his bench.

Palms drenching the inside of her gloves, Farah worked her throat over a desperate swallow that pushed against the gem-encrusted collar of her fine dress. She hoped to look more dignified than she felt as she walked the few paces to stand in front of Justice Rowe. Or below, rather, as the seats of the High Court were intolerably high.

A rustle of skirts told her that Lucy Boggs now stood next to her, but Farah didn't dignify her presence by acknowledging her.

"Answer me this one question, and I'll recommend to this court and to Her Majesty that your title and lands be returned to you." Though he spoke in a conversational register, his voice carried through the silent hall.

He narrowed his eyes at Farah. "You referenced my thirtieth birthday party in which you were in attendance at Northwalk Abbey."

"Yes, my lord," Farah rasped.

"Which one of you can recall the birthday present I gave you that year? I'll provide a hint to jog your memory, it was inside that little jewelry box with a painted ballerina on it. I recall little Farah Townsend's fondness for ballerinas."

Farah's heart sputtered and died. She frantically searched her memory. When that produced nothing, she searched the face of the justice in front of her, who seemed as cold and stoic as Dorian. Her breath began to fail her. This couldn't be. Her future couldn't be slipping through her hands because of the faulty memory of a five-year-old girl. She looked back at Dorian, who studied her intently. What she read in his face almost caused her to faint.

It was the closest thing to helplessness the Blackheart of Ben More could convey.

Turning back to look up at the three imposing wigged men, she couldn't form the words that would crush her credibility in front of all these people. Tears burned in her eyes. A stone of terror and loss formed in her throat, threatening to choke her. Oh, if only it would hurry!

"Yes?" Rowe prodded sharply.

"I—I—" A hot tear spilled from the corner of her eye and burned a trail down the side of her face. "My lord, I do not recall receiving such a gift on that birthday or any birthday. From you or—or anyone else."

Farah couldn't stop a glance at Lucy next to her, whose blue eyes now glittered with malice and victory. "It was a trinket, my lord," she guessed in a prim voice, her gaze searching the man's face with obvious assessment. "My childhood memories are vague, so much has happened since then, and I am recovering from a head wound." She held a lace glove to her forehead with an overdramatic flare "But it was a necklace, wasn't it? One that sparkled, or a bracelet?" She shrugged her shoulder with a coy blink of her lashes. "I was so small and my memory shoddy due to the injury, you see, so I simply can't remember which."

Farah had to swallow convulsively. It was a good guess, as guesses go. Convincing and probable, if not likely. The excuse of the head wound was a good one.

Damn it, why couldn't she remember? Why had she failed so utterly? A jewelry box? Ballerinas? She'd been such active girl that any jewelry she'd been given would have been lost or broken right away. It was Faye Marie who'd loved—

"My *sister,*" she gasped, then louder. "My sister!" She clasped her hands together in a pleading gesture. "My lord, I beg pardon of you, but you're mistaken. I believe you gifted that treasure box to my older sister, Faye Marie. *She's* the one who loved ballerinas. I was obsessed with—"

"Pegasus." The old justice's eyes melted from cold to kindness. "It was a trick question. I'd forgotten your birthday was so close to mine, and shared my spice cake out of pure guilt." His lined face wrinkled as he smiled with a fond memory. "You were a kind little soul, unspoiled for a girl raised in such wealth. You forgave me instantly and informed me that spice cake was, indeed, your favorite present ever received."

Farah began to tremble, great quaking shivers of relief making her legs unsteady. Dorian was there, his strong, gloved hands propping her shoulders up.

"Thank you," she whispered, unsure to whom she was speaking as the room tilted and swayed. "Thank you."

"You have your father's shock of light hair and your mother's lovely gray eyes," the justice continued. "I've been half convinced it was really you since you walked into the courtroom."

The lord chief justice cleared the surprise out of his throat before rapping his gavel to silence the wave of whispered exclamations echoing in the hall. "Nothing is final until I have the writ of the Queen," he said. "But I don't think I'm presumptuous in offering my congratulations, *Lady* Farah Leigh Blackwell, Countess Northwalk."

"Thank you, my lord justice!" Farah's face split into a smile so wide it made her cheeks ache. She turned to Dorian and threw her arms around him. "Thank you!"

He stiffened inside her embrace and she remembered herself, pulling away quickly. She didn't dare look up at him just then, remembering he was still angry about something. Reaching for him in this public forum couldn't have helped the situation.

"Arrest this woman, Lucy Boggs, and hold her for investigation," Rowe commanded.

The lord chief justice leaned over his desk toward Farah. "May I ask you, Lady Blackwell, just where you have been all this time?"

"I—took a job at Scotland Yard under an assumed name," she answered honestly.

"Why in God's name would you do that?" he asked with an incredulous laugh.

Dorian cut in. "My lord, I've brought two more witnesses who would speak to an evil conspiracy on the part of Sir Warrington. Lady Blackwell was in hiding because she knew he was a threat to her life. My agent Christopher Argent and Inspector McTavish of Scotland Yard are both willing to testify that Warrington approached them about payment for the assassination of Lady Blackwell. I request he be arrested—for his own safety as well as hers," he added.

"So ordered!" The lord chief justice banged his gavel one last time. "And may I add my congratulations to you both on your nuptials?"

CHAPTER NINETEEN

Dorian looked out of the third-story window of his London home and pondered the storm clouds gathering over Hyde Park. He'd tried to open the window and let in the cool wind of the approaching storm, but the ancient, wrought-iron lock handle had been stuck in the upright position for so many decades it may as well have been welded.

He ached for Ben More. For the concealing mists and the untamed sea. For the cold stone fortress whose halls he haunted at night like a restless spirit. There were too many people down there in the city. Too much color and noise, pleasure and pain, need and want and movement. Chaos in its purest form. So many suffered bereft of care. So many lived without a name. So many died, *everyone* died.

Even the powerful Dorian Blackwell. Though he'd made a name that was recognized in every corner of the realm and beyond, one day fate would pay him back for all the trouble he'd caused. And the empire would churn on, expanding and accumulating. Perhaps reaching to encompass the world, somehow. It wasn't impossible. With their intrepid and enterprising cousins across the pond to the west, and their far-reaching interests in the east, perhaps in a hundred years or so, they'd all be connected. The economy would expand. Telegraphs would improve. Technology advance. And the world would become a small and manageable place, nothing but a ball trapped in the hands of greedy men like him until they closed their fists and crushed it.

And where did that leave him? What part of that inevitability did he control? More than most. Less than he'd like. A truly insignificant amount in the grand, global, eternal scheme of things. Damned irritating, that. The more one conquered, the more conquest was presented. Where did it end?

Taking his eye patch off, Dorian scrubbed his tired eyes and plunged his hands through his hair, scoring his scalp in frustration before leaning against the windowpane on one outstretched hand.

He'd done this for as long as he could remember. Controlled, dominated, and manipulated all those within his purview. First Newgate. Then Whitechapel, stretching his influence to the entire East End. It was never enough. None of his victories had ever made him feel safe or satiated his incessant need for *more*. Not manipulating members of Parliament. Not fixing judicial appointments or socially and economically crushing members of the peerage. Not reaching across the Atlantic and dominating Wall Street.

What was left to take? Without a Napoleonic motion of conquest on a corporate and imperial scope, he'd reached a sort of pinnacle.

And he felt as lowly as he ever had.

A blue eye reflected at him from the windowpane. The ghost of a boy long dead, and yet who lived on. Perhaps not in name, or perhaps in name only.

Who knew anymore?

For at this moment Dorian realized that, though he controlled the machinations of so much, he'd lost control of one small, four-chambered organ. One whose existence had been in doubt until now. It wasn't that the Blackheart of Ben More hadn't been born with a heart. It was that he'd not been in possession of it for nearly twenty long years.

And he had to abandon it, before the one who held it uncovered the secret buried within.

A tingle at the base of his neck and a quickening of his blood alerted him to her approach before the rustle of her skirts swept into the long solar.

"Dorian?"

A distant growl of thunder answered her. He didn't.

Of course, Farah was never one to be deterred by brooding, scowling men. Damn her. She moved closer when she should flee. She soothed when she should scold. It had always been thus.

"Dorian, I know you're cross with me," she began. "Today was quite a victory, and I'd like to celebrate it as friends."

She came to a stop behind him. Close. Too close.

"Tell me what I've done? What may I do to put things right between us?"

She could stop torturing him in that fucking dress, for one. She could cease smelling like lilac water and springtime. She could cease being the voice in his head, encouraging his repressed humanity to take root.

"You can leave," Dorian clipped. "Go to your father's in Hampshire. Reclaim your birthright."

"Won't you—come with me?" she ventured.

"I'd rather not."

Her sharp intake of breath pricked a hole in his own lungs.

"I know that being locked up yesterday must have been rather awful for you." She changed tactics. "I am sorry that you had to go through that because of something I asked you to do. I want to thank you for saving my friend and I hope that, in time, you'll forgive me the pain it caused you."

He didn't look at her. Couldn't look at her. Not now. Let her think what she would. If he ignored her for long enough she'd give up and leave.

"If you think about it," she continued, forcing brightness into her tone. "It all ended rather well as Gemma was able to help us expose Lucy Boggs for who she really is and so—that was helpful—at least."

Dorian continued staring, the jutting iron latch of the window his focal point. Maybe if he became cold enough. Hard enough. The ice he'd formed would turn him to stone. The vibrating that seemed to begin in his soul and ripple through his veins would freeze and still. He would have some fucking peace. The thoughts that tortured him. The emotions that heated him. The urges that tempted him. They would be encased behind an impenetrable fortress of his own making. He was a stone. He was a glacier. He was—

"Dorian. Please!" Farah seized his arm, tugging at it in an attempt to turn him toward her.

Before he was fully aware of his actions, he spun and seized her wrist, brandishing it between their bodies. "How many times do I have to tell you *not* to reach for me?"

Farah was staring at where his hand gripped her most delicate wrist with something like awe. Dorian glanced at it, too.

He wasn't wearing gloves. The first time he'd actually touched her, and it had been in violence.

Fuck.

"I know," she acknowledged with only a little regret. "I'm sorry. I can't seem to help myself. It's like you call to me, like you *need* me to reach out." She uncurled her fingers, stretching them toward him.

The anger Dorian had been fighting since his most recent arrest flared anew. "Did you reach out to Morley?" he growled, tossing her wrist away from him.

Her brow furrowed as she rubbed at the skin he'd just released. "What?"

Dorian advanced, fury tightening his chest and lungs, deepening his voice to a snarl. "I know you were alone with him."

"How do you know that?" she hedged.

His fear flared to all-out suspicion. "How do you *think*? I have informants everywhere." But not inside that office. Not behind that closed door. The possibilities had been driving him mad. "Did he put his hands on you? Did you kiss him again?" What had she had to do with Morley to get the chief inspector to release them so quickly? What promises had she made? What demands had she fulfilled?

"No!" Her eyes widened, filled with uncomfortable doubt. "I mean—I hugged him good-bye. I touched his face."

The picture of even that made him crazed. He searched for a lie in her liquid-silver eyes. "Did you tell him you regretted marrying me? That you wished you'd said yes to him? That you *belonged* to him?" Dorian felt like a monster. The ice wasn't there anymore. It hadn't just melted, a foreign inferno had disintegrated it with alarming swiftness and intensity. Now he was flooded with liquid fire. Boiling with jealousy. Where was his chill? Where was his armor of ice and calm? Why couldn't he control this tempestuous firestorm of possession and fear and anger and despair?

She should not have reached for him.

"I—I . . ." Farah stared at him as though he'd become

a foreign creature. A monster of darkness and rage and loss.

And lust. He was so fucking hard.

Dorian reached behind him and ripped the golden-tasseled silk rope that held the drape back from the window.

Farah retreated a step, but he seized her before she could turn and run. "You'll never belong to another, Farah." He growled, looping the thick cords around each of her thin wrists as she struggled.

"Dorian—"

He jerked her toward him, cutting off her protest with his lips. Letting her feel the true strength of his hands for the first time as they shackled her arms. He could break her. So easily. Her bones were so small, like a bird's, her skin so soft and translucent. The tiny webs of blue veins on her wrists and throat so delicate in contrast to the thicker ones pulsing beneath his skin.

How could someone so damned fragile hold the power to destroy a monster like him?

"You're *mine*!" he snarled against her surrendering mouth. "*Only* mine."

He might have been able to stop if she hadn't kissed him back.

Even while grappling with this new beast of fire she'd provoked, she didn't know the danger she toyed with. Didn't know the consequences of her actions.

Dorian fought with the strength of a drowning man, but in the end, the beast won out. He'd always known it would.

Bending her over the window seat, he looped her bound hands over the ancient iron window latch, imprisoning her there.

She let out a whimper as he flung her skirts above her waist, and another as her underthings disintegrated in his hands.

He tested her slit as he freed his erection. A river of moisture drenched his fingers and his desire flared impossibly hotter.

He breached her body with one brutal thrust. Claimed her with the second. Branded her with his third. She cried out only a little. Her feminine muscles bearing down against his invasion for only a moment before drawing him in.

Mine. He drove forward.

Only mine. He seized the soft flesh of her ass, spreading it for his view. Watching his cock spear into her with deep, devastating thrusts.

The sight was too much, and he roared his brutal anger out against the window as pulses of fire poured into her receiving body. Sweat bloomed beneath his clothing, his hair fell into his eyes. His hands clutched at the globes of her ass with bruising force, as agonizing torrents of pleasure burst through him.

Thunder roared back at him from the sky, and the first drops of the coming storm pelted the window. It cooled his fire, but only a little. Once the orgasm passed, Dorian paused only to pull the pins out of her tidy hair, remaining buried deep inside her warm, wet flesh.

He bent over her, the width of his shoulders engulfing the slimness of hers. "I'm like this all the bloody time around you. I hate it. Do you know that? I have no control. I just want to fuck and fuck and fuck until nothing matters anymore. Until we can no longer move our limbs or lift our heads to eat." He flexed his still-hard cock inside of her. "This is supposed to go away after I come. But it doesn't. Not with you, *wife*. My passion is this insatiable perversion."

Her hair tumbled down her back, falling in a tumultuous curtain of silvery ringlets across her face and onto the red window seat.

"It will destroy you," he bit out, burying his hand in her hair as he surged forward again. "It will consume you."

"Dorian—please!" Her voice trembled, her muscles clenched around his shaft.

"I'm sorry," he gasped as a new blaze ignited on the embers of his previous climax. She would hate him. He already hated himself. But she felt so good, and he'd waited so long. "I'm sorry but I—I can't stop."

"No," she gritted out, her voice low and guttural. "Please—faster."

He fucked her then. One hand bracing her hip, the other grasping the hair at her scalp, imprisoning her head and exposing her throat as he pistoned into her tight body again and again.

Little pants of demand escaped her. Tight whimpers of pain or pleasure. Then she bucked against him, a reedy cry becoming a shrill one. She twisted and writhed, pulled and arched as her intimate muscles drew another soul-shattering climax from him. He could feel his seed leaving him and pouring into her. He sank deep enough to touch her womb with his own flesh. That such a thing was possible seemed like a miracle. *She* was a miracle. He'd found her. After all these years.

Mine.

His body and mind, for once, were in agreement. She could never doubt his claim on her. A claim he'd staked seventeen long years ago.

My Fairy.

The words echoed against the window. They both stopped breathing.

A tremor visibly ran down her spine and passed between where they were connected, undulating up his spine and ending at the base of his neck.

"Dougan?" she gasped.

CHAPTER TWENTY

He was gone.

Farah leaned her weight on shaking, outstretched arms and tried to absorb the paralyzing shock. The brittle sound of breaking glass and splintering wood echoed down the hallway and carried for some distance. Then all was silent.

This couldn't be real. Couldn't be happening. Had she really heard that name whispered against her neck? Felt the truth of it shudder through her in that unmistakable voice?

Against the soft window cushion, she struggled to catch her breath. Aftershocks of the mind-shattering climax still caused her inner muscles to clench and pulse. The slick leavings of their sex quickly became cold, exposed to the empty solarium with its marble floors and many windows.

That name. She'd never forget how he said that name. Farah realized that Dorian Blackwell had been very careful never to utter that name to her before.

And now she knew why.

She had to get to him. Now.

Shimmying her back and legs so that her skirts slid back into place, she began to tug at her bindings. She could say one thing about her husband, he certainly knew about restraints.

Shouldn't this window latch give? In her stupefied desperation, she simply struggled fruitlessly for a moment. Grunting and straining, she pulled this way and that. She needed just a few inches and she could probably shimmy off the point at the top. Damn her short legs. Maybe if she could somehow lift her skirts over her knees so she could climb over the window seat and stand on it . . .

She froze as heavy footsteps shuffled down the hall.

"My lady!" Murdoch's horrified exclamation echoed in the solarium.

"Please release me." She pulled against the cords biting into her wrists as she struggled to look back at him. Remembering her discarded drawers, Farah grimaced with mortification. However, if anyone was to find her in such a state, she could only ask it be Murdoch. It wasn't like he hadn't done it before.

"There are limits to my loyalty," the Scotsman growled as he climbed onto the ledge and began to work at her husband's masterful knots. "I'll kill him for this."

"No, Murdoch," Farah admonished as her hands finally slid free and she pressed them against a protesting back as she stood. "You must forgive him for this."

"Never!"

Farah searched the floor around her until she snatched up her ripped eggshell-blue drawers. "You *must*," she insisted. "Just as I must forgive you for not telling me who he was all this time."

He turned the color of a jaundiced turnip. "I—I doona know what ye mean, lass."

"Oh, do give it up, Murdoch!" she huffed. "Now tell me which way he went."

"Christ, Jaysus," the old man moaned, looking quite unwell.

"Which way?" She brandished her unmentionables at him in a threatening manner.

Murdoch pointed out the west doors. "Follow the devastation," he said rather dazedly. "Though when he's in such a state, I wouldna advise being in his path."

Despite everything, Farah was unable to suppress a grin and planted a kiss on Murdoch's balding pate. "Don't follow me," she ordered before dashing out.

The devastation did, indeed, mark a path toward her husband. Antiques were pushed over. Pictures pulled off walls. Priceless glass vases and stone statues lay smashed in the middle of the hallways.

Ducking into an unused guest room, she used her ruined undergarments to clean herself and discarded them in the rubbish basket before resuming her search.

The path ended at the back stairs, and Farah followed them down to where the garden door flapped against the storm.

Of course, Farah knew exactly where she'd find him.

The stone walls of the terrace gardens stood higher and in better repair than those ancient mossy rocks at Applecross. It made sense to Farah, in a way, as she approached the man slumped against one. He stood higher, too, these days, impossibly so. But *this* sable-haired man was once a sable-haired boy she'd known better than any other, and he still retreated to cold stone walls in times of crisis.

His white linen shirt and dark vest were plastered to his torso and outlined powerful shoulders along with the dips and swells of thick arms. His limp hands dangled over splayed knees. Locks of hair dripped rainwater onto the grass beneath him, hiding his downturned face. The posture of defeat didn't diminish the potency of his masculinity.

An acute ache opened a pit in her chest and spread until she had to swallow to keep it down.

Here they were again. A cold storm. A stone wall. A wounded boy. A lonely girl.

"Tell me why you're crying?" She whispered the first words she'd ever spoken to him.

And he gave her the same reply, without looking up. "Go. Away."

A ragged gasp escaped her and she rushed to him, sinking to her knees next to him in a cloud of expensive midnight skirts.

He snatched his hands back and fisted them at his sides. "I mean it." The dangerous growl rumbled from deep in his chest. "Get out of here."

She swallowed a lump of tender, painful joy. "Let me see your hands."

He lifted his head like a man with the weight of a mountain on his shoulders and turned it on his straining neck to spear her with those unsettling mismatched eyes. He *wasn't* crying. Not yet. But muscles twitched in his face and his lips pulled into a hard white line as he visibly fought the pool of bright moisture gathering against his lids. "I'm warning you, Farah."

"You should know me better than that," she murmured, slowly moving her fingers across the grass toward where his fist clenched at his side.

Neither of them felt the rain or the biting cold as she picked up his big, white-knuckled fist. Her hands looked so small in comparison. Both of them clutching his one fist and still not engulfing it. Farah's heart didn't pound so much as it quivered inside her rib cage, struggling to move her blood through veins tight with hope and awe and terror.

Her long, slim fingers covered his thick, scarred ones and one by one, coaxed them to uncover his secret.

A breath as jagged as the long seam across his palm broke from her throat, then another. She could feel her face crumbling as hot tears mingled with the cold rain on her cheeks. The wounds Dougan had suffered the day they'd met. The scars she'd traced as a girl more times than she could count.

"Oh, my God," she sobbed, pressing her lips to his scarred palm. "My God, my God." The exclamation became a chant. A question. A prayer. Punctuated with kisses and strokes of her fingers as though his hand were a holy relic and she a pious disciple at the end of a long pilgrimage.

Finally she held it to her cheek as she sat back on her knees and stared into the face of the boy she'd given her heart to, and the man who'd begun to steal it.

His entire body shook, though his features were still as granite, but for a twitch in his strong chin he couldn't seem to control. He regarded her as one might a strange dog, unsure of whether its next move was to nuzzle or attack.

"Is it truly you, Dougan?" she pleaded. "Tell me this isn't some kind of dream."

He turned his face from her, a drop of moisture leaving the corner of his eye and slowly following the blade of his cheek to join the rivulets of rainwater running down his jaw and neck.

"I am Dorian Blackwell." His voice matched the stone, gray, flat, and cold.

Farah shook her head against his palm. "I knew and married you as Dougan Mackenzie, all those years ago," she insisted.

His throat worked over a difficult swallow and he pulled his hand out of her grasp. "The boy you knew as Dougan Mackenzie is deceased. He *died* in Newgate Prison." His gaze swung back to hers. "Too many times."

Farah felt her heart become a fragile thing. More fragile even than the vases and sculptures that lay in shards along the expensive flooring of his home. "Is there nothing left of him?" she whispered.

He stared at a point over her shoulder for a moment, before reaching out.

Farah didn't dare move as he pulled a wet ringlet over her shoulder and wound it around his finger. "Only the way he—remembers you."

Hope swelled and tears overflowed her lashes again, blurring her vision until she blinked them away. She felt like a woman ripped in two by opposing forces. Exquisite pain and agonizing elation. Dougan Mackenzie had been returned to her arms. Alive. Broken. Powerful. Unable to bear her touch. Unwilling to give his heart.

Were the heavens truly so cruel?

She reached up, smoothing the wet streams of his hair off his wide brow. "You don't look a thing like him," she murmured with awe. "He was so small, his face rounder. Softer. And yet, I see him in your dark eye, that dear, mischievous, intelligent boy. So, you see, he *cannot* be dead. I must have known that somehow, all this time. It's why I never let you go."

"That's impossible," he said.

Farah lifted the hem of her blue skirt and found a white petticoat beneath that was not yet drenched. Gently, she covered a finger with the hem, much as she had when they were children, and knelt up to wipe the rainwater from his face.

After a cautious wince, he remained unmoving. Unblinking. *Unbreathing* as she parodied her prior ministrations to him from all those years ago.

"Of course it's possible," she said. "It was your Gaelic spell that you said to me in the vestry at Applecross. Those last words."

May we be reborn,
May our souls meet and know.
And love again.
And remember.

"*I* remember, Dougan. And I know *you* never forget."
She let the petticoat fall away and traced the lines of his
brutal face with fingers soft as feathers, learning and memorizing this new incarnation of him. "My soul recognized
your soul—and was reborn. I knew there was something
behind those eyes, beneath those gloves, that would give
back to me what I've been missing all these years." Farah
launched herself at him, wrapping her arms around his
neck and clinging like a burr. Their first kiss tasted of salt
and desperation. Tears mingled, his or hers, she couldn't
tell. Lips fused. Bodies melded. And finally, a miracle.

His thick arms encircled her, pulled her to him, then his
hands plunged into her hair as he claimed her mouth with
his tongue. He was as big and hard as the stone wall behind
him, a mountain of ice melting beneath her warmth. But his
mouth neither punished nor demanded. This time, his kiss
was full of darkness and hesitancy. It was as if all the emotions he couldn't understand or allow poured from his
mouth into hers in a tumble of chaos.

Farah accepted them all. Savored them. Would hold
them and help him identify and sort through them later,
when they'd finished discovering just who they'd become.

She felt safe here in the arms of this dangerous man. It
was like returning to a home that had been destroyed and
rebuilt. The same bones, same structure, but a new core
that felt more foreign than if you hadn't ever known it from
before. Walls and obstacles constructed by hands that were
not her own.

But it didn't matter to her. She'd learn this man he'd

become, renovate with her love what could be improved upon, and accept and adapt to what she could not repair.

"I love you, Dougan," she murmured against his stroking mouth. "I've loved you for so long."

He released her hair and shackled her shoulders with his strong hands, thrusting her away from him so abruptly she felt it in her bones. The scar interrupted by his eye was deep enough to catch the rain, and the expression on his face finally forced the storm's chill beneath her skin. His breath came in ragged pants, and his lips were colored with the heat of a kiss. But any other effect had disappeared, and that fact struck Farah's heart with dread.

"I am Dorian Blackwell." He shook her shoulders a bit, as though that would give his words more weight. "I have been for the entirety of my adulthood and will be until this wretched life is over."

"How is that possible?" she asked gently, setting her hands on his chest to stabilize herself. Curious ridges in the hard planes of muscle called her fingers to investigate. Seams? Scars? She found herself firmly planted away from him as he prepared to stand.

"That's just another story full of blood and death," he warned.

"Tell me," she insisted, fisting her hands in her skirts, promising herself that no matter how badly she ached for it, she would not reach out until he finished.

The rain beat them with a steady staccato, dripping down the stones of the wall in dark streaks that evoked images of bloodstains. The grass beneath them cushioned the hard ground and fragrant hedges hid what walls could not. It was a lovely garden, just awakened to the first nudges of spring with blooms not yet blossomed. But as Dorian spoke, a grim pall covered the whole world, one that not even this lovely corner could brighten.

"I wrote to my father, the Marquess of Ravencroft,

Laird Hamish Mackenzie, before they sentenced me. I begged him not only for help on my behalf, but also for his help in locating you. In keeping you safe." His eyes touched her for a moment, but then swung to fix on a weathered hedge, stubbornly holding on to the barren kiss of winter.

"I never heard a word from my father, though as my situation became more desperate, I wrote to him more often. Turns out, instead of the paltry sum it would have taken to hire a lawyer for me, he paid exponentially more to his friend and associate Justice Roland Cranmer the Third to be rid of me. Cranmer, in turn, paid the three most corrupt and vicious guards in Newgate to beat me to death."

Farah gasped, holding a horrified hand to her heart to keep it from bleeding out of her chest. "They—killed Dorian instead?"

"He happened to be working on a cipher for outside communication with my cell mate, Walters, and so we switched for the night, knowing the lazy guards had a hard time telling the difference between us."

"Walters, you mean—Frank?"

His lids shuttered for only a moment. "Walters used to be brilliant and brutal and prone to manic episodes of extreme artistic genius. One of the best forgers ever captured. They tried to kill him that night, as well, but he survived to become the gentle simpleton you met. I suppose they left him alive because he can't remember what happened, and therefore couldn't speak against them."

Farah couldn't tell which was more responsible for the moisture on her cheeks, the relentless rain, or her tears. "Dear God." She sniffed. "Your own father caused all this?"

A frightening satisfaction lifted her husband's satyric features. "He paid his price, and was the first to experience my wrath. He funded my rise and, needless to say, there is a new Marquess of Ravencroft. His legitimate heir, Laird Liam Mackenzie."

Farah didn't even want to know what happened to the old one, and couldn't exactly summon pity for the man who'd paid for the violent death of his own son.

"Liam Mackenzie is . . . your brother?" she breathed.

"Half brother," he answered tightly. "I am only one of countless Mackenzie bastards out there. We tend to stay out of Laird Mackenzie's way."

"Why?" Farah asked.

He looked away, signaling that the matter was closed. She wisely moved on. "Now Cranmer's gone missing?"

"Dead. And they'll never find the body."

Farah wasn't surprised. "How were you able to take on Blackwell's identity?"

His lip curled into a snarl of disgust. "There are no words to describe the filth of the railway mixed with that of the prison. Infection killed more men than violence." He swallowed obvious revulsion. "We truly could have been brothers. The Blackheart Brothers. And we smeared our faces and skin with soot and mud to protect it from the sun and cold when we worked. The added benefit was often men didn't realize to whom they spoke if we weren't standing next to each other. I lost all traces of my Highland brogue and learned his mannerisms and accent very early on. Once I grew to roughly his size, there was no telling us apart."

"Who knows who you really are?" she asked.

"Murdoch, Argent, Tallow, and—well—Walters is confused most of the time. We *were* the five who *ruled* Newgate. The fingers that made a fist." He curled his fingers over his scar, squeezing until the creases whitened. "We all knew it was supposed to be *me* who died in that cell. And we all wanted revenge, so we took it. And we've never stopped taking since."

Farah found it difficult to digest his story, her mind threatening to regurgitate its ugliness onto the ground like so much rancid meat. "You won't say his name," she murmured. "Dorian Blackwell, the boy who died."

"You don't seem to understand. Whoever was left of the boy I was is buried in that mass grave along with his body. You did not marry Dougan Mackenzie."

"Yes I did," Farah insisted in a gentle whisper.

He pushed to his feet, standing over her like a reluctant executioner, about to carry out the sentence of a dark soul. "*I* am Dorian Blackwell. I will always *be* Dorian Blackwell. He lives on in me."

Farah lifted to her knees, meaning to stand, but froze when he took a retreating step. "Then—I'll love you as Dorian Blackwell," she offered. "For I married him, as well."

A quiet and painful desperation speared through her as his face hardened. "Do not speak of love, Farah. For it is something I cannot give."

Stunned, she fell back on her haunches as though his words had physically pushed her down. "What?" Of course, Dorian had told her that before. But—things were different now.

"I can offer you protection. I can offer you revenge. I've given you your legacy. But I cannot offer you my heart, because I am not capable of giving something I don't possess."

Bleeding for him, Farah forgot to be proud, forgot to be strong, and prostrated herself on her knees in front of him, clasping her hands in supplication. Ready to give him anything. Her heart. Her soul. Her life. He was her soul mate, back from the dead. It would kill her to lose him again. She didn't care what he'd done, what life had driven him to do. She'd take those sins upon her own head; carry the burdens of his memories on her slim shoulders. "You can have *my* heart," she offered.

"You'd be a fool to give it to me," he mocked, twisting his features into something foreign and frightening.

"Then I am a fool," she insisted. "For I already have."

"I do not suffer fools!" he hissed. "You gave your heart to *Dougan,* before you even knew what it meant. It is not meant for me."

She seized his fist, pressing a kiss to the scarred knuckle. "But Dorian has begun to steal it, thieving highwayman that he is."

"Then take it back!" He wrenched his fist from her grasp, pulling her off balance and forcing her to catch herself on the grass with her outstretched hands, soiling them with the mud beneath. "In my hands it will become corrupted. Poisoned. I'll blacken it until you hate me almost as much as you hate yourself for giving it to me." He thrust a finger at her to silence her reply. "Every part of my life has been bleak, brutal, and bloody—except you. I'll not add your ruin to my many sins."

"We can change that," she cried. "Together."

He bent and thrust his strong, cruel face into hers, water falling from his hair onto her skin. "That's what you're too blind to see. I don't *want* to change. I like being the Blackheart of Ben More. I relish making the imbeciles that run this empire into my puppets. I feed on the fear of others. I love to crush my enemies and outwit the police. I am not the redeemable hero, Farah. I am *not* the boy who loved you. I am the *villain*—"

"Fine!" Farah held her soiled hands up. "All right. I'll take it, all of it. I'll take you just as you are. Dorian Blackwell, the Blackheart of Ben More. I've seen the kind of man you are, how you take care of those whom you pretend not to care about. I'm your *wife*. I've been your wife for *seventeen* years. I love you."

His next words made her doubt the twitching flicker of agonized emotion that struggled to peel itself from his bones before he crushed it behind his mask of ice and stone. "I know what you're thinking, Farah. Don't you think it has been offered to me before? Maybe if you love me enough. Accept me enough. Set a good example of compassion and kindness that you'll make me a better man."

He was so astute, so brutally correct, that Farah had to force herself not to cringe from him.

"There *is* no better man under this." He gestured to his scarred eye. "In fact, with you here, I'm much worse. I lose control around you, Farah. You make me blind. The thought of touching you dissolves me into madness. The thought of another man touching you . . ." He grabbed her wrists and held the raw skin in front of her eyes. "Look what I've done. What I—*forced* you to do upstairs."

"You didn't force me," Farah breathed. "I—wanted you."

"I would have."

"You *can't* have done," she argued. "Dorian, I'll never deny you. I'm yours. *Only yours.* Just like you've always said."

Before her eyes he became a stranger. The vestiges of the angry, possessive Dougan Mackenzie disappeared. And even the cold, aloof, and dominant Dorian Blackwell gave way to someone new. It wasn't just the light and life that disappeared from his eyes, but the shadows and mystery, too. It was almost like watching him jump off the edge of a cliff. She'd never in her life felt so utterly helpless. Not with her hands bound to the bed. Not when they'd taken the boy she'd loved away from her. Not ever.

"What about your promise?" she reminded him desperately. "You *promised* me a child."

"Consider this the first time of many that I'll disappoint you."

"But you said that you always keep your promises."

"I was wrong to say that."

Farah panicked. He wasn't just retreating. It was like watching him die. Right there, in front of her. Severing the ties with the last of his humanity. With the part of himself that still searched for her after all these years.

"Why?" She hated the pleading note in her voice.

"As I said before." He straightened, his hair hanging down into his eyes. "I do not suffer fools."

He stepped over her like one would a sopping puddle and strode toward the house. Farah watched his drenched clothing molding to the wide back he held as straight as an arrow.

She fought her heavy, sodden skirts to stand. The ache in her heart echoed in the falls of his feet on the wet flagstone walk to the house. It was like she'd thrown her heart beneath his boots and each beat was the stomp of his heel.

Well, she wasn't a flame to be stomped out so easily. "Then why marry me?" she called after him, pushing her wet ringlets out of her eyes. "Why capture me and bind my life to yours if you planned to cast me away? What's the bloody *point*?"

"The point is, I'm a bastard," he replied over his shoulder. "In *every* sense of the word."

CHAPTER TWENTY-ONE

"Why doona ye go with her?" Murdoch asked for maybe the millionth time. "It'd be a damned sight better than staying locked up here and working yerself to death."

Dorian looked up from where he unpacked crates of books he'd unloaded this morning, and swiped a forearm across his sweating brow. He'd been up and down the library ladder possibly hundreds of times today, and planned to climb it a hundred more, until every book had been placed where it belonged. Maybe then, he'd expand the wine cellar. Regardless of his past, there were times his hands ached for the feel of a sledgehammer or a pickaxe again. Perhaps he'd dig a tunnel to France. By himself.

"Blackwell—"

"It's this, or drinking," Dorian interrupted. "Pick one."

"Drinking yerself to death would certainly be more enjoyable," his steward muttered.

A flurry of dust erupted as Dorian dropped a pile of gold-leafed hardcovers on the table with a loud *crack*. "Is there something that needs attending?" he asked irately.

"Yer *wife*," Murdoch challenged.

Dorian paused, a pang of pure agony spearing through him with such force he couldn't bring himself to lift his head above the book spines in front of him. "Careful, old man."

"Ye aren't even going to say *good-bye*?"

"She's going to Hampshire, Murdoch, not the Indies. It's an hour or so by train." Dorian sorted through books he could not see, moving them from pile to pile just to avoid the knowing stare of his oldest living friend. "It's better this way," he finally murmured.

"Ye're a bloody idiot," Murdoch declared.

"And you are *this* close to losing your—"

"She's yer *Fairy*, Dougan. How can ye possibly let her go now?"

"Don't call me that." An abyss that could encompass the night sky had opened up in his chest a week ago, on that day in the gardens, and Dorian rubbed at his sternum, wondering when it would burst from his rib cage and swallow the earth. "You've seen what I've done to her." He fingered a page, receiving a cut for his troubles. "It was never part of the plan to keep her with me. She wants to make me a father. We both know that's a terrible idea. I'm not—whole."

"She loves ye," Murdoch offered.

"She loves her memories of Dougan. She's known Dorian for such a short time, and I've already done more damage than can be repaired."

"But, what if ye—"

"What if I broke her?" Dorian seethed, advancing on Murdoch. "What if I hurt her in my sleep, or worse? What if I lost my temper? What if I lose my mind?"

"What if ye let go of yer past and she made ye happy?" Murdoch retorted. "What if she gave ye peace? Maybe a little hope?"

Dorian swiped a bottle of Highland scotch he'd been

nursing and took a deep, burning swig before turning toward the window overlooking the drive. Maybe he *would* drink himself to death. At least then the fire in his belly would be something other than this numb sort of despair. And wouldn't Laird Ravencroft be glad to hear of his demise? By his own whisky, no less.

"There *is* no hope for a man like me," he told his reflection, and the pathetic bastard in the window seemed to agree, looking back at him with disgust. "No peace to be had."

After a hesitant moment Murdoch asked, "Are we going back to Ben More, then?"

A black coach and four pulled into the circular drive and rolled to a stop beneath the portcullis. Dorian watched its progress with a sinking desolation. "I will likely be, but you're to accompany Lady Blackwell to Northwalk Abbey."

"But sir!" Murdoch argued. "I havena packed."

"I had them pack your things this morning," Dorian informed him. "I don't want her traveling alone and Argent is—occupied."

"Very well," Murdoch acquiesced. "But she should get used to the idea of her being alone. Ye've just cursed her with a life of nothing *but* isolation. She'll be the unwanted wife of the Blackheart of Ben More. How lonely do ye think that'll be?"

Dorian took another swig, his books forgotten, his head swimming in scotch and misery. "Have a safe journey, Murdoch," he said in dismissal.

"Rot in hell, Blackwell," Murdoch tossed back before quitting the room and slamming the door.

He already was, Dorian thought with a wry huff before taking another swig. He didn't think he stood staring out at nothing for that long, but before he knew it Farah stepped from under the front awning.

There couldn't be a picture of a more elegant and refined

countess. Her traveling dress, a jewel green with gold ribbing at the hem of the jacket, matched the hat covering her intricately pinned hair. A tasteful black feather flowed from the hat and matched the gold and black bobs at her ears.

Dorian drank in the sight of her. Committed it to his memory as he had none other. The indent of her waist. The fourteen ruffles of her pelisse. The delicate curve of her neck and the way a few lone ringlets draped down her shoulder.

Don't look back at me, he begged, unable to tear himself away from the window. *Don't give me another memory of your eyes to haunt my dreams.*

It had been at his insistence, hadn't it, that she go and properly claim her father's Hampshire castle? He could no longer stand her presence beneath his roof. No longer watch her while she slept and not be tempted to take her. To hold her. To curl against her body and lose himself to the oblivion she found so easily.

The blood of the dead and dying didn't haunt her dreams.

And he had to make certain it stayed that way.

Don't look back.

If she did, he wouldn't be able to let her go. He'd lock her in the tower like some pirate's captive and—and— well, it didn't bear thinking what he'd do. All manner of debauched perversions, that's what. He'd use her in all the dark and devious ways he'd been trying not to obsess about since that first night.

He took another swig.

Murdoch took Farah's hand to help her into the coach. She paused, her chin dropping and tilting toward where he stood at the grand library window.

He put his hand on the windowpane, feeling more like

that boy at Applecross than he had in years. *Don't look back at me.*

And she didn't. For there was nothing to see.

Farah stood on the banks of the river Avon and enjoyed a few minutes of rare and blessed silence. It wasn't that she minded all the callers and well-wishers who had swarmed upon Northwalk Abbey; in fact, they provided a lovely diversion. One could not dwell on a broken heart when there was a house to put in order and a past to reclaim.

Breathing in fragrant air chilled by river water and sweetened with bluebells, Farah turned back to admire the gables of Northwalk Abbey. Diversion only took one so far. The mind was a powerful tool, but altogether useless when it came to matters of the heart.

Farah had done everything she could think of to keep herself occupied. Renovations to Northwalk Abbey, working with Murdoch to transfer, claim, and understand her finances, which were more vast than she realized, and acquainting herself with Hampshire society. She was requested to every drawing room, solarium, and dining table, as the Countess Northwalk became the latest and most stylish controversy. Not just because of who she was, but also because of to whom she was married.

Deciding to head back, she kicked at a rock with the toe of her walking boot. She certainly didn't *feel* married. It had been two extremely busy and exhausting months since she'd left Blackwell House in London. Busy because of all she'd accomplished, and exhausting because of the sleepless, lonely nights.

Northwalk Abbey seemed immense and empty, even after she'd requisitioned Walters and Tallow from Ben More to help, and installed Gemma with Walters in the kitchens. In truth, she'd thought that might anger Dorian enough to come after her and reclaim his staff for Ben More. But he didn't. According to Murdoch, he remained in London, becoming such a recluse, people feared him a prisoner of his own home.

More like a prisoner of his own mind, Farah thought.

"When do ye think we should go back to London?" Murdoch had asked at the end of that first dreary month.

"Probably the first week of *never,*" Farah had retorted, hating the bitterness in her voice. It covered a wound she felt like she'd never be rid of.

"My lady . . ." Murdoch had begun, but in the end, hadn't been able to think of anything to say.

"I mean it. I'm not going back to him. Northwalk is my home now. He can sit in his bloody castle and brood his life away." She couldn't believe how angry the subject made her. How utterly disappointed and frustrated. Farah had always considered herself a calm and reasonable woman, prone to curiosities and independence, but not fits of temper and ranting. "We were given a second chance at life—at happiness—and *I'm* going to grasp it. Whether he does or not."

Farah would have regretted those initial words to Murdoch except they'd seemed to galvanize him, somehow. And he'd, in turn, taken his second chance with Tallow.

The footman, now turned butler, smiled more these days, and stuttered less. Though he and Murdoch kept their relationship very much to themselves, Farah didn't miss the way they protected or encouraged each other, the light brushes of one's hand against the other's shoulder as they passed, or the fact that Tallow's room hadn't been slept in for ages.

It had taken her another month to admit that she *wasn't* happy. Not even close. A desperate loneliness haunted her quiet moments, and had begun to stalk her regardless of how many people she surrounded herself with.

Picking her way through the gardens, Farah veered for the kitchen doors as she smelled Walter's baking. Perhaps he'd prepared some spring fruit and cream. Or, if she were lucky, followed through on his threat to make an olive oil cake with preserved cherry compote that he'd read about in an Italian cookbook. They'd just received a shipment of dark Spanish chocolate. He'd probably worked wonders with that.

Stomach rumbling with anticipation of what she might find, she swung open the door to the entry and was rendered speechless by the scene that greeted her.

A towering Frank held Gemma in his embrace from behind, his chin resting on the curve where her neck met her shoulder as he watched her fold confectioner's sugar into some kind of concoction.

Farah observed them from the doorway, neither of them having noticed her yet. Ingredients splayed across the wooden island in disarray, and Farah knew that this was Gemma's doing, as Frank tended to be fastidious to the point of compulsive with the cleanliness of his kitchens.

The basins, sinks, stove, ovens, and cutlery of Northwalk Abbey had all been his own requisitions and they eerily resembled those at Ben More.

Gemma hadn't so much transformed in two months as adapted. Her dresses were newer, her skin and hair more luminous, but she maintained her stubborn sense of self and wielded her bawdy personality like a weapon.

Yet, as Farah watched her with Frank, she spied an expression on the woman's face she'd never before imagined. A vulnerable insecurity.

"You whisk it too rough," he guided gently, engulfing her stirring hand with his gigantic one. "Slow. Like this."

"I told you I ain't no good at this," Gemma protested churlishly. "I can roast the bloody hell out of a bird, but baking gives me a fever."

Frank turned his head and kissed her jaw. "You're good at this," he said with absolute conviction. "You're good at lots of things."

"Get on with you," Gemma chided. But the woman smiled down at their joined hands, and relaxed into his arms.

Farah glided backward until she was certain they wouldn't notice her and pulled the door shut as quietly as she could.

Gemma and Frank? Frowning, she made her pensive way to the front entrance. She'd been too wrapped up in ignoring her own problems to notice their attachment. Or perhaps she just hadn't wanted to see the affection and hope blooming here at Northwalk. Everyone was seizing their second chances at life. And love. Murdoch and Tallow, and now Gemma and Frank.

Farah was happy for them. If any man would treat Gemma with kindness and infinite patience, it was Frank. And the former prostitute likely wouldn't mind his slow speech or simple ways. A gentle giant like Frank Walters would allow her freedom, protection, and would more often than not defer to her for all decision making. Gemma would finally have control over her life, and the pure kind of love only a man like Frank could give.

Farah couldn't pretend that all of this romance didn't make her solitude that much more pernicious. She didn't want to be bitter. Didn't want to resent the good fortune of those she cared about. Such tendencies were beneath her.

And yet . . .

The tender intimacy of a gentle embrace like the one she'd just witnessed caused a yearning so palpable her skin ached with it. Every affectionate touch Murdoch and Tallow shared felt like a blade sliding between her ribs and nicking at her heart.

Farah knew she possessed a capacity to love that was

greater than most. Sometimes, she was filled with so much care, so much brimming affection, she thought it might encompass the entire world. She wanted to hold every unloved child, to save every wounded soul. She wanted to embrace the man she loved, and have him return that love in kind.

But he didn't. He couldn't.

Tears stung behind her eyes and only managed to irritate her.

Enough of this, she told herself. Hurrying up the wide marble steps to Northwalk, she swept past Tallow. "Do you know where Murdoch is?" she asked him.

"T-t-the study, my lady."

She was already halfway up the grand marble staircase when she thanked him, gripping the black banister to propel her faster.

Murdoch looked up from the big oak desk in the study as she entered. Once he took in her troubled expression, worry lines appeared between his brows.

"Are ye well, my lady?"

"Quite well, thank you," she lied, suddenly uncertain why she'd sought him out.

"Is there something ye needed?" he asked carefully, following her restless pacing from one end of the study to the next.

"No. Yes." Farah paused her pacing, then started again, nearly unsettling a globe unlucky enough to be in her path. "I—I'm not sure." She'd just been so melancholy. Felt so— abandoned. But now, staring into the patient gaze of her friend, it all seemed so silly, and also hopeless.

It wasn't the understanding in his eyes that unraveled her. It was the pity.

"Why don't ye sit down?" He motioned to the plush bronze settee and pulled the cord to ring for a maid. "I'll call for tea."

Farah didn't want to sit down, but was suddenly too tired and heavy to stand. Murdoch ordered tea while she stared at her hands, then settled himself next to her. He was quiet while she gathered her thoughts, her courage, knowing that she'd speak as soon as she could.

"I miss him," she admitted to her lap.

"No more than I'm certain he misses you."

"A part of me hoped he'd come, and a part of me knew he wouldn't." She turned to him, dashing at angry tears. "He was right, you know. I *am* a fool."

"Doona say that, my lady." Murdoch reached for her hand. "*He* is the fool. Love and fear are the two strongest emotions known to the heart of man. I've never seen Blackwell afraid, it's part of what's made him so dangerous. No matter how much he's acquired, he's lived like he's had nothing to lose. Like he didna fear death."

Farah stood, too restless to sit any longer. A hot ire speared through her like a lance, settling close to her heart. "He doesn't fear death, but he fears life? That's so ridiculous!"

"He's a dangerous man, my lady. He's afraid he'll hurt ye. He's afraid to let himself hope, to lose ye again. He almost didna survive the first time."

Farah wrapped her arms around herself and leaned against the desk. "All the terrible things that happened to him—they were a result of his love for me. Do you think that's why—"

"Nay." Murdoch put a staying hand out, but didn't go to her. "Many different circumstances and forces converged against him. His path may have been similar whether ye were a part of it or not. Such is the lot of so many bastards and orphans."

"It just makes no *sense*," she lamented. "Why be so afraid of *losing* something, you deny yourself of it? Everyone is entitled to a chance at happiness. Even the Black-heart of Ben More. Especially him."

"So are ye, my lady."

"So I am." Farah straightened, galvanized by a moment of self-discovery. "I'm so angry with him. He thinks he's done me such a favor by restoring my birthright, and it isn't that I'm not grateful. But his methods have stolen from me the one thing I've ever wanted." She was gesturing wildly, ignoring Murdoch's growing alarm.

"What's that?" he asked hesitantly.

"A *family*, Murdoch." Farah marched behind the desk and extracted a sheet of monogrammed paper and pen. Two monthly courses had come and gone since Farah had last seen her husband, and each one had been a reminder that her thirtieth birthday approached, and her child-bearing years were numbered. "If he's too afraid, too stubborn to love me, that's his prerogative. But if Dorian Blackwell thinks he can deny me what he promised, he has another thing coming."

"What do ye plan, my lady?" Murdoch rose slowly.

"I'm writing a letter."

He eyed the paper dubiously.

"I am going to live my life, Murdoch," she announced. "I intend to have my family, whether he's a part of it or not."

Murdoch sat down like a man readying for the gallows. "No one gives Dorian Blackwell an ultimatum who doesna regret it," he cautioned.

"This isn't an ultimatum, Murdoch. This is his last chance. And while *he* might be afraid to seize it, *I'm* not."

"Ye might destroy him, lass. Doona tear him down."

Farah glared up at Murdoch, though she understood and appreciated his loyalty to her recalcitrant husband. "I have worked with nothing but men for over a decade," she informed him. "I know exactly how to dismantle them, and how to put them back together. You think it's difficult? I would have built him back up, Murdoch. We could have had the future that was stolen from us." She took the tall seat at the desk.

Murdoch stroked at his close-cut beard for a moment before reaching for the pen and unscrewing the cap with infinite slowness and handing it to her. "I think all this time, I've been afraid of the wrong Blackwell," he mused.

"You look like hell," Christopher Argent observed mildly as he puffed on a cigar in Dorian's London study.

Dorian bloody well knew what he looked like. He cringed at the memory of what he'd seen in the glass this morning. He'd lost weight in the past two months. His skin clung more tightly to his sharp, heavy bones and caused every scar and line of age to stand out. He did, indeed, look like some dark creature that'd dragged himself from the bowels of hell. He ate little. He slept less. He worked, he drank, and he haunted the streets of London in the dark looking for trouble.

Sometimes he found it. Sometimes, it found him.

And yet he lived. He yearned.

The torture of *her* absence was worse than the cause of any mark left on his body. He was obsessed, *possessed*. His skin burned and his heart ached. He wanted. He needed. He *craved*.

"When's the last time you shaved?" Argent queried, running an elegant hand over his own shadow beard, this a bit lighter red than the auburn of his hair. Cropped close to his sharp jaw, it made him look more like a rawboned, ferocious Celt than a gentleman.

Dorian ignored his questions. He'd bathed today after his work on the wine cellar. That was all he could muster. "Any sign of him?" he demanded.

Since Harold Warrington had paid for his release pending investigation on suspicion of conspiracy to commit murder, he'd simply disappeared.

A corrupt judicial system was somewhat of a double-edged sword. Any judge willing to accept bribes or blackmail from one villainous reprobate, namely Dorian, certainly would turn coat for another.

Though the judge who'd released Warrington should have known better than to go against the Blackheart of Ben More, Dorian thought darkly. He'd deal with *that* later.

"That's why I'm here." Cigars always lent Argent's rough voice even more gravel. "The bobbies fished a body out of the Thames this morning. McTavish says it's Warrington."

Dorian's head snapped up. "Are they sure? Did you see the body?"

Argent nodded. "He was wearing the monogrammed jacket the villain disappeared in. You were right about him. Fat bastard was even more bloated by the water, took five coppers to lift him."

A tension that had resided in Dorian's shoulders these past months released, resulting in a throbbing headache.

Argent regarded him with those trademark cold, shrewd eyes that seemed less like he saw you as a human, and more like a creature he'd like to dissect.

"Why don't you go to her?" Argent queried. "Now that Warrington is no longer a problem?"

"I—can't," Dorian admitted wryly. His body was strung too taut for that. Once he'd tasted the sweetness she had to offer, the oblivion that bliss afforded, he couldn't even be trusted in the same room with her. Even now, his body responded.

Argent shook his head and unfolded his tall form from the chair, crushing his cigar on the tray. "Never thought I'd see the day Dougan Mackenzie gave up his Fairy." He flicked a concerned glance toward Dorian.

"The next person to call me that is going to lose his tongue," Dorian snarled. "I haven't given her up. We're married. She's still *mine*."

An amber brow conveyed skepticism, but Argent wisely kept his own counsel.

"A letter for you, Blackwell." His butler brought in a flat envelope on a silver tray. Dorian took it, his stomach taking a dive at the sight of the Northwalk seal.

Why wasn't she using his seal? he wondered as he broke the wax and unfolded the letter.

Why would she?

"I'll take my leave, then." Argent pulled the bell and requested his coat from a footman as Dorian read the words that drove rail spikes of rage through his temples.

> *Dorian,*
> *I have given our situation a great deal of consideration, and have decided to subsequently release you from your promise. My intention to raise a family still remains. As such, I will be accepting another candidate to fulfill the required vocation until my objective has been attained.*
>   *It is my sincere hope that this letter finds you well and that you are able to find peace.*
>
>   *Yours,*
>   *Lady Farah Leigh Blackwell, Countess Northwalk*

Crushing the paper in his hand, Dorian stood and hurled it into the fireplace. A fury the likes of which he'd never before felt bolted through him with such violence he physically jerked. Beneath the cold logic and cruel calculation of every villain lay slumbering a mindless beast of wrath, greed, and lust. This beast was cultivated in a more barbaric time, one where a man had to fight with his hands to keep what he claimed. He had to use rocks and weapons to crush his enemies. This beast surged through him now.

He would rip the limbs off any man who dared touch his wife.

Mine. His blood sang with the words. His breath flowed with them. His heart, the one he'd not thought to possess, beat the staccato of what he'd known since the moment he'd seen her on the Scottish moors all those years ago.

Only mine.

Argent's words were nothing but the buzzing of an insect as he hurled himself past the man, reached for his coat, and bellowed for his horse.

He should have known she wouldn't accept his terms, should have guessed she'd be obstinate. But he hadn't considered that she'd dare to fill her bed with another man for the sake of a child.

Farah wanted a family? He'd plant a manor full of children in her belly. He'd take her until she could no longer walk. He'd tried the honorable route. Done his best to keep her safe from the menace and perils of his life.

No more. She'd won her dangerous game. She wanted the love of the Blackheart of Ben More? It was hers, and all the danger and darkness that came with it.

CHAPTER TWENTY-TWO

Farah stood on the round dais in her dressing room long after Madame Sandrine had left, staring at her figure in the long mirror.

A velvet, late-spring evening settled into her Hampshire valley, turning the emerald fields into black squares of shadow. Only a dark blue stripe of light remained on the western horizon, and Farah had left the doors to her balcony open to let in the soft breezes to tease her hair.

The lavender lace sheath she wore brought out a violet tone in her eyes that she'd never before seen. Her hair spiraled around her arms in wild ringlets, reflecting the light from the candles with an almost luminescent glow. As nightgowns went, this one was rather scandalous. Though the neckline was high, the diaphanous fabric clung to her every line and curve, even accentuating the press of her nipples against the slight chill in the mobile air around her.

Though she slept and rose alone, generally eschewing the use of a ladies' maid, she couldn't help but try on the lovely undergarments that Madame Sandrine had brought with her to Northwalk along with several newly commissioned gowns. She only modeled them for herself, but she liked the sensual feel of the fabric against her skin. The glide of the hem on her ankles. She could imagine a masculine hand gathering the fabric in his grip to uncover the flesh beneath.

Lord, but her mind drifted to such things often these days. She supposed once she'd tasted the pleasures of the flesh, it became more difficult to live without. Farah knew, of course, that not all sexual encounters were as intense and climactic as hers had been, and she realized it would be excruciatingly difficult to allow anyone but her husband into her bed.

She wanted him. More than she wanted a child. More than she wanted her title. She wanted her Dougan back. Not only that, she wanted the sleek, predatory criminal Dorian Blackwell. She missed his cool arrogance, his sharp wit, and the way his eyes tracked her.

Watched her.

She wanted him to see her in this gown. Wanted to tantalize him by standing in front of the candles and pulling it across her skin while he watched, wondering when his control would snap and waiting for him to pounce like her jaguar.

The fantasy caused her thighs to clench and a moist warmth to rush between them. She really did look like a fairy in this gown. She wanted to show him that, too. That she still could be *his* fairy. That she could teach him how to love, just like she had once before.

A click interrupted her thoughts, and she whirled in time to see a shade move in the darkness beyond her candle. Who would lurk in the shadows of her rooms? "Dorian?" she called.

"You still haven't accepted that your bastard husband has forsaken you?" The voice from her nightmares stepped from the shadows. "Pathetic."

Reacting on impulse, Farah lunged for the bellpull that would bring a footman running. A revolving click stopped her cold.

"One more step and I paint those mirrors with your blood."

"Warrington," she gasped. She'd known he'd been released, and that he'd disappeared, but she'd been told by Murdoch that he'd been found dead.

"How did you get in here?" She'd been facing her door, and the balcony was two stories high. The stone walls were flat with no trellises to climb.

His eyes were two dark pits of rage in his large, ruddy face. "I've lived in this house longer than you've been alive, you spoiled bitch." He took a threatening step forward. "This is *my* home."

"This was my father's home," she argued.

Warrington scoffed. "But I know all her secrets."

Farah's eyes swung to the bed, her arms crossing over her breasts in an attempt to cover herself. Her limbs felt weak, her neck frozen and unable to move as terror locked her muscles into place. "What—what do you want?"

"I want what's *mine*!" he raged, advancing on her until the metal pistol pressed against her temple in an icy kiss. "I want what your father promised me."

He meant *her*. Panic stabbed deep into her belly, nearly doubling her over.

"You'd better escape before my husband returns," she threatened, hoping she'd improved upon her lying skills somewhat. "He's a dangerous man. I won't send him after you if you leave now."

Though he had to be inching toward fifty years, Warrington had retained a powerful build, if not a bit softer and heavier than in his youth. Farah remembered that he'd fought with her father in the war, that he'd saved her father's life. Was that why Robert Townsend had kept him around? Out of gratitude?

Now that he'd stepped into the dim light, Farah could see that his skin looked worse than it had months ago. Sores covered one side of his neck, and his breath smelled foul. Like rot and death.

She cringed as he lowered his face to hers. "That disfigured bastard you married can't stand the sight of you. He doesn't love you. He's not coming to save you. No one will even notice you're missing until it's too late."

The truth of his words terrified her more than the gun at her head. She'd turned in for the night. Even if the maid, Margaret, peeked in to check on her, she likely would just assume Farah had gone to use the necessary before bed.

No one would look for her until Warrington had done his worst.

"I cannot give you what you want."

"I know that," Warrington snarled, his eyes rolling in a way that made her doubt his sanity. "Don't you think I know that?" Clawlike fingers grasped her arm and pulled her toward the east wall against which her large wardrobe stood. "I will die before getting what I want, but at least I'll claim the vengeance I deserve."

Farah struggled, knowing that if she went anywhere with him, her life would be forfeit.

A soft knock sounded on her door. "My lady?" Murdoch called.

"Get rid of him," Warrington hissed, shoving the gun so hard against her, it wrenched her neck.

"I—I've turned in, Murdoch," Farah called, her voice surprisingly steady. "I'll talk to you in the morning."

"Ye'll want to know this," Murdoch pressed. "I've a

telegram from Argent in London . . . It's about your husband."

"Murdoch, please, I can't be bothered. Don't come in here!" she cried, praying that he would find the urgency in her voice strange and send for help.

A second ticked by before her door exploded open, shattered by the strength of Murdoch's burly shoulder.

Warrington fired, and Murdoch fell.

Farah screamed. She tried to jerk out of Warrington's grip, but his hand clasped about her arm like an eagle's talon. Blood spread from Murdoch's side, seeping into the gray wool of his vest. He was breathing, gasping for air, the shock of the bullet having knocked the wind from his chest.

"Murdoch," she cried. "Murdoch, can you hear me?"

The pistol was shoved through her curls and against the back of her head. "You'll come with me, or the next bullet goes in his eye."

Panic faded, and a cold sort of calm resolution stole through Farah's veins. Murdoch couldn't leave Tallow, not when they'd just found each other. The gunshot would bring the household, and the next person through that door would be Warrington's next victim.

"I'll go," she said. "Just don't kill him."

Warrington jerked her toward the wardrobe, opened the latch with one hand, keeping the gun trained on her, and hurled her through her new dresses until she tumbled out of the false back, barely maintaining her balance.

The other side of her papered wall and velvet drapes was nothing but cold stone lit by a few sporadic torches. It was like stepping back in time two hundred years.

"What is this?" Her tremulous voice echoed down the dank stone corridor, interrupted by only a few other openings, presumably from different manor rooms.

Warrington gave her shoulder a rough shove forward. "Walk," he commanded.

The cold of the stones and close, arid stench seemed to reach through the thin fabric of her gown. Farah hugged herself and plodded forward, the dank, uneven earth beneath her slippers making sounds she dare not identify.

"Northwalk Abbey was built in the sixteenth century by a papist earl," Warrington informed her conversationally. "It's said he hid condemned Catholic priests here, and smuggled them out of the country by way of Brighton."

"Surely you didn't bring me here for a history lesson," Farah said imperiously. "Where are you taking me?"

Warrington's gun jabbed at her shoulder. "Just like you entitled monarchists. Don't even *know* where your titles come from. Don't acknowledge the innocent blood that's been spilled so you can have your castles and your tenants."

"That's not me," Farah argued. "I only want what my father intended for me to possess. What makes you more entitled to it than I?"

They came to an abrupt drop, a steep set of wooden stairs that led down into a dark abyss. Farah glanced over her shoulder at Warrington, who kept the gun trained on her as he took a torch from the wall. "Climb down." He gestured to the stairs with his pistol.

Farah stared into the dark. She didn't *want* to go down there. What if she never came back out?

"Move, or I'll set those pretty ringlets on fire."

She could feel the heat of the torch on her skin as he thrust it toward her. Gathering her gown above her knees, she gripped the rough wooden banister tightly as she took the first step.

The light from his torch followed her down, and Farah could hear the heavy bouts of his breath as they descended.

The smell hit her first. Death, filth, and excrement. She held a hand to her mouth to contain her gag reflex. The torchlight touched a pile of animal bones she'd rather not identify. Then the rough pallet of filthy blankets, and finally, the old bucket he must have been using as a chamber pot.

Her stomach heaved, and Farah swallowed against the sting in her cheeks and the saliva flooding her mouth. "You've been *living* here?" she asked, horrified. "All this time?"

"I told you, Northwalk is *my* home." He placed the torch in an ancient metal sconce, never once looking away from her. "Your father, Robert, promised it to me." He spat the name. "Promised *you* to me, so that I may be part of its legacy."

"Why did he do that?" Farah asked the question that had been on her mind since she'd been old enough to understand. "What did you have on him to get him to acquiesce?"

Warrington spat on the ground, his eyes becoming wells of black hatred in a face that was ghostly white for lack of sun. "You would think so, you useless bitch." He stepped toward her, and she backed away, her heart pounding wildly. "I was eighteen when you were born, and had already been licking your father's boots for a year. Did you know that in the queen's army it's money not aptitude that makes you an officer? Your father was a privileged earl who'd only ever shot at foxes and peahens, and I'd been infantry since I was fifteen, having lied about my age. I had to shine his shoes, brush his coat, pin medals he never earned. And all the while, I pretended to love him like a brother. Convinced him he couldn't do without me."

This shocked Farah. "You mean—he betrothed us because . . ."

"Because I convinced him I could love, protect, and adore a spoiled git like you." He stood in front of her now, the pistol pressed into the tender flesh beneath her jaw. Farah could feel it as she swallowed, and morbid, terrified thoughts crowded out all else.

"I didn't know all this," she whispered, trying not to focus on which was worse, his breath or the smell of the bucket in the other corner. "Please," she beseeched him with her eyes. "It doesn't have to end this way. I can give you the money that you would have been promised as my dowry. You can start over somewhere on the Continent or America. Stake a claim on land that's your very own. Have something no one can take from you."

"It's too late for that!" he screamed in her face, the vibrations echoing off the stone walls and being absorbed by the dirt floor. "Too late for me," he said in a quieter, flat tone, trailing the nose of the pistol down her neck, past her collarbone, and resting it in the valley between her breasts. "Too late for *you*."

"It's never too late," she told him. "As long as you're alive, you can choose to *live*. To be happy, even if it means starting over." She truly believed that. Though she felt as though she could see her chance at life draining away along with the last of the sanity in his eyes.

"That bitch I married gave me a whore's disease. The doctors say I'll be dead within a month, but it'll steal my mind before it takes my body."

With every breath, Farah's chest pressed against the pistol, now warmed by the heat of her skin. The sensation terrified her, paralyzed her body, but her mind raced for a way to survive.

He had nothing left to lose. He lived only for revenge.

"I *was* going to rape you," he informed her in a voice as soft as death. "I was going to make you waste away with me, rotting from the inside. But it seems that I am no longer able, the syphilis has stolen the use of my cock."

Grateful for that small mercy, the threat had bile crawling up her throat, and a moan of disgust escaped her lips.

The weight of the pistol left her ribs as he backhanded her across the mouth so hard she had to blink against spots of blindness and regain her bearings. When her vision cleared, the pistol was inches away from her forehead at the end of his outstretched arm. She could only focus on it or his face, but not both.

"Don't act like you're better than lying beneath the likes of me," he snarled. "You may be a countess by birth, but you've already wallowed in the mud with the lowest kind of filth. You've corrupted that perfect body with his touch and shamed the Northwalk title and the Townsend name by becoming a Blackwell. It would disgust me to lie where he's already been."

Farah wiped a trickle of blood from the side of her mouth. A cold rage blocked out the pain and sharpened her vision, even in the dim light. "Do not speak ill of my husband," she warned in a voice so hard it didn't even sound like her own. "You're not even fit to lick his boots, not worthy to speak his name. He's better than the law, more powerful than any lord, and more of a man than you'll *ever* be."

Warrington's lip curled, unveiling teeth barely rooted in a rotting mouth. "Too bad he'll never hear you say that. I imagine Dorian Blackwell will always wonder what became of his pretty wife. For he'll never find your body down here. We'll rot away together, buried in the same grave for eternity." His finger tightened on the trigger, the pad turning white with the beginnings of pressure. "Goodbye, Lady Northwalk."

$\mathscr{C}$HAPTER $\mathscr{T}$WENTY-THREE

Northwalk Abbey glowed against the night sky as Dorian pounded up on the back of his Thoroughbred. Every window blazed with light, and frantic movements from within prickled the hairs on the back of his neck.

Something was amiss.

Clattering into the cobblestone courtyard, Dorian leaped from his horse and threw the reins to a stable boy, his focus on the men clustered in the yard studying a map in their hands.

"What's going on here?" he demanded.

Peter Kenwick, an employee he'd installed to watch his wife, led the handful of men. His dark eyes widened as Dorian approached. "Blackwell!" he exclaimed, crumpling the map. "It's Murdoch, he's been shot."

"Is he alive?"

"Yes, we sent for the doctor, and to get word to you. Tallow's with him now."

Dorian ripped off his riding gloves and mounted the

stairs two at a time. "Where is my wife? Who did this? I assume he's been dealt with."

The men followed him up the steps, their silence screaming a warning. "Murdoch was found in Lady Black-well's bedroom," one of the men was brave enough to answer. "She's missing."

Speared by an arrow of cold dread, Dorian spun at the top of the stairs and glared down at them. "What do you mean, *missing*?"

No one met his eyes.

"Answer me if you value your lives."

Kenwick, more accustomed to Dorian's visage, stepped ahead. "All we know is we can't find her, or the gun. The house is being scoured, sir, and we were going to start a search of the grounds. She can't have gone far."

The prick of dread turned to a douse of icy fear. "How long since the gunshot?"

"Minutes," Kenwick answered. "If that long."

Whirling so fast his black cloak flared, Dorian plunged into Northwalk Abbey, bellowing Murdoch's name. The bedrooms had to be on the second floor, so he dashed up the stairs, his boots barely touching the carpets. "Murdoch," he roared. "Farah!"

Tallow ran around the bend of the hall to the right. "B-Blackwell! He's here!"

Murdoch sat propped against the wall outside a splintered door barely clinging to the hinges. A maid held pressure to his side with a heavy cloth.

"Murdoch." He dropped to one knee next to the injured man. "Who did this?"

"Bullet grazed me flesh." Murdoch waved him off. "Go. He has her," his steward bit out through drawn, white lips. "Warrington."

The bastard isn't dead.

"No!" Dorian exploded to his feet, his ice becoming

that foreign fire, the one that stole his thoughts along with his breath. "Where did he take her? Which way?"

Murdock shook his head. "They never—left the room. I was by the door." He winced and swore as the maid pressed harder on his side.

Dorian leaped into her bedroom, lit by a lone lantern. Walters and Gemma were already searching the balcony and beneath the bed. "She's not 'ere." Gemma moaned fretfully. "We looked everywhere. There's no way anyone could have leaped off the balcony and lived, it's too high."

Every muscle in his body tightened. "Murdoch," he gritted out. "Is there a chance you lost consciousness? No possibility that they might have gotten past you?"

"Not a one," Murdoch rasped. "Passing out would be a mercy."

Panic threatened to choke his rage, and Dorian refused to let it. "Warrington's a dead man," he announced to the men who'd only just crowded in through Farah's bedroom door. "And so is the imbecile who allowed him in. Which one of you was it?"

"It's impossible, Lord Blackwell," Kenwick marveled. "We've attended our posts like you ordered. Not one of us has been late or remiss. We wouldn't dare fail you."

"My wife is in the hands of my *enemy*." The truth of it burned through his blood, making him wish a man could die more than once. He'd murder Warrington exactly the number of times he'd put his hands on Farah. The man's soul would expire before his body gave out. There were *ways*.

And this time, he'd stay dead.

"We'll find her," Kenwick promised.

"You'll answer for losing her," Dorian vowed.

The man went whiter than Murdoch. "Blackwe—"

A shot volleyed through the castle, freezing them all. Then another.

"Farah," Dorian gasped. It had come from *inside* the castle, from inside the *walls*. Dorian walked to the east wall and pressed his hands against it, then his ear. She was behind there. He knew it. She wasn't dead. That shot wasn't for her. She was alive! She was alive because *he* was still alive. And if her heart ever stopped beating, his soul would follow her.

Feeling like an animal trapped in a cage, he hurled his body against the wardrobe, shattering the wood. He would tear this bloody castle apart brick by fucking brick. Starting with her bedroom.

"Good-bye, Lady Northwalk."

Farah reacted before she thought, slapping at Warrington's wrist as he pulled the trigger.

The gun went off right next to her ear. She could no longer hear, but she could *kick*. And so she did, her foot coming up as hard as she could drive it between Warrington's legs.

Another bullet pinged off the stones, but Farah felt no pain, and so she lunged for the pistol, easily pulling it from Warrington's hand as he crumpled to the earth, clutching himself.

Fumbling for a moment, she got the pistol pointed in the right direction, and slowly backed away from Warrington. "Don't move," she yelled, the sound still muffled. Every limb shook with a violence she'd never before experienced. Her left ear rang loudly, and another sound, like rushing water, competed for dominance, but she was alive.

She was *alive*.

The foul words that spilled from Warrington's lips rivaled the filth of the pit. And Farah began to wonder just how she was going to climb the stairs—they were almost as steep as a ladder—while still training the gun on him. Should she run first and get help? Or make him climb at gunpoint? Should she just kill the bastard and be done with it?

The idea held appeal, and yet her stomach protested.

A loud explosion, like the shattering of wood and brick, startled her. Warrington took that moment to lunge toward her, his teeth bared as if he planned to bite.

Farah leaped back toward the corner, screamed, and pulled the trigger.

Warrington staggered, a hole opening just below his sternum, and fell. She felt rather than heard the vibrations of footsteps sprinting toward her.

The ringing had started to fade, and she might have heard a man scream her name, but she just stared and shook, wondering if she shouldn't empty the gun into the fallen man, just in case he rose again.

Warrington's eyes blinked rapidly. His mouth, ringed with blood, worked over words, though she couldn't hear any of them. The world began to spin, the ground beneath her feet pitching like a ship rolling on an angry sea.

A dark shadow leaped from the stairs, his long coat flowing behind him like demon wings, landing in between her and Warrington.

Dorian.

He looked like the devil, come to take his minion. His hair black as obsidian. His scarred eye glittering with so many dark things, Farah couldn't identify a single one through her shock.

"Give me the gun," he growled. "His life is *mine*."

His words seemed to snap Farah out of whatever threatened to pull her under. "No." She scowled at him. "He attacked *me*."

"Farah, you're not a killer," Dorian soothed, a desperate tenderness glimmering from his onyx eye. "Now give me the gun."

"I've—reconsidered my position on that." She looked

at Warrington's twitching leg, could hear the breath gurgle through his throat, and she felt woozy all over again.

In a flurry of swift and magical movements, Dorian took her gun, shoved her behind him, and shot Warrington squarely between the eyes like he was a dog that needed to be put down.

Farah took her hands from her ears and pushed at his broad back, fighting elation at his presence that rose through her fear, shock, and anger. "You needn't have done that," she charged. "He wouldn't have survived my shot."

Her husband turned on her, his eyes devouring every inch of her barely clad body as he tucked the gun in his belt. "He should have died slowly," he said. "But he is still a stain on *my* soul, not yours."

They stared at each other for a dark, tremulous moment.

"Dorian." She breathed his name, and the sound of her voice seemed to unleash a torrent of raw, brutal emotion from within him.

She was at once trapped between the chilly stones and six feet of burning, aroused male. On a primitive groan, he took her lips in a fierce, possessive kiss. His gloved hands were everywhere, almost clinically, as though checking for injury, then he crushed her to him in an embrace that threatened to squeeze the breath from her.

"Fairy," he groaned against her lips, and Farah thought she detected the brogue of their childhood. He seized her mouth. Possessed it. Drove his tongue into her with deep, drugging thrusts.

Farah wanted to leave this place. To escape the smell and the death and the fear. But she felt her husband's ribs expanding with heaving, painful breaths against her chest, and detected bone-deep tremors running through his solid frame, and so she stood passively in his arms, submitting to his scorching kisses.

He said her name almost incoherently between rough drags of his hard lips and bristly chin. "Fairy. *My Fairy.*"

She tried to answer him, to soothe him, but each time she took a breath, he claimed her lips again. His own breaths began to slow to a less alarming rate, rattling out of his broad chest in deep, ragged pants.

Farah wasn't aware that they weren't alone until some rather loud throat clearing echoed off the castle walls. "Blackwell . . ." She recognized Kenwick, one of her handymen, who addressed her husband. "What do you think we should do with this?" He kicked at Warrington's limp body with the toe of his boot.

Dorian lifted his head, his eyes clearing of their clouded frenzy. Inspecting her again, he seemed to only just notice the thin translucence of her nightgown.

"Get rid of it, Kenwick," he said darkly, taking off his cape and settling it around Farah's shoulders.

Farah lifted an eyebrow as the enveloping warmth instantly sank through her gown and into her skin. She shivered, not from the cold, but a deep, intense relief. "Kenwick? You know my handyman?"

He didn't even have the decency to look sheepish, and Farah narrowed her eyes at him. "Just how many of *my* staff are in *your* employ?"

Dorian didn't answer. Instead, a strong arm swept beneath her knees and lifted her until she was cradled to his thick chest.

"I'm perfectly capable of walking," she informed him, wriggling in his grasp.

"Hold still," he ordered, climbing the stairway.

She did as he said, only because she didn't want to survive all this only to die from a fall down the stairs. Now wasn't the time. She had a few choice things to say to her husband.

CHAPTER TWENTY-FOUR

"Murdoch!" Farah cried, as they stepped through her shattered wardrobe. She struggled to be let down, but Dorian held her in a vise grip.

A pile of rumpled dresses lay strewn about the floor like bright casualties of a horrific battle. Her room was torn apart, as though tossed by a frenzied thief searching for treasure.

"He's being seen to," Dorian said.

"He could *die*." She thrashed about in his arms. "I must go to him!"

Her husband subdued her resistance with embarrassing ease, his jaw set in a hard line. Shards of timber crunched beneath his boots as he carried her into the hallway where a standing Murdoch was being supported by Frank and Tallow. Gemma held a cloth to his side, and Farah was overjoyed to see that the blood hadn't soaked through yet.

"Doona ye worry about me, lass," Murdoch admonished. "I've enough flesh around my middle. The bullet just took a bit of it, 'tis all."

Relief doused her with alarming force, renewing her struggles with vigor. He still looked alarmingly pale, and sweat glistened on his brow. "Murdoch! You need a *doctor.*"

"Bah!" He motioned with his head to be led toward his rooms at the far end of the hall. "Nothing some whisky and a few stitches willna fix. It was more the shock of the shot than the bullet itself that took me down, I'm ashamed to say. I'm getting too old for this sort of thing."

Desperate to see for herself, she pushed against her husband's unyielding chest. "Blast it, Dorian. Put me down!"

"No." His strong arms held her impossibly tighter, but he glowered at Murdoch. "You *will* be seen by a doctor and that's final."

"A-a doctor's been c-called for," Tallow informed them, looking in no better shape than Murdoch, who wore the most stubborn look Farah had ever seen.

"Send him for Lady Blackwell once he's finished with Murdoch," Dorian ordered sharply. "And have a basin and soap brought."

"No, no. Don't bother. I wasn't hurt in the least," Farah insisted. "You'd *see* that if you set me down."

Dorian stared down at her with a startling expression of possession and mystification. "I—can't."

Murdoch's unmistakable bark of mirth startled them all. "Go see to yer man, Lady Blackwell. I think he's had the worst scare of us all tonight."

Blackwell scowled at his steward, though he didn't argue as the wisely silent crowd suddenly found a new interest in helping the wounded man to his rooms.

Murdoch had been correct. Though Farah had stopped trembling, her husband's muscles still twitched as though being shocked with unwanted tremors. He stood in the middle of the hall, clutching her to him, looking like a man overcome by too many forces to endure.

"The master's rooms," Dorian ordered.

"I was using the master's rooms." Farah motioned toward the chaos of her chamber. "Take me in there." She pointed to the countess's suite. It would be cold from lack of a fire, but they'd have to make do.

The only light was provided by a bright spring moon, filtering from the windows and casting the white counterpane with silver and blue. The sudden stillness and quiet jarred them both, and they took a moment to adjust.

Dorian's heavy breaths broke through the darkness, painting the night with the myriad of emotions Farah didn't have to see in order to understand.

"You can set me down now," she assured gently. "It's safe."

It took him two breaths to reply. "I—can't seem to release you."

Reaching up in the darkness, she pressed her palm to his hard jaw, now rough with a few days' growth of beard. "You don't have to release me."

Reluctantly, he lowered the arm beneath her knees until her feet reached the floor, though he didn't release her shoulders. "He *dared* strike you." Dorian's savage voice didn't match the extreme gentleness of his thumb as he drew it against her faintly swollen lip.

Farah was hoping he hadn't noticed. She should have known better.

"It's nothing," she soothed, pressing her hand against his glove.

"I wish I could resurrect the bastard and slaughter him again," he growled. "Slowly."

Farah stepped into him, still surrounded by his rough cloak. He didn't pull away.

"Did he touch you, Farah?" Dorian asked in an agonizing groan. "Did he—hurt you anywhere else?"

"There wasn't time."

"When I heard those shots, I thought—"

She stopped his hard lips with a gentle press of her fingers. "Let's not dwell on the terrors of the day." She pulled her fingers away. "Why are you here, Dorian?"

His already tense body hardened against her, his hands grasping her shoulders in a punishing grip. "Don't pretend you don't know. The *letter*," he snarled. "Have you already taken a lover? Because I swear to Christ, Farah, if you value his life—"

Her fingers found his lips again, hope beginning to seep into her chest. "It would be impossible for me to invite someone into my bed so soon after you broke my heart," she confessed.

"But you would have," he accused, his lips moving against her fingers. "Eventually."

"I thought so," she whispered. "I truly *meant* to, but it took me seventeen years to even consider another after losing you the first time." She put her head against his solid chest, marveling at his height and breadth. "I was hurt and lonely when I wrote that letter. I was angry with you for rejecting me. I wanted a child more than ever, because I *needed* someone who would accept my love. Someone who wanted it. Who wanted *me*."

Dorian grasped her shoulders and drew her away, giving her a little shake. "*How* can you think I didn't want you?"

Farah gaped. "You sent me *away*," she reminded him sternly. "I haven't seen or heard from you in two months."

He bent until his face was close to hers. His white scar and blue eye caught a shaft of moonlight, and what she read in the stark hollows of his face told her everything she needed to know.

"*I* want your love," he declared fiercely, clutching her arms with desperate fingers. "I came to claim what's *mine*."

Farah's heart glowed and her body rejoiced. "Not if I claim you first." She lifted up on her tiptoes and captured his mouth, twining her arms around his neck and shackling him to her.

He stood frozen in her embrace for a breathless, undecided moment before melting against her, around her, pulling her into the hard curve of his body with a deep groan of surrender.

Yes. At last. The feel of her arms around him, her tongue entering his mouth, her body locked against his, was a sweeter victory than she could have imagined. It wasn't only desire and need she tasted on his kiss, but trust.

And that word was a foreign concept to a man like Dorian Blackwell.

For a boy like Dougan Mackenzie.

A soft knock on the door interrupted them, and Dorian turned to admit a maid laden with a basin of fresh water, linens, soap, and a candle. "You want us to lay a fire?" she asked.

"No," Dorian clipped. "You may leave us."

"Thank you, Molly," Farah added as the maid bobbed a hesitant curtsy and scampered out.

Farah stepped to the basin, more than ready to wash the memory of that fetid hidden chamber and the very breath of Harold Warrington from her flesh.

Dorian followed, silent as a whisper, standing so close his chest grazed her back. "Let me," he rasped in a voice made husky by darkness.

Farah reached for a soft and absorbent cloth and dipped it in the water. "It's all right, you don't have to."

A warm hand reached from behind and covered hers. His gloves had disappeared, and only scarred male flesh rested against her skin. "Yes, I do," he breathed against her ear.

New trembles seized Farah's body as he eased her fingers open and let the cloth fall into the water. These had nothing to do with fear or cold, but a budding relief. A powerful hope. Farah knew the significance of his gentle movements as he eased his cloak from her shoulders. A few soft tugs, and her nightgown floated to the floor.

Her eyes stung with hot tears, her vision blurring until she allowed them to pour down her cheeks at an alarming rate. He'd come for her. Just when she'd thought all was lost.

Using his hands, those strong, scarred hands, Dorian took her bare shoulders in the softest grip and turned her to face him. A tenderness she'd never before seen glowed unnaturally bright in the dim light of the lone candle. His skin against hers felt foreign and familiar all at once. Dorian Blackwell was *touching* her. Of his own volition. No fear flared in his eyes. No revulsion curled his lips.

Rough knuckles lifted to her cheek. "Why are you crying?" He crooned her first words to him with a look so warm and earnest she could see her Dougan staring out through his eyes. "Did you lose something?"

The tears fell faster, harder, drenching the fingers he brushed against her face. *"Yes,"* she sobbed. "I thought I'd lost the only family I've ever really known, the very moment I'd found him again. And it was worse that you weren't dead. That you sent me away."

"What a fool I've been." His hand lifted to cup her jaw, his thumb hovering over the bruise swelling around the small split there. "I thought you were safer without me. That, for once, I was doing the noble thing. It took almost losing you—God, Farah, I've never been so afraid." His jaw clenched and his own eyes seemed to glitter with raw, agonizing emotion. "I thought I could live without you. But there *is no life* without you. Only existence. And that is a greater hell than what awaits me after death."

Farah's breath was stolen by a small hiccup. "Well." She sniffed. "If you're feeling noble in the future, just—stop. You're rather terrible at it."

That drew the devilish sound of amusement that Farah had come to recognize as Dorian's chuckle. He gently pressed her down with his palms until she sat on the cushioned trunk at the foot of the bed, truly feeling naked for the first time since he'd undressed her.

"I mean it," she admonished as she watched him rub the cloth along her favorite lavender-scented soap and wring it into the basin. She wrapped her arms over her breasts and crossed her legs, feeling rather brittle and exposed. "How are you supposed to keep me safe if you're far away?"

She submitted as he softly brushed the cloth against her lip and chin, and then wiped away the tears from her cheeks, rinsing the fine patina of suds with a clean section of the linen. He noted her nakedness with a banked heat in his eyes, but his concern seemed to outweigh his baser instincts.

"You'll never be rid of me now." It would have been a tease from a less serious man, but coming from Dorian, it sounded like a dire warning. "You may come to regret it. My demons will haunt our lives."

Farah reached for his wrist, stilling his hand and capturing his eyes with her own to make certain he understood her words. "I don't mind battling a few demons when I'm living with their king." She smiled. "And I think, after a time, we'll chase them away together."

He was silent, pensive, as he continued to wash her. His eyes and hands discovered parts of her for the first time. Parts that, while generally innocuous, became instantly arousing and sensual beneath his touch. He found places that made her gasp. The thin skin on the underside of her forearms. The dip of her waist. The curve behind her knee. The arch of her foot and between her toes.

Though she was generally clean from a previous bath, his ministrations seemed to be as much ritual as they were practical. He washed the fear from her skin. The taint of an evil man. The remembered smell of death and rot. All the while truly discovering her body with his fingers for the very first time through the thin veil of cloth and water.

Farah could tell by the flare of his nose and the strain in his neck and jaw that he struggled to be gentle with her. To complete his task without turning it into an advance. He was being careful, flicking concerned glances from beneath his lashes.

He stopped doing that once Farah poured invitation into her gaze.

She was a puddle of need and sentiment by the time a second knock preceded Gemma's flounce into the room.

Biting out a curse, Dorian stood to block the view of Farah from the door and opened his mouth to, no doubt, commit a horrid form of verbal abuse on her friend.

"Calm your britches." Gemma tossed her wild brown curls and held up a simple cotton wrapper. "I brought this for the lady as the doctor's on the other side o' that door. It was you wot called for 'im."

"Bless you, Gemma." Farah stood, reaching for the wrapper.

Gemma's face split into a wide smile as she handed Dorian the robe. "Guess you already been examined," she intimated with a wink.

"See the doctor in," Dorian clipped.

Though the rather elderly country doctor, a Sir Percival Hancock, tutted and blustered over Farah's ill-treatment and small bruise, it didn't take long for him to announce that she was hale and hearty. He left some sort of syrupy substance to help her sleep and calm her nerves, but Farah disposed of it the moment he tottered out to confer with Dorian about Murdoch. She'd seen the dangers of dependence on the opiate contained within, and couldn't bear the thought.

Dorian returned almost immediately with a wilder cast to his features, kicking the door shut behind him and blowing out the candle.

Farah wrinkled a brow at his almost manic behavior. "What's wrong?" she queried. "Is it Murdoch?"

"He's fine." Dorian reached her in two long strides and pulled her to him, fusing their mouths for the second desperate time that night. A rough tug preceded the chilly kiss of the night air as her robe dropped to the floor.

Not breaking the seal of their lips, Doran lifted her off her feet and carried her to the bed, setting her gently upon it. Pulling back, he stood above her, as he'd done once before, his gaze roaming her body as his fingers curled into familiar fists. "I want to touch you."

Moonlight cast his features silver and shadow, and illuminated the vulnerability lurking beneath the lethal ruthlessness. He was once again that starving boy, trapped between his hunger and his fear.

Slowly, so as not to spook him, Farah rose to her knees. "Then touch me."

His mismatched eyes dropped to her breasts, swaying with her careful movements. His tongue wet his lips, and yet he didn't move. "I—shouldn't."

Farah tilted her head to the side in confusion. "You already have."

He winced. "I couldn't stop myself. I wasn't in my right mind. I was mad with worry." He turned his head and studied the bright moon shining through the window like a shameless voyeur.

They had a few things in common, her husband and the moon. They dominated the night. Created shadows and, yet, illuminated the darkness.

"Maybe I should order a proper bath," he offered, not looking at her.

Farah shook her head in confusion. Now? She was naked, offering her flesh to him. "I bathed this afternoon. You only *just* washed me. I can't be much cleaner than I am now."

"Yes, you can." His tormented gaze found her again. "I touched you, Farah."

"I've been touched by you before," she reminded him suggestively.

"You don't *understand,*" he said through his teeth, and Farah feared that he might bolt again.

"You're right," she said gently. "You keep saying that, and I truly don't understand why you're repulsed by touching me."

"No." He stepped toward her, as though wanting to argue, but stopped himself. "That isn't it."

"Tell me," she entreated him. "I deserve to know."

He came to his decision looking like a prisoner readying himself for the gallows. As though, with his words, he would bring about irrevocable ends. When he spoke, it was with the voice of a dead man. "For a time I was the youngest inmate at Newgate Prison. The smallest. The softest. The—weakest. I won't describe the hell that distinction brings."

Farah held her breath to trap a sob in her lungs, knowing that the pity conveyed by her agony on his behalf would insult him.

"To say it was a nightmare would be kind. The brutality was all-encompassing. Sexual, physical . . . mental." He lifted his eyes to her, covering the flicker of shame behind those familiar walls of ice. "Can't you see how it changed me, Farah? Not only physically, but essentially."

Aware of her nudity, Farah didn't give in to the impulse to wrap her arms around herself, in case the motion conveyed the wrong message. "I remember our conversation at Ben More," she said carefully. "You so much as told me about all that. And, you forget, I've worked at Scotland

Yard for a decade. I'm aware of what happens in those prisons, how criminals prey on each other. It breaks my heart, Dorian, but it doesn't color my opinion of you with darkness. You were young. You were small and helpless." She inched toward the edge of the bed. "You are none of those things anymore."

"You are such a fucking angel." He said these words with his lips pulled back in a snarl. "And so you still do not *see*. I did not remain helpless for long. I took my vengeance."

"Yes." Farah nodded. "Yes, you told me about the guards, about other prisoners."

"Those guards, that judge, they were lucky to die as swiftly as they did." He stared into her eyes, unblinking, making certain she marked the horror of his every word. "I repaid all the sins committed against me in kind, Farah. My brutality surpassed that of anyone else. I didn't hurt people, I broke them. I didn't kill, I murdered. I didn't punish, I humiliated, until only those loyal to us were left. Do you understand *now*?" he demanded. "Don't you see? Everywhere my fingertips touch your sacred flesh, blood and filth is left behind like so much hot tar. Impossible to remove. I can't do that to you, Farah." He jammed fingers through his hair, his volcanic emotions preparing to erupt in front of her eyes. "I can't—"

"*Stop*," Farah ordered, holding up her hand. "Stop it and listen to *me*, Dorian Blackwell."

His eyes widened with dangerous warning, but his lips slammed shut.

Farah wanted to hold him more than she'd ever wanted anything in her entire life, but she clenched her own fists to keep from ruining the moment and overwhelming him. She, instead, held his gaze with the earnestness she injected into her words. "You *survived*," she said adamantly. "You survived when others didn't. You had no other means

with which to keep yourself alive. In order to stop the per-
secution, you *had* to become a man with a black heart. I
don't . . . sanction violence, but neither can I condemn you
for the past. Especially when it was my fault you were
there in the first place."

"Don't say that," he growled. "Don't ever say that!"

"It's true." She shook her head. "Look at me." Holding
her hands out to her sides, she bared her body to the moon.
"You have touched me, and yet my flesh is unmarred."

The tormented hunger in his gaze caused a thrill of
hope and possessive need to warm her skin against the
night.

"Mine isn't," he muttered. "There is nothing pure left
of me. Not my flesh. Not my hands. Not my soul. Why
would you want that anywhere near you?"

"The darkness you see in your touch is only in your
mind," she said gently. "Perhaps we can fix that."

"It's impossible," he lamented, shaking his head.

"Come closer," she entreated.

He didn't move.

"If I've learned anything in my life, it's that there is no
darkness so absolute that it cannot be dispelled by the
faintest of light," she explained.

His face softened as his eyes touched her, and his boot
slid forward. "My sweet Fairy." He exhaled on a painful
breath. "You can't imagine darkness. You are the only light
I've ever known."

His tender words didn't match his pitiless features, but
Farah still found hope. "You must believe that my light is
more powerful than your darkness. And so let me touch
you, instead. And everywhere that *my* fingers touch your
flesh, they will clear away the blood and filth that you see,
and will leave behind the light I've always wanted to give
to you."

He didn't grant her permission, not verbally. But he

slowly stepped back to the edge of the bed, holding a breath trapped in his wide chest, and a wary uncertainty banked in his eyes.

Farah held a similar breath captive as her fingertips found the lapels of his coat. Gently, with infinite care, she parted the unbuttoned folds and pushed it from his shoulders, letting it fall to a heap on the floor. He wore only a black shirt, no cravat, unbuttoned at the collar, and a charcoal vest.

"I don't want you to restrain me this time." She kissed his throat, the sinew straining and twitching beneath her lips. "*I* want to touch all of you, Dorian. Will you allow me that?"

He remained silent and still, uttering no promises, but making no move to stop her, either, as she reached for his vest and deftly undid it. His eyes burned like blue flame and glittered like volcanic stone. His nostrils flared and fists remained clenched at his sides.

A powerful need to see the man beneath the black seized her. He'd hidden so many secrets. Concealed as much as she'd ever exposed.

Now was the time to reveal the Blackheart of Ben More.

Her fingers reached for the button of his shirt, but her wrists were seized in a swift move. "No," he gasped. "I can't do this. You don't want to see . . ."

"Dear husband." Farah inched forward on her knees until she was on the very edge of the bed, and he allowed her to reach her captive hands toward his face. "You can't know how terribly wrong you are."

He shook his head. "My skin. It's not like yours. It will—repulse you."

Farah remembered the strange texture she'd felt beneath his shirt that day in the gardens.

She closed her eyes against a well of pathos for his tragedy. "Your hands are the same, Dougan Mackenzie," she whispered. "I have always loved your hands, scarred and savage as they can be. I've missed your touch for seventeen years." She twisted her wrists against his grip and uncurled his palm to press her lips against the scars of his boyhood wounds. "Trust me?" she whispered against the scars she'd treated so long ago.

Farah reached for his shirt and he stolidly allowed it, closing his hand as though to hold her kiss in his grasp and returning it to his side. Farah's heart sped with each button she liberated, but she let his chest remain in shadow until she'd undone the last one before the rest of his shirt tucked into his trousers.

Carefully, she peeled both his shirt and vest from the mountains of his powerful shoulders, and slid them down the swells of his arms.

It wasn't the many slashes and scars marring his chest that caused her sudden gasp, though she felt the pain of each one. It was the unparalleled beauty of his physique that stole her breath. Dorian's body was rendered by some ancient god of war. No Greek sculpture could compare, no artist could re-create the sleek, predatory masculinity rippling through the complex landscape of his torso.

"You're beautiful," she marveled.

His head snapped to the side as though she'd slapped him. "Don't be cruel," he said stonily.

Her hands trembled as she reached for him, not out of fear, but of eager anticipation. The first time she ever truly felt like she *touched* her husband was when she laid her hand flat over the hard swell of his chest, right above his heart.

The muscle flexed and jumped beneath her palm. Farah followed a raised slash that cut from beneath the flat of his nipple across the wide expanse of his ribs. Her other hand found a large patch of roughly webbed skin on his opposite shoulder that appeared to have been badly burned a long time ago. "I'm sorry for all you have endured." She couldn't see all the details of his past wounds by the wan moonlight, and she was glad of that. Some were hidden in shadows and grooves. Though her heart ached, a hot trickle of desire had bloomed between her legs, and the muscles there began to rhythmically clench.

"My touch will *never* bring you pain," she vowed, slowly smoothing her hands over the inconceivable expanse of his chest.

Dorian's eyes closed, as though he couldn't face the moment. His breaths were short and labored, and his heart kicked like the hoofbeats of a racing stallion beneath her palm. He lifted his hands to cover hers, making as though to pull them away from his skin. But he didn't.

Farah realized this gave him control. That he took an active participation in her experiment, and he could guide her to touch him, or allow her own exploration, depending on how it affected him.

Aware of his hesitation, she caressed down wide ridges of his ribs, and stopped to explore every divot created by the clenched muscles of his stomach. She found more nicks and creases, but ignored them, focusing on the hard male beneath the scars.

His trousers hung low on his hips, and she let her fingers wander over them.

His hands fell away and his breath sped as she found the column of his arousal. She loved the feel of him. Hot like a branding rod, straining for release against his confines.

His body jerked, and his breath caught audibly in his throat, as she explored the linen-covered shape of him. Pressing another kiss to his throat, she followed the valley in between his smooth chest with her lips. "My hands will only offer you pleasure," she promised, her curious fingers working at his trousers.

He moaned her name as her mouth followed the entic-
ing trail her exploring hands had blazed. When she reached
the linen barrier of his trousers with her lips, he took a step
back so abruptly it was almost a leap. "What do you think
you're doing?" he rasped.

"I want to taste you," Farah divulged, feeling heat touch
her cheeks. "Like you tasted me that first night."

His eyes peeled wide, the muscles in his arms flexing
with intriguing strain. "N-no," he stuttered. "That's . . . No."

Farah hooked a finger in the waistband and pulled him
back toward her. "Yes," she replied saucily. "I'll not be denied." The last resistance fell away beneath her hand and
she easily slipped his trousers over his lean hips, his shirt
falling to the floor with them.

Lines of roped muscles led from his hips to where his
thick member jutted toward her. Moonlight shaded the
particulars of the shaft of flesh, but she reached for it with
gentle fingers, knowing the turgid heat and steely hardness
she would find.

"Farah." Her name tumbled almost incoherently from
his lips on a tortured gasp. "*Don't*. What if—I lose myself—in your mouth?"

The thought was so scandalous, so utterly wicked, she
was rocked by a wave of lust so hot she had to clench her
fist in the covers to keep from touching the aching flesh
between her own thighs. "You, husband, are the villainous Blackheart of Ben More," she told him in a voice she
barely recognized as her own, it had become so husky with
need. "You may lose yourself *wherever* you like."

The curses he released as she closed her lips over the
thick head of his shaft were not all entirely in the Queen's
English. At least, Farah didn't think so, and she was pretty
certain she'd heard them all.

He tasted like salt and sin.

The jerk of his hips as he bowed against her pressed

him as far into her mouth as she could take, and still she didn't hold the half of him.

"Farah," he groaned. "Oh. *Fuck*."

His profanity made the act that much more delicious.

Unsure of exactly how to proceed, she pulled back and was glad when a ripple of movement seemed to unconsciously flow down his spine and press him deeper into her mouth before retracting. Farah let her tongue explore him. The curious ridge on the underside. The weeping slit at the tip of the ridged head. The give of skin at the top and the unyielding rigidity of the rest of the shaft.

His hands rested on her curls, and then wound into them. Strong fingers dug against her scalp in erotic demand. No matter how an act unsettled Dorian Blackwell, he would not be passive for long.

He bit out a harsh noise as she began a rhythmic, sucking massage with her tongue, even the basest of language seeming to abandon him. His cock jerked and flexed in her mouth. Swelled and pulsed and thrust, slick with moisture, both his and hers.

Hands tightened in her hair and ripped her away from his sex. "Stop," he gritted. "I'm going to . . . Holy *Christ*."

"You can," she encouraged, drunk with power, inflamed to the point of madness by his pleasure. "Let me."

Farah enjoyed the strain of his muscles as he stooped to lift her away from him.

"Lie back," he commanded. *"Now."*

Swollen lips parted with the force of her breaths, she slid herself up the counterpane, staring in awe at the man she had married.

Any trace of boyish vulnerability had vanished. In its place stood a tower of dominant muscle and lust.

She shivered, partly from the silken feel of the cool linen beneath her skin, and mostly because of the inevitability of the man who was about to claim her as his own.

CHAPTER TWENTY-FIVE

Dorian lay naked for the first time since he could remember, enjoying the cool air against skin heated by movement and pleasure. He wrinkled his nose as a silvery curl tickled it, but was unwilling to let go of the woman draped across his chest even to move the offending lock.

He didn't know how long they had been silent like this, long enough for the moon to move from one side of the window to the other. Their breathing had slowed, and little pricks of chill bumps began to make him consider tucking her under the covers. But that meant moving, and he couldn't stand the idea of parting with her skin for even a moment. Also, he was pretty certain she'd drifted to sleep, and he would freeze to death before he disturbed her.

How had he made it two months without her presence? How had he survived *seventeen years* of unadulterated hell? It was like the fibers that constructed his body required her nearness in order to function.

He'd not only endured her touch tonight, he'd *enjoyed* it. She'd been so right. Farah could never be corrupted, was hips as he buried himself only a handful of times before seizing on a shuddering convulsion, and burying her name against the counterpane.

Fairy. My Fairy.

too pure to be touched by his darkness. But *he* felt less revolting, like some of the rifts in his soul had been stitched by her hands.

Dorian closed his eyes, berating himself for his stupidity. All this time, he hadn't been afraid of her, he'd been afraid of himself. Afraid that intimacy would bring the violent fears of his years in prison roaring to the surface.

He should have known better. This was his *Fairy*. His soul *remembered*. He was a killer, a violent man, but he'd slit his own throat before harming a hair on her head.

He pictured the lust in her eyes when she'd bared his body. The honest appreciation. His desire for her didn't make him feel vulnerable and weak. But powerful. Virile. Like he could conquer the stars and all the unknown powers beyond them.

"I hope you realize, Madame Sandrine is going to be very irate with you," she said on a lazy yawn.

He nuzzled her curls, taking the scent of lavender so deep he hoped it knitted into the corners of his lungs. "I thought you were asleep," he murmured, bemused that those were the first words out of her mouth. Likely, she was trying to put him at ease by creating a light moment after the intensity of everything just past.

She was so fucking precious to him.

"Don't try to change the subject," she reprimanded with a teasing poke. "*You're* going to have to answer for destroying my entire wardrobe in one night."

His hands roamed the silken skin of her back, creating chill bumps of his own. He'd never tire of the feel of her. Never cease to marvel at the unnatural softness of her fairy skin. It was like stroking a miracle. Holding an angel. A woman like this just—didn't belong on this wretched earth. "You won't be needing clothing for quite some time," he informed her. "For I plan to keep you naked for as long as I'm able."

She pulled herself out of his embrace to execute a dramatic flop onto her back with her hand held to her forehead. "Maybe you should reconsider a harem of courtesans." She sighed. "I don't think I'll survive the bed of the infamous Blackheart of Ben More."

Dorian rolled to his side to lord over her prone, pale flesh, his hand tracing the distracting underside of one perfect breast. "Do you want to help me interview them?" he asked lightly.

She swatted his hand away with a dangerous look. "Of course not!" she huffed, only half joking now. "I'd scratch the eyes out of any woman who dares to touch you."

Dorian's hand returned to her breast, his fingers working their way toward the other one. "I had no idea you were so ruthless, Lady Blackheart," he teased, lapping at a nipple and then blowing on it for the sheer joy of watching it pucker.

"Oh my, yes." Her boast was interrupted by an airy gasp. "I've shot a man, you know, and stabbed one. I can be *quite* dangerous when I need to be."

Dorian sobered, his lungs deflating as he ran his large hands down the delicate line of her arm. It struck him again how fragile she was, how easily broken, how easily lost. "Is being a woman just terrifying all the time?"

Farah's smile faded, but a playful glint still remained in her sweet, silvery eyes. "What a question. Whatever do you mean?"

"You're so—soft, so frail," he marveled. "Like a morsel of the rarest delicacy just waiting to be preyed upon. And we men, we are nothing better than wolves—no, vultures. Bloody predators," he cursed. "How do you ladies muster the courage to leave the house? Better yet, why do I allow it?" He started thinking of all the dangers the world possessed for her beyond his arms and his palms began to sweat.

She traced the long scar he'd received from a dock pirate blade years ago. "Don't you think you're letting your—

singular life experiences cloud your view just a little? I lived among dangerous criminals and bohemians for almost twenty years without being preyed upon." Heat warmed the silver of her irises to a darker gray-green. "And more's the pity, as I find I quite enjoy being *your* prey."

That unsettling possessive instinct flared, the one he'd first felt in Applecross's library. "Only mine," he declared to the night.

"I've only ever been yours," she affirmed.

He stared down at her, his heart in his throat. "I—love you, Farah."

She blinked rapidly, a mist appearing in her eyes. "I love you, too, Dorian."

He captured her chin, forcing her to look into his face. "You don't understand. I've always loved you. From the moment I saw you in that graveyard I loved you with the strength of a man. So much, it terrified me more than you can imagine."

To his astonishment, her face fell, a troubled wrinkle appearing between her brows. "Did you just not realize?"

"I've always known." He captured a ringlet with his finger, the action something he'd dreamed about for years and that he planned on doing for the rest of his life.

The wrinkle only deepened. "Then—why did you deny it before? Why did you break my heart when I offered it to you?"

Shame pierced at him, and he couldn't bring himself to meet her eyes. "In my world, if you care for something, it is a weakness your enemies can use against you."

"I don't care about that." Farah covered his hand with hers. "What else?"

"It's what I've said before," he muttered, trying to find the words to express the depth of his dysfunction. "I was—am broken. I'm not only afraid of causing you harm in my sleep, but that if I allowed myself to love, to hope, the force of my love would consume you, destroy you, somehow. I don't know. Smother or repulse you."

She soothed his agitation with her touch, and he loved that he no longer flinched away, but melted into the warmth of her caress.

"That's not what love does," she whispered, lifting her head to press a kiss above his heart. "Of course it's all-consuming, but love—real love—doesn't destroy or smother. It's the very opposite of a weakness. Love strengthens. It liberates. It molds itself to every fiber of your being and fortifies you where you may be broken. It is as necessary to the body and soul as food or water. It couldn't repulse me. I can only be humbled and awestruck by the most precious gift of your love." Her voice cracked and her eyes spilled tears she'd been holding back. "It is what I always desired the very most in this world, from the moment I saw *you*. Angry and wounded in the Apple-cross graveyard. I wanted to keep you, to hold you like this and teach you love."

Dorian's throat burned. Her words. Her eyes. Her tears. He couldn't stand the sight of them without his heart expanding until his chest might burst. Jaw clenched, he blinked at a foreign blurriness in his eyes.

Panicking, he bolted upright, ready to flee.

"Dorian, no!" Farah shocked him by flinging a long, smooth limb over him, wrapping her body around his so tightly he'd have to hurt her in order to disengage. "Do *not* run from this."

"Farah," he croaked, the warning lost in the barrage of emotions crowding his throat.

"You are *mine*, Dorian Blackwell," she said with savage possession so foreign to her angelic face. "Only mine."

He tasted salt on her tongue when he kissed her, felt a cold wetness on his cheeks as she took him into her body, fusing her limbs around his trunk.

He gripped, she clung. Their hands roamed and explored. It didn't take long before pleasure bloomed and blood sang. A simultaneous culmination so sweet and prolonged peeled away any barrier left between them, fusing their souls and their voices into an archaic song of pulsating bliss.

Dorian kept her body wrapped about him as he maneuvered them beneath the covers.

Once they were settled, he kissed her eyelids. "I love you." Her cheekbones. "I love you." Rooted in the soft curve of her shoulder. "I love you."

She lifted her head, a luminous smile baring her small, even teeth. "I'm glad you're getting used to the phrase." She kissed his jaw. "You'll have to say it at least once a day. For the rest of our lives."

He'd already planned on it, but lifted his brows in mock surprise, enchanted that she'd swung back to being playful. "Every day, you say?"

"And much more often on the days when I'm cross with you," she warned sagely.

"Why are you going to be cross with me?"

She slanted him an imperious look. "Trust me, there will be occasion."

His laugh sounded foreign, even to his own ears. "Fairy?" he mumbled, a drowsy languor stealing through his bones, her tiny body warming him.

"Mmmmmm?" She struggled with her own heavy lids, apparently unable to open them wide enough to see him properly.

"I love you."

Her yawn cracked her jaw and she patted his chest. "So you said."

"I said it as Dorian. But I must tell you once per day for Dougan, as well."

Her chin wobbled, but this time the tear that rolled

down her cheek contained no sadness, only joy, and so he kissed it from her cheek, and moved to roll her over and leave her to sleep.

"Sometimes you watch me sleeping, don't you?" she asked, more alert now.

Dorian didn't answer her.

"Couldn't you do that tonight, but hold me, as well?"

"I really shouldn't . . ."

She put a hand to his chest, imprisoning his back to the bed. "Stay."

"What if I hurt—"

"You *won't*," she insisted, and dropped her cheek against his chest, her legs still split over him. She was asleep in the space of an instant, just like when they were children.

Dorian did stay up and watch her. His fear melting into true realization. She *wasn't* his weakness. Through his entire godforsaken life, she'd been the source of his strength, and now that they were reunited he could conquer anything. Even the past.

Especially the future.

Dorian closed his eyes, identifying the space in his soul as peace and—hope.

Before sleep took him, he whispered the vow into her ear that he would repeat every night until time claimed its due.

I make ye my heart
At the rising of the moon.
To love and honor,
Through all our lives.
May we be reborn,
May our souls meet and know.
And love again.
And remember.

$\mathcal{E}$PILOGUE

"For God's sake, Blackwell, quit pacing and have another drink!" Murdoch slurred, swatting at a shushing Tallow. "Ye're making the room spin with yer to-and-fro. If you doona quit, I'll be seasick."

"I t-t-think that's the whisky making the room spin." Tallow took the bottle from Murdoch and handed it to Frank Walters who, in turn, handed it to Christopher Argent.

"Lady Blackwell ordered that ye had to be at least one or two sheets to the wind afore she lets ye in to see her. I'm upholding *my* end of the bargain," Murdoch bellowed.

Dorian paused in pacing across Ben More's gallery hall only to scowl at his drunken steward. He'd picked this open space to await Farah's labor as the tapestries on the walls muted her distress. "Since when did everyone in this bloody castle start taking orders from the wrong Blackwell?" he snarled, still infuriated that he'd been tossed from the birthing room by his wife and a gaggle of bossy women.

In the way, they'd called him. *Making things worse with his glowering and ordering them about,* they'd said.

He didn't fucking glower.

In a smooth movement, Argent poured them each a crystal glass of liquor and handed one to Dorian. "This is Laird Ravencroft's best Highland vintage," he said in a voice as dark and rich as the scotch in their glass. "He sent it to you for just this occasion. Now stop glowering and have a drink."

"I don't fuc—"

"I'm all done!" A powerful voice echoed through the great hall, and had each of the former Newgate convicts averting their eyes as quickly as they could, studying the tapestries or their boots with great interest.

Dorian tossed back his drink and set his glass down as a bundle of sable ringlets and sticky hands barreled into his arms.

"Papa, Nanny made me scones and peach jam!" Dorian's four-year-old daughter, Faye, slapped a preserve-smeared hand over his scarred eye.

"I can see that." Dorian laughed and scooped her up, holding her close to his chest as her chubby legs bracketed his ribs.

"You can't see!" she reminded him plaintively. "I'm covering your fairy eye."

Dorian smirked, pulling his daughter closer as it eased some of the crippling fear in his heart. "That's right, but I can certainly feel the jam you're smearing on my face." He kissed her warm cheek, which also tasted like Frank Walter's amazing peach preserves. He thought she'd grow out of this game by now. They'd invented it when she was a toddler and had been afraid of his scarred, milky-blue eye. He'd told her that she and her mother were fairies, and he had to have the magical eye to see them as they could choose to be invisible to everyone else, but he could always see them. Now, when she was feeling cheeky, she covered his eye to "hide" from him.

"Who are you talking to, Blackwell?" Argent asked in an exaggerated tone. "I don't see anyone."

Everyone at Ben More Castle and Northwalk Abbey had become very adept at pretending not to see the girl as she scampered about. It surprised Dorian that Argent joined in the game, but the deadliest assassin in London seemed to bear more than a few surprises, even after all these years, not the least of which was his choice in a wife.

"Don't be invisible today, little Faye, your mother is having a baby," Dorian cajoled.

"Oh, all right." She sighed, her lovely gray eyes twinkling at him as she literally peeled her hand away from his eye. "I'm not invisible."

Everyone "started" at the appearance of a tiny fairy girl in Dorian's arms, and then greeted little Faye Marie appropriately, which caused her no end of amusement.

"Papa, can I name my little sister Kitty?"

"You want to name your sister after a cat?" he asked, accepting the offered cloth from Nanny.

"Don't be absurd." She laughed as he helped her to wash the stickiness from her hands. "I want to name her after *all* the cats." She threw her arms wide to encompass all the beloved living creatures, and almost threw herself out of his arms in her exuberance.

"Of course you do," he muttered wryly.

Her smile brightened, if that was at all possible. "That's what Mummy said."

Gemma appeared at the top of the stone steps. "Your wife is askin' for you," she announced.

"Is she well?" he demanded, clutching his daughter to him until she squirmed.

Gemma's lips split into a wide smile, but she only motioned to the hall. "See for yourself."

Heart hammering wildly, Dorian took the stairs two and three at a time, Faye squealing with delight in his ear.

When he reached the hall, the midwife, a middle-aged woman so thin and brittle he could barely understand how her bones didn't clack, beckoned to him from the bedroom doorway.

Dorain found Farah reclined against a mountain of pillows, bleary-eyed but smiling.

Relief swept through him like a firestorm, and for a moment he wondered if he might pass out from the strength of it.

His Fairy had been washed and had fresh linens, her hair, tightly braided before the birth, now haloed by damp, escaped ringlets.

She looked like an angel about to drown in a cloud of fluffy white linens.

"Come in, my love," she encouraged faintly. Her arms were wrapped around a tiny bundle huddled on her chest. "Come and meet your son."

"Son?" He felt ridiculous, but it had somehow never entered his mind that he'd father a boy. Faye Marie had been so certain she was getting a sister that, somehow, she'd convinced her parents that it was so. He looked down and met his daughter's surprised look with one of his own.

A son.

He was just getting used to being powerless against the will of a wild female creature that barely reached his knees. His "little Faye" might have her mother's angelic ringlets and soft gray eyes, but ebony hair and lack of regard for rules branded her a pure Blackwell. She was everything to him, a dynamic mix of curiosity, mischief, and unconditional love. She'd stolen his heart from the first moment he'd seen her. He'd known his role, his place in her life. To love her. Protect her with his life. To offer her sanctuary and an education.

But a boy? How did someone like *him* teach a boy to become a man? Panic lanced his chest, and he had to fight bright spots that danced in his vision.

Faye Marie squirmed to be put down, and Dorian allowed her to slide down his leg and rush to the bedside.

Farah lifted the soft blanket to uncover a pinched, sleeping face and an impossibly small fist.

Dorian couldn't seem to make his feet move.

"Isn't he beautiful?" she whispered.

"Not really," Faye piped rather dramatically. "He's so red. And wrinkled."

Farah gave a soft, exhausted laugh. "He'll look better in a few days."

"I certainly hope so." Faye returned to Dorian and tugged on his hand. "Come see, Papa."

He allowed himself to be led to Farah's bedside, where he gingerly lowered himself to the counterpane, trying to remember how to blink. How to breathe. It still astounded him that the pleasure he and his Fairy shared produced such an extraordinary result.

Life. He put *life* inside her, and she miraculously created someone else for them to love. Someone else to give them love.

With a trembling hand he reached for his son, covering the hand she held against the boy's back. God, but he was tiny, the entire body almost engulfed by the span of Dorian's fingers.

The smile Farah gave him contained the pride of a legion of conquerors and all the love of a saint. "His name is Dougan."

His racing heart stalled and he stared at her, unsure of how to land on the emotions rocketing through him. "What?"

"Dougan Mackenzie Blackwell," she informed him gently but firmly. "I named him after a boy who deserves a second chance at childhood. And maybe, through this one and our little Faye creature here, Dougan and Fairy will be able to experience all the happiness and magic of a childhood that we lost."

As it often did when with Farah, uncertainty and fear drained away, replaced by the love that spilled from her touch. "I lost nothing," Dorian said as he reached for his wife and twirled a ringlet around his finger. "I found *my Fairy,* and that's all the magic I'll ever need."

$\mathcal{T}$urn the page for a scintillating look at
the next exciting novel from Kerrigan Byrne

THE HUNTER

$\mathcal{F}$eaturing the dark and dangerous
Christopher Argent!

$\mathcal{C}$oming soon from St. Martin's
Paperbacks

Reconnaissance. Argent answered his own question. That's what he was doing at the gin-soaked dance hall at midnight. The Sapphire Room was little more than a veritable mélange of shadowed nooks and private rooms sprouting from the main dance hall with no shortage of cushioned furniture on which to drape oneself or another.

The cacophony of the revelers packed beneath the crystal chandeliers all but drowned out the chamber musicians. Everything sparkled. From the gowns of the waltzing *demimonde*, fashionable in their jewel tones, to the ladies' intricate coiffures, to the champagne, all glimmered and winked like fallen stars beneath the new electric lights of the Sapphire Room.

Argent had to suppress a wince as a woman's high, fake cackle breached his eardrum. He never understood why people pretended amusement or hilarity. It was as though they believed if they laughed loudly enough, they would create happiness where there was none. Their worthless lives wouldn't seem so meaningless if they could drown out the sound of their own cognitive dissonance with enough champagne and laughter.

Fools.

Times like this Christopher appreciated his uncommon height, as he could stand a head above the crowd, and scan the herd for his prey. It wouldn't be difficult to find *her* here. Millie LeCour's hair was an uncommon shade of ebony. Her eyes, though nearly black themselves, shone with such life, they reminded him of volcanic glass.

Those eyes. He'd watched the abundant life drain out of them as Othello had strangled her with his large, dark hands. Above them, alone in his box, Argent had held his own breath as the light that captured all of London dimmed and extinguished to rousing, thunderous applause.

He'd leaned toward her then, gripping the railing of the box. Willing her to wake, truly wondering if he hadn't just watched someone carry out his own charge to murder her in front of an audience of hundreds.

Argent had seen the real thing so many times he'd lost count, and she captured the dull lifelessness so precisely, *he* didn't breathe again until the curtain lifted for a final bow. And there she was, her smile brighter and more prismatic than Covent Garden's crystal chandelier.

He'd actually slumped back into his chair. Relieved.

She'd turned to him, pressed her hands together, and curtsied with such grace, her eyes sparkling with unshed tears. Alive. Not only alive. *Full* of life. Brimming with it. Pressing her rouged lips to her hand, she'd tossed a kiss to the crowd. And again, he could have sworn, she turned and tossed one to him.

She'd been happy. He'd observed enough of humanity very closely to recognize the emotion. The true glow of transcendence. And as she'd waved at the boxes, *his* box, beaming that elated smile at him, he'd felt the most peculiar impulse to return it.

He'd. *Felt*.

Shaking his head, he took up a silent guard against the far wall, hoping the odd sensation would dissipate. That she could affect him so was an impossibility. What was she? A liar. A blackmailer. A charismatic narcissist dancing with a death sentence. A mark with private rooms above Bow Street. It was all he needed to know. He should kill her at home.

So . . . why was he here?

Oh yes. *Reconnaissance*.

A murmur of pleasure and surprise swept through the crowd, followed by a swell of applause directed toward the entrance.

The first thought that occurred to Argent was that Millie LeCour couldn't be more porcelain-white if she were, in fact, a corpse. His second, that the crimson-and-white-striped dress accented her pallor so absolutely, she brought to mind the Countess Bathory, a woman famous for bathing in the blood of virgin peasants to maintain her skin's youthful perfection.

Her smile was brilliant in every sense of the word, and Argent found himself with his hand pressed to the chest of his jacket. It happened again. That curious little jolt in the cavern of his ribs. It was the same when she'd smiled at him from the stage. A startle of sensation. A current of awareness that singed along the nerves.

It seemed, if she was the Countess Bathory, tonight he was Vlad Tepes, dead but for strange, lethal animation and his insatiable hunger for blood. Not for physical sustenance, like the vampire, but just as necessary for survival.

Beaming, Millie LeCour let go of her foppish escort to execute a curtsy at the top of the stairs before descending down to her adoring public, rouged lips pursed to receive and return a plethora of air kisses.

Of all the jewels on display at the Sapphire Room, she

gleamed the brightest. Christopher had marked the tired cliché that men would often tell their female companions. They would say that she lit up a room. In the past, it confounded him that such a sentiment would occur to either party as a compliment.

But now . . .

What was once a tepid room, filled with the press and stench of people flirting with debauchery, now seemed to glow with whatever luminescence was contained beneath her nearly translucent skin.

Objectively, it was a shame to rid the world of such beauty. Such talent. Though her smile was an illusion, and her graciousness amounted to artifice, her loss would further tip the scales toward the desolation of humanity by means of mediocrity.

It wouldn't stop him, though. She wouldn't live to see the dawn. He could do it here. Draw her into a corner and snap her pretty neck, drape her limp body across a chaise, and disappear before anyone raised the alarm.

Though surrounded by people, she found him at once. Her head snapped up like she'd heard his thoughts articulated above the drone of the crowd.

But Argent was certain she knew nothing of his intentions, because her eyes became warm midnight pools of pleasure the moment she noted him.

Excusing herself from her adoring public, she pressed through the throng as the orchestra began to play once more. She didn't stop until she stood in front of him unaware, or uncaring, that all eyes were on them both.

"I've found you," she announced with a coy smile.

Argent had no idea what she meant. Maybe she knew why he was here. Maybe someone had warned her of the contract drawn against her life. Perhaps she was as unafraid and unfeeling as himself. A human free from the chains of pathos.

It still didn't change anything.

"It is I, Miss LeCour, who have found you."

And it is I who will end your life.

Millie couldn't believe her luck. Here *he* was, the night's audience of one. She'd never had the pleasure of actually meeting one of them before. Could it be that he somehow had felt that strange, electric connection that she had from the stage?

That would be terribly romantic, wouldn't it?

"I thought this was a private gathering, Mr. . . . ." She looked at him expectantly, offering her hand for an introduction.

"Mr. Argent," he answered, leaning over her hand, but not kissing it. "Christopher Argent."

Millie was unable to hold in a sound of mirth.

"My name amuses you?"

Everything about him amused her.

"Not at all." She rushed to cover any offense. "It's only that you don't look like you'd be named Christopher."

"Oh? And what name would you deem appropriate for me?"

Millie regarded him with gathering interest, somehow unable to answer his question. He didn't look like he'd have a proper English name at all. He was nothing like the slim, elegant, fashionable men-about-town she usually met at these parties. Indeed, with his thick locks of hair the most uncommon shade of auburn, startling blue eyes, and raw, broad bones, he seemed as though he belonged on a Celtic battlefield wielding a claymore against Saxon intruders. Though his handsome features were relaxed into a mild expression, something dangerous shimmered in the air about him. Something . . . she couldn't quite put her finger on. It wasn't violence or anger. Nor was it anything unbalanced or wrong. Could it be that when he smiled, it didn't reach those fiercely blue eyes?

She searched those eyes. They were like ice, and not because of the color. A glacial chill emanated from behind them. Charm and geniality warmed the slight curve of his hard mouth, but looking into those eyes was like staring across an endless arctic tundra. Bleak and empty.

Suddenly she was anxious, and more than a little intrigued. "I fear I'm drawing a blank at the moment," she admitted, surprised how breathless she sounded as she pulled her hand away from his.

He seemed to loom over her, a threat with a nonthreatening air.

"How did you say you came to be here?" she asked.

His expression changed from mild to sheepish, which sat uncomfortably on a face as brutal as his. "I was invited by a friend of a friend, actually. I forget her name. Quite tall, fair hair. Younger than she looks, but then older than she claims." He winked at her, his eyes crinkling with endearing grooves. Not yet a smile, but the promise of one.

"Oh, do you mean Gertrude?" she asked.

"That's the one," he nodded, then scanned the crowd as though halfheartedly looking for the lady in question. "We have a mutual acquaintance by the name of Richard Swiveller, do you know him?"

Millie shook her head. "I'm afraid I don't."

He shrugged a gigantic shoulder and the movement rippled under his expensive evening suit. "No matter. These private parties are hardly intimate, are they?"

Millie took a moment to scan her surroundings, taking in the hundred or so dancers and revelers in various stages of drunkenness and excess. "I suppose that depends on your interpretation of the word," she remarked wryly.

There was that sound of amusement again. It hailed from deep, deep in his cavernous chest. A sound more suited to the shadows of the jungle than an English ballroom.

recover while supported by the strength of his astonishingly solid body. Regaining the rhythm of the waltz, she threw him an appreciative glance.

"It seems, Miss LeCour, that it is *I* who should have been worried about injury to my feet."

She laughed, dipping her forehead against his shoulder. Her heart sped along with the tempo of the waltz, sending warm flurries of nerves flooding through her. Perhaps her scruples about him had been as mistaken as her worries over his dancing capabilities.

"Tell me, Mr. Argent, what is it you do?"

"I'm a longtime partner in a business enterprise," he answered.

"Anyone I've heard of?" she pressed.

"Undoubtedly. My partners handle the day-to-day running of the business, meetings, mergers, acquisitions, and so forth. I'm over contracts, damages, and . . . personnel."

"My," she flirted, "you sound like an important man to know. Tell me more." She used this ploy often. Men loved to talk about themselves. But this time, she found that she truly was curious about him. About how he spent his days. His nights.

And with whom.

"It's all rather dull and workaday compared to what you do." Millie felt, rather than saw his head tilt down, inching closer toward her. The din and atmosphere of the Sapphire Room suddenly melted away. Everything seemed darker, somehow. Closer. Their feet waltzed over shadows and their bodies synced in a flawless rhythm that felt, to her, sensuous. Sinful, even.

His scent enveloped her, a warm, masculine musk of cedar trunks, shaving soap, and something darker. Wilder. Something that smelled like danger and sex. The kind that marked you afterward. The kind she'd heard in the wailing of ecstatic obscenities and pounding of headboards

"Would you care for a waltz, Miss LeCour?" He stepped closer, invading her space, towering over her like a wall of heat and muscle.

Millie hesitated. This time not because she was afraid, but because she very much doubted that a man of such height and width and—she looked down—large feet could waltz worth a damn.

One tread of his heavy soles upon her feet and she feared he'd break them.

"I'll step lightly," he murmured, reading her mind.

She looked up, and up, into those unsettling eyes. There. Not a feeling, not an emotion, per se, but a glimmer. One of enjoyment . . . or regret, she couldn't be sure.

Lord, but he was fascinating.

"See that you do," she teased. "One cannot act if one cannot walk."

He took her gloved hand in his—enveloped it, to be accurate—and led her to the floor. She paused to wait for an opening among the swirling couples, and gasped as he pulled her forward, seizing a place and twirling her into it with powerful arms.

It became instantly obvious that her fears regarding his dancing skills were completely unfounded. Indeed, he was the most graceful, skilled man on the floor . . . or perhaps on any dance floor in London. He held her close, scandalously close, his hand on her back securing her to him like an iron clamp. The warmth of that hand seeped through the layers of her clothing and corset, an undeniable brand. Yet the hand that held hers was gentle, but just as warm.

The arms beneath his suit coat were even harder than she'd guessed. The swells of muscles where her hands rested flexed and rolled with his movements, and Millie found herself entranced by them. So much so that she stumbled and lost her footing around a turn.

He pulled her even closer, allowing her to seamlessly

the man she'd been waiting for, the hero who would sweep her off her feet and capture her heart.

His fingers tightened again, just a little, and she gasped. Then moaned as a thrill of fear titillated down her nerves and settled as a pool of moisture between her thighs.

"Again," she demanded, her arms winding around his neck, her body rubbing against his like a cat demanding to be stroked.

His curse was lost in the cavern of her mouth and she knew in that moment that they both needed to see whatever this was to fruition.

A commotion warned them before the door from the hall burst open. Two female bodies spilled into the entryway floor in a heap of skirts and spitting, swearing, scratching violence. One of them they'd seen kissing another in the hall.

The other was another woman.

Millie and Mr. Argent leapt apart, suddenly surrounded by a riotous group of men crowding behind them, shouting pleased and lusty approval and encouragement to the fighting women. Millie watched them for a moment. Stunned that ladies could be so vicious to one another.

But, she supposed, jealousy was a powerful emotion.

"Well," she called over the din, looking back over her shoulder to her would-be lover "Would you like to—"

Her words died away, as there was no one to offer them to.

He'd disappeared.

chest and shoulders, the calluses on his palms abrading her flesh and unleashing chill-bumps everywhere.

And *still* he didn't kiss her.

Millie released a whimper of need, unashamed of the frenzy beginning to build within her. Who could have known? That desire would be this delicious? That anticipation could lock you in its hands, its large, calloused hands, and strip away your pride until you wanted to beg?

"It won't hurt, I promise," he whispered as his fingers gently reached the nape of her neck, and then her jaw, and paused there.

Millie's breath had now been reduced to little more than needy pants. "If you don't kiss me, I'll *die*," she demanded.

He froze.

Vibrating with frustrated arousal, she surged against him, lifting to her toes and grinding her lips against his.

The kiss was as hungry as it was sudden. While his eyes might have been cold, his mouth was hot and tasted of wine and male. She kissed him with abandon, enjoying the way his entire body stiffened.

From the fingers at her throat to the sex in his trousers.

At the press of his arousal against her, Millie's sensitive breasts swelled beneath her corset, becoming full and heavy. Her clothes felt confining; her skin itched to be bared to him. Demanded it.

His tongue invaded her mouth and she moaned her approval. His thumbs, at first resting against her clavicles, caressed the dip of her throat, the curve of her chin, the line of her jaw, all while tasting her with the insatiable gluttony of a hedonist.

Millie had a sense that he was as lost as she was, moreso even, and the sensual, feminine power that surged within her fed her desire. She wanted him gone for her. Drunk on her. Atop her, beneath her, and within her.

Perhaps they were *meant* to meet tonight. Maybe he was

That shadow became theirs as they claimed the darkness.

Gasping, Millie found herself pressed against the wall, imprisoned between it and Argent's unyielding torso. A willing prisoner.

Lord, she never did this. Certainly, she'd stolen a few kisses, or gifted them as favors. She'd shamelessly flirted, openly admired, and allowed the pursuit of men on occasion. But never like this. Publicly, with a man she barely knew whom she wasn't using for money or gain.

Just pleasure.

He stood like that for a moment, or it could have been an eternity. Their breath mingling in the darkness. Wine and port and desire.

She couldn't see his face clearly, backlit as it was by the chandelier that cast a halo around his light hair. Millie knew for a certainty that neither of them were angels and with a man as mysterious as this one, she could pave her way to hell in only an evening.

Best get started then.

She strained toward him, lifting her mouth in invitation, but he didn't allow her to move. He just stood against her, his chest pressing her breasts higher as those big hands rested on her waist.

Millie knew he could see her a little, and she didn't have to fake the come-hither look this time, and finally, those hands began to move.

This man never seemed to do what she expected him to. Even now, his hands weren't exploratory, but purposeful. They spanned the indent of her waist. Then her ribs, increasingly confined by her ever-quickening breath. His own breath hitched when he reached her breasts, but he didn't stop there. Didn't cup or test them, didn't reach beneath her low bodice to find the straining, aching nipples. His hands merely kept moving upward, across her bare against thin walls in the days before she could afford her own apartment.

Tilting her head back, she'd meant to smile an invitation into his eyes, but her gaze never got that far. They snagged on his lips. Soft against several hard, almost cruel, brackets of rough skin.

Those lips would mark her. The russet stubble of his shaven face would redden her tender skin and tickle any flesh she exposed to him.

"I believe," she whispered, breathless again for the second time in his presence, "I believe that you want to kiss me, Mr. Argent."

His answer wasn't the witty flirtation she'd expected. Just as suddenly as she'd found herself whisked onto the dance floor, he twirled her away from it. The crowd melted before them, artists and actors mixing with lower nobility or wealthy merchant men. Those with money, power, influence, but not burdened by the more strident social mores of the upper class.

Eyes followed them as they left. Millie was used to it; people watched her wherever she went, but this time, she had a cloying suspicion *she* wasn't the center of attention for once.

The further into the Sapphire Room they ventured, the darker and seedier it became. In a corner of the hallway, two bedazzled women were locked in a passionate embrace, one lovely head buried in the other's neck. There was desperation in their passion. One born of unfulfilled desires denied too long.

Millie found an echo of that surging within her own body as she followed Mr. Argent's wide back into a narrow nook beneath the grand stairway. Here, the entry chandelier was dimmed to create a wicked atmosphere, but it provided enough light to cast their corner in shadow.